**He shoved the rest of the cupcake in his mouth.
I watched him chew and swallow.**

Then he asked, "Would it piss you off to know that right about now I'm wondering if I walked in here yesterday because I missed my Tess or if it was because I missed her cupcakes?"

I grinned at him.

Then I answered, "No, because I *am* my cupcakes."

And it hit me right then. I was. On the outside it could be tees, jeans and flip-flops or pencil skirts. But on the inside, it was all about mountainous swirls of delicately colored frosting on top of rich, moist cake. And as that understanding settled inside me, that made me feel warm and gushy too.

"Come here, baby," he murmured. When I got close, his arms folded around me and he pulled me deep. Then his head dipped and he gave me a sweet, delicious, long, deep cupcake kiss.

When he was done, against his mouth, I whispered, "You taste good."

To which he replied, "I know."

I smiled against his lips and he returned the gesture. Then he lifted his head an inch, his arms gave me a squeeze and he said gently, "I wanna spend the night."

Praise for the Dream Man Series

"[*Law Man* is an] excellent addition to a phenomenal series!"
—ReadingBetweentheWinesBookclub.blogspot.com

"[*Law Man*] made me laugh out loud. Kristen Ashley is an amazing writer!" —TotallyBookedblog.com

"Run, don't walk...to get [the Dream Man] series. I love [Kristen Ashley's] rough, tough, hard loving men. And I love the cosmo-girl club!" —NocturneReads.com

"I adore Kristen Ashley's books. She writes engaging, romantic stories with intriguing, colorful, and larger-than-life characters. Her stories grab you by the throat from page one and don't let go until well after the last page. They continue to dwell in your mind days after you finish the story and you'll find yourself anxiously awaiting the next. Ashley is an addicting read no matter which of her stories you find yourself picking up."
—Maya Banks, *New York Times* bestselling author

"I felt all of the rushes, the adrenaline surges, the anger spikes...my heart pumping in fury. My eyes tearing up when my heart (I mean...*her* heart) would break."
—Maryse's Book Blog (Maryse.net)
on *Motorcycle Man*

"There is something about them [Ashley's books] that I find crackalicious." —Kati Brown, DearAuthor.com

WILD
MAN

WILD MAN

KRISTEN ASHLEY

FOREVER

NEW YORK   BOSTON

Copyright © 2013 by Kristen Ashley
Excerpt from *Law Man* copyright © 2013 by Kristen Ashley

Forever
Hachette Book Group
1290 Avenue of the Americas
New York, NY 10104

www.HachetteBookGroup.com

Printed in the United States of America

Originally published as an ebook
First Mass Market Edition: October 2013
10 9 8 7 6 5

OPM

Forever is an imprint of Grand Central Publishing.
The Forever name and logo are trademarks of Hachette Book Group, Inc.

The Hachette Speakers Bureau provides a wide range of authors for speaking events. To find out more, go to www.hachettespeakersbureau.com or call (866) 376-6591.

The publisher is not responsible for websites (or their content) that are not owned by the publisher.

To Erika Ann Moutaw Wynne and Roy Gilbert
"Gib" Moutaw, my big sister and my little brother.
*Everything we are is based in love and
history and loyalty. Thank god.*

PROLOGUE

Wild Man

"OH MY *GOD*," I breathed as I came, my mind blanking, every inch of my body tightening as bliss like I never felt before coursed through me.

When I was done, my eyes slowly opened and I saw him still moving over me, in me, God, *God,* he looked good. Beautiful. And he felt good. Amazing.

His gorgeous, silvery-gray eyes were locked to mine, heated, intense, glittering, searing into me, all of this in a way he'd never looked at me before. Not once in the four months we'd been together.

And I knew, feeling the burn of his eyes, what that look meant. I knew this man, this fantastic, striking, wild man, was mine.

Mine.

I felt it in my blood.

"Jake," I whispered, my limbs gripping even tighter around him, one of my hands sifting up into his thick, dark, unruly hair. His eyes closed at my voice sounding his name and they did this in a way that seemed like he was in pain.

Um... what?

Then he shoved his face in my neck, moving faster, thrusting harder, his breath labored against my sensitive skin and my mind turned to his body, my hands glided across his skin, my legs gripped him harder as I clenched his driving cock with my sex.

"*Fuck,* Tess," he growled against my neck then I heard him groan as he kept thrusting and he came.

I held him tight.

He gave me his weight.

I held on tighter.

Then he pulled out and rolled off me, falling to his back. The instant he did, eyes on the ceiling, he lifted the butts of his palms, pressed them to his forehead, and closed his eyes.

Um. Not good.

"Jake?" I called softly.

"Yeah?" he grunted, not soft and also not opening his eyes or moving his hands.

Okay, uh, what was going on?

Feeling suddenly exposed and vulnerable even after just moments before feeling like I'd finally, *finally* found my dream man, he was there, in my bed, in *me* and the joy that brought evaporated. I moved quickly. Nabbing the throw at the bottom of the bed, I pulled it over my naked body.

"Is everything okay?" I whispered.

"Fuck no," he answered, and I felt my body go still.

He dropped his hands, his head turned to me, the look in his eyes not heated, glittering, intense, burning into me. It was conflicted and—I stared, not believing it but seeing it—filled with regret.

Oh no. Oh God. Oh shit. Oh no.

I pulled the blanket closer to me, thinking Martha had been right.

Damn. She'd been right.

His eyes dropped to my hand clutching the blanket to my chest, then lifted to my face. I watched them melt to quicksilver as they lingered, his face gentling, his body turning my way, his hand coming out and then his phone rang.

His hand stilled and he muttered a pissed off "*Fuck*."

He rolled the other way and reached out with a long arm to grab his jeans. I was staring at the contours of his back, the sleek skin, the defined muscles, thinking that wasn't for me. It wasn't for me. None of it.

I knew it.

I'd always known it.

From the instant four months ago when his silver eyes hit me, traveled the length of my torso, all he could see of me behind the display cabinet, and when his eyes again came to mine, he'd smiled sexy, lazy, and slow, I knew it.

He wasn't for me.

There was no dream man for me.

But he was so beautiful, I went for it anyway.

"Yeah?" he asked into the phone and I felt his mood hit the room and it grated against my skin like sandpaper.

In the four months we'd been together, Jake did not hide his moods. Ever. Not even in the beginning. And Jake had a lot of moods. If he was pissed, you knew he was pissed. If he was happy, you definitely knew he was happy. If he was feeling playful, annoyed, frustrated, amused, distracted, content, whatever, you knew it, you sensed it. It was like he controlled the atmosphere of the room.

And whoever was on the other end of that phone was pissing him off *and* frustrating him.

"Give me an hour," he said into the phone, paused then went on. "No, man, I'm tellin' you, I need an hour." Another pause then, "Fuck, you've got to be fuckin' *shitting* me." Pause then, "This can't happen now." A very short pause, then, "I'm tellin' you, this *cannot* fuckin' happen fuckin' *now.*" He shifted his powerful body to sit on the edge of my bed, back bowed, elbows to knees, phone to ear, and he growled low, "All right, motherfucker, but you fuck this up, you fuck *her* over, mark this, you answer to me."

He flipped his phone shut and bent forward to grab his jeans.

Then he announced to the other side of the room, "Babe, gotta go."

I closed my eyes.

Okay. Okay.

When Jake got into a mood, you knew his mood. And when Jake had to go, Jake went.

This was nothing unusual.

Okay, so, we'd been seeing each other for four months and this was the first time we made love.

Sure, that seemed weird, considering he was all man, a wild man, but he was always gentle with me, *very* gentle, and it was like he sensed I needed that. I needed him to take it slow. And I *did* need that. Boy, did I need that. So I didn't think anything of it.

And sure, we'd made out. We'd fooled around a lot. *A lot,* a lot and it was good. The best. And he'd made me come with his hand, though he'd never let me touch him that way, saying he liked to watch and the first time

I made him come, he wanted to be inside me. Just him telling me that nearly made me come. But I'd never been naked with him, not even close, until now.

So, any girl would expect, after all that time with a wild man unlike any man she'd ever been with, a wild man who tamed that beast in order to be gentle with her, that he'd hang around after the big event.

But not Jake.

I knew that about him.

But this was something different.

I knew that too.

"Tess," he called, his deep voice gentle and my eyes opened.

He was somewhat fuzzy. I didn't have my glasses on but I knew he was still unbelievably gorgeous. The sight of him was burned on my brain in a way I knew I'd never forget.

"Yeah?" I replied and watched him, now fully clothed, lean into a hand on the bed toward me.

I held still as he got closer and came into better focus.

"Grab your glasses, darlin'," he whispered and I must have narrowed my eyes to focus on him or something.

Jake, I also knew, didn't miss much.

I forced my body to come unstuck, rolled as I kept the blanket pressed to me, nabbed my glasses off the nightstand, and slid them on. I rolled back to him.

Seeing him focused, I saw his eyes were no longer conflicted and remorseful. They were quicksilver still but affectionate, gazing at me like they did when I fancied he was thinking I was cute. Or at least I hoped it was that.

He liked me wearing my glasses. He'd told me that flat out. Said he never had a woman who wore glasses. He told me it was like stepping out with a sweet, sexy school teacher.

I'd never felt sexy, not in my life. Not until Jake.

"We'll talk later, yeah?" he said quietly.

"Yeah," I answered, hope budding in my heart at his look, his tone, his words.

"We'll talk later, Tess. Yeah?" he somewhat repeated, and I blinked.

"Yeah," I repeated too.

"Promise me, babe."

I stared at him, not sure why he needed that. I didn't play games with him, not at all. Not even when Martha told me I should, repeatedly. Test the waters. Test *him*. Don't be too available. Don't let on how much I liked him.

But I was too old for that shit and I'd never had a man like Jake. There was no way I was going to fuck it up with games.

So now I didn't get where he was going with his need for a promise.

But still, he asked and I'd give him anything he asked. Anything. Even from the very beginning.

"Promise," I whispered.

He nodded.

Then he asked, "You sleep naked?"

A shiver I couldn't quite read slithered over my skin. It wasn't bad but it also wasn't good.

"No," I answered.

"Don't start tonight," he ordered.

Then he leaned in, his hand not in the bed coming to cup the back of my head. He pulled me to him and kissed me hard and wet.

His mouth released mine but he allowed me to pull

back only an inch before his hand, still at the back of
my head, put pressure on to stop my retreat and his eyes
locked with mine.

"We'll talk later," he whispered.

Then his hand disappeared because he disappeared.

Gone.

I listened to my front door close.

Then I collapsed back on the bed and stared at the
ceiling.

One could not say that Jake Knox was not a complicated man, he was. And although I knew him, I had no
freaking clue.

But that whole scene was *wild*.

Then again, Jake—with his motorcycle boots, his
bike, his beat-up pickup, his old T-shirts that fit way too
well, his faded jeans that fit better, his dark brown, long-
ish, unruly hair, his silvery-gray eyes that told a million
stories without giving away a thing, his capacity to drink
beer, down shots, eat hearty, howl at the moon, and kiss
so hard it was like he knew it was the last moment for
every being on earth and he was going to make the most
of it—was wild.

Being with Jake was like the ride I once took on a
mechanical bull. You could not even begin to guess which
way that thing would buck. All you could do was hold on
as tight as you could and enjoy the ride for as long as you
had it.

So I needed to cool it.

It would all be okay.

I got up, put on underwear and a nightie, went to bed,
and turned off the light.

It took a while for me to find sleep even after having

a very, *very* sweet orgasm, one given to me by Jake, one I'd waited a long, *long* time to have and after him leaving after kissing me like it was the last moment on earth and him telling me there was more to us because we were going to talk.

But after I fell asleep, I woke when my front door was busted open, a large cadre of bulletproof-vest-wearing men surged into my house, and minutes later, I was hauled to the police station for questioning.

CHAPTER ONE

Fucking Great Actress

THE DOOR TO the interrogation room opened and a man wearing slacks, a shirt, a tie, and an ill-fitting sports jacket strolled in, eyes glued to me, manila folder in his hand.

He dropped the folder on the table I was sitting at and sat across from me.

I kept my eyes on him and, like I'd been doing since I'd been led into that room what felt like hours ago (and what I didn't know actually *was*), I kept them away from the mirror. I'd seen enough cop shows on TV to know that that was where recording equipment and possibly other police officers were watching.

"Mrs. Heller," he said and I felt my heart skip at hearing that name.

"Ms. O'Hara," I replied and his gaze didn't leave mine.

"Sorry, ma'am?" he asked, but he wasn't sorry. I knew he wasn't sorry.

"Ms. O'Hara, my name," I answered, and he nodded, still not releasing my eyes and I didn't tear mine from his.

"You *were* Mrs. Heller," he stated. "Do I have that right?"

"Yes," I told him. "You have that right."

"For ten years," he went on.

I didn't reply, just lifted my chin a little, wondering what the hell was going on.

"Married to Damian Heller, is that correct?"

Uh-oh.

I wasn't sure this was good.

"Yes, I was married to Damian Heller," I agreed, then enquired, "What's this about?"

"Funny," he said quietly.

I wasn't thinking anything was funny, including him weirdly saying the word "funny."

"Funny?" I prompted.

"Funny you didn't ask that first," he observed. "Usually folks wanna know right off why they're sittin' in a room like this."

I stared at him.

Then I returned, "Well, seeing as you opened with the knowledge you didn't even know my name, I thought it important to get that straight before we got started with whatever is going on here."

I watched his eyes flare with annoyance as his mouth got tight.

Jerk.

"So," I pushed, "would you mind telling me why I'm here?"

"There're a few things we need to know."

I lifted my brows. "And those would be?"

"Can you tell me if you've been in contact with your husband recently?" he asked.

Damn it all to hell. Damian. God!

My ex-husband. A pain in my ass. Would I never get rid of that man?

"Yes, I can tell you that I've been in contact with my *ex*-husband recently," I answered.

"And what did you discuss?" he went on.

"We didn't discuss anything except me asking him repeatedly to *stop* contacting me," I replied.

He studied me.

Then he asked, "So was this on the phone or did you meet?"

"On the phone," I told him.

"You didn't meet?" he pushed.

"No."

He opened the folder in front of him and my eyes dropped to it. He flipped some papers over and finally he pulled out some black-and-white eight-by-tens, turned them, and slid them across the table to me.

In them were photos of me and Damian having lunch.

Okay. This *was* not good. Why were people taking photos of me and Damian having lunch?

And second, this was not good because I really had to consider never wearing that top again. It didn't do me any favors even in black and white.

"Would you like to amend your last answer?" he offered, and my eyes went to him.

"No," I replied, his brows went up but his head turned slightly to the side, toward the mirror.

Yep. People were watching.

Damn.

"Mrs. Heller—" he started but I interrupted him.

"My name, sir, is Ms. O'Hara. Actually, it's Tess because no one calls me Ms. O'Hara. And I'll explain those photos and my answer," I stated, then went on before he could speak. "You asked if I'd been in contact with my ex-husband recently. I have on several occasions, as he calls me frequently. Sometimes I pick up and tell him to stop calling me. Sometimes I don't. I was married to Damian for ten years. He dislikes being ignored and he's not skilled with catching hints. He responds better to direct communication, although this endeavor unfortunately takes time because he doesn't respond well if that communication happens to be something he doesn't want to hear. Those photos"—I lifted a hand out of my lap and gestured to the photos on the table before dropping it back to my lap—"were taken of me having lunch with Damian what I believe was at least six months ago. That is not, in my definition, recent. If your definition of recent is different, I apologize that I didn't give you the answer you expected, but even so, I still gave you one that was honest."

He didn't hesitate after I spoke before he asked, "Can you tell me what you discussed during this not-recent lunch?"

"Can you tell me why I'm here?" I returned.

"I prefer to ask the questions *Ms. O'Hara.*"

I stared at him then I pulled in a breath before I answered, "Damian wanted to discuss reconciliation."

"He wants you back," he stated.

"That is what reconciliation means," I informed him and his mouth got tight again.

Then he observed, "I would assume from your asking him not to contact you via the phone that you declined this reconciliation."

"You would assume correctly."

"And that was it? That's all you discussed?"

"No, he asked about our dog, who I got custody of in

the divorce and who has since died. I told him he died. Other than that, yes. Pretty much. That's all that we discussed."

"Pretty much?"

"Sir, it was six months ago and at that time I hadn't seen him in person in over four years. His contacting me at all was a surprise and not a good one. His reason for wanting to meet was a surprise too and *definitely* not a good one. I'm sorry I didn't take note of everything we discussed but the reason for the meeting kind of rooted itself in my brain, forcing out everything else."

"You hadn't seen him in over four years," he noted.

"Yes, that's what I said," I confirmed.

"So, if you didn't wish to reconcile, why did you agree to lunch?"

I pulled in a breath and I stated, "I forgot."

He stared at me.

Then he repeated my words in a question. "You forgot?"

I nodded.

"I forgot how Damian is. When he contacted me and told me his father wasn't well and that he wanted to meet me for lunch, I forgot that Damian is, well..." I threw out a hand. "*Damian.* Or maybe I didn't forget. Maybe I blocked it out, considering I spent those years trying to block out everything about Damian. But I know how close he is to his father. I was close to his father, though I haven't seen him in over four years either. So I felt badly he wasn't well and I wanted to know what was happening. Damian refused to tell me any details over the phone so I met him. Then I discovered nothing was wrong with his father and Damian used that to lure me to lunch."

He stared at me again, likely letting the news that my ex-husband was that big of an asshole sink in before he changed tactics. "It was you who filed for divorce."

They'd looked into me.

Good God. They'd looked into me.

What was happening?

"Yes," I confirmed, thinking that with whatever was happening, honesty was definitely the best policy, so I kept with it.

"Infidelity?"

I nodded and added verbally, "Yes."

"Repeated," he stated.

"You've obviously read the court documents so you know that's also a yes. But, yes, I'll confirm that Damian cheated on me repeatedly."

"Yes, Ms. O'Hara, I have read the court documents and the sheer number of them indicate that the papers you filed were contested. He fought the divorce. It went before a judge."

"Yes, he did."

"He didn't wish for your marriage to be dissolved."

"No, he didn't."

"But it was."

I sighed, then said, "Yes, it was."

"And you walked away with nothing except money enough for your legal fees. Did I read that right?"

It was at this point I was beginning to get scared. That was to say I was beginning to get scared in addition to the scared I already was, which was layered on top of the massive freak-out created by my home being invaded by what appeared to be about three teams of multiagency SWAT (because some had the word *POLICE* on their vests, some had *FBI*, and some had *DEA*), pulled out of my bed, and hauled to the Police Station to be questioned.

Therefore, my bravado melted and it came out as a whisper when I asked, "Please, can you tell me what's going on?"

He didn't tell me what was going on. Instead, he queried, "Did you ever regret that, Ms. O'Hara?"

"What?" I asked.

"Accepting nothing from your husband but your legal fees, did you ever regret that?"

I shook my head. "No, I . . . no. I didn't. I wanted a fresh start. I wanted—"

"Why?"

I blinked at him. "What?"

"Ten years with him, multiple infidelities, he made six figures and you lived a very nice life. You could have cleaned up. But you took the dog and took off. Didn't you think he owed you? Didn't you think you should have part of the life you built together?"

I shook my head again. "No, I wanted a fresh start. I just wanted to . . . go," I answered. "Is something . . . has something happened to Damian?"

He didn't answer my question. Instead, he remarked, "Ten years is a long time. That's a lot to invest in a life, a marriage, a home just to walk away with nothing but the dog. Seems strange you wouldn't lay claim to *something*. The wedding china. The dining room set. You didn't even take a car."

"Damian paid for the cars," I said quietly.

"And you wanted nothing to do with him," he noted. "Nothing to remind you of him. Am I right?"

I nodded, staring at him, trying to read his face, but he wasn't giving me anything.

"Lotta women, they wouldn't feel like you. Lotta women, kind of money he made, kind of lifestyle they were used to, they'd feel something different," he observed.

"I'm not a lot of women," I told him.

"No, seems to me you definitely aren't. Leaving all that behind, taking nothing but the dog. Seems to me it wasn't so much leaving him as running away. Were you running away from your husband, Ms. O'Hara?"

I felt my chest compress like a hundred-pound weight had settled on it.

"No," I breathed out on a wheeze. This the first lie I'd uttered since he came in and his eyes sharpened on my face.

He knew I was lying.

"Clearly, we had someone taking photos of you at that lunch. This did not go well. We know this. You didn't finish your lunch, Ms. O'Hara. You left early, looking agitated. Hurried. Like you were running away. He tell you something at lunch that would make you wanna run away?"

"I didn't run away," I denied. My second lie, I did. "I just didn't . . . when he told me that he'd lied about his father and he wanted to reconcile and I knew I didn't, I didn't think there was any reason to stay."

He sat back in his chair and threw out an arm. "Ten years together, he screwed around on you, that's tough but you married him, spent ten years with him. Time had passed. Time heals wounds. It wasn't cool he lied about his dad but he went out of his way to get you. You couldn't shoot the breeze over salads? Talk about old times?"

"Please tell me what's going on," I begged softly.

"I'd like to understand why you left your husband and why you left that lunch in such a hurry."

"I told you and so did the court papers. He cheated on me and I didn't want to have lunch when I learned the theme," I reminded him.

He leaned toward me and said softly, "I don't believe you."

Oh God.

Something had happened to Damian.

"Something's happened to Damian," I whispered, and he smiled.

I didn't like that smile mainly because it wasn't the kind of smile you liked.

"Now, why would you think that?"

I threw up my hands and lost a bit more control.

"I don't know. Because we're talking about him in an interrogation room in the middle of the night, maybe?"

"You know someone who would want to hurt Damian Heller?" he asked.

"No," I told him, the truth.

"Sure about that?" he asked.

I nodded. "Yes, I am."

"No one?" he pushed.

I shook my head. "No one."

"Why'd you want a fresh start, Ms. O'Hara?"

"My husband was cheating—"

"Why'd you want a fresh start?"

"Like I said, he was unfaith—"

He banged his hand on the table, so, wound up and freaked out, my body involuntarily jumped in shock at the sudden movement and loud noise and he clipped angrily, "Why'd you want a fresh start?"

"Because he raped me!" I shrieked.

It just came out, those four words. They just came right out of my mouth, even surprising me.

The first time I said them to anyone.

He shot back in his chair blinking and I heard a loud crash outside the room so my head jerked toward the wall.

My heart was beating fast and my chest was moving deeply with my heavy breathing as I stared at my pale face in the mirror.

And I stared for a long time at my pale face in the mirror.

God, I hadn't really looked in the mirror for ages. Not really. Not for years.

Was that what I looked like?

"Ms. O'Hara," he called, his voice different, quiet, weirdly gentle, but I kept staring at my pale face in the mirror, stunned by what I saw. "Tess," he whispered and my head turned, my eyes sliding to his. "Your husband raped you?" he asked softly.

"I know it sounds funny," I found my lips whispering. "He was my husband but it happened." I held his eyes and kept whispering. "It happened."

"It doesn't sound funny," he whispered back. "Not the least bit funny."

I held his eyes and said nothing.

"You ran away," he stated.

"Yes," I whispered.

I ran away. Fuck yes, I ran away.

"Had he hurt you before?"

I nodded. "He was changing. Something was happening." I hesitated, then repeated, "He was changing."

"What was happening?"

.

I shook my head. "I don't know. I tried to talk...we had...we fought. He would get..." I paused. "Suddenly, it never happened before, but suddenly when we fought it would get physical so I stopped trying to talk."

"He fought the divorce."

"Damian doesn't like losing hold on what he thinks is his."

He studied me with eyes now as gentle as his voice.

Then he said quietly, "But he left you alone for four and a half years."

"Yes, he left me alone," I whispered.

"Then he wanted you back."

"Yes."

"Did he explain why he approached you after all this time?"

I shook my head but said, "He said he was...he said..." I pulled in a deep breath, then told him, "He said he loved me, missed me, messed up, and wanted to make it up to me."

"And since that lunch, he's been contacting you regularly in an effort to do that?"

"Yes."

His head tipped slightly to the side. "And after what he'd done to you, you took his calls? You had lunch with him?"

Suddenly, needing to know, needing to know since I'd told him something I'd never told anyone before, I asked, "What's your name?"

"Sorry, I'm Agent Calhoun."

"Well, Agent Calhoun, the answer to your question is yes. I took his calls and I had lunch with him. Damian is who he is and I know who he is. I didn't want him showing up at my house. I didn't want him sending presents and flowers. I didn't want him anywhere near me. He thought, throughout the whole time we were getting divorced, that I'd come back. He told me so and he worked at it. Only when I saw it through did he leave me alone. Whatever this is, whatever he wants from me, I had to see it through until it sank in with him that I wasn't coming back and he left me alone. So, I was seeing it through."

He studied me again and then he remarked, "That took a lot of courage."

"He raped me, Agent Calhoun. He hit me, but he didn't kill me. As long as I'm breathing, I've got fight in me and luckily I'm breathing."

It was at that he whispered, "You *aren't* like a lot of women."

"Yes, I am," I whispered back. "I'm like all women. You see this, but inside there's something else that I won't let you or him see, but it's the mess he left me. But that's mine. No one gets to it. Everything you get and he gets is a show. One thing you learn really quickly and really well when that kind of thing happens to you is to be a fucking great actress. You don't have a choice in that because a man like that does something like that to you, you lose having choices. The only choice you have is what role you intend to play. I picked my role and that…that, Agent Calhoun, is what you see."

I watched him draw in a breath but he didn't respond.

So I asked, "Now, will you tell me what's going on?"

He held my eyes as he finally answered.

"Tonight, we swept up your ex-husband's entire operation. He's the top narcotics distributor in Denver, with ties direct to Colombia."

I blinked.

Then I breathed, *"What?"*

"As far as we can trace it, after a number of years being a low-level dealer to high-end clientele, mostly colleagues, he entered the game in a serious way ten years ago and crawled his way to the top."

I felt my lips part as I stared at him.

He kept talking. "Your name is joint with his on all his offshore accounts. There are four of them totaling seventy-five million US dollars."

"Oh my God," I whispered.

"You hit our radar with your lunch and when we started monitoring his calls. We were aware you were in regular contact with him over the phone for the last six months. And we were aware your name was on his accounts. However, we didn't know what your involvement was in his operation. As the disintegration of your marriage and your divorce coincided relatively closely with his moves to elevate his position in the business, we thought you'd discovered what he was doing. But, considering your behavior at lunch, we couldn't know why you and he resumed contact."

"I don't have any involvement in his operations." I was still whispering.

He reached into his inside jacket pocket, pulled out a tri-folded piece of paper, and set it on the table. "Search warrant. We're searching your house, car, business premises, and computers. We'll also be taking a sample of your handwriting because someone signed your name to open those offshore accounts and they did this approximately six months ago."

I kept staring at him and then I closed my eyes and turned away while shaking it.

Damian.

Evidence was suggesting that I would, indeed, never get rid of him.

"I don't...I can't..." I sucked in a deep breath, looked back at Agent Calhoun, and said, "I don't believe this."

"If what you say is true, our searches will bear this out. However, I will have to ask you to remain here until those are complete. This could take some time, Ms. O'Hara," he stated while standing. "Can I get you some coffee while you wait?"

I had tipped my head back to look up at him, too shocked by what I'd learned to respond.

"Tess," he prompted quietly. "Coffee?"

I kept staring at him then I shook my head sharply once and looked at the table, murmuring, "Yes, thank you."

"Someone will be in shortly with your coffee," he told the top of my head.

"Thanks," I told the table.

I didn't see him but I also didn't feel his presence leave for several long moments. Then I heard his feet hitting the floor as he walked to the door. The door closed and I was alone in the room with nothing but the table, the chairs, the mirror, and whoever was behind it.

I didn't move and continued to stare at the table.

And luckily, when the one tear I couldn't control fell, it coursed down the cheek that was on the opposite side to the mirror.

CHAPTER TWO

Exit. Stairs.

I STARED AT the table for a long time and I kept staring at it after they brought my coffee and asked me to write my signature on a blank piece of paper. I did that, drank my coffee, and then kept staring long after I was alone again.

But in my head, even with all that was happening, all I could see was my pale face in the mirror.

God, was that really me?

The door to the room opened, my head came up, and Agent Calhoun was standing there.

"You're free to go, Ms. O'Hara," he said quietly. "I'm afraid we'll be working with your computers for a little while longer and we'll need to ask you not to leave town in case we have follow-up questions but you can go home now."

I stared at him a moment before I stood. Grabbing my purse, the only thing they'd let me bring with me, I walked his way but he didn't move out of the door so I stopped two feet away.

"We'll contact you when we're done with the computers

and arrange a time to return them. It shouldn't be more than a day or two." He was still talking quietly and I nodded. "You want me to call you a taxi, or do you have a friend who'll come pick you up?"

No way I was phoning any of my friends. Not about this. Not when it had to do with Damian. Not when questions could be asked and answers would be expected and lies might need to be told.

No way.

"I'll call a taxi," I told him. "Thank you, Agent Calhoun."

He didn't move. Therefore, I didn't either.

Then he offered, "I know it's been a long night, Tess, but you give me twenty minutes, I can get away. Take you home."

I studied him and really saw him for the first time. A little salt in his pepper hair, not much. Tall. Broad shoulders. A bit of a belly. Nice wrinkles by his eyes, saying he either needed to wear protective eyewear in the sun more often or he laughed a lot. Older than me by maybe five years, maybe more and he was good at hiding it, maybe less and he didn't take great care of himself. No wedding band.

This was the kind of man for me. This was the kind of man who might take on that pale-faced woman in the mirror and handle her with care.

Not Jake Knox.

Never Jake Knox.

Agent Calhoun was a decent-looking man, probably a good man, maybe a safe man and, above all, I needed a man who made me feel safe.

But not being a bitch or anything, he was no dream man.

I'd fucked up once, gravitating toward a man who blinded me with his charisma if not his looks.

But if that night taught me nothing else, it taught me I needed to learn to play it safe in order to *get* safe.

Something tight and uncomfortable was sitting coiled in my belly. But it was squirming like it was about to unfurl and I'd had enough experience with that poisonous snake that I knew I didn't want it to do that.

But it was going to happen. I knew that too.

"I'll be okay," I said softly.

His head tipped to the side and something shifted through his eyes, disappointment, maybe, concern, possibly.

"Sure?" he asked, and I nodded.

He opened the door farther but stepped out of my way.

I stepped into the hall and dug into my purse for the phone. Lucky for all citizens of Denver, the taxi companies had easy-to-remember numbers they plastered on the sides of their cars.

I'd never called a taxi.

Until now.

I punched in one of the numbers as I walked down the hall. I put the phone to my ear, listening to it, eyes on the elevators in front of me as I walked out of the mouth of the hall and into a bustling open room filled with people, phones ringing, fingers tapping keyboards, and low conversations.

My eyes moved through the room unseeing. They blinked as I heard the taxi company answer in my ear and I stopped short.

My eyes were pointed through the window of an office, taking in the back of a man I knew.

Hell, I knew that old T-shirt and I'd committed that

fine ass in those faded jeans to memory. I'd been pressed to that back on a bike. My hands had moved across the skin of that back and that ass just that night after I'd removed that shirt and after he'd removed those jeans. My fingers had moved through that dark, messy hair that night too, and other times, countless times in the last four months.

He turned toward the door and I didn't see his face.

No.

I saw the shiny badge on his belt.

"You sleep naked?"

"No."

"Don't start tonight."

Oh.

My.

God.

He left the office he was in and my eyes went from his badge to his face. Since that thing in my belly was unfurling, growing, swelling, filling my stomach, slithering up my throat, I didn't notice the look on his face or feel his mood hit the room like a slap.

I just knew a man like Jake Knox would have not one thing to do with the pale-faced woman who was me.

Unless it was his job.

His eyes caught mine and he stopped dead.

I'd been stopped dead, but the minute his eyes hit mine I moved.

Rushing quickly toward the elevators, I hit the button at the same time my eyes scanned.

I found what I was looking for.

Exit.

Stairs.

I dashed to the door, opened it, darted through it, and then down.

I heard my heels echo on the stairs then I heard his boots.

One flight and around, I went faster. Two stories. Three flights to go.

"Tess," I heard his voice call and I went faster.

Another flight and around.

"Goddammit, Tess," he clipped, and I kept going.

Another flight and around.

His boots were getting closer.

Another flight, the last one. I raced down them and had a hand to the door, opening it when my wrist was seized in an iron grip, yanked away, my body with it. I was pulled from the door and pushed against the wall, Jake's tall, lean frame fencing me in.

I looked to the side.

"Let me go," I whispered.

"You promised we'd talk," he growled.

I shook my head and kept my eyes averted. "Let me go," I demanded.

His voice dipped gentle and his other hand curled around the side of my neck. "Tess, baby, you pro—"

My eyes shot to his and whatever he read in them made him stop talking and flinch.

"Let . . . me . . . *go*," I hissed.

He let me go and stepped back.

I walked instantly to the door and pulled it open.

Standing in it, I turned to him to see his eyes on me; his face unreadable, except his strong jaw was set in granite.

"Is your name even Jake?" I asked quietly.

His silvery-gray eyes, not melted, not quicksilver, not affectionate but glittering and hard, held mine.

I held my breath until he finally shook his head.

Then, without another word or a glance back, I walked through the door.

CHAPTER THREE

Kentucky

Three months later...

I was in my kitchen when I heard the knock at the door.

My eyes went to the clock on the microwave.

Holy crap.

Martha was early. Martha was never early. In fact, I told her to be there at three because I actually needed her to be there at three thirty. Martha kept a steady schedule of being at least fifteen minutes late but had an average of being half an hour late (I'd known Martha a long time, long enough for it to happen so often I could actually calculate that average, which I did) and, therefore, it wasn't unheard of for her to rush in, winded and filled with excuses forty-five minutes or an hour late.

It was ten to three and I didn't even have the cake ready.

Damn.

This meant one of two things.

Man trouble or wardrobe malfunction.

Both of these did not bode good things, for both of these

meant Martha would be in a more than the usual Martha tizzy. And the usual Martha tizzy, which was the result of the crazy, out-of-control life Martha lived, was bad enough.

Fuck.

"I'm elbow deep in icing, honey!" I shouted toward my front door, bending back over the cake with my pastry bag. "Let yourself in, it's open!" I finished as I continued to dot every third fluffy white buttercream frosting star with a point of pale yellow icing.

The door opened as I spun the cake around to get to more stars.

I was standing at the island in my kitchen, my head bent to the cake, when I felt her presence hit the room but stop in the doorway.

"I'm running a bit late," I told the cake. "Get yourself a pop or something. In fact, get me one. Cherryade. Crushed ice," I ordered, dotting more stars at the top border of the cake, then moving down to the bottom.

Martha didn't move.

My eyes lifted and my mouth opened to say something but the words and my breath got clogged in my throat when I saw not Martha but Jake Knox, arms crossed over his wide chest, one broad shoulder resting against the doorjamb, lean hips hitched to the side, motorcycle-boot-clad feet crossed at the ankles.

I said not a word and didn't move as I took in all that was him.

Ratty-assed, faded black T-shirt with the peeling words "Charlie Daniel's Band" over an equally peeling American flag fitting just right over his torso, a pair of mirrored shades shoved in the collar by an arm and dangling down. Jeans so faded they were their own unique shade of blue with frayed bits around the pockets and delicious worn patches at his crotch, the length of them fitting loose or snug in all the right places on his slim hips and long legs. Unruly dark hair about an inch longer than I remembered, so it was curling low on his neck and around his ears. Below his sharp cheekbones, along his strong jaw and chin, and down the column of his corded throat was, from my experience, at least three days' worth of stubble.

Silvery-gray eyes pointed right at me.

Fuck.

I straightened, filled pastry bag in my hands, and stared at him.

He stared back.

He did it better.

So I blinked and when I was about to say something, do something, maybe even yell something, he got there before me.

"You ready to talk now?"

I blinked again.

Then I whispered, "Sorry?"

"Talk, Tess." His deep voice rumbled across the kitchen at me. "You promised we'd talk. I wanna know if you're ready to do it now."

I dropped my pastry-bag-filled hands to the counter and kept staring at him.

Then I asked, "Have you lost your mind?"

He ignored my question and told me, "Name's Brock Lucas."

I closed my eyes and dropped my head as that knowledge filtered through me, knowledge I lay awake at night wondering about, knowledge that had been kept from me as I fell in love with an imposter.

"Tess, babe, eyes," he growled. "Now."

My eyes opened and my head came up as I felt a shaft of steel rip down my spine.

My eyes narrowed on his hard face as the electric feel of his mood finally made it through the cocoon of surprise shrouding me and sparked against my skin.

"Oh my God," I whispered. "Are you angry with me?"

"No," he bit off. "I *was* angry with you, seein' as I fucked my woman for the first fuckin' time, she made me a promise when my cum was still inside her and then just hours later she reneged on that promise. Now I'm here 'cause there's a goddamned for-sale sign planted in your front lawn and I walk in here and see you lookin' like this so, gotta say, babe, I'm not angry. I'm fuckin' *pissed*."

Did he . . . ?

Did he . . . ?

Did he just fucking say what I thought he just fucking said?

"Sorry?" I whispered again, but this whisper was different.

He didn't repeat himself. Instead he asked, "Where are your glasses?"

"What?"

"Your glasses, Tess. Where the fuck are your glasses? You never decorate a goddamned cake without your glasses."

"I got contacts," I snapped.

His head tipped back and he clipped to the ceiling, "Jesus," before I saw his jaw get hard.

Why in *the hell* were we talking about my glasses?

I didn't care. Nope. I didn't.

I only cared about one thing.

"Get out," I ordered. His chin tipped down and his eyes locked with mine.

"No."

I felt my eyebrows go up. "No?"

"Yeah, Tess, no."

"You have," I told him. "You have lost your mind."

He ignored me again and asked, "What the fuck are you wearing?"

"What am I wearing?"

"Yeah, babe, what the fuck are you wearing?"

I looked down at my T-shirt and jeans then I looked back at him.

"T-shirt and jeans..." I hesitated then spat, "*Brock*."

"No one calls me Brock. They call me Slim."

I blinked and something about that took me right out of our current scenario and into la-la land.

Therefore, I breathed, "What?"

He pushed away from the doorjamb while speaking. "No one calls me Brock. Mom, Dad, brother, sisters, friends since I was a kid called me Slim."

"You're not slim," I told him.

Although he was lean, he wasn't what I'd call slim.

"No, I'm not and I wasn't when I was a baby, seein' as I was over ten pounds when I was born. It was a joke 'cause I was a big kid. My family's screwy that way."

Whoa. He was over ten pounds when he was born? That was one huge kid.

He was tall, at least six one, maybe six two. And muscled. He wasn't slim at all. His body was built of lean, compacted muscle that had some bulk to it, sure, but I wouldn't call him huge now.

Since babies didn't come out muscled, I wondered if he wasn't a *big* baby but a *long* one.

It hit me then that, while I was distracted, he'd rounded the island and was getting close. I stopped thinking about his weight as a baby and his current size and started retreating at the same time I came out of la-la land and back into our current scenario.

"I want you to leave," I stated firmly.

"Yeah," he replied, still coming at me and I hit the side counter as he kept coming and talking. "I get that, but clue in, Tess. I ain't leavin'."

Then he was right there. So right there that I could feel his heat and I had to tip my head way back to look up at him, seeing as I was barefoot and not six foot one or two but five foot six.

"Please leave," I stated a fair bit less firmly.

He leaned in, settling his hands on the counter on either side of me and I lifted my hands (and the pastry bag) between us.

He also again ignored me. "You didn't call."

I stared into his angry eyes. "I didn't call?"

He glared at me with his angry eyes. "No, babe, you didn't call."

"I didn't call," I whispered. My heart, already beating fast, started to pound.

"Three months," he declared but said no more.

I stared into his glittering, silver eyes.

Then I lost my ever-lovin' mind.

"*Are you nuts?*" I shrieked.

"Tess—"

"Fuck you!" I shouted and pushed at him with my pastry-bag-filled hands. A thin stream of pale yellow icing shot out onto the floor beside us as well as on his Charlie Daniels tee.

I found the bag not in my hands and watched him twist his torso and toss it on the island next to the cake and twist back to me.

That was when I put my hands on the hard wall of his chest, shoved, and repeated on a shout, "Fuck you!"

He rocked back a couple of inches, then moved right back in. His face got into my face and he growled, "Fuckin' listen to me."

"No!" I yelled. "No way. No *fucking* way. You *used* me."

"It's my job," he ground out.

"Do you think I give a shit?" I asked.

"Maybe, if you'd calm the fuck down and listen for a goddamned minute, you'd understand why I *do* think you should fuckin' give a shit."

"I can assure you, Brock Lucas, that nothing you can say will make me understand why I should give a shit," I informed him.

"Your ex, Tess, that motherfucker needed to be taken down. That motherfucker is serious bad news."

My body went completely still at his words and I held his eyes as my next words trembled. "I know that, *Brock. I* know."

And it was then I watched with rapt attention as his eyes immediately melted quicksilver and his hands moved from the counter to my head, palms at the base of my neck, fingers in my hair, and his face dipped an inch away from mine.

Then he whispered a ragged, tortured "baby," and that one word cut through me like a jagged knife.

Oh God.

He knew.

Of course he knew.

Of course, of course, of course.

That thing tight in my belly uncurled, filling me up, slinking up my throat and this time it wasn't filled with the paralyzing poison of fear or despair. It was something else.

Panic.

I tried to tear away but Brock held on. One hand still at my head, the other arm sliced around my back, he shuffled me down the counter and pressed me into the corner.

With no way to escape, I held my body tight, hands pressed against his chest, and kept my eyes glued to his throat as I whispered, "Let me go and get out."

"No one knows that shit happened to you, do they?" he asked softly.

"Let me go and get out."

"You haven't told any of your girls."

Eyes firm on his throat, I demanded, "Let me go, Brock, and get out."

"Kept that shit buried deep," he murmured.

My eyes lifted to his and I screeched, "*Let me go and get out!*"

His arm around my back tightened and his hand shifted so his fingers were still in my hair but his thumb swept over my cheekbone.

"I was the first you let in there, wasn't I, baby?"

Oh *God*.

"Let me go and get out," I whimpered.

"Tess," he whispered.

I fell silent.

"You need to let that shit out," he advised and my gaze

slid to his earlobe. "Eyes," he ordered and my gaze slid back.

I still didn't speak.

He held my eyes.

Then he said softly, "I held back takin' us there, Tess. I didn't want us to go there until the shit with Heller was done and you were cleared and we were good to move on. But your goddamned glasses and that cute fuckin' look you'd get on your face every time I kissed you that made you look like you just experienced a fuckin' miracle, *shit*." His hand tensed on my head. "Shit, baby, you got to me and I couldn't hold back." His thumb swept my cheekbone. His eyes went from warm to hot and his voice went deep when he told me something, but he said it like he was talking to himself, "That look gets way fuckin' better after you come."

"Please let me go and get out," I whispered.

He shook his head. "It's the job and it's a shit part of the job and I'll tell you, Tess, I knew he violated you, no way I'd have played you. No way, Tess." His voice got lower and his face got closer when he said, "You gotta believe that, babe. I wouldn't have played you if I'd known."

"But you did," I said quietly.

His hand tensed on my head. "I didn't know."

"You still did it." I leaned into the counter, pulling back my head. "I didn't play you. I never played a single game with you. But you played me from start to finish."

His hand tensed on my head again as his eyes started glittering. "That's not true, Tess, and you fuckin' know it."

"You're right, *Brock*. Earlier with what you said, you're right. You're the first person I let in there and when I did, I didn't even know your fucking name."

"That fuckin' guy had to go down," he growled.

"Yes, he did but it doesn't warm my heart to think the first man I trusted with my time and attention after a very, *very* bad marriage was with me only to investigate my possible criminal relationship with my definitely criminal ex-husband."

"It started like that, yeah, it did and that lasted about a goddamned hour. You cannot stand there lookin' in my eyes and tell me you don't know the fuckin' second it stopped bein' that, because, if you do, you're a god-damned liar."

He was not wrong. I knew. I knew the exact second. I'd lain in bed at night thinking about that too.

Therefore, I didn't respond.

He kept speaking. "I had a job to do and we wanted a clean sweep. I knew you weren't gonna be swept up in that but I also knew they had to make certain, so *I* had to make them certain before they hauled your ass in and you finished them off."

"So you're saying you did what you did to protect me?"

"No, I'm sayin' I did my job. You weren't dirty, no need to protect you. And I'm sayin' for four fuckin' months I *liked* my job a whole fuck of a lot."

That took my breath away. So much so, I couldn't speak.

Brock didn't have the same problem. "You didn't have my name, Tess, but all that time you had me and you know it."

I looked back at his throat.

"Baby, *eyes,*" he growled and my eyes lifted to his.

"Why are you here?" I asked quietly and he sighed.

Then he asked back impatiently, "Honest to God?"

"What do you want from this talk?" I pushed.

He shook his head, but as he stared at me, I saw his eyes light and felt the sharp flickering voltage of his mood shift out of the room as the sweet hum that came with his humor started pulsing through it.

"How many conversations do you think I have with women I corner against a counter, hold in my fuckin' arms, and do it with icing all over my favorite fuckin' tee?" he asked.

Oh God.

I had to move this away from Brock being sexy and amused and back to Brock being out of my life somehow. So I did the best I could do.

"I don't know. Turns out, I don't know you very well."

He held my eyes and replied, "Well, lettin' you in a little more, the answer to that question is none. A bitch throws attitude at me, shouts in my face, and gets icing on my Charlie Daniels tee, that bitch isn't you, I walk out the door."

"I'm not fond of being referred to as a bitch," I snapped.

His face dipped close and I saw his eyes were now full on lit with his amusement. "And right now, darlin', you're just holdin' on to hold on and we both know it."

Damn. He was right.

I held his eyes.

Then I tried a different tactic.

"I can't do this now. I've got a cake to finish decorating. I need to change my shirt because now that icing is on me. And I have a baby shower to get to," I informed him and his lips tipped up as his hand at my head became fingers that slid through my hair. Then it moved down and around so he was holding me in both arms.

Damn, I missed this. He could be sweet, a lot. When he got in a good mood it was the best, the best ever. And he could be touchy, a lot. He held me. He held me close. He held me loose. He held me while he laughed. He held me while I laughed. He held me while he kissed me. And he held me just because.

And I missed it.

Damn.

"When're you gonna be home?" he asked.

"Later," I answered.

"When later?" he pressed.

"Later, later," I evaded.

His arms gave me a squeeze and he said low, "Tess."

Crap.

"I don't know. Later. Seven? Eight?"

"I'll be back at nine," he declared.

Damn.

"Why don't we make a date to meet for coffee?" I suggested.

"Maybe because I'm not stupid?"

Damn!

I was totally going to bail on coffee and he knew it.

He kept speaking. "But right now you're gonna tell me why you put your house on the market."

"I need a change," I told him.

"Yeah." His arms gave me a squeeze. "I see this. You've shifted ten pounds that looked better when it was on your ass and tits. You're in a tee and jeans and not your fancy-ass clothes and heels. You lost the glasses and got contacts. The only thing I like, babe, is the hair. Looks good longer and lighter."

He liked my hair.

I tried not to let that make me feel tingly but it ended up more like me pretending I didn't feel the tingles that made me feel.

"Brock, seriously, can we talk about this later?"

"Where you movin'?" he asked, telling me that no, we couldn't talk about it later.

"I haven't decided yet," I lied, and the pulsing hum of his humor and good mood went flat as his eyes narrowed.

"Christ, Tess, did the three months you spent lickin' your fuckin' wounds erase the four months we spent together so you don't remember you can't pull shit over on me?"

My eyes narrowed too and I informed him, "That was not cool."

"No, what was not cool was you taking three fuckin' months to lick your wounds and makin' me haul my ass to you, but we'll talk about that tonight."

I felt my body go stiff. "If that's why you're coming over tonight then don't bother."

"Okay, no," he said on a low rumble. "I see this shit shook out some sass in you, babe. My Tess was sugar sweet from the minute my eyes hit her to the minute I kissed her good night. I know what happened was fucked and it fucked with your head, so I'm willin' to ride that with you. But you gotta know now, once we clear a bump, you're not draggin' us back time and again so we become intimately acquainted with it. We're over the bump. We move the fuck on. We're agreed I'm over tonight, nine o'clock. We sort shit out we shoulda sorted out three months ago and see where we are. But right now, you're tellin' me where you're movin'."

"*We* didn't agree to anything, Brock. You said you were coming over. *I* want to have coffee."

"Don't shit me, Tess. You'll bag on coffee."

"See!" I cried. "Is this sinking in that maybe I'm try-ing to move on in a variety of ways, including moving on from Jake Knox slash Brock Lucas?"

Way, way, *way* wrong thing to say.

I knew this when one of his arms got tight, the other one slanted up my back, his hand cupping the back of my head as he leaned deep into me, pressing me over the counter, and his face got in mine.

"I was observing," he snarled. "Calhoun promised he'd handle you with care. I was keepin' an eye on him 'cause, he didn't, I told him I'd rip his fuckin' throat out and I wanted to make sure, he fucked with you, I didn't fuckin' delay."

My body froze except my lips, which parted, and my eyes, which I felt grow round.

Brock kept talking.

"He didn't. He pushed and you broke and what you said when you broke, babe, I didn't know. Calhoun didn't know. No one fuckin' knew. But I'll tell you this. Those four words you said I'll *never* fuckin' forget. Those four fuckin' words soldered themselves deep in the walls of my gut in a way they'll never be cut loose. They had to drag me outta there so I didn't go after him or try and get to you."

I continued to stare up at him, stunned.

"Then you walked away and I knew you needed that even as it pissed me off you did it and broke your promise to me when you did. But you needed it. Then you stayed away and I see now you took that time to build your wall but I don't give a fuck. That night, I found out my woman had been violated and for three fuckin' months I've lived with that and I'm done livin' with it and lyin' awake wonderin' where your head is at. I'm done, Tess. So tonight, at nine, I'm back, we're talkin' shit through, and then we're gonna see where we're at. You're clear of Heller. You don't know dick. You aren't a part of that investigation. We're free and clear and we're gonna explore that. But now... now darlin', you're gonna tell me why you got a goddamned for-sale sign in your yard when you told me you love this house so much you didn't mind livin' in it until you die."

"The crash," I found my mouth whispering and I watched him blink.

"What?" he bit out.

"During... when Agent Calhoun... when I..." I stopped and licked my lips. "There was a crash outside the interrogation room. That was you."

"Yeah, babe, that was me throwing a chair against the wall."

That was him throwing a chair against the wall.

That was him.

That was him throwing a *chair* against *the wall*.

I closed my eyes and did a face-plant into his chest as my body relaxed in his arms.

That was Brock throwing a chair against the wall when he heard me admit to being raped.

As this knowledge flowed through me, it did it like a warm gush of clean water wiping away years of filth.

Oh my.

"Tess," he called as his hand at my head tensed and his arm around me gave me a squeeze.

I opened my eyes and saw tee.

"Is this really your favorite tee?" I whispered against the fabric.

I felt his body still for a brief moment before I felt his whiskers pull at my hair as he slid his jaw down the side of my head.

Then he whispered in my ear, "Yeah."

"It's old and ratty-assed," I informed him.

"Exactly," he informed me.

I closed my eyes again. Then I smiled. The smile faded from my lips as I opened my eyes and tilted my head back. His came up with mine and I looked into his quicksilver eyes.

"Do you want me to stop by the store and pick up some Bud on the way home from the shower?" I asked softly and the mood shifted in the room again. It got warm and heavy, sultry, sweet.

My favorite mood of his. Bar none.

Damn, I missed that too.

"Yeah, baby," he answered softly.

"Okay," I whispered.

He closed his eyes and then he opened them and dipped his head.

He kissed me, light and gentle at first, then warm, heavy, sultry, and sweet.

My toes curled and my fingers did too, right into his ratty-assed tee at his back.

Okay, okay. Seriously.

I missed this most of all.

He lifted his head and his hand at mine shifted around to the side of my neck, taking my hair with it, his thumb moving out to catch me under the chin and keep me facing him.

"Where you movin', darlin'?"

"Kentucky."

He did a slow blink. Then he asked, "Kentucky?"

I shrugged.

He grinned.

Then he said quietly, "All right, baby, we'll talk about that later too."

"Okay," I said quietly back.

His eyes moved over my face before his hand shifted up so his thumb could glide over my cheek, my lips. He dipped his head and put his lips where his thumb was for a brief touch and pulled away.

"Later, babe," he whispered.

"Later, Slim."

That got me a full-blown, striking white smile.

My toes curled again.

Then he was gone.

CHAPTER FOUR

Committed to His Job

"This cake is so beautiful it's a shame to cut it!" Ada cried right before she dug right into the huge cake I'd made for her shower.

I smiled a polite smile as the abundance of women tittered around me excitedly at the thought of getting their free slice of a Tessa O'Hara cake. Not to brag or anything but my cakes and cupcakes had been written up in the local papers because they looked as good as they tasted. My bakery was shoulder to shoulder from open to close, ten to seven, seven days a week. That cake was homemade yellow cake with vanilla buttercream frosting. Simple but a winner. Even I knew they were in for a treat.

That titter changed as they watched Ada cut miniscule slivers and put them on the paper plates with the big blue teddy bear on them.

There you go.

That was Ada.

She told me how many people were coming so I made a fourteen-inch, four-layer cake, plenty for everyone to have a nice thick slice. But Ada was cutting slivers so she could have half a cake as leftovers for her and Vic.

I sighed, wondering what the heck I was doing there at all since three years ago, when Ada met Vic, and because she was thirty-six and her biological clock was ticking so loudly the personnel at NORAD were tracking it, she immediately dedicated herself to the sacred quest of making him her fiancé. Then her husband. Now the man who was the father of her unborn child. Through this, Ada pretty much checked out of my life.

She called me to make the cake for her engagement party then for her bridal shower, her wedding, and now this. Only two of those cakes she paid me for and she asked for (and stupid me, I gave her) a discount on both.

I'd only seen her on those occasions and all of them required me bringing a present.

Other than that, Ada was all about sculpting (with chisel and hammer if she had to) Vic into the perfect suburban husband, through wedding planning, house hunting, house decorating, and baby making. She didn't have time to be a friend unless it was to call on all of us to buy her presents and celebrate milestones of her life.

I didn't even think she sent me a Christmas card last year.

And I had my own milestone to think about. I didn't need to be here.

Okay, maybe it wasn't a milestone. But whatever it was, it was a big, huge, stinking deal because no way that scene with Brock "Slim" Lucas in my kitchen was not a big, huge stinking deal.

I knew it.

I started thinking about how and when I could get out

of there while handing around plates with slivers of cake and baby-blue plastic forks on them.

But when I gave one to the woman sitting beside me, she muttered an annoyed "Muthafucka."

As it would, this surprised me. So I looked at her, to see her staring down at her nearly transparent slice of cake and I was right. She appeared annoyed.

I didn't know her but had met her that day. Her name was Elvira, mocha skin, hair in stylish crop with blonde highlights at the long bangs, fabulous tangerine top that showed even more fabulous cleavage, skintight skirt that showed this baby had back, and she would have been shorter than me if she wasn't wearing four-inch killer stiletto-heeled sandals. She came to the party with a cadre of beauties, all of whom I'd met in passing before at Ada's milestone celebrate-me celebrations. A knockout blonde named Gwen, a tall, svelte, modelesque blonde named Tracy, and another modelesque, tall, svelte African American named Camille.

But I'd never met Elvira.

"How do you know Ada?" I asked and her eyes came to me.

"Don't know the bitch and don't wanna know a bitch who puts out bowls of peanuts, no honey roast, no salt, just motherfuckin' peanuts with the motherfuckin' skins still on them, and some corn chips for a party. Then she gives me a sliver of cake. Shit. What? Crazy," she replied and I stared at her mainly because her answer was crazy. Honest, but crazy.

Then I asked, "You crashed a baby shower?"

"No. Got dragged here by Beanpole." She jerked her head at the tall, svelte, modelesque Tracy. "She didn't

wanna come alone. Gwen and Cam didn't wanna come
at all. I'm seein' now why. Trace has got a heart of gold
but no capacity to get it when people walk all over her,
even when they're doin' it in high heels. She talked us into
it with promises of employee discounts at her store. She
works at Neiman's."

"Mm-hmm," I mumbled, thinking that would do it.
There was a time in my life when I'd go to a really bad
baby shower with the promise of an employee discount
at Neiman's. That time was over, though. As I had done
frequently through the years, starting at around age six,
I'd entered a new phase in my life. This one was one
where Christian Louboutin didn't factor, but Harley-
Davidson did.

As I was thinking this, she suddenly and bizarrely
announced, "Done with this shit. Let's have cocktails."

Before I could open my mouth, she shot up to standing, grabbed her enormous purse that clunked and clinked
when she did, hefted it up on her shoulder, grabbed my
hand, and pulled me out of the couch.

When she had me up, she declared loudly, "Smoke
break!"

Everyone's eyes came to us, some of them shocked,
seeing as these days you could light up a doobie and no
one would blink, but if you lit up a smoke, you courted
being publicly stoned to death. But most of the eyes were
envious and probably not because they smoked. Probably
because they, like me and obviously Elvira, wanted to
escape.

"Smoke break?" Ada asked, her face twisted in
revulsion.

"Yeah, back deck, okay?" Elvira asked, but didn't wait

for an answer. She started tugging me to the sliding-glass doors at the back of Ada's picture-perfect suburban home while jerking her chin at her posse.

I had no choice but to go but I did manage to bug my eyes out at Martha as I went—my nonverbal invitation for her to get her ass up and follow.

I'd known Martha since we were in fifth grade. I moved out to Denver to be with Martha. Before marrying Damian, I lived with Martha. After leaving Damian, I again lived with Martha. Therefore, Martha read my nonverbal invitation and got her ass up.

"Ice," I heard Elvira order.

Tracy nodded and peeled off as Elvira tugged me out the door.

She let my hand go and sashayed to the picture-perfect lawn furniture on the deck, and folded then shoved my slice of cake into her mouth all in one go (though, it was so small, this wasn't hard). Then she dropped the plate to the table and plonked down her massive purse, which again clinked and clunked. I watched in unconcealed astonishment as she started unearthing the ingredients for cosmopolitans (including a stainless-steel cocktail shaker) from her purse as Martha, Gwen, Camille, and I rounded the table.

"Ohmigod, I'm *so* gonna kill Tracy for this. I didn't like Ada even *before* that bitch hooked up with Vic. But this party is so bad, if ex-prisoners of war attended it, they'd reminisce nostalgically about the days shit was shoved up their fingernails," Camille muttered.

"Have you *seen* Vic?" Gwen asked Camille and got a head shake to her question so she continued. "Shadow of his former self. He used to live and breathe Broncos,

Nuggets, Rockies, and his vintage Chevy Chevelle. Now he's wearing button-downs instead of Elway jerseys and driving a minivan and Ada hasn't even popped that kid out yet."

"Poor Vic," Martha muttered.

"Poor Vic, my ass," Elvira stated while pouring vodka into her shaker. "Needs to man up, take charge of his woman." Her eyes sliced through Camille and Gwen and she proclaimed, "You bitches know what I'm sayin'."

Both "bitches" nodded in a way I found interesting since they clearly did know what she was saying and I did not and wanted to know more. Before I could ask, I heard the sliding glass door open. I twisted to look as it closed and saw the gorgeous, glamorous Tracy carrying two big glasses filled with ice strutting out like she was on a cat-walk and not on a picture-perfect back deck.

"Okay, just gotta say, I'm glad we're out here because I wanna know what the frig is up with you," I heard Martha say and I looked to her to see she was looking at me and, therefore, talking to me.

This was probably not good.

Martha was Elvira's height, which was to say five foot four. She was also now taller than me, for I was wearing a pair of flip-flops with a black base and glittery silver on the straps and she was wearing a pair of platform pumps with a six-inch heel and two-inch platform. She was rounded just right, and had curly dark brown hair that looked fabulous against her pale skin and bright blue eyes.

She also knew me better than anyone in this world (or, at least, the parts I let her know). She was always late. She was always in a tizzy. Her life was always filled with drama. But I loved her and she loved me, always and forever, no matter what. I'd been through the thick and the thin with her, all of it, and there was a lot of it, riding her killer waves, holding her hand the whole time. She was grateful for it and didn't have a problem with letting that show.

That said, although she could be immensely gentle, insightful, and thoughtful, that didn't mean when she had something to say, even if that something might be uncomfortable, she didn't say it.

Which I was getting the sense she was gearing up to do now.

So I asked a fake innocent, "What?"

"What?" she asked back, not buying my fake innocent for a second and I knew this when her eyebrows shot up and she kept speaking. "Girl, I walked into your house and you had a face... a face..." She shook her head. "I don't even *know* what was up with your face and you still got that face."

Then, as if I didn't know what a face was, she lifted a finger and jabbed it toward mine, going on as she dropped it.

"All I know is, three months you've been hell on wheels, no one could keep up with you, and now you look all foggy, like you're living in a dream world."

Damn.

I really needed to remember that even as Martha lived out her ever-present drama, that didn't mean she didn't pay attention.

"I don't know what you're talking about," I lied.

"Sure you do," Elvira stated, dumping ice into her cocktail shaker.

"Uh..." I mumbled to Elvira, a little surprised since

I'd met her an hour before and she couldn't know anything about me, especially not about this.

"I got the gift," Elvira informed me, answering my unasked question. "Can read people's faces." She topped the cocktail shaker and started shaking. "And yours is sayin' you know *exactly* what your homegirl is talkin' about."

Oh crap.

I felt all eyes on me but it was Martha who spoke next.

"All right, Tess, I backed off because you *know* I did not like that Jake. But that look on your face, I'm done backing off."

Oh *crap*.

At this point Martha looked to the beauty parade of women around the table and shared, "She got hooked up with this guy...hot and when I say hot I mean—"she licked her finger and then sliced it through the air making a sizzle noise and went on—"*smokin'* hot. But bad news."

It was safe to say I didn't want to talk about this at all but it was safer to say that I didn't want to talk about this drinking clandestine cosmos on Ada's picture-perfect back deck with a bunch of women I didn't know during a very badly hosted baby shower I didn't want to be at. But instead, I wanted to be home preparing for nine o'clock when Brock would be back and we would be talking.

Therefore, I started, "Martha—"

"No, girl," Martha cut me off, lifting a hand in my face to which Elvira muttered, "Oh shit, this is serious. She's givin' the hand."

Martha continued, dropping her hand and looking back at the bevy of beauties. "This guy had it all. The walk, the voice, the hair, the ass. Kid you not, I'd sell

my soul just to run my fingers along his forearms." She
leaned in and semi-whispered, "He's got these veins that
pop out on his hands and forearms, freaking *delicious*."

Oh jeez.

Totally paid attention.

"Mm-hmm, I hear you," Elvira and Tracy muttered in
unison, their eyes rapt on Martha's face as were Gwen's,
but Camille was looking at me.

Martha went on. "But did he take her to his pad? No.
Did she know where he worked? No. Did she meet any of
his friends? No. Family? Unh-unh. Always her place or
some dive. Never a nice meal. Never got dressed up and
took my girl on the town. He met *her* friends. He showed
up at *her* bakery. But for all she knows, he's a lone wolf
livin' off his family's inheritance and, from what I could
tell, it wasn't a generous one. If he called, she answered.
She couldn't and he left a message, she called straight
back. He wanted to meet, she asked where and what time
and then she was there."

"Oh boy," Gwen muttered, clearly disappointed I'd let
down our side.

"You got *that* right. Oh *boy*," Martha agreed. "Did she
listen to me when I told her to play it cool? No. Did she
listen to me when I said in four months you should see your
man's pad, at the very least meet a friend, just one? *No*.
I get it. She was into this dude. Hell, Melissa Etheridge
would be into this dude. He's the walking, talking, breathing definition of a dude you…would…be…*into*. But a
girl's gotta play it cool and not put herself out there."

I tried again. "Martha—"

She turned her bright blue eyes to me. "Unh-unh, Tess.
You put yourself out there and I know, seein' as for the

last three months there's been no talk, no sightings, Jake Knox all of a sudden fell off the face of the earth." She leaned into me. "I *know*." Then she leaned back. "It's ended. Because off you go, hell-bent on whatever you're hell bent on."

She turned back to the girls and kept going.

"Suddenly, after twenty-five years of me talking to her about it, she gets contacts. Suddenly, she's at kickboxing classes three days a week. Suddenly, she's looking at places to open a new bakery and expand her business at the same time she's put the house she loves on the market and is waxin' on about movin' to Kentucky. Suddenly, she's off to a new hairdresser, spends three hundred friggin' dollars for a new friggin' look. Suddenly, she's not shopping at Nordstrom's but scrounging through the racks of Biker Babes 'R' Us."

Martha settled back on her heels and kept right on talking.

"Now, we all know, a girl gets dumped by a serious hot guy she's got two options. She deposits her ass at the nearest LaMar's and steadily eats her way through the inventory until she's gained fifty pounds and gives up on men until she finds herself a beer-bellied loser who worships the ground she walks on. Or she gets herself a new look, kickboxes her way to a new ass, and throws herself into her job. That means she's living and breathing for that moment when she sees him again and she can say, 'Look what you gave up, asshole.'"

Martha's eyes came back to me.

"And that's what you've been doin'."

That wasn't what I was doing.

Or not *exactly*.

"Honey—" I began again only to get cut off again.

"But today, I see it in your eyes. Something is up and my guess is that something is that guy's back. You're in your head again, livin' the dream that he's going to be all you want him to be when everything about him screams he...is...*not*."

"Tell it like it is, sister," Elvira encouraged.

"Um...not to be rude or anything, but..." I looked at the girl gang. "I don't really know you all and maybe—"

Elvira cut me off. "Nope, you don't know us. That's the damned truth but I'll tell you, from what I hear your girl sayin', it's intervention time and we all got tits and ass—except Camille, she's just got ass, but lucky for her, God gave her plenty 'a that—so we're in the club and anytime a member gets herself in a situation where she needs an intervention, it's our duty to kick in even if we don't know the sister," Elvira stated then her eyes scanned the table and she asked, "Am I right?"

I stared at Elvira, not happy to admit that what she was saying was sheer lunacy but it was also right as most anything that had to do with women was. And this included her observation that Camille was light up top but she made up for it by being generous on the bottom.

"You're right, Elvira," Tracy chimed in.

"I think—" Camille started but Elvira talked over her.

"Spill," she ordered me. "This Jake back?"

"Kind of," I found my mouth saying, and Elvira's eyebrows shot together in a scary way.

"Kind of? How can a boy *kind of* be back?"

"Um..." I muttered, avoiding Martha's eyes since she was right. I didn't share anything about what had happened with Brock, Damian, and being investigated by a multiagency task force that came together to dismantle my ex-husband's drug operation and I was seeing, just then, this was probably something girlfriends shared.

Elvira yanked off the top of the cocktail shaker and then extended her arm across the table, offering it to me. "Suck some of that back, girlfriend, and let 'er rip."

That was when I found my hand reaching for the cocktail shaker. Then, as told by a somewhat scary Elvira, I took it and sucked some back.

She made good cosmos.

I handed it off to Tracy, who was standing beside me so she could partake, and I pulled in a breath and started.

"Okay, well, see, I didn't tell you..." I turned to Martha, "because I... well... it was messed up."

"Oh boy," Gwen muttered again.

"Keep talking," Martha said quietly, her eyes on my face, her body braced, and I knew she was worried.

Damn.

"His name isn't Jake Knox. It's Brock Lucas," I whispered and felt something weird and tense coming from the table but since Martha was blinking at me and looking more worried, I hurried on. "He was... okay, here it is. Damian is a drug kingpin and he called me nine months ago, lying to me that his dad was sick. I met him for lunch and he told me he wanted to reconcile."

I stopped talking mainly because Martha shrieked a very loud, "*What?*"

I put my hand on her arm and talked quickly. "Honey, it was... it was nothing."

"That jackass calls you, Tess, it's not nothing," she snapped, her bright blue eyes flashing.

She was right. She didn't know the worst of it with

him but she never liked him either. Said from the beginning he was a bad seed. Told me while she was trying on maid-of-honor dresses that she was performing her duties under protest. She always hated Damian.

Which was why I never told her he hit me and raped me. She'd lose it and I needed her breathing free air, not serving time for manslaughter.

"You're right," I agreed.

"Damn straight I am," she shot back.

I pulled in more breath. "Anyway, I told him, obviously, I wasn't interested. But you know Damian."

She shook her head then told the girl posse around the table, "Dick never gives up. Sinks his poisonous fangs in you and doesn't let go until he injects *all* the venom."

"Oo, lawdy, seems you don't got good radar when it comes to pickin' 'em," Elvira muttered.

"No, her radar is beyond not good. Beyond malfunctioning. It's straight out broke," Martha agreed and I was wondering if perhaps Elvira and Martha were not such a good match. Denver was relatively peaceful. I'd never heard of riots or sieges or militant hostile takeovers of land and I was foreseeing this if these two got together and rallied the female population of the Denver metropolitan area as a protest to shelter all women against dickhead assholes.

"Go on, girl," Camille prompted quietly and I looked around to see her, Gwen, and Tracy's eyes gentle on me.

I nodded and went on. "It gets worse."

"Oh boy," Gwen whispered.

"Shit," Martha muttered.

"You don't say," Elvira mumbled.

I kept talking. "Like I said, Damian is a drug kingpin who's in jail, or was. Now he's out on bail awaiting trial."

Martha glared at me. She knew this. Everyone did. It had been in the papers. She'd only broached it with me once. I told her he wasn't in my life, so I didn't care, and she'd backed off about that too.

I kept going. "But since he contacted me and *kept* contacting me, the task force investigating him thought maybe I was involved in his operation."

"Oh boy," Gwen whispered.

"Shit," Martha muttered.

"You don't say," Elvira mumbled.

I continued, "So, they, um...well, they sent someone in undercover to get close to me and that someone they sent was Jake slash Brock."

"*Holy fuck!*" Martha shouted.

"Honey, keep it down," I whispered, my body getting tight.

Martha leaned across the table, snatched the cocktail shaker out of Camille's hand, and downed a huge gulp like it was Kool-Aid before she dropped her hand and her eyes cut to me.

I took that as my cue to keep going.

"Well, um...that was it, really. They did their sweep. I was caught up in it. They searched my house, my car, the bakery, did a forensic search of my computers and another of my finances, brought me into the station to talk to me and I found out who he was. We had a few words and I walked away."

I stopped talking, which meant Martha started.

"I gotta tell you, Tess, I knew Damian was a bad seed. When I read that shit about him in the paper, it did not surprise me."

I held her eyes and settled in for the "I told you so's."

I was not disappointed.

"And I gotta tell you, I knew somethin' was *not right* with that Jake slash Brock slash whoever-the-fuck."

I pressed my lips together.

"And I gotta tell you, I cannot *believe* you did not share any of this shit with me."

I bit my lip.

"Now, what I wanna know is, how is he back?"

I released my lip only for both to slide to the side. Martha's eyes narrowed.

I decided, since I'd kept so much from her, and I really shouldn't have, that it was the right thing to do to answer.

"He stopped by today to explain," I said quietly.

"Yeah? And what'd he say?"

"Um... well, he was, uh... well..."

I petered out.

"Oh boy," Gwen whispered.

I started talking again when Martha got a look like her head was about to explode.

"He wants us to talk stuff out and see where we are."

"Where you are?" Martha whispered and I shrugged, even though I knew that was not my best play. "Okay, where are you?" she asked.

"He's coming over tonight at nine," I informed her and she rolled her eyes to the heavens.

"Oh boy," Gwen and Camille said in unison.

I took in another breath.

Martha rolled her eyes back to me. "Don't do this," she said softly.

"Martha—"

She shook her head. "I'm tellin' you, Tess. Do not do this."

"I—"

She grabbed my arm. "Listen to me, okay, seriously, open your ears for once and *listen to me*. This guy is bad news. *Bad news*. Okay, so he's not up-his-own-ass-dickhead bad news like I thought. Instead, he's a coplike, up-his-own-ass dickhead who played you. Just because he's on the right side of the law even though I thought he was on the wrong side doesn't mean he's right for you."

"Honey—"

She shook my arm and shook her head.

"*Listen to me, Tess*," she hissed. "I do not get why you live your life with your head buried in the sand but I love you and that's you, so okay, you do. But because you do it's my job to look out for you when you're buried, and right now, I'm looking out for you."

She moved closer to me and her eyes got intense before she kept talking.

"You are beautiful. You are so sweet, damn, honey, too sweet. I love that about you. *Everyone* loves that about you. You're forty-three years old, you had a rotten marriage to the king of all assholes who's finally proven he's truly the king of all assholes, and you're still naïve and innocent and that's cute. It is. Trust me. Guys think so too. But that makes you a mark for players out there and you've managed to steer clear because life scares the fuckin' beejeezus out of you and now when you take the leap it's with someone who is *not* good for you. Someone who any woman who's not got her head in the sand would take one look at, know was fun to play with, and then move the fuck on."

She shook her head and her hand on my arm gave me a squeeze.

"Not you. You have visions of white picket fences and making him extravagant birthday cakes until he dies. He started this shit with you as his mark and I know why he's back, because you're naïve and innocent and he thinks it's cute. But he's going to chew you up, Tess. Chew you up and spit you out. He already has, and girl, my sweet girl, you gotta pull your head outta the sand and see him for what he is and that he's gonna do it again."

"Mm-hmm," Elvira muttered.

I turned my eyes to her.

Then I said what I knew to this group would sound stupid. "You all don't know him."

"Uh . . . sorry to say, but we do," Gwen said quietly and I turned surprised eyes to her.

"You do?" I asked.

"Well *I* do. It was a while ago but . . . uh . . ." She looked at Elvira then back at me. "He was . . . my man is in the business and there was a situation where I got involved and Lucas was also involved. He was undercover then too and . . ." She paused, pulled in a soft breath and finished softly. "Sorry, Tess, he was also with a girl during that operation. Her name was Darla and she was a skank, total skank, total bad-news skank, but he was pretending to be with her while actually *being with her* in order to take down the bad guy. It's cool he's committed to his job. But Brock Lucas is known by all to be seriously *committed to his job*."

I stared at her and I knew what she was saying.

I knew exactly what she was saying.

That thing tight in my belly started unfurling again, hissing, bearing its fangs, preparing to strike.

Damn.

I had to get out of there and get it under control before it choked me, or worse, poisoned me.

"I've gotta go," I whispered, stepping away from the table.

Martha's hand still on me tightened. "No, honey."

I pulled carefully free and took another step back as I felt all their eyes soft on me.

"I've gotta go," I repeated.

"Not thinkin' that's a good idea, hon," Elvira said gently.

I looked to Martha and whispered, "I'll call you later."

"Tess, honey—" she started to whisper back but I turned and hightailed it through the door.

I caught Ada and told her I had a headache.

Then I grabbed my purse and went out to my car.

I hoped Elvira, Gwen, Camille, or Tracy would drop Martha at my place to pick up her car.

And I stupid, stupid, *stupidly* stopped by the store and bought a six-pack of Bud in bottles, Brock's preference, on the way home.

CHAPTER FIVE

The Light of a Warm, Sunny Day

I STARED AT myself in the mirror of my bathroom.

I now did this a lot. Ever since I came back from the police station after catching sight of myself in the one-way mirror, I did it. Looking at myself for the first time ... no ... actually *examining* myself for the first time in my whole life.

Martha was a little right but mostly she was wrong.

The last three months hadn't been about building a Tessa O'Hara who, if Jake slash Brock saw her again, he would think, "Whoa, shit, I fucked up screwing over *that*."

It had been about finding out who I was.

No, not even that.

It had been about not *being* who I was becoming.

The day after I got interrogated by a member of a multiagency task force regarding my ex-husband's criminal exploits, I looked in the mirror, examined myself, and came to the uneasy knowledge that I had no fucking clue who I was, no clue where I was going, and no clue who I wanted to be.

The only thing I knew, looking in the mirror that day and all the days since, was that I knew I didn't want to be me.

So I was trying a new me on for size.

In all this examining, I knew I'd been doing this unconsciously for a while, drifting through life just as Martha said, with my head in the sand. But along the way I was apathetically trying on new versions of me. I wasn't paying a lick of attention, so unlike other women, sometime in my late twenties or my thirties, I did not find the me that fit.

I liked decorating cakes. I got off on the fact people thought they were beautiful and loved to eat them. I was really proud of my bakery, how it looked, how inviting it was inside and the fact I could do something I loved and make a decent living with it.

But that was as far as I'd gotten.

I got derailed along the way, and during my three months of mirror examinations of my face, my hair, my body, and my soul, I knew it was when I met Damian.

He wasn't hard on the eyes but he wasn't hot either.

What he was was charismatic.

He could so totally be the leader of a cult of fanatics who were disenfranchised and needed to latch onto someone strong and compelling so they could let go of the struggle of daily decisions, their consequences both good and bad, and allow someone to show them their path.

I knew this because it happened to me.

He was a stockbroker then, youngish but already successful, going places, driven. He sucked me in with his charisma and big personality and nice car and great clothes and large lifestyle. But it was me who kept my head buried in the sand and didn't notice he had a very short fuse, an explosive temper, and his drive was unhealthy. He had to have the nicest car, house, clothes and he needed to prove his manhood in a variety of ways—with me, fucking other women, and besting other men.

Even though, early, this started to crawl through my skin, gather in my belly, and tighten up, curling in on itself and sitting there, poisoning me all the while I kept my head buried and ignored it. Until it got to the point he was backhanding me to end an argument and then he raped me one night when I told him I was not in the mood. We argued about it. This argument escalated beyond reason. He suddenly and terrifyingly lost his mind and took what he wanted anyway.

So that happened.

And that was then.

This was now.

Was I right back where I started? Starting something, eyes closed, head buried, hope springing eternal with a magnetic, moody, driven man who was going to suck me into his captivating but dysfunctional vortex with him not giving a damn how banged up I got swirling around in his personal cyclone?

On this thought, I heard the knock on the front door.

Perfect timing.

I gave myself one last long look in the mirror. Then, stupidly hopeful or intuitively right, either way, feeling cautious, unsure, and hesitant, my feet took me to the front door.

I got up on my toes and looked out the little square window to see Brock standing there, head turned, eyes aimed to the street. I opened the door and saw what his eyes were aimed at.

Martha and Elvira were standing beside Martha's car, and even in the light cast only by a Denver streetlamp, I could see Martha was glaring daggers at Brock and Elvira was summing him up and I knew with them being there that their timing was planned.

Well, on the bright side, it was good to know my friend got a ride.

"Hey," I whispered, and his head turned to me.

His mouth was twitching before he noted, "I take it you filled in your posse."

"Uh..." I mumbled.

His lip twitch became a grin. He planted a hand on my belly and shoved me inside as he entered.

"Hey, guys!" I called in order not to be rude.

"Be smart!" Martha shouted back, clearly not feeling the need not to be rude, for her words could have only one meaning and Brock firmly shut the door.

Well, I guess that conversation was over.

I looked up at him. He was still grinning.

Damn.

"You get beer?" he asked and I nodded.

He left me at the door and walked through my living room to the kitchen in the back.

I went to the window and saw that Martha and Elvira were conferring.

The good news was, if there was a way to buy explosives and fuses on the Internet, they had not had time to send in their order and receive it. The other good news was, unless you had contacts in the criminal underworld or with mercenaries or the like, such items were not available on the open market. I knew Martha had no such contacts. Elvira was a wildcard.

The bad news was, for Martha to have so much drama in her life, that meant she was a creative person and I figured Elvira was too. And I didn't think this was good.

"Babe, you want one?" I heard Brock call, and I called back, "No," as I kept watching the terrible twosome plotting outside.

Apparently I did this long enough for Brock to pop the cap on a cold one and return to me, for suddenly my blinds were snapped shut.

I blinked at the closed blinds. Then I turned to him just in time to watch him lean in to me. He grabbed my hand and pulled me to the sofa.

He sat.

Then he did what he used to do. That was, tug me down so I was sitting astride him.

Brock liked to talk like this and I couldn't say I hated it. In fact, I liked it. There was an intimacy to it that was nice, a connection that felt good and, I had to admit, it was comfy.

And as I said, he was touchy. I always thought it was a little weird, but in a good way, that this tough, rough, wild man liked closeness so much and so often. I thought it said a lot about him and all of it was good.

Now I wasn't so sure.

He took a drag off his beer, his silver eyes not leaving my face.

When he dropped his hand, both came to rest on my thighs. But the one not holding a beer was open, moving slowly and soothingly up to my hip, down my thigh, and back again (something else he used to do, something else I used to like and now something I still liked).

He remarked, "I see my sweet Tess has spent some time gettin' her head filled with shit."

Hmm. I didn't know if he was right or wrong about that.

"Brock," I whispered, but said no more.

This obviously was okay, for Brock was in the mood to talk.

"Lot about women I do not get. The biggest is that they listen to each other's shit. No one knows what goes down between a woman and her man except that woman. Only thing they know is what went down with their own men. This colors what spews outta their mouths when they're yammerin' about their friends' men even when what they're sayin' has got fuck-all to do with the situation at hand."

"I'm not sure that's true," I replied. "Martha is my closest friend and I know she has my best interests at heart."

"She know you when you married Heller?" he asked and I nodded. "Your girl had your best interests at heart, babe, she woulda tackled you when you were walking down the aisle."

"She did her best," I shared, then kept sharing. "She told me she was a bridesmaid under protest. She always hated Damian."

"How's she feel about me?" he asked, a question I knew he knew the answer to because Martha had been around him on several occasions and she was not one of those girlfriends who pretended to like their girlfriend's boyfriend when she didn't like him. She was one of those girlfriends who stared at the men in their friends' lives balefully, made catty comments under her breath that were meant to be heard, and pounced on any possible failing the man had, lighting it up like a beacon.

Damian had hated her nearly as much as she hated him. And since Brock didn't miss much and he'd been around her on more than one occasion, including just now, I figured he didn't miss this so I didn't answer.

He knew why I wasn't answering, apparently took no offense, and went on. "How long have you known her?"

"Since fifth grade."

"She doesn't wear a wedding band."

"She's never been married," I admitted.

"She's your age and never been married. Clearly a winner when lookin' for man advice."

"Brock," I whispered again, and suddenly his hand snaked up, caught me behind the neck, and pulled me down so my face was close to his.

"*You* know what's goin' down with you and me. *You* know what you feel when I kiss you. *You* know what you feel when you sit with me like you're sittin' right now. *You* know what you felt when you were watchin' me move inside you after I made you come. And *you* know how you felt in your fuckin' kitchen six fuckin' hours ago. *She* does not know any of that shit."

"I haven't been exactly good at picking men," I pointed out then instantly wished I hadn't. In fact, I wished I had the power to grab my words and shove them back in my mouth when his hand got tight at my neck, his eyes got hard and glittering, and the extreme voltage of his anger started snapping in the room.

"I am not Heller," he growled.

"I know," I whispered, my hands moving to rest on his chest.

His eyes seared into mine. His were molten and not in a good way.

"Okay," I said softly. "You're not Damian, but right now, I have to admit, you're freaking me out."

"Yeah?" he shot back. "Well, you just linked me to a man who supplied Denver for years with shit that fucked a lot of people's lives *and* the lives those people's shit fucked in turn and who also took his hands to and raped my woman. Sorry I'm freakin' you out, babe, but you gotta get that doesn't make me too happy."

God, for years, no one knew about what happened to me and now...

Now, it was right in my face and it was Brock who kept putting it there.

I closed my eyes and twisted my head away.

Brock kept speaking.

"I know why you aren't lookin' at me, Tess, but that shit happened to you. You gotta face it, and for this shit to work between us, one of the people you gotta face it with is me," he declared. I opened my eyes and turned them back to him.

"So, you're a law enforcement officer *and* Denver's resident sage on how to deal with being raped? Is this what I'm learning about you now?" I asked sarcastically, finding myself no longer hesitant, cautious, and unsure but totally pissed off.

"Yeah, since my sister and a girlfriend of mine both got raped, both of them were bad as that shit always is, but only one of them was by someone they thought they could trust. I think I know something about it," he fired back and I blinked in shock as this unwelcome but somehow crucial knowledge filtered through me.

Then I whispered, "Sorry?"

He didn't repeat himself.

Instead, he shared, "My sister got help, she talked about it, she faced it, she dealt with it. Now she's married and has three kids. Her life's a fuckin' mess but it's a mess of the grape jelly smears on her car upholstery variety. My old girlfriend didn't get help, she didn't talk about it, she buried it deep, and her life went right down the toilet. He took what he took from her but, babe, with her not fightin', she *gave* him the rest."

Oh man.

"Brock—"

He cut me off to announce, "Straight up, baby, I wanna explore this with you. I liked what we had. I fuckin' missed it when it was gone. I want that back and I wanna know how it feels to have it not havin' my job comin' between us. This is why I'm here. You want that too. We have to have this conversation. Because I'm in your bed, you're in mine, I'm in your life, you're in mine, that motherfucker isn't going to be there too. You get what I'm sayin'?"

I got what he was saying.

And I also liked that he wanted to explore this with me with everything clear between us and that he missed me when I was gone. I liked it a whole bunch because for three months I felt the same exact way.

"I've moved on," I assured him and just like that, the snap of angry electricity left the air and the sweet, steady hum of his humor hit it.

"Right, my sweet, sexy, totally clueless Tess with her glasses and thick fuckin' hair and great fuckin' rack, who can bake a cake most men would trade their balls for and who looks at you like you're the only motherfuckin' guy on earth, goes six years without a fuckin' date when half the guys at your bakery probably come on to you and you have no fuckin' idea, *that* Tess has moved on. I see this. Totally. We're obviously good."

Okay, there was a lot there that I liked.

A lot.

But there was some of it I didn't like.

At all.

Therefore, I snapped, "I'm not clueless," and pulled back on his hand at my neck, which only served to make it tense and bring me closer.

"Tess, darlin', of all the men who walk into your bakery or come in contact with you through your life, the last one you should take one look at, he smiles at you and asks if you wanna get a beer, you should never have said yes to."

"That's you," I informed him acidly.

He grinned. "I know. I'm the only person lucky you're totally clueless."

Contradictorily, I felt all warm and gushy inside from his earlier Brock-like compliments and at the same time I was totally pissed.

The totally pissed won out so I pushed against his chest with my hands while announcing, "I've decided I want a beer. Let me up."

He ignored *my* mood and I knew this when his hand with his beer wrapped around my back and he brought me even closer.

"I'm also lucky my girl had a craving to take a walk on the wild side," he muttered, his quicksilver eyes dropping to my mouth.

Mm. I knew what that meant.

I also knew that for three months, one of the things I *seriously* missed was making out with him.

And, last, I knew at that moment I was not prepared to go there.

"Brock," I hissed and again pushed.

He ignored my push, his eyes lifted to mine, and he whispered, "I can't make any promises about where this is gonna go but what I can do is give you me, keep you safe while you walk on the wild side, and work my ass off to do what I can so this never goes bad for you."

His quiet words made me stop pushing. They also made that warm gushiness warmer and gushier and I stared at him.

Brock kept talking. "That's all I got to give, babe, but I'll also tell you the only thing I'll take is what you're willing to give back. Except you need to give me what that asshole left in you so you don't have to carry it around anymore."

Oh *God*.

Okay, maybe he *did* know a little something about women who'd been violated.

I felt my body ease in his hold, but still, I told him honestly, "I don't think I can give you that."

"Yes, you can, Tess," he replied softly. "He cut you deep and that kinda cut leaves an ugly scar but my girl hasn't drifted clueless and without a man for six years because of a scar. I didn't get it because you didn't talk about him when we were together but I get it now. My girl's done that because he left something ugly with you and you have to unload it, Tess. You have to let it go so you can see me right now the way I really am and how I am with you. You have to let it go so when you let me in and, baby"—his hand squeezed my neck—"when I say that, I mean when you let me *in*, the only thing you feel is me moving inside you and the only thing you see is me likin' right where I am."

"I already let you in." I whispered my reminder and I saw a shadow pass through his eyes before he replied.

"Yeah, darlin', you did but after you came, you looked at me like I was the only guy in the whole fuckin' world and then you called me Jake."

"I thought that was your name," I defended and his hand and arm gave me a squeeze.

"I know that but when I'm inside you, I wanna hear you say *my* name. That was between us then, for me. And now that's gone. I wanna clear the path of what might be between us for you. Can you get that?"

That was when my mouth suddenly formed the words "Who's Darla?"

The heavy warmth of his mood disappeared in an instant and the static came back.

"What the fuck?" he asked softly.

"Who's Darla?" I repeated.

His eyes narrowed and his jaw turned to stone before he clipped out, "Who told you about Darla?"

I stared at him and I decided that what I saw I did not like.

Then I whispered, "Right," and started pushing again.

This didn't go well for me mainly because he let me go with one arm only to lean us both to the side to put his beer on the table. He whipped me around so I was on my back in my couch and he was not only on top of me but also his hips were between mine.

Our last position wasn't conducive to us having an intense chat about the future of our relationship in a way where he couldn't boggle my mind with his hotness, sexiness, and outspoken honesty but this one was *way* worse.

"I'll ask again, Tess," he growled. "Who told you about Darla? Was it Elvira?"

"Um…" I mumbled. His eyes narrowed so I rushed

on. "She was at the shower with her girls and one of those girls was a lady called Gwen. Gwen told me."

His neck bent back so his eyes could look over my head and he snarled, "*Fuck*."

"Brock—" I started and his eyes sliced back to me.

"Who Darla is, is not you," he bit out.

"But—"

"No, Tess, she is not you. I told you earlier I liked my job for the four months it meant me bein' with you. Suffice it to say, I did not *at all* like my job when the only play I had to make was bein' with her."

"You're hot," I said softly.

"What?" he clipped roughly.

"You're hot," I repeated. "I can see them sending you in when they—"

"Unh-unh." He shook his head, pressing his body into mine as the electricity snapped and sparked through the room. "I am not the DEA's resident prostitute with a dick," he growled. "The play I made with Darla was my choice, a long job, a sacrifice I decided I had to make 'cause the life I was livin' bein' under that cover I had to get out of. It was sucking me under. It was suffocating me. That shit, those people I had to spend time with, no contact with clean air, decent living, good folk, it was dragging me down. I had to make a Statue of Liberty play and I made it. And the fuck of it was, I made that sacrifice and the whole thing got fucked in a bad way, Tess, where I had to watch those morons take a good man down and almost take him out."

His face dipped closer and he kept going.

"*You* were not that. My assignment with you was light cover. Getting close. Nosing around. They investigated your finances, your bakery, and they knew you were less likely a suspect involved in his operation and more likely a possible witness and knew he was jacked. But the amount of communication and your name on his accounts, they had to be sure. I took it where it went because, after about an hour with you, I knew you were clean and I knew where I wanted to take it after the investigation was over. I came in late on this one because I'd just come off that last one. And when I took that job, you were the light of a warm, sunny day, Tess. Darla was the dead of a cold, dark fuckin' night." His face got even closer and his voice got low when he finished. "It felt good to feel the sun again."

I stared into his glittering eyes.

Then my mouth whispered, "Your job is pretty intense, Slim."

He stared into my eyes. The sparks disappeared, the warmth invaded, and he rolled to his side, back to the back of the couch, taking me with him, his arms tight around me, his legs tangling with mine.

"Yeah, baby, it is. And it can fuck with your head. That's why when I met a woman whose house always smells like there's a cake in the oven, who holds tight and presses her tits to my back when she's with me on my bike, who looks at me like I can make the rest of the world melt away and for her its only me, I know I wanna hold onto that woman."

To those sensational, warm gushiness-inducing words, I blurted, "It's in my belly."

I watched him do a slow blink before he asked, "What?"

"It's a poisonous snake curled up tight. It can get really small. So small, I forget it's there. But when it uncurls, it swells and gets so big it fills me up, crawls up my throat. So deep up my throat, Brock, sometimes I think it's going to choke me, and when it starts uncurling, I'm always terrified it's gonna strike."

One of his hands slid up into my hair and the skin around his eyes got soft before he whispered, "What he left you?"

"Yeah," I whispered back.

I watched him lift his chin as his fingers sifted into my hair against my scalp and then he shoved my face in his throat.

When he spoke again, his voice was thick. Thick in a way I knew what that meant, thick in a way I knew what it meant to me and I pushed closer to his long, lean body as he asked, "You gonna work that shit out?"

"I..." His hand tensed on my head and my fingers curled into his tee before I whispered, "Yeah."

"You gonna let me help?"

I closed my eyes.

Then I repeated my whispered, "Yeah."

His arms got tight, drawing me close and I held on.

"You scared, baby?" he asked.

I didn't repeat my "yeah," I just nodded.

His arms got tighter and his voice got thicker as I felt his neck bend and his lips say against my hair, "Don't be. There's a wild that's fucked and there's a wild that's just plain wild. You just hooked yourself to a different kind of wild, Tess, and I swear, baby, *swear*"—his arms squeezed before he finished—"I'll show you that's a good, safe place to be."

I sighed deep and I did this because I believed him.

Then I whispered, "Okay."

Brock had no response. He just held tight. He did this for a long time. Long enough for me to relax in his arms. Long enough for my fingers to uncurl and settle flat on his warm, hard chest. Long enough for me to realize that cosmopolitans on a back deck at a really bad baby shower with girls who were good to the core and wanted the best for me didn't shed even a little light on what I had on that couch in that moment.

The only people who knew what was happening were Brock and me.

And after that time went by, he pushed up, grabbed his beer then settled with his back to the couch, his head on my toss pillows at the armrest, me mostly on his body, his beer in his hand resting on his chest, and when I lifted my head to look at him, I saw his quicksilver eyes on me.

Then he muttered, "All right, babe, now tell me about Kentucky."

I bit my lip.

Brock grinned.

I quit biting my lip and grinned back.

Then I whispered, "I have to take my contacts out and get my glasses."

His eyes went warm and his mouth got soft as his arm around me loosened and he whispered back, "All right, darlin', I'll be right here."

That made me grin again.

Then I jumped up to take out my contacts and get my glasses.

CHAPTER SIX

Drawback Cancelled

"FUCK," I HEARD muttered and my eyes drifted open to see Brock's tee-covered chest.

We were still tangled together on the couch. Apparently we fell asleep there because early-morning sun was shining through the blinds.

I also knew that it was morning because I could hear Fiona Apple singing "Fast as You Can" from my bedroom and I knew my alarm had gone off.

"Damn," I mumbled, shifting and preparing to push up, getting a knee underneath me and a hand in the cushion when suddenly two strong arms locked around me. I found my soft body colliding with Brock's hard one. His hand slid up into my hair and it guided my mouth to his.

He kissed me, long, sweet, deep, and wet.

My toes curled, my belly got warm, and my body melted into his as one of my hands slid up his neck into his hair curling around the back and holding on.

When he broke the kiss, my head lifted away an inch, my eyes lazily opened, and I heard Fiona Apple was getting way louder (and I didn't care).

"You passed out before we got to the fun stuff, babe," Brock informed me in a deep, sexy, sleepy, rough whisper.

"I did?" I asked.

"Yeah." I watched his mouth grin. "Right in the middle of talkin' you just faded away."

Crap.

How embarrassing.

I stared in his sexy, sleepy eyes and bit my lip.

Brock's eyes dropped to my mouth.

Then I found myself on my back in the couch, Brock on top, and he was kissing me again, longer, sweeter, deeper, wetter and he added some pretty freaking great hand action.

Mm. It felt nice waking up this way.

Fiona quit singing "Fast as You Can" and "Get Gone" started, sounding loud from my adamant alarm clock that was a fancy one where you could shove in an MP3 and it woke you soft and nice with music you liked. But the longer you let it play, the louder it got.

And we'd let it play for a long time and Fiona's changing tempo in "Get Gone" from sweet and melodious to pissed off and pounding was filling the house so much even Brock's fantastic kisses couldn't block it out.

Clearly mine couldn't block it out for Brock either since his mouth broke from mine and he muttered, "Fuck, babe, sorry but I gotta turn that shit off."

"Fiona Apple isn't shit," I told him.

He gave me a look, knifed off me, and prowled to my bedroom.

I watched his ass as he went, thinking it would not be good if that look meant he didn't like Fiona because I loved Fiona. It wasn't like I played her 24/7 but she got a lot of airtime in Tess O'Hara's house.

No, that wasn't entirely true. I was thinking about Brock and Fiona Apple but mostly I was thinking about how great his ass looked in his faded jeans.

Once I quit thinking of this (around about the time he disappeared), I looked around for my glasses, saw Brock had taken them off and put them on the table at the side of the sofa. I nabbed them, slipped them on my nose, got up, and walked to the kitchen.

I was at the sink filling the coffeepot with water when he made it into the kitchen.

It took a bit of effort but I didn't drop the glass pot into my ceramic sink when I saw a smokin' hot, clothes-disheveled, usually sexy and unruly haired, now sexier and unrulier-haired (due to sleep and my hands running through it), heavy-eyed Brock Lucas saunter into my kitchen.

Whoa.

I'd never woken up with Brock but just looking at him in the morning was nearly as good as one of his kisses.

I turned off the water and moved to the coffeemaker, covering this reaction by asking, "Do you not like Fiona Apple?"

His response was, "Is this a deal breaker for you?"

I'd flipped up the top of the coffeemaker and turned to him while I poured the water in seeing he was preparing to open the fridge.

That was when I said, "I'll take that as a no."

He stood, fingers curled around the fridge's door handle and his eyes leveled on me. "Babe, I listen to Credence, the Eagles, Santana, Stevie Ray Vaughan, Thorogood, shit like that and pretty much anything country if a chick ain't singin' it. Does that sound like a man who'd like Fiona Apple?"

"No," I replied. "It sounds like a man in dire need of a crash course in three decades of music. The boys are back from Vietnam, Brock. Follow me into the new millennium."

He grinned at me and muttered, "Smartass," before he opened the fridge door and stuck his head into it.

I was feeling warm gushiness in my belly due to his grin and seeing his head stuck in my fridge when I heard my cell ring.

I shoved the coffeepot under the coffeemaker and moved to my purse on the kitchen counter, wondering who was calling me at that ungodly hour and why. Then I pulled out my phone, looked at the display, and saw it was Martha.

Damn.

I hit the button on the screen to take the call and put it to my ear.

"Hey, honey," I greeted. "What's up?"

"His filthy, rusted, beat-up, in *desperate* need of a trade-up truck is still in front of your house, that's what's up," was Martha's greeting and my eyes moved out the kitchen doorframe and toward the front window that was still covered by closed blinds.

Then I asked, "How do you know that?"

"Because I swung by your place on my way to work to check and see how crazy stupid you're being with a smokin' hot guy and I found out you're being off-the-charts crazy stupid with a smokin' hot guy."

"Martha!" I snapped.

"Am I wrong or did his truck not start last night and he hitched a ride home?" she asked.

My eyes went to the microwave then they went to the

kitchen counter. "I cannot believe you. *You* are the one who's crazy. First, you don't leave for work for an hour, and second, my house is thirty minutes out of your way to get to work."

"I am committed to the mission of stopping you from making another very bad mistake," she returned.

I heard the fridge close but I didn't need to hear it to be very aware that Brock was in the room and he could hear every word.

"I can't talk about this now," I told her. "Come by the bakery tonight after work. We'll have a cupcake and a chat."

"Girl, I'm single and my best friend just dropped ten pounds and got a three hundred dollar hairstyle. There is *no way* I'm eating one of your cupcakes because eating one means eating four and I don't need those cupcakes on my fat ass when I'm out on the prowl with you. No one looked at me before, what with you and your bodacious ta-tas and the look on your face that says to all comers, 'Isn't it sweet, the whole world is like Disneyland!' I eat your cupcakes, which never fail to settle on my ass, I'll become invisible."

"That isn't true," I told her.

"Which part?" she shot back.

"All of it," I answered instantly.

"Girl, wake…*up*."

I sighed. My eyes moved to Brock to see him, hips against the counter, open jug of milk in his hand, and I was pretty certain I missed him drinking straight from it.

A drawback.

He grinned at me and I felt the sweet hum in the air, saw his eyes dancing, and knew he was grinning in order not to burst out laughing.

Okay, cancel drawback. He could drink straight from the milk jug all he wanted as long as he filled my kitchen with that great vibe and grinned at me while looking all morning hot guy.

"Hello!" Martha snapped in my ear and I jerked my eyes away from Brock.

"I'm here," I told her.

"Ohmigod, he's right there muddling your head," she muttered.

She wasn't wrong about that.

Time to get serious.

"Martha, really, honey, we need to talk."

"Shit." She was still muttering.

"It's important," I whispered, and felt the amused Brock vibe flatten but the kitchen filled with warmth.

Martha heard my tone, read it, and immediately gave in. "All right, but we're not meeting at the bakery for cupcakes. You're coming over and I'm making salad."

I blinked at the counter. "You're making salad?"

"I'm making salad."

"Honey, the last time I had dinner at your house, you fried celery."

The warmth in the room remained but the hum came back and it was heralded in by Brock roaring with laughter.

My eyes cut to him and I bugged them out but he ignored my hint, kept laughing, and did it shaking his head.

"I hear he found that amusing," Martha noted irritably.

I looked away from Brock and pointed out, "Martha, babe, you fried celery. *Anyone* would find that amusing."

"I'm an experimental chef," she fired back.

This was true. But she was not an altogether successful one.

I sighed again.

Then I suggested, "How about you come over here and I'll make salads."

"Will smokin' hot guy be there?"

"His name is Brock," I whispered.

"Will smokin' hot but bad for you Brock be there?" she amended.

"I don't know," I told her, the truth. "But what I have to say won't wait and he knows about it anyway, so if he is, you'll deal. If he isn't, he isn't. Yeah?"

Silence.

Then, "So this isn't about him?"

"No, it isn't. It's about something I should have told you a while ago but I didn't and I need to..." My eyes slid to Brock and saw his were on me as I saw he was moving toward me. Then he made it to me. His arm wrapped around my belly, the front of his body hit the back of mine, I felt his heat, then I felt his face in my neck. Only then did I continue. "I need to get rid of it, so it's time to tell you about it."

Straight off the bat, she whispered her guess. "Damian."

That's when I knew she knew. Or she might not actually know but she sensed there were deeper issues at play but she backed off and let me deal with them. And when I stuck to my guns and got shot of my ex-husband without sinking into the depths of despair, she gave me that play.

"Yes," I whispered back.

Brock's arm gave me a squeeze.

I closed my eyes.

"All right, babe, I'll be there at seven."

"Martha?" I called.

"Yeah, Tess," she answered.

"Love you, honey."

"Love you too, babe."

"But you keep stalking me, that love will die," I warned on a tease.

"Whatever," she muttered, knowing it was a tease, then disconnected.

I hit the screen to end call and dropped my phone on the counter. When I did this, Brock turned me so we were face to face and both his arms were around me.

"Not my biggest fan," he muttered but he didn't appear the least broken up about it.

"You want to hang with me, you might want to put some work into that," I suggested.

"Right," he replied, then said, "No, babe. I'll tell you now, she don't like me, she don't like me and I don't give a fuck."

Hm. Another drawback.

"She's my best friend," I reminded him.

"If she is, she'll come to see what's good for you and she'll sort her shit out. If she's a different kind of woman, she won't. Instead, she'll see green and won't clue in that men do not want high-maintenance drama queens so much they steer well clear and until she shifts that shit outta her life, it's gonna be a lonely one. Unlike her friend who sees a man drinking outta her milk jug, processes that it's highly unlikely she's gonna break him of that habit, seein' as he's forty-five and still does it and has since he was a kid, lets it go, and moves on all in the expanse of about a second. Instead of throwing a shit fit about it, which gets her nowhere, is a waste of energy, and leaves both involved feeling like garbage."

Well, I had to admit, all that was interesting and insightful and weirdly mature.

Still.

"Well, now that we're on that subject, it's somewhat unhygienic for you to drink out of the milk jug."

"Babe, I had my tongue in your mouth for ten minutes this morning. How's that any different?"

I tipped my head to the side while considering this point.

Then I shared, "Your point holds merit."

He burst out laughing, and in the middle of it buried his face in my neck so when he was done he could kiss me there.

This was nice as in *way* nice.

He used to do that all the time too.

And I'd missed it.

His head came up and his eyes captured mine.

"You all right with me jumpin' in the shower before I head out?"

Brock naked in my shower and all the delightful visions that would generate that I could pull out and turn over in my head anytime I wanted?

Uh…

Yeah!

"Sure," I said.

His mouth hitched up on one side and I liked that too.

Then his semi-smile faded, his arms squeezed, and he asked, "You want me here for salad?"

"Do you want to be here for salad?" I asked back.

"What I want is for you to tell me what you want," he replied.

I thought about this.

Then I said hesitantly, "Maybe not."

"Right," he muttered.

"It's not that I—" I hastened to add but he cut me off with another arm squeeze and dipped his face close.

"Baby, it's cool. I'll show tonight around the same time as I showed last night. Good?"

I nodded.

"Tomorrow, no plans with your girls. Tomorrow night is mine," he declared.

My belly got warm and gushy and I nodded again.

He grinned and muttered again, "Right." He dropped his head more, touched his mouth to mine briefly, and murmured, "Shower," against my lips.

A thrill slid up my spine.

Brock let me go and sauntered out of the room.

I stared at the coffeemaker and smiled when I heard the shower go on in the bathroom.

Then I made coffee.

*   *   *

An hour and a half later, I was sitting in my car staring at the side of my bakery, my phone in my hand, deliberating.

I had never played games with Brock. Never. Not from the very beginning.

I took one look at him, liked what I saw a whole lot, and the minute he showed interest, I showed it back and never veered from that path.

I did this because, since I saw it and all the times I saw it since, the scene in *My Big Fat Greek Wedding* when Ian asked Toula out and she immediately answered yes, no games, no subterfuge, exposing straight out she was not only interested but the idea of spending time with him excited her, I thought that was the sweetest thing I ever saw.

And I also did this because I was me.

So I was sitting in my car with my phone in my hand thinking that what Brock said was right. What he and I had had been fucked and for three months it fucked with my head.

But seven months ago, when he brought me home after our first date and kissed me in his pickup and that kiss lasted half an hour (this is no joke) and he finally tore his mouth from mine, shoved his face in my neck, and growled, "*Fuck,*" against my skin with his strong arms tight around me, I knew what we had was real. I also knew that it had started good and it was only going to get better.

Like Toula and Ian knew in *My Big Fat Greek Wedding.*

That had been what Brock was talking about in my kitchen yesterday. That was what he meant when he said I knew the exact second I stopped being someone he was investigating and started being someone who might grow to mean something to him.

And I *did* know and that was the exact second I knew.

And last night he'd proved that what I felt in that second was no lie.

And playing games hadn't got me that.

And playing games didn't bring it back.

I got it and, being only who I was with him, I kept it.

So I touched the screen on my phone, went to favorites, and my fingertip touched the word "Slim" (I'd changed it, obviously).

I put the phone to my ear.

It rang twice before I heard, "Yeah, babe."

"Hey," I replied.

"Everything cool?" he asked.

"I need to tell you something," I told him.

Pause, then, "I'm listening, Tess."

I bit my lip.

Then I shared. "The reason I don't really care about your drinking from the milk jug isn't because it's debatably ridiculous the reasons a woman doesn't like a man drinking from a milk jug. It's because I don't much care what you do because I like you in my kitchen."

This was met with silence.

I held my breath.

I got more silence.

That was when I considered maybe not letting it all hang out anymore.

Then I heard Brock ask, "Debatably ridiculous?"

The tightness forming in my chest released and I felt my lips form a smile as my eyes closed.

I opened them and said, "I will grant that just you drinking from it isn't all that bad. But we didn't get into other options, say, should you be eating cookies or cake and you get backwash into the milk. That's gross. No one wants to drink someone else's backwash, even if it's cookie or cake backwash. This is where it becomes a gray area."

An attractive, low chuckle sounded in my ear through which I also heard, "Babe."

"Just saying," I said.

"Noted," Brock replied.

"Okay, I have cakes to bake."

"All right, darlin', and I got the hint your girl is avoiding your cupcakes but your man is not so if you bring some home tonight, they will not go unappreciated."

"Will you drink milk out of a glass when you eat them?"

Another attractive, low chuckle sounded through which I heard, "We'll see how it goes."

"Right," I whispered.

"Go bake cakes."

"Okay, later, honey."

"Later, babe."

I disconnected.

Then I smiled

I exited my car, entered my bakery, and commenced baking cakes.

CHAPTER SEVEN

Mountainous Swirls of Frosting

I STOOD AT my front door waiting.

Then it came. Martha stopped folding her body into the driver's seat, and her eyes came over the roof of her car, up the steep rise at the edge of my front yard, the four steps up my front stoop to me at my arched front door.

She pressed her fingers to her lips, stretched them my way, and blew me a kiss.

My throat got clogged but I blew one back.

She folded her petite body behind the wheel, started up her car, and rolled away.

I watched until I lost sight of her brake lights and then I watched for longer.

Suffice it to say, my best friend Martha Shockley did not take the news very well that my ex-husband had hit me and raped me even if it happened over six years ago. She had not been mad at me. She'd been devastated for me. Upon the news, she crumbled instantly. She hated this for me and watching her absorb the burden of this information I was reminded why I didn't tell her.

Then she enveloped me in her arms and forced me to promise never, and I mean *never*, to hold something like that to myself again.

"It's always been you for me, Tess, and I can't bear thinking it isn't me for you," she whispered. "I'm done backing off, hoping you'll sort your head on your own, honey. You gotta let me be there for you and from now on, I sense something's wrong, I'm gonna *make* you let me be there for you."

I held her close and I gave her that promise.

Seriously, what else could I do?

Needless to say, salad did not really go with confessions of the soul so Martha ate four of the dozen cupcakes I brought home for Brock.

But learning this news had not put Martha off her game and when Brock showed, she watched him like a hawk, waiting for him to fuck up in some way so she could pounce. She did this with eyes constantly narrowed so much I feared she'd give herself a migraine.

Brock, however, was who he always was (even when I called him Jake). He was Brock.

Sensing he was not going to fall at the first hurdle and expose the screaming dickhead he was hiding within, Martha finally gave up and left.

Which led me to now.

I closed the door, locked it, and turned to my living room.

I lucked out. Four years ago, after the bakery caught on and life started to get a lot less scary, I went house hunting and the second house I looked at was this one.

The couple who had previously owned it spent years fixing it up and getting it to exactly what they wanted it to

be. Then the husband received word he was being transferred just weeks before the finishing touches were put on
the last of the loving care (and scads of cash) they'd put
into their house—a brand-new kitchen.

They were devastated at having to leave.

I was elated (though I didn't share this).

The dark wood floors had all been redone. The walls
had all been reskimmed. The bathrooms were updated
and fabulous. The basement had been finished into a huge
family room where I kept my TV. Also down there was a
powder room, laundry room, and a guest room that had
its own bath. The furnace had been replaced. The roof re-
shingled. The yard landscaped. And a swamp cooler had
been installed.

But it was the kitchen that did it for me. The kitchen
was phenomenal. An abundance of white cabinets, the wall
ones all glass fronted, quirky ones handcrafted to set in corners and spots that were tough to fill. Slate floors. Fabulous
black-and-white-tiled splashbacks. An enormous island in
the middle. Shiny marble countertops. Restaurant-quality
stainless-steel appliances, including a narrow but fabulous
wine fridge. Inlaid cookbook holder. Built-in microwave
and double oven, one fan assisted.

A baker's dream.

My dream.

It was fifty thousand dollars over budget but I bought it
because I thought it was worth it. Since then, even though
the first year it was rough going, I never regretted it.

As I walked through the front living room off of which
were two bedrooms and a bath to the double doorway that
led to the kitchen, I thought the same thing.

And when I hit the kitchen and saw Brock resting

faded-jeans-clad hips against the back counter, teeth sinking into a cupcake, half of a mountainous swirl of silver-dusted, pale lilac frosting, sprinkled with pastel candy confetti disappearing behind his full lips, I made an instant decision. I was going to go through my paperwork, find out the day I signed on the dotted line that made that house my home, and celebrate it with a huge, honking party every fucking year.

"She's gone," I informed him, stopping on the other side of the island and putting my hands on it.

I watched with admittedly captivated attention as he licked frosting from his lips after he swallowed and then he asked, "How long's it take her to get home?"

"Twenty minutes," I answered.

His eyes locked with mine and he said quietly, "You need to call her in twenty-five minutes, babe."

My gaze held his as more warm gushiness hit my belly, knowing he got it, he read her mood, he knew she was hurting, and he wanted me to check in on her.

"Okay," I whispered.

He studied me and I let him.

Then he asked, still talking quietly, "How you doin'?"

"Sharing that with her was not fun," I admitted.

"I could guess that part, Tess," he told me, again quietly.

I nodded and took a breath. Then I added, "I'm glad I did it. I'm sorry I didn't do it earlier. I'm glad it's done and I'm glad I never have to do it again. That's as far as I've got."

"Right," he whispered.

He shoved the rest of the cupcake into his mouth. I watched him chew and swallow.

Then he asked, "Would it piss you off to know that right about now I'm wondering if I walked in here yesterday because I missed my Tess or if it was because I missed her cupcakes?"

I grinned at him.

Then I answered, "No, because I *am* my cupcakes."

And it hit me right then that I was. On the outside it could be tees, jeans, and flip-flops or pencil skirts, complicated designer blouses, and high-heeled strappy sandals or, me being me, just about anything. But on the inside, it was all about mountainous swirls of delicately colored frosting with sprinkles of candy confetti, edible fairy dust, all on top of rich, moist cake.

As that understanding settled inside me, that made me feel warm and gushy too.

"Come here, baby," he murmured.

I caught the feel of the room and the look on his face and didn't delay in rounding the island and going there.

When I got close, his arms folded around me and he pulled me in deep. Then his head dipped and he gave me a sweet, delicious, long, deep cupcake kiss.

When he was done, against his mouth, I whispered, "You taste good."

To which he replied, "I know."

I smiled against his lips and he returned the gesture.

Then he lifted his head an inch, his arms gave me a squeeze, and he said gently, "I wanna spend the night."

My belly dropped and I felt a convulsion between my legs.

Then I replied, "Okay."

His eyelids got heavy, his arms got tighter, my arms around him got tighter, his head descended, and he kissed me again, this time longer, deeper, sweeter, and even more delicious.

This went on for a while. Long enough for me to get my fingers in his hair. Long enough for Brock to get one of his hands up the back of my tee and the other one clamped tight on my ass. Long enough for my nipples to swell and the area between my legs to get wet. Long enough for me to think the bedroom was way, way, *way* too far away and to be glad I kept the kitchen floor mopped because that was where I wanted him to take me.

But unfortunately not long enough that we were still making out standing up in the kitchen rather than somewhere either naked or semi-naked and thus at the point of no return when a knock came at the door.

Brock's head came up on a low, short, frustrated growl and his eyes went over my head toward the front door. I blinked at this unwelcome turn of events and twisted my neck to look in the same direction.

It was closing on ten. Too late for a caller. Unless that caller was Martha, who forgot something, and Martha was the kind of gal who consistently forgot something no matter where she was, like her wallet, purse, credit card, and other such nontrivial items.

Another knock came at the door and I felt Brock's arms squeeze. This also happened to coincide with his fingers digging pleasantly into my ass. That felt great. So great, I forgot someone was at the door and I looked to him to see him looking at me.

Oh my.

He was still turned on too.

And let's just say that look on his face was *nice*.

"Hold that thought and, for fuck's sake, whatever you

do, hold that look," he growled before he let me go. I tee-tered slightly but managed to stay standing, turn, and watch him stalk toward the door.

I walked the few feet to the island and put my hands on it as he unlocked the front door. Then my eyes dropped.

On the corner of my island was a white, ceramic pedestal cake stand with glass dome. Sweeping lines. Simple and elegant. It cost a fortune and I didn't care. I baked cakes. I needed fabulous cake stands. At that moment in my life, I owned seven of them (in my home, at the bakery I had tons more). All of them fantastic, most of them expensive. They rotated to the top spot on my island depending on my mood.

In the one now were six cupcakes with mountainous swirls of frosting, glittering, edible fairy dust, and pastel confetti. Two had mint green frosting, two had pale pink, two baby blue.

This meant Brock had a cupcake while I was saying good-bye to Martha, before I made it to the kitchen when he was eating his second one.

I felt my face go soft as I realized I missed that too. He had a great body, the kind of body that no matter what age, but especially at forty-five, you worked on. He didn't shy away from his food, his beer, or his bourbon. He lived his life like he appreciated it. But he still took care of himself. I'd phoned him enough times when he told me he was at the gym or just got back from a run to know this was true.

But he had a weakness for my cupcakes. And my cake cakes. And my cookies. In fact, anything that came out of my oven, he made no bones about liking it, liking it more than anything else that I'd noticed he liked and he didn't do this by handing me flowery compliments. He did this by consuming them with relish.

And in that moment, I found I *loved* that.

On that thought, I heard Brock snarl, "You have got to be *shitting* me," and my head snapped up.

"Who are you?"

At the sound of the familiar voice asking that question, my hands slid down the counter and curled tight around the edge as my chest compressed so deep it felt like I was being crushed.

Damian.

"It doesn't matter who I am. What matters is that you are not here. You are never here. You are never anywhere near this fuckin' house, Tess's fuckin' bakery, or *Tess*. I see you or I hear you are, honest to fuckin' God, I'll deal with you and you do *not* want me to do that." Brock was still snarling, it was vicious, biting, and I could feel his mood all the way across the living room, through the kitchen, and to me. It was filling the house. Beyond his pissed-off snap of electricity, this was rough and abrasive, scoring at my skin.

"I beg your pardon?" Damian asked.

Oh no. Oh God. Oh *no*.

Damian was at least three inches shorter than Brock. Damian was probably twenty pounds lighter if not more. Damian was lean in the sense he was lean, not muscled, no bulk. He was fit but there was no power to his frame like there was to Brock's. In a physical tussle, Brock would take him, easy.

And Damian wouldn't give one flying fuck. Damian spent most of his time pissing in corners. Damian would *not* take to a threat well.

Not at all.

I started to move around the island to instigate damage control, my eyes on Brock's back, seeing he had his body between the door and the doorjamb, his big frame blocking Damian from view, his back to me.

Still, he lifted an arm out behind him like he had eyes in the back of his head and could see me starting to approach and he barked, "Tess, do not fuckin' move."

I halted at the side of the island.

"If Tess is in there, I'd like to speak to her," Damian, voice tight, requested.

"Did you not hear me ten fuckin' seconds ago?" Brock asked.

"Who *are* you?" Damian demanded to know.

"You didn't hear me ten fuckin' seconds ago," Brock decided.

"All right, I'll ask politely. Please move aside so I can talk with Tess," Damian asked.

To that, Brock stated, "In five seconds I'm closing the door. You're not in your Escalade and on the road sixty seconds after that, I'm on the phone with the cops. No joke, no delay. Got that?" Then, as he promised, he stepped out of the door, closed it in Damian's face, and locked it.

I stood where I was at the side of the island.

Brock moved to the window and yanked hard on the cord to the blinds to expose the glass. He stood in it, arms crossed, feet planted.

I licked my lips.

Brock didn't move a muscle.

I put a hand out to the counter and held on.

Brock didn't twitch.

I counted to ten. Then to twenty.

Brock leaned to the side, yanked the cord, and the blinds dropped with a crash.

He turned and prowled through the living room toward me, one hand to his back pocket. He had his phone out by the time he stopped a foot away.

I held my breath when I saw his face up close.

"Honey—" I whispered but stopped speaking when his hand came up abruptly.

I tensed as it came to me but, whisper-soft and unbelievably sweet, his fingertips skimmed my cheek on their way to glide into my hair where his hand curled around the back of my head and he pulled me closer.

I went because I didn't have a choice and because I wanted to. When I got near, I put my hands to his abs.

"Mood's broke, sweetness," he muttered. "And I need to make some calls. If you're tired, go get ready for bed, or if not, give your girl a call. I'll be in in a minute and we'll get some shut-eye. Yeah?"

"Is he gone?" I asked.

"Yeah."

I swallowed.

His hand gave me a squeeze and I watched his eyes flare.

Then he asked, "He won't stay gone, will he?"

I shook my head.

His mouth got tight.

Then he said gently, "Give me a minute to make some calls, baby."

I nodded. His hand gave me another squeeze and then sifted through my hair until it was gone.

I moved to my bedroom.

Okay, it was safe to say I wasn't tittering with excitement nine months ago when my abusive ex-husband who raped me contacted me for the first time in over four years, shattering the illusion I'd built that I was safe in a life that no longer contained him. And it was also safe to say I deliberated at length about going to lunch with him.

But I loved his dad.

Donald Heller was a good man. He adored me openly and it cut to the quick when, to erase Damian from my life, I had to break ties with anything that had anything to do with Damian, including his dad. Donald tried to keep up a relationship with me but I did not encourage this and he finally quit trying. News that he was unwell broke my heart, gave me guilt, and just as Damian knew it would, spurred me to show at lunch.

It was a mistake that I would pay for quite a bit, it would turn out. And this settled in my soul the troubling fact that I'd allowed myself to be played, *again*, by Damian.

I left him the day after he raped me. My dog and I lived with Martha for the year and a half it took finally to get a divorce then I moved to my own apartment. And for that year and a half, Damian stopped at nothing to "win me back."

I couldn't take another year and a half.

Unfortunately, this current scenario wasn't conducive to me finding that perfect nightgown to wear the first time I slept the night with Brock Lucas. We had slept together, twice, both times me falling asleep with him on my couch while watching a movie. No, strike that, three times adding last night.

But, except for last night, he'd always been gone before I woke and we had never slept together in a bed.

This was a momentous occasion that I should mentally, and arguably more important, *fashionably* prepare for. But at that moment, I didn't have it in me.

I sorted through my nightgown drawer with trembling hands and luckily my inherent girl power kicked in and my fingers honed in on my cotton-candy purplish-pink embroidered eyelet nightie with its empire waist, spaghetti straps, and teensy-weensy ruffle at hem and bodice. Cute, girlie, comfortable, therefore it seemed a casual choice, like it was any other night, but it bared lots of skin, showed serious leg and a hint of cleavage, all of which stated plainly I was making an effort for my man.

Freaking perfect.

I grabbed it and my glasses, took them to the bathroom, and did my nighttime gig, contacts out, face washed, teeth brushed and flossed. I changed clothes, slid my glasses on, and walked out.

I heard Brock's rumble when I did.

And this was what it said: "No shit, Calhoun."

I pressed my lips together at that name, scurried into the bedroom, dropped my clothes in the hamper, and scurried out.

I knew he wanted to protect me but I was forty-three years old. I was in a situation. This situation was unlike the last. Now people knew. People who cared about me. People who had my back *and* people willing to take my front and act as a shield.

But it was high time I got my head out of the sand.

Somehow, I'd managed to be a survivor. But I was thinking that was pure luck and it only had to happen because I'd left my head in the sand too long with a husband who was no good for me from the start and I knew it. I just didn't do a thing about it.

I needed to get my shit together.

So I stopped in the kitchen doorway and leaned against it, doing this with my eyes on a Brock Lucas who had his fist to his waist and his eyes on me.

Then he did something beautiful.

He trusted me and the strength I was building inside enough to keep talking.

"You call the DA and you tell him to tell that asshole's attorneys that if he doesn't desist in harassing Tess, his boatload of legal problems will become a shitload. He already forged her fucking signature on bank documents. And we already got taped testimony and phone records that show for six months he's been dicking with her. So, when the DA talks to his legal team, he needs to use the words stalking, harassment, assault, and sexual assault."

I felt my chest rise with my indrawn breath and I knew Brock saw it but he kept trusting me and thus talking.

"Statute of limitations is not out on that. No way in fuck that Tessa O'Hara, who runs a bakery and sprinkles fuckin' confetti on her cakes, will take the stand, describe her nightmare and he won't go down. I don't give a fuck if we have no physical evidence. She'll have any jury eating out of her hand. His lawyers will know that. Now, I smell that guy's fuckin' cologne, Calhoun, she's pressing charges. This ends for her tonight. Make the fuckin' call." He listened for about two seconds, then grunted, "Yeah," and flipped his phone shut.

I waited for him to shove it back into his pocket before I asked softly, "Are you okay?"

"No," he answered harshly. "I had my tongue in my woman's mouth and my hand on her ass for the first time in three months. I like your ass. For three months, I spent a good deal of time thinkin' about havin' my hand back on your ass. What I *didn't* spend time thinkin' about is havin' my hand on your ass and someone knockin' on the front door and that someone being your slimeball motherfucking ex."

Well, there you go.

"Are you all right?" he asked.

"Kentucky is becoming more attractive."

He stared at me.

Then he grinned.

His eyes swept the length of me and back again before he said low, "Great nightie, babe."

"Thanks," I replied, tipping my head to the side then, to shift the mood and probably breaking all the rules of the game by doing something that would get me kicked out of the sisterhood, I shared, "If I'd have known you were spending the night I would have carved out some time to take a trip to the mall to buy a silky, sexy nightie that shouted, *occasion*." With this, I lifted up my hands and shook them then dropped them and continued. "Though it would be carefully selected so when you saw me in it you'd think that was what I wore to bed every night when it isn't. But since I didn't know, I had to make do and this is what you get."

To that, I flicked my hand to my cotton-candy nightie.

"I'm thinkin' you did all right in a pinch," he noted.

"I'm glad," I said on a smile.

"So what do you wear to bed every night?" he asked.

"Well…" I thought about it, then finished, "various

versions of this. Though, I will warn you so you don't get your hopes up, some of them don't have ruffles."

To that, he burst out laughing and he did it while walking to me. He stopped laughing and walking a half a foot away.

With his head tipped down to me, he said quietly, "Call your girl, sweetness, and then let's hit the sack, yeah?"

I nodded but asked, "I'm sensing our earlier activities have been scheduled to recommence at a later date."

He lifted a hand and curled it around the side of my neck as he dipped his face close to mine.

Then he said, "It sucks but yeah." His hand gave me a squeeze while he went on. "You're right, this is an occasion. It's important and that douchebag showing marred it. When that happens between us again it's gonna be just you and me without the ghost of that guy tarnishing it."

I liked that. I liked that he wanted to give me that. I liked knowing us connecting in that way was as important to him as it was to me. And I liked holding the knowledge that he wanted to make it special.

I liked it so much, my hand came up, my fingers curled around his wrist at my neck, I got up on my toes, and I touched my mouth to his.

When I rocked back, I whispered, "Okay. I'll call Martha and meet you in bed."

He bent forward an inch, touched his forehead to mine then pulled back and dropped his hand. I released his wrist and he moved around me and toward the bedroom.

I went to my purse and dug out my phone. Then I called Martha. She was home. She wasn't fine but she'd just opened a bottle of red wine in an attempt to get that

way or at least put herself to sleep. We chatted until I
heard the tremble go out of her voice. Then I hung up.

I walked to my bedroom to find a bare-chested Brock
"Slim" Lucas in it, on his back in my bed, sheets to waist
but hands to his face rubbing.

Those hands dropped when I hit the room but not
before I remembered the last time he was in my bed,
pressing the butts of his palms to his forehead, his manner conflicted and his expression would provide further
evidence of that when he'd turned it to me.

This made a curl of apprehension writhe in my belly.

He rolled to his side and got up on a forearm while asking, "Babe, you gonna sleep on your feet or get in bed?"

I came unstuck, moved to my bed, pulled back the
covers, and got in cross-legged. I took off my glasses, set
them on the nightstand, grabbed my tub of moisturizer,
and commenced moisturizing my face.

Face moisturized, I sucked up the courage to ask,
"When I came in, what was on your mind?"

To my surprise, he didn't hesitate to answer.

"What was on my mind was that Calhoun was the lead
on the investigation into Heller. Calhoun is a good man.
A dedicated man. He and a lotta guys spent three years
building up to that takedown. They made twelve arrests
with that sweep and ten of those twelve are major players
in Heller's operation. That takedown was huge. Planned
and orchestrated with precision and the man-hours behind
it are incalculable. No case is rock solid but what they got
on all those guys is the closest I've ever seen. And I was
thinkin' that if that asshole fucks with you and I do what
I had the near overwhelming urge to do tonight when I
looked at his motherfucking face seeing he had the balls

to be standin' right at your front door at ten o'clock at night, I'll fuck *all* that."

I was watching him as he spoke.

When he stopped, I asked, "What urge?"

Brock blinked up at me.

Then he asked a repeated, "What urge?"

"Yeah, what urge?"

He stared at me three seconds before he leaned into me, grabbed the tub of moisturizer out of my hand, and leaned deeper, half tossing, half placing it on my nightstand. With his strong arm tight around my belly and hip, he pulled me into the bed and into him.

Once he had me settled, arm still firm around me, he said softly, "I am not a normal guy, Tess."

I'd already got that.

"Okay," I whispered.

"I'm the oldest boy. I got two sisters, a brother, and Mom got us all in the divorce. Dad's a decent guy but that didn't mean he didn't jack her around. He did. A lot. Too much. He and I have come to uneasy terms and, since he jacked her around so much, this took a while but because of his shit, I grew up bein' the man of the family. I did not learn to be the man I am from my dad. The man I am was ingrained in me, starting at seven."

I wasn't sure I understood what he was saying but I was sure I thought it was fascinating, and furthermore, I very much liked lying pressed close to him in my bed with his arm tight around me while he told me stories of his life.

"Okay," I whispered again when he didn't go on.

"What I'm sayin' is, you do not fuck with a woman who means somethin' to me. And when I say that, I mean, you do *not* fuck with a woman who means somethin' to me."

Oh my.

I got it.

"You wanted to hurt Damian," I said quietly.

"Hurt? Yeah. In a way he'd feel that pain every fuckin' day for the rest of his motherfuckin' life. In a way he'd never forget me. In a way he'd never forget the lesson I taught him. And in a way he'd think about you and instead of you giving precious headspace to wishin' you never met him, his headspace would be filled with wishin' he'd never fucked with you."

Before my mind told me to do it, my body pressed closer to his. But if my body asked my mind, my mind wouldn't have argued.

I slid my hand up his hard chest, along his corded neck to come to rest on his stubbled jaw.

Looking deep into his eyes, I admitted, "I don't have words."

His arm got tighter and his face tilted on the pillow to get closer before he whispered, "Tess, I learned somethin' early about you. You are the only woman I know who doesn't need words. Everything you do speaks for you and it never lies. Just your hand on me, babe, said it all."

He held my eyes and I held my breath because he said that like he liked it, not a little, a whole bunch.

I nodded. His face got soft. It dipped to mine where he touched my mouth with his.

When he pulled back, he murmured, "Hit your light, darlin'."

I nodded again and rolled. I turned out the light then curled on my side, pulled the covers over my shoulder, shoved my hands under my cheek and called, "'Night, honey."

Half a second later, I found my body hauled across the

bed, my ass in the curve of his hips, his knees cocked into mine, his front pressed to my back, his arm tight around my belly and his lips at my hair.

Only then did he murmur, "'Night, Tess."

Brock Lucas spooned.

I fell asleep smiling.

CHAPTER EIGHT

Wild Thing

THE SOFT STRAINS of Fiona Apple's "I Know" forced my eyes open to the early-morning light. I listened to her contralto, her piano, the soft strum of a bass, and the slow gentle beat of a drum for a few long moments before the volume started to increase. Then I got up on a forearm, reached out, and hit the button that would freeze the volume like I usually did so I could listen to my music in the mornings.

When I reached for the covers to shove them off, my body moved backward across the bed and hit something very, very solid and very, very warm.

Oh man.

How could I forget?

Brock was there.

And boy was he there, his hard, heated body behind me, his strong arm around me. I felt his lips at the skin of my neck.

"Honey," I whispered. Those lips trailed up then I felt teeth nip my earlobe.

A shiver slid through me.

Then, a rough, sleepy, deep, "'Mornin', baby."

Oh my.

His lips slid to behind my ear as his hand at my belly slid up my ribs and I held my breath until his hand stopped. I let out my breath and held it again when the backs of his knuckles started stroking feather light at the bottom swell of my breast.

Oh my.

I pressed back into him as he pushed into me and his tongue touched the skin behind my ear at the same time his thumb disengaged from his knuckles and swiped my breast *just* under my nipple.

At that, a throb pulsed through me.

"Brock," I breathed.

"Unless you got an early-mornin' emergency cake to bake, sweetness," he growled in my ear, "our earlier activities are scheduled to recommence right about now."

"The White House tends to give me plenty of advance warning," I quipped breathily.

"Fuckin' fantastic," Brock muttered, rolled me to face him, his hand went in my hair, twisted gently, and tugged back but he didn't have to do that. My arm was winding around him and my head was dipping back so he could have my mouth.

And he took it.

Brock had not lied with what he said in my kitchen when he came back. The first time he made love to me had not been planned. It wasn't a seduction. It started as usual. We were just messing around, but before that night, he'd always kept it under control. It had usually been about me, him exploring me or him helping me to get off. But something happened, and even as much as I thought about it, to that day, I had no idea what it was. But whatever it was, it snapped his control and he picked me up from the couch, carried me to the bedroom, and off we went.

This was different from all of that except the last.

Because Brock didn't have a plan. Brock wasn't protecting me from exposing myself, giving too much to a man whose name I did not know. There was no reason for Brock to control the situation, his reaction or mine.

So he didn't.

And even bigger than that night when his control snapped, now he didn't need it. With one touch of our tongues, lying in my bed in the weak, early-morning light of dawn, it exploded.

And even better than any other time, this wasn't about him exploring me and helping me to get off. This was about us exploring *each other*.

For the first time ever, I was free to give as good as I got.

So I fucking did.

It was wild. It was heated. It was energetic. There was a lot of rolling, groping, tongues, teeth, fingers, moans, groans, whimpers, sighs, and gasps as he took, I took, he gave, and I gave.

And it was when I was giving, crouched low between his cocked legs, my mouth taking him deep when he knifed up. His hands came under my armpits, and he hauled me up his body between his legs at the same time he rolled me to my back. I wound my arms around his shoulders as I opened my legs and his hips fell through.

His eyes locked with mine the second before he thrust deep.

My neck arched, my arms spasmed around him, and I lifted my knees to press my thighs tight to his sides.

"Tess, mouth," he growled.

My neck righted and his mouth was on mine, his tongue in my mouth as he rode me deep. God, so deep. Hard, *God*, so hard. And sweet, God, *God*, so unbelievably *sweet*.

It built, it was fast, it was hot, and it was going to be incredibly good.

Before it swept over me, I tore my mouth from his, shoved my face in his neck, and moaned, "Brock."

"Oh yeah, baby, *fuck* yeah," he grunted, thrusting deep, I drew in a sharp breath and came hard.

Then I came down, my head dropping back to the pillows, and I had the opportunity to watch his face as I felt him move inside me and I saw, clear as day, Brock Lucas liked right where he was.

A lot.

A *whole* lot.

He had an arm around my waist, grinding me down, his weight in his other forearm in the bed. I wrapped my legs around him, tilting my hips up for him, and this made him growl deep from his chest. His eyes locked with mine. I kept one arm tight around his shoulders and my other hand went to his face, thumb sweeping his cheek then his lips.

He buried that face in my neck, groaned, "Tess," and planted himself to the root on another groan as he came.

I slid my hand from his face into his hair, tipped my head so my face was in his neck, and I pressed my lips against his heated skin, feeling the tickle of the long hairs that curled there.

Then I closed my eyes and took him in with three senses, smelling his skin, feeling him all around and buried inside me, and listening to his heavy breaths.

He gave me his weight for approximately two seconds before he gathered me in both his arms, miraculously got up to his knees, taking me with him, still connected, and, keeping our bodies linked, he twisted, falling to his hip and dropping to his back with me on top.

Nice.

"Nice," I whispered into his neck.

I heard his deep, attractive chuckle before I heard his head move on the pillow then I felt his lips against my hair where he kissed me.

Oh my.

That was nice too.

He had one arm wrapped around the small of my back and when the other hand drifted up my spine to play with my hair, I lifted my head to look down at him.

He tilted his chin, his quicksilver eyes catching mine, and he grinned, sated, content, and amused.

The sweet, sultry, warm hum of that mood saturated the air and settled like bliss against my skin as he muttered, "Wild thing."

I blinked.

Then I asked, "Sorry?"

"Baby, *fuck*"—his arm gave me a squeeze—"you were all over me."

I blinked again.

Then I felt my body get tight.

Damn.

I was a follower, not a leader in bed. Careful, thoughtful, keeping ears and eyes open to make sure what I was doing was enjoyed and noting what my partner liked when I did it so I could keep doing it or cataloguing it to do it again.

I did not lose control. I did not let go.

This meant the two times I'd had sex with Brock were the two best times of my life, by far. Like, far as in an ocean far. In fact, without a fair amount of work from my partner (and, usually, they gave up), I rarely climaxed during sex or any part of the festivities.

But, just now, I had not been in my head and paying attention. I had been in the zone and acting on instinct. My body, what it was feeling and its needs, ruled my mind and my mind had totally checked out.

Totally.

Damn.

I started to pull up when Brock's hand cupped the back of my head but slid down, taking my hair with it so his fingers were curled around the back. His palm was warm on my neck under my ear and his thumb was against my face by my hairline.

As his hand positioned, he whispered, "Hey." My eyes slid through his to come to rest on the pillow by his head and I inched up again but his hand tensed and he semi-repeated, "Tess, hey." I stilled but kept my gaze on the pillowcase to which I got a squeeze of his arm around my back, pulling my body close, and a growled, "Eyes, babe."

My eyes slid to his.

His looked deep into them.

Then his hand at my head brought my face super close to his and he whispered, "What the fuck, baby?"

"I—" I started but a shadow shifted into his eyes and stayed there as he cut me off.

"Jesus, did I hurt you?"

I shook my head slightly and said, "No, it's just…"

I trailed off because I didn't know what it was.

His thumb started skimming my cheek light and sweet as he prompted gently, "It's just what?"

"I don't know what," I whispered.

He held my eyes and didn't say anything.

Then I found my mouth telling him, "I lost control."

He did a slow blink.

Then he asked, "Is this a bad thing?"

"I don't know," I began, watching him closely, then whispered, "Is it?"

He stared at me, eyes widening in unconcealed disbelief. Then, quick as a flash, both of his arms were super tight around me even as he pressed his head back into the pillows and roared with laughter.

About two seconds into his hilarity, he rolled us both, losing our connection as he did but settling with his weight on me, his hips between my legs, and his laughter sounding against the skin of my neck where he shoved his face.

"Brock," I wheezed. "I...can't..." He lifted his head and looked down at me, smiling huge as he planted one forearm in the bed, taking his weight off me, and curled his other hand around my neck right under my jaw. "Breathe," I finished.

His thumb stroked my jaw as he kept smiling down at me but he didn't say a word.

"Um...I think I should get up and—"

"Yeah, babe, you can get up in a second," he interrupted me. "But first, let's get somethin' straight, all right?"

I held his eyes and bit my lip.

He looked at my mouth and pressed his lips together as his eyes danced.

Then he unpressed them to say, "I intend to spend a

lot of time doin' just what we did, adding variations, positions, different locations, and I'm gonna be creative."

Oh my.

I felt the walls of my womb contract.

He went on. "You ever"—he dipped his face close, mouth and eyes still smiling—"*ever* lock onto your control while we're enjoyin' each other, I'll know one thing. And that is, I'm not doin' it right."

Oh *my*.

"Brock—" I whispered, but stopped when his face dipped even closer.

"Baby, that was fuckin' *phenomenal*. Nothin' you did, not one thing, I didn't like and most of it I fuckin' loved. Mark this, sweetness, I like it wild and you... were...*wild* and I loved every fuckin' minute of it. I do not know what the other men you took to your bed taught you but whatever it was, it was fucked. Lose that ghost in your eyes, Tess, because, baby, you're a goddamned natural."

Because his words made that warm gushiness invade my insides, I lifted my hand to his neck then slid it into his hair and lifted my head as I pulled his down to me. My head tilted, his slanted and I kissed him, wet and hopefully sweet. He gave me his weight as his arms wrapped back around me. He rolled me again to the top and he took over the kiss and his was also wet, his was deep and his was *definitely* sweet.

He broke the kiss but not the connection of our mouths so his lips moved against mine when he whispered, "Totally a natural."

I smiled against his mouth and into his eyes.

Brock smiled back the same way.

Then he muttered, "Shower," to which I did a full-body tremble right on top of him.

He felt it and I watched close up as his smile got lazy.

He hauled us both out of bed, out of the room, into the bathroom and then into the shower.

After that, I made him coffee and toast and later made out with him on my doorstep in full view of a waking neighborhood. My arms around his shoulders, my body pressed deep, our tongues tangled. His arms were tight around me, with one hand carrying coffee in a travel mug and the fingers of his other hand holding a half-eaten slice of toast.

He lifted his head, looked in my eyes, and whispered, "I'll text you the address to my place. Come prepared to spend the night. I'm doin' dinner."

"All right," I whispered back. "But I'm doing dessert."

His mouth twitched before he agreed. "You got it, sweetness. Now let me go before I do something we'll both get arrested for, like throw you on the lawn and give your neighbors a show."

I let him go.

He chuckled low, tipped his chin up at me, turned, and jogged down to his pickup at the same time taking a bite of toast.

I watched him drive away and I didn't give one shit that I should have played it cool and walked right into my house and shut my door. I stood there and watched until I couldn't see his truck anymore.

Only then did I go in.

I turned on my music and I didn't turn on Fiona Apple.

I was an equal opportunity music lover and what-ever struck my fancy normally didn't unstrike it. So, considering "The Devil Went Down to Georgia" and "In America" were kickass songs, I owned the Charlie Daniels *Super Hits* CD.

And that was what I listened to while I got ready to face the day.

I couldn't say it was all my gig but I sang "The Devil" and "In America" out loud and one could not say "The South's Gonna Do It Again" was not the shit.

Dressed and ready to go forth and bake cakes, I got in my car thinking that was the best morning of my whole...

Fucking...

Life.

CHAPTER NINE

Dinner at Brock's

I WAS SITTING in my car looking up at the apartment building, scanning the numbers on the doors, looking for number sixteen.

Brock's apartment.

I was trying really hard not to make a judgment about the state of his apartment complex, if one could call it that.

It was off the one-way section of Lincoln just up from Speer and perpendicular to the road. There was a small spread of tarmac in front of a very deep, long, two-story building, eight apartments on bottom, eight on top. The doors faced an exposed walkway. The stairs leading up to the top level on the ends of either side were iron, rusting, and looked more than a little scary. And the two padlocked sheds off the parking lot, one smaller one with the stenciled word "Laundry" and the other one bigger and maybe not too intelligently having the stenciled word "Storage" on it did nothing for the feel of the place.

Sometime in the summer, someone clearly made an

effort. However, they also just as clearly got side-tracked. In Denver, if you planted flowers, in the arid climate you needed to tend them and this tending mostly had to do with adding copious amounts of water but it also didn't hurt to pull weeds. Now it was a still warm mid-October and in the two half barrels that flanked the short entry from Lincoln to the building and the four that "decorated" the top and foot of both stair-wells had a riot of a green, healthy weeds. An equal riot of brown, dead bits. And some straggly, weak petunia blossoms that had obviously struggled valiantly against the odds but clearly should be put out of their misery and not only because autumn had settled on the Rocky Mountains.

Oh well, whatever. He was a man. A single man. A single man with a Harley Fat Boy and a beat-up pickup truck that Martha was right about; it needed to be traded up and that trade-up should have happened around a decade ago. This wasn't a big surprise and, truthfully, I might be concerned if he had a picture-perfect house in a suburb that looked like Ada haunted the place.

That would be bad.

I was turning to gather my overnight case, purse, and the white bag with the robin's-egg-blue ink stamp of hum-mingbirds and hibiscus blossoms around the words "Tes-sa's Cakes" when my phone rang.

It was probably Brock, though why I thought this, I didn't know. He said to be there at six and although I took time out for my kickboxing class and extended that with a side trip to the mall, I still left the bakery early to go home and get ready. The kids who worked for me were good, and the shelves, displays, and cake stands were stocked with plenty of goodies to see them through so I didn't have a problem doing this and did it often. So it was now two to six. I wasn't late. I was actually, if you got down to it, early.

Maybe there was a change of plans. In the four months we were seeing each other, this happened. Not regularly. Brock didn't usually miss seeing me and if he had to change plans, it usually meant he had to see me later or leave early but it was rare he'd cancel.

In fact, thinking about it, I didn't recall that ever happening.

Therefore, curious, I pulled out my phone and saw it said "Unknown Caller."

I touched the screen as I felt my brows draw together, put it to my ear, and greeted, "Hello."

"Yo, bitch. You got Elvira."

I blinked at my dashboard.

Then I said, "Uh... hey."

"Uh... hey right back at 'cha. Listen, your homegirl gave me your number 'cause I called her 'cause Gwen and me were doin' a little lookin' around in Cherry Creek durin' my extended lunch break and we saw you in the lingerie section of Nordstrom's."

"Oh," I replied. "Okay."

"So?" she asked, and I felt my brows draw together again when she said no more.

"So?" I asked back.

"So, what gives?"

"What gives?"

"Yeah, what gives? You *were* drinkin' cosmos with us in Stepford country when we were talkin' 'bout your bad-news boy and I do *not* think it bodes well two

days later that you're in the lingerie section of Nordstrom's," she stated, then announced, "This here's a phone
intervention."

"A phone intervention?"

"A phone intervention. See, I work for Hawk Delgado
and Hawk's Gwen's man, which, incidentally, is why
I'm allowed to take extended lunch breaks in the lingerie section of Nordstrom's with the company credit card.
But, anyway, Gwen pumped Hawk for intel about your
bad-news boy and so did I and we put our heads together.
Hawk...well, he says your boy is bad news, not that we
didn't know that already. But Hawk agreeing, considering
he's Hawk, confirms it."

Damn it all to hell.

It was only me who could run into a well-intentioned
but nosy, inappropriately meddling and slightly frighten-
ing black woman at a really bad baby shower and it was
only Martha who would give her her number and then, in
turn, give her mine.

"Elvira, I...well, thank you for...I mean, I don't
really know you but thanks for looking out for me but it's
unnecessary. It's all good."

"Just you sayin' that means it's all *bad*. We've decided
its cosmos at Gwen's. Trace and Cam are in and so is
Martha. Tonight. Eight o'clock. Don't worry about eatin'
'cause I'm doin' boards."

"I can't make it because I'm having dinner with
Brock."

This was met with a moment of silence, then a muttered, "Oh boy."

I looked through the windshield up to the top floor and
saw it. Apartment sixteen, on the end next to some tall,

bushy pine trees that meant if he had side windows, those trees would block out the light.

I pulled in a light breath.

Then I looked at my dashboard and whispered, "I left my husband the day after he raped me." I heard her suck in a breath and hers wasn't light. "This was after eight years of a not-great marriage then two years of him hitting me, not regularly, but when he did it, he did it hard. This came out during the questioning at the station and Brock was observing. When he heard me say I'd been raped, he threw a chair. I heard it. I heard the crash. He threw a chair and they had to drag him out so he wouldn't interrupt the questioning to get to me."

Elvira, for once, was silent.

I, for once, was not.

"His sister was raped, as was an old girlfriend. His father jacked his mother around and he assumed the role of man of the house at seven years old. When a woman means something to him, he takes care of her. He told me this and I believe him. I mean something to him. I don't know what you've heard or who this Hawk guy is but I know who Brock is to me. Now I'd love to have cosmos with you and the girls. But I won't listen to anyone trash talking Brock because he also means something to me and only he and I know what's going on between us. All that other shit, well, Elvira, it just doesn't matter."

She, again, was silent.

I, again, was not.

"Honey, you're the third person in six years I told that to. Martha just found out last night. Brock heard me say it and he's unfortunately got experience with this kind of thing. He knew I'd buried it and he's helping me to move on from it. This is not a man you don't trust. He has my back, he has my front, and he's handling me with care. Trust me."

"All right, girl," she whispered.

"And thank you again for being cool. Any other time with any other guy when all this other stuff isn't happening, I'd appreciate it. But this isn't what it seems. It's something a whole lot different."

"Okay," she said quietly.

"Okay," I whispered.

"We didn't mean—" she started but I quickly cut her off.

"I know you didn't, honey."

"I won't say anything to them about, you know," she assured me and I closed my eyes.

Then I opened them and told her, "You don't have to keep this secret. I did for too long. I didn't do anything to be ashamed of so there's no reason it shouldn't be in the open."

"Still, girl, I'll let you do the talkin'."

Okay, maybe she was nosy, meddling, and a little scary. But she was also very sweet.

"All right," I replied.

"Over cosmos at Gwen's."

"Sounds good."

"Another night."

"Yeah."

Silence then, softly, "He threw a chair?"

I smiled at the dash but my smile was for me. Then, softly back, I replied, "Yeah, he threw a chair."

"I'm thinkin' Hawk don't know that," she remarked.

"Well, maybe you should tell him."

"Bet yo' boots I will. I got one on Hawk. I *never* got one on Hawk."

I laughed softly.

Through this, Elvira said, "Have fun with your hot guy."

I smiled again. That one was for her even though she couldn't see. Then I said, "I will."

"Later, girlfriend."

"Later, Elvira."

I took the phone from my ear and hit END CALL. I dropped it in my purse, gathered up my stuff, was sure to bleep the locks on my car, and I braved the rickety steps.

I stood in front of door number sixteen and knocked.

Two seconds later it was thrown open by a tall, gorgeous, rounded, dark-haired, silver-eyed woman with a flushed face and a visible desire to kill.

I took a step back.

She whirled to face the apartment and shrieked, "*Dylan! You do that to your brother one more time and it won't be the naughty step when we get home! I don't know what it'll be I just know you . . . won't . . . LIKE IT!*"

I checked the impulse to grab my phone and inspect the text Brock sent me to make certain I got the apartment number right when she turned back to me, smiled sweetly, and said, "Hey, you must be Tess."

I blinked.

She went on. "I'm Laura, Slim's sister."

My entire body seized and I feared an acute onset of epilepsy when I heard Brock's rumble coming from deep in the apartment. "Jesus, Laura, what the fuck?"

To which Laura (apparently Brock's sister!) turned

back to face the apartment and snapped, "Slim, we try not
to drop the f-bomb in front of the kids."

"Great, you're in your house or at little league or
wherever-the-fuck, try not to do it. Your hooligans are
systematically tearing up my place, anything goes."

He appeared in the door by his sister, grinned at me,
leaned out, extending a long arm. His fingers closed on
my wrist and he pulled me into the apartment whereupon
his arms locked around me and he shuffled me in deeper.
And, before I knew it, his mouth was on mine and he laid
a hot, sweet, deep, but short wet one on me.

"Gross, Uncle Slim!" a child's voice shouted.

"Yeah! Gross!" another one chimed in.

"I like her shoes," another one, this one clearly female
and clearly having good taste, observed.

Brock's head lifted and I had three thoughts. One,
even with an audience of family members, some of them
being children, he could really kiss. Two, I was obviously
meeting members of Brock's family and I was in no way
prepared. And three, I was glad I gave the flip-flops a rest
and was wearing a pair of sexy, strappy sandals, really
good jeans, and a complicated designer blouse.

Before I could utter a noise or, perhaps, gather my
thoughts, Brock divested me of the purse and overnight
bag on my shoulder (both he dumped on the floor), the
white bag filled with my famous bakery-fresh snickerdoodles (this he tossed on the coffee table) and turned me to
the apartment. One arm sliding around my shoulders and
holding my front close to his side, he made introductions.

"Babe, this is my sister, Laura, her hooligans Grady
and Dylan, my princess, Ellie, and my Mom, Fern. Everyone, this is Tess."

His mom, Fern?

He kissed me *with tongues* in front of *his mom, Fern*?

I scanned the room and a lot forced itself into my brain. Too much to process. So much, my mind started to shut down and it took every bit of effort I had not to lapse into catatonia.

First, the door had been closed and Laura, Brock's gorgeous sister, was standing by it grinning like a madwoman.

Second, there were two dark-haired boys on the floor. Both of them in little-boy football uniforms (*sans* shoulder pads). Both of them appearing at some point in the not too distant past to have rolled around in the dirt for a good length of time and my guess was that was at least five hours. Both of them appeared to be arrested in mid wrestling match. And both of them had green Kool-Aid mustaches.

Third, there was an adorable little dark-haired girl wearing a princess dress costume, complete with fake satin top and masses of tulle skirt, this ensemble complimented by clickety-clack, little girl plastic high-heeled shoes. She was sitting on the couch with her legs straight in front of her, feet bouncing while she gamely licked a melting Popsicle but was struggling in this endeavor as evidenced by it dripping purple on the fake satin of the top of her dress.

Fourth, an older woman with thick silver hair, blue eyes, and an overall look that screamed, *"Grandma!"* was standing in a doorway grinning at me like a madwoman.

And last, Brock's furnishings were, at a glance, approximately two point seven five steps up from the overall feel of his apartment complex. But at least the place appeared clean if not tidy. And when I say "not tidy" I say this in the sense that it also reflected that Brock was a single man with a Harley Fat Boy and a beat-up pickup truck that Martha was right about. It needed to be traded up and that trade up should have happened around a decade ago.

"Uh…hey," I greeted.

"We're a surprise, we know. We were on our way back from junior football league practice and we thought we'd stop by," Fern said, coming farther into the room and I saw she was holding a dishtowel. "We brought KFC because the kids had to eat. We didn't know Slim was expecting company."

"Um…okay," I told her, then added stupidly, "Cool."

She made it to me and held out her hand. I took it and her fingers closed around mine. Her other hand came up and closed around our clasped hands. As she did this, she looked into my eyes and did a Mom Scan, which left me feeling mildly ill at ease considering the fact that I was pretty sure her blue eyes read all the words written on my soul. Therefore, she knew I'd lied to my mother when I was ten and told her I didn't try to shave my legs (when the nicks on them proved this to be false) and that I let Jimmy Moriarty get to second base at the homecoming dance my sophomore year in high school.

She released me from The Scan, let go of my hand, stepped back, and luckily didn't announce to the room I was a floozy who lied to her mother.

"They're about to leave," Brock stated, to which Princess Ellie shouted, "No, we're not! We're watching *Tangled*!"

And to this, Dylan (or Grady, it had not been pointed out who was who), shouted in return, "We're not watching *Tangled*! We watched *Tangled* this weekend *five times*." He swung his head to Laura and whined, "Moooooom! I'm sick of *Tangled*!"

"I'm not sick of *Tangled*. That movie is awesome," I found my mouth (again) stupidly muttering.

"*See!*" Ellie shrieked, gesturing to me with her Popsicle, off which flew a massive chunk of purple ice that plopped on the shag (yes, *shag*) carpet a foot away from Brock's motorcycle boots. "Uncle Slim's girlfriend wants to watch *Tangled*!"

I didn't exactly say that but then again, she was probably five and five-year-old girls heard what they wanted to hear. In fact, lots of fifty-five-year-old girls heard what they wanted to hear.

Fern rushed to the ice on the floor with her dishtowel while Laura scolded, "Ellie! Careful with that Popsicle."

"Do we have to watch *Tangled*? Do we? *Do we?*" Dylan (or Grady) whined.

"Dylan, pipe down. We're not watching anything. We're going home and getting cleaned up for bed."

"I don't wanna go to bed!" Dylan *and* Ellie shouted in unison.

At this point, the front door opened and a tall, beer-gutted older man with dark hair shot with not a small amount of silver and silvery-gray eyes strolled in shouting, "Jesus H. Christ! What's the commotion?"

"Grandpa!" Ellie and Dylan screamed, Ellie tossing the Popsicle aside only for it to land with a plop on Brock's couch in her haste to scramble off said couch and race Dylan to hug the older gentleman's legs. But when they did this, with the velocity and force they hit him, he went back two paces before they successfully latched on. Luckily, disaster was averted and he kept his feet.

I was rooted to the spot, looking at a man whose somewhat withered good looks stated firmly he was Brock's father as I felt the slap of attitude hit the room and heard Brock mutter under his breath, "Fuck."

For once, the mood in the room didn't come from Brock. When my head woodenly turned in the direction from whence it emanated I saw it was coming from Fern.

"Tell me he is not here," she hissed.

Uh-oh.

"Mom—" Brock started.

"Slim, tell me…he…is not…*here*," she somewhat repeated with scary mini-pauses and equally scary emphasis.

Brock's arm gave me a squeeze.

My head tipped dazedly back to look up to him and when I caught his eyes, he immediately informed me, "This is why I'm never fuckin' home."

Well, that answered one question. If Brock was never home he didn't need a fabulous pad.

"Heya, Laurie, honey. Heya, Slim. Heya, Grady," Brock's father greeted with smiles.

"Hey, Grandpa," Grady returned.

"Hey there, Dad," Laura said hesitantly, her manner watchful.

Brock's father's look became cautious when he muttered, "Hey, Fern."

"Cob," she bit off, clearly deciding not to go with the

option of leaping forward and scratching out his eyes as
this would scar her grandchildren for life, but I could tell
she was hanging on to that control by a thread.

Brock's father's gaze hit me. His head tipped to the
side and his eyes flashed back and forth between his son
and me about seven times before he said, "Uh...hey
there, little lady."

"Dad, this is Tess," Brock introduced.

"She's Uncle Slim's girlfriend!" Ellie shouted, her fingers curled into Cob Lucas's pants, her back arched at an
impossible angle, her grape Popsicle-stained mouth smiling huge up at her grandfather.

He looked down at her, put a big hand gentle on her
head, and asked softly, "Is she, my Ellie?"

"Yeah!" Ellie cried. "And she wears pretty shoes *and*
she's gonna watch *Tangled* with me *right now*!"

Cob's eyes came to me. They were curious, searching
even, but like he looked at Fern, hesitant as he muttered,
"That's fantastic, sweetheart."

Into this conversation, Fern asked acidly, "There a reason you're here, Cob?"

"Well, actually"—his eyes moved from Fern to Brock
to me and back again—"yeah."

"I'll bet there is," she mumbled bitingly.

I caught sight of Laura bugging her eyes out at Brock
and with that I decided to take action.

I slid out from under Brock's arm then leaned and
carefully took the dishtowel out of Fern's hand.

I walked to the couch and grabbed the bag of snickerdoodles at the same time I swiped up the Popsicle
and announced, "All right, kids, in this bag are bakery
fresh snickerdoodles I made at my shop for your uncle.

Whoever gets to the kitchen and gets their hands and mouths clean gets a cookie. Who's with me?"

Dylan and Ellie instantly abandoned their grandfather and raced to the kitchen, Ellie, hindered by her heels, nearly taking a header twice. Grady got to his feet eyeing the bag and his mother, clearly weighing cookies versus hanging with the adults in a tense situation and, not surprisingly, cookies won out. So he sauntered after his brother and sister. I followed them and didn't look back as I was confronted with a kitchen Fern obviously just cleaned and shut the swinging door behind me.

I set about hiding nine of the dozen snickerdoodles (Brock's favorite) and setting out the other three at the same time supervising cleaning up three tired, wound-up kids.

When they were clean and sitting at Brock's scarred, wooden kitchen table eating cookies and sucking back milk from glasses I'd poured, Grady, the oldest (my guess, Ellie around four or five, Dylan around six or seven, and Grady around eight or nine) informed me, "Grandma isn't Grandpa's biggest fan."

Hmm. How did I respond to that?

"Well, sometimes things get complicated with adults," I told him lamely.

Grady kept the information flowing. "Dad isn't his biggest fan either. Dad says he's a douchebag."

I pressed my lips together to stop the giggle escaping then I said, "Douchebag isn't a really nice word, but that said, your father is entitled to his opinion."

Grady kept speaking. "Uncle Slim puts up with him but I think he does it for Mom and Aunt Jill 'cause they like 'im but Uncle Levi thinks he's a douchebag too. I heard him and Uncle Slim talkin' when Uncle Slim told Uncle Levi to cool it about Grandpa because it was bothering Aunt Jill. But Uncle Levi said that Grandpa never paid child report and he had a bunch of girlfriends other than Grandma so he didn't owe him anything and neither did Aunt Jill."

Apparently, Grady had a mind like a sponge, though he got one thing wrong. Child report I was guessing was child *support* and I was also guessing having a father that didn't pay it and played around on your mom was not good.

"I like Grandpa!" Ellie piped up.

"Of course you do, honey," I said, smiling at her from my place leaning against the counter.

"I put up with him like Uncle Slim," Grady announced.

"Grady's gonna be Uncle Slim when he grows up," Dylan, sporting a milk mustache, shared.

Grady did not challenge this information. Instead, he declared proudly, "He played first base and I play first base. He played linebacker and I play linebacker. His job is scary, Mom says, but he does it to keep kids like me safe so that's what I'm gonna do too. When I get old, I'm gonna keep kids safe."

I was feeling warm and gushy again.

"That's a fantastic goal, Grady," I said quietly.

"Do you got kids?" Dylan asked.

"No, honey, I don't have any kids."

"That's good. When you marry Uncle Slim, you can be mom to Rex and Joel," Grady offered and I blinked.

"Sorry, honey, who?"

"Rex and Joel, Uncle Slim's kids, our cousins," Grady told me. My body went completely still, including my heart and lungs, the warm gushiness evaporated, and Grady kept talking. "Aunt Olivia used to be married to Uncle Slim and Mom, Dad, Grandma, Grandpa, Aunt Jill, Uncle Fritz, *and* Uncle Levi aren't her biggest fans. I'm *really* not allowed to say the word Mom calls her. Dad too. And Uncle Levi said if he saw her again, he'd break her neck."

I stared at him.

"She has a pinchy face," Ellie added to the conversation, making her own scrunchy face that stated clearly she felt the same about Aunt Olivia as everyone else did.

"She never brings snickerdoodles to the family reunions," Dylan put in, then sucked back more milk before he musingly went on. "Or anything."

"She wouldn't think about snickerdoodles. She doesn't care about snickerdoodles. Mom says she only cares about looking good and that's why she's always gettin' her nails done," Grady authoritatively told Dylan.

"She has pretty nails," Ellie told me. "I like her nail polish even though it's almost always red. She should try pink."

Although I was nowhere near processing the information they'd provided me, Grady kept spouting it. "She brings Rex and Joel to the family reunion every year and she stays and Mom says she stays even though she's not family anymore just to show off her fancy outfits and be a wet blanket. I can't say why Uncle Levi said she does it because most of the words are bad."

Uncle Levi clearly had a mouth much like his brother.

And Brock Lucas had an ex-wife and two sons. A pinchy-faced ex-wife who had a perma-manicure and two sons.

This, I did not know. This, a thing you shared. This, I did not know what to do with.

To be fair, I had known Brock as Brock for three days. Still.

"Can I be your flower girl when you marry Uncle Slim?" Ellie asked.

Again, my body, lungs, and heart went completely still and then the latter two started pumping and when they did this, they did it *hard*.

Damn! Now how did I answer *that*?

I decided on honesty.

"Right now we're just seeing each other, Ellie, but I'll keep a line open to you if it looks like it's getting serious," I promised and she giggled.

Then she placed her order. "Okay, but I want my dress to be pink."

"I'll keep that in mind," I told her and she grinned at me.

She had a milk mustache too.

I grinned back.

The door swung open and people flooded through, starting with Laura and ending with Fern, Brock sandwiched in the middle. He came direct to me, eyes on my face and my eyes slid away. Fern went direct to the table to gather glasses. Laura started herding kids.

"All right, kiddos," Laura started, snatching a towel from a rack, "wipe off those milk mustaches and inspect Uncle Slim's living room for your stuff. We're packed up and in the car in five minutes. March!"

Grady grabbed the towel, swiped his face, tossed it vaguely in his mother's direction, and raced out. Dylan followed suit. Ellie skipped to her mother like she had all the time in the world to tiptoe through the tulips, rubbed the towel across her face once mostly smearing milk and not lapping it up then she skipped out.

"So sorry about crashing your date, Tess," Laura said, pushing the towel back on the rack. "We were just driving by, saw Slim's truck and bike, and that's unusual so we took our shot. We'll be out of your hair before you know it."

"Not a problem," I told her on a smile, feeling Brock leaning into the counter with a hip, the front of his body facing my side but I kept my eyes glued to his sister at the table.

Laura smiled back and stated, "I'll have to bring the kids to your bakery. They'll love it. I've been in a couple times but never with the kids, just to pick things up. Ellie talks about your pink cupcakes all the time."

"Give me a warning call and I'll batten down the hatches," I quipped and her smile got bigger as Brock's body got closer. When I say this, I mean his arm circled my rib cage, he turned me so that now *I* was leaning one hip against the counter and the rest of me was pressed back against him.

Laura's eyes dropped to his arm. They warmed, and she looked back at my face and was grinning like a madwoman again.

At this point, Fern dampened the mood by proclaiming, "Slim, I hope that doesn't happen often."

I turned my head to see her at the sink. She had rinsed the glasses and loaded a rickety dishwasher that might, though I wasn't certain, have been the first of its kind, and she was currently shutting its door.

"Mom, we'll talk about it later," Brock said in a warning tone.

She turned and tipped her head back to look at her son. "Does it happen often?"

"Did I say we'll talk about it later?" Brock asked.

"Simple question, Slim," she returned and he sighed.

"If you mean does he stop by? Not often. But he does it. If you mean does he ask for money? No. Not anymore," he answered.

"Not anymore?" Fern prompted and Brock sighed again.

"He saw my truck and bike just like you, Mom," he said quietly. "He's an old guy with not a lot of friends left that he hasn't fucked over. He comes by. We sit around, drink beer, and watch a game. This does not happen often but it happens."

She stared at him. Then she stated, "I remember a time when you wouldn't even look at him."

"Yeah, well, I've grown up. He's my father. I don't like that he's lonely. What can I say?" Brock replied.

Fern studied her son before her eyes shifted to me. She seemed to realize this was not the time or place and that was when *she* sighed.

Then she said, "I'm sorry, Tess. You must think we're all nuts."

"My parents are divorced, Fern, and my mom hated my dad from when I was nine to the day he died and even then she announced she wanted to go to his funeral so she could spit on his grave. Luckily, the next day, she got the flu and was bedridden for a week or she might have done it," I told her. She stared at me, Brock's arm got tight around my ribs, and I finished. "I guess what I'm saying is, I get it."

Her eyes warmed, her mouth got soft, and she nodded.

Then she whispered, "Thanks, sweetheart."

"Mom! Dylan's pulling my jersey!" Grady shouted from the living room.

"Cue exit," Laura muttered and I looked at her. "See you later, Tess?"

"Yeah, Laura, nice to meet you."

"You too," she replied, then rushed out.

Brock pushed me gently in front of him, slid out from behind me, and went to his mother, bending low for her to kiss his cheek.

"Have fun, honey," I heard her whisper.

"Right," he murmured and she moved away from him and her eyes came to me.

"Have a nice night, Tess. Lovely to meet you."

"You too, Fern," I replied.

She made to move out. Brock caught my hand and followed her, pulling me behind him. We hit the living room and got separated as the kids shouted good-byes to me, went into attack mode in order to give Brock's legs hugs (this, he allowed from his nephews but he swung his niece up in his arms, gave her a fierce hug while he kissed then blew into her neck, through which she giggled with childish abandon and while observing this I fought a tidal wave of warm gushiness). A brief period of pandemonium ensued for what appeared to be no reason at all then I stood in the middle of Brock's shabby living room as he closed the door.

He locked the three locks (knob, deadbolt, chain) and turned to me.

"Your mom wanted to spit on your dad's grave?" he asked, eyebrows up.

"In the bitter divorce department, although your folks

clearly have a solid contender, my folks beat anyone by a mile."

He grinned at me.

I tipped my head to the side and asked, "So . . . Rex and Joel?"

His grin spread to a smile then he moved and before I knew it, in fact, even after it happened I wasn't sure how I got flat on my back on the couch with Brock on top of me. All I knew was that I was there.

"Rex and Joel," he stated, his eyes holding mine, his holding mirth, his hands moving on me in ways not conducive to relaxing or having a life-sharing chat. "My boys. I was married to their mother for five of the most miserable years of my life. Then I was divorced from her and she made the next five years the second most miserable years of my life. Two years ago, she got remarried and now she's making her new husband's life miserable, and lucky for me, she's not able to multitask. Rex is ten, Joel is twelve. They're good kids. I get them every other weekend, two weeks in the summer, and whenever Olivia's at the spa, which, considering her new victim is loaded, is often. This works for me because I think the world of my boys and clearly my genes are dominant because they aren't pains in the ass like their mother is."

"I'm reading from that you two did not have an amicable divorce and remain friends," I noted and the mirth in his eyes hit the room and also hit his body, which shook over mine with suppressed laughter.

"Yeah, babe, sorry I didn't make that more clear."

"So being with her was the five most miserable years of your life?"

"Yeah, and she made being without her miserable too but being without her was not the miserable part."

"So why did you marry her?"

His head tipped slightly to the side and his face got slightly more serious.

Then he answered, "Because there was the Olivia I met, dated, fell in love with, and asked to marry me. Then there was the Olivia who I went on my honeymoon with. Night and day. Dark and light. Kid you not, sweetness, it was like she wasn't even the same woman. It was whacked."

I stared at him, shocked and intrigued by this story.

"Really?" I asked.

"Really," he answered.

"That's kind of..." I hesitated. "Scary."

"You're tellin' me," he stated with feeling and I thought about Ada and Vic and how Ada showed Vic everything he wanted to see then the minute she got his ring on her finger, Ada showed him Ada and set about making him the Vic she wanted *him* to be.

"Why do women do that?" I asked.

"Seein' as I have a dick, I was hopin' you'd answer that question," he replied.

"I've no idea," I told him.

His mirth came back through his smile and his body shaking on mine.

Then he asked, "Are you gettin' it yet?"

"Getting what?" I asked back.

His roaming hands stopped and one came to frame the side of my face as he dipped his close.

Then, he whispered, "With Tessa O'Hara, what you see is what you get. No bullshit. No games. No masks.

No lies. No nothin'. Just her, all of her. I'm forty-five years old and, baby, I gotta tell you, I'm so sick of that shit you wouldn't believe it. Meeting a woman who doesn't have a clue how to even initiate a play was fucking refreshing."

Oh my.

At that point, for some totally unhinged reason, my mouth blurted, "Ellie has ordered a pink flower girl dress."

Brock stared at me. Then he burst out laughing and shoved his face in my neck to do it. While still doing it, he rolled to his back so I was on top and I lifted my head to watch as the laughter died to chuckles and his hands came up to gather my hair at the back of my head.

When he controlled his hilarity, his warm, quicksilver eyes locked on mine and he said quietly, "There it is. My sweet Tess doesn't have a clue how to initiate a play. No bullshit. No games. No masks. No lies."

"Brock," I whispered.

"Thanks for dealin' with the kids so I could deal with Mom and Dad."

"You're welcome," I murmured and he pulled my face to his for a lip touch then moved it back an inch, where-upon I informed him, "Just a heads up. Grady hears stuff. So much of it, he might go out of his way to listen and he doesn't forget much."

Brock pulled in a breath before he shared openly, "We got dissension. Laura and my older sister Jill want my Dad back in the fold. My younger brother Levi, Laura's hus-band Austin, Jill's partner Fritz and obviously my mom disagree. Austin because he's overprotective of Laura. He met her two years after she was raped. She was still raw but he liked what he saw, put on the kid gloves, and hasn't taken them off. He's a good man, a family man, and he loves her. He doesn't like the history and he didn't like it when my dad came around and asked for money. Fritz because Fritz likes his money and that's because he works his ass off for it and anyone comin' around and askin' him to give it away isn't real popular. Levi because my brother hasn't worked shit through. He's got a short fuse, carries a mean grudge, and takes loyalty to extremes. Shit's comin' to a head. There's a lot of talk. Grady's a smart kid, he feels deep, he loves his mom, and he's gonna hear and be confused." He paused then said, "I'll have a word with Laura."

"Why is this happening?" I asked. "I mean, you're all adults. Can't those who want your dad in their fold do it and those who don't—?"

Brock cut me off with, "Dad's got cancer, Tess."

My body stilled on top of his and I whispered, "Ohmigod."

"Yeah," he whispered back. "This is the second time. It's come back. First time, he beat it easy. This time, they say it's more aggressive. He wants to make amends, wants his family back, wants peace in case he passes. There are those in our ranks who question his motives and timing. There are those who see our dad is gettin' old, he's sick, he's not only fucked us over but also a lot of other people so he's lonely and he's a social guy. But even if he wasn't, lonely isn't good when you're sick. So we got dissension. It's bringin' up shit that's been buried awhile and emotions are high."

I slid my hand up to curl my fingers around his neck as I whispered, "I'm so sorry, honey."

"I am too. This shit sucks."

"Yeah, it does," I agreed, still whispering and I saw his eyes intense on me.

Then he asked quietly, "How'd your dad pass?"

"Hepatitis C," I answered. "No one knows how he got it but he was an EMT when he was younger so maybe something happened on a call. He had it for ages before they caught it. He was close to dying when he got a donor liver but it attacked the new one and still, he lived twelve years after that before it beat him."

"And your mom hated him because...?"

"Mom hated him because he fell in love with his partner in his ambulance and they got married two weeks after the divorce was final. She was humiliated and I get that. But he also genuinely loved Donna. I mean truly. He adored her and it just sucked that he found her after he found Mom. Mom isn't a bitch or a crazy person. She just wasn't his other half and Donna was. He felt guilty all his life and made that clear but she never let it go. She isn't like that with anyone else, but unfortunately for her Dad was *her* other half and she genuinely loved him so her heart just broke and never mended."

"Makes you wonder why we do this shit," he muttered and I had to admit, there were a lot of times I agreed.

Though, the four months with him and the last three days, I didn't.

"Why does your brother want to break your ex-wife's neck?" I asked and he shook his head but smiled.

"Because he loves me and she made me miserable for ten years. The four of us kids were close growin' up and sometimes, honest to God, Tess, sometimes I could swear the only things Levi wants in life are to see Jill, Laura, and me happy. He's not married, never has been, has dedicated his life to his career, his summer softball league, his season tickets to the Broncos, gettin' laid as often as he can, and his family. He's the one we all call to babysit. He's the emergency contact at all the kids' schools. He never fails to prop his latest piece in a chair at the dining room table at Mom's house for Thanksgiving dinner. And he runs his ass ragged to get to every house on Christmas."

"I don't know if that sounds nice or a little crazy," I shared cautiously.

"You and me both, babe. I get his struggle. There were times I wondered if I'd grow up to be Dad. Let a good woman down and fuck over my family. Because none of us know why the fuck he did all the shit he did. As a man, you watch the man whose seed made you and you think that shit's in you. Then again, you also gotta live your life and if that beast lives within, you gotta have the balls at least to try and tame it."

He pulled my face slightly closer to his and his silvery eyes grew intense as he continued.

"But the beast doesn't live within. This is not to say that I didn't think of steppin' out on Olivia, who was a pain in my ass, but I didn't have it in me. And when it got so miserable I couldn't take it anymore and I had the choice of eatin' shit my whole life and teachin' my sons eatin' shit was the right thing to do, which it isn't, or getting out from under that mess and showing them it was important to be a man and find my own happiness, I made that choice for me and for them. Levi doesn't get that life will always be fucked one way or another and you can't run away from it. He's living a life that's been over for years. We aren't livin' with Mom and doin' our homework at the kitchen table. That family's changed and that life is gone and he needs to make his own life and his own family."

"Have you told him this?"

"Getting my brother to listen is like convincing him to let it go about Olivia or Dad. It is just not gonna happen."

"My sister lives in Australia and my mother lives in Florida," I told him.

He grinned and let my hair go as his arms wrapped around me.

"Finally, two things that show my Tess can be lucky."

My body relaxed into his and I shared, "I miss them every day."

His eyes moved over my face as he murmured, "Yeah."

"Thanksgivings suck. I either go to Florida, where it's just Mom and me and that's okay but that isn't like having a full table with kids being loud and wondering what girl your philandering brother is going to bring to dinner. Or she's in Australia and I have to find a friend close to mooch dinner from. Those are worse."

The skin around his eyes went soft and he muttered, "My poor Tess."

I moved my face a half an inch closer and my fingers tensed into his neck for a second before I said quietly, "I guess what I'm saying is, all this *seems* like it sucks but it doesn't. It's all based in love and history and loyalty so really it's kind of beautiful because the alternative would be not having any of that and then where would you be?"

Brock didn't answer. No. Instead, his eyes looked into mine for long moments before his hand slid up in my hair, his body rolled me so I was again on my back, he was again on me, and his mouth had captured mine, and he was delivering a hard, deep, wet kiss that took my breath away.

When he lifted his head, I fought for my breath as well as control of several areas of my body and he asked, "You hungry, babe?"

"Yes," I breathed because that was the truth. I was. But I was happy to eat later, as in, lunch the next day.

Brock grinned and the sight of it with his handsome face close, his hard body pressed the length of mine, and my lips (and other places besides) still tingling from his kiss, I again lost control of those several areas of my body.

Therefore, to move my mind from him and what he was doing to those places, I blurted, "I think I've got Popsicle juice on my back."

"I'll pay for the dry cleaning."

"That's okay. I kick ass with hand wash."

He grinned again.

Then he asked, "Snickerdoodles?"

From the look in his eyes I knew that he knew I'd marked they were his favorites.

Therefore, I shrugged and said, "The first time I made them, you ate, like, seven and you gravitate to cinnamon. It doesn't take a mind reader to figure out you like them."

He shook his head, still grinning but now muttering, "No games, no lies, no bullshit."

What could I say? This was true.

So I didn't say anything.

He did and this was a murmured, "Let's get you fed."

He knifed off me, grabbed my hand, pulled me off the couch and into the kitchen.

Then he fed me.

Then he ate three snickerdoodles.

Then he took me to bed.

*   *   *

Oh God. Oh my *God*.

"Fuck, Tess," Brock growled, and not able to hold myself up anymore, I fell forward into a hand in the bed beside him as I kept riding him hard, grinding down to take him deep, his fingers on one hand clamped encouragingly around my hip as his thumb on the other continued to press and roll against my clit.

My dazed eyes focused on him as the sensations between my legs trembled down the tops of my thighs, warmed my belly, glided up to swell my breasts, making the silk covering them beautiful torture at my nipples and up farther so even my scalp tingled.

I ground down on his cock, rolling my hips as my free hand went to his face.

Sliding my hand down his throat then farther to explore the sleek, solid wall of his chest, I held his heated, mercury eyes and whispered, "God, honey, you're so fucking beautiful."

At my words, he bucked his hips so forcefully, I nearly went flying. His torso knifed up, his arm clamped around me, and he whipped me to my back. His hips driving into mine, his thumb still at my clit, he captured my mouth in a searing hot kiss and didn't let go even as I whimpered the warning of my fast-approaching orgasm into his mouth.

And he still didn't let go as one of my arms convulsed around his back, the other hand drove into his hair and fisted, my feet planted themselves in his bed, my hips surged up, and I exploded with a sharp cry against his tongue.

Still coming, Brock's thumb disappeared and both his hands yanked my legs up and around his hips. He gave me his weight, then both hands went to my ass and he jerked my hips up, deepening his pounding thrusts. His mouth finally released mine in order for his to grunt. Each noise he made throbbed into the walls of my sex and the subsiding wave built and, to my shock, started crashing in again.

"Brock." His name came from somewhere deep, breathy with surprise and low with pleasure as the second orgasm rolled over me.

My nails dragged his back and my neck started to arch but one of his hands left my hip and slid into my hair, fingers fisting and holding my head steady so he could watch.

The wave receded again just as his thrusts lost their rhythm but increased their violence then, still driving deep, I watched his head tilt back and listened to his release.

When it stopped being vocal and his thrusts regained a rhythm, this one slower and starting to gentle, I lifted my head and pressed my lips against his throat.

He let me do this but when my head dropped back to the bed, his face moved to my neck and, still gliding slowly in and out, his hands started to roam over the silk at my sides.

I held him tight in three limbs, my hand in his thick hair sliding through repeatedly as both our heart rates slowed, our breath evened, and finally he stopped stroking and stayed planted inside me.

Against my skin, with a gentle tug on the material at

one side, he asked, "To sleep, you gotta change outta this into a normal nightie?"

I laughed softly and stopped stroking his hair to wind my arm around his shoulders.

After dinner and snickerdoodles, he took me to his bedroom where we fooled around on his bed until we were fooling around partially unclothed then we were seriously fooling around because we were totally naked. He took his time, I took mine and only at the end when it was skin against skin and breathing was so labored there were no whispered words that it got wild and energetic.

This, of course, totally blew out of the water the plan I came up with while kickboxing. Undeterred, after we were done, when I hit his bathroom to take out my contacts and prepare for bed, I slid on the short, deep-lavender nightie with slits up the sides, thick edges of delicate black lace, and a pair of black lace panties, all of which cost a fortune because it was pure silk and the lace was extraordinary.

In glasses and wearing what I thought was an in-joke, I walked into Brock's bedroom only to find Brock didn't think my nightie was funny. I knew this when his eyes hit me, his whole face got dark, the air in the room became so sweltering it felt like it was pressing against my skin, and the minute I got close to the bed, he moved. Lunging toward me, his arm hooked me at the waist and he yanked me into the bed, pulled off my glasses, tossed them unheeded on the nightstand, and we started up again. This time, from start to finish, it was wild and energetic. No pleasant exploration, no lazy caresses. It was hot, heavy, and completely abandoned.

I answered his question with, "Actually, it's kinda comfy."

His head came up and he looked down at me. "Good, 'cause I like it."

I grinned at him and whispered, "I kinda got that."

He grinned back and his head descended so his mouth could touch mine then it slid down my cheek to work at my neck, slow, lazy, and sweet.

His hips moved slightly as he pulled out gently and I drew in a soft breath at the feel of it and the fact I didn't like the loss of him. My arms gave him a squeeze as my head turned.

In his ear, I whispered, "I have to go get cleaned up."

His head came up, his sated eyes caught mine, and he whispered back, "All right, baby."

His face dipped to my throat, his lips touched me there, and he rolled off.

I rolled the other way, got off the bed, snatched up my panties, and headed to his bathroom.

The good news was, his bathroom was clean, though he could use new towels since he clearly bought his in the same year he bought his pickup and his furniture. Not to mention, the bathroom had been installed before *The Brady Bunch* was in reruns.

Still, it wasn't icky, which was what I decided to focus on.

I did my thing, slid on my panties, and bent over the basin to look at myself in the mirror.

Hair wild, face flushed, lips swollen, nipples still hard against the silk, I stared and for the first time in my entire life, taking in my reflection, I thought I might be a little bit of all right.

Then I grinned, turned out the light, and walked back into the bedroom.

Brock was leaning across the bed and turning off the light at my side. As I joined him, he was faced the other way and turning off the light at his.

When he was done, he reached out to me, gathered me in his arms, pulled my front close to his, tangled his long legs with mine, and his arm slanted up my back so his hand was in my hair, pulled me deeper as he pushed my face against his chest.

I turned it so I was resting my cheek there and slid an arm around his waist.

"Thanks for dinner," I whispered against his chest.

"Best part about it was dessert," he whispered back and I smiled.

Then I sighed.

Then I told him, "I like your family."

His fingers tensed against my scalp before he murmured, "Good."

It was then, keeping it real, which was the only way I knew how to do it, I shared, "Just FYI, and I'll preface this by saying this is not an act of a psycho woman invading your life but a rescue effort, I'm buying you new towels and, uh...new dishtowels as a priority-one mission."

His voice held a smile when he asked, "A rescue effort?"

"Someone needs to put yours out of their misery."

There was a short, deep chuckle I not only heard but also felt before. "Sweetness, I got an ex who cleaned me out seven years ago, a job that means I'm rarely home and this includes me bein' under deep cover on an assignment that lasted a year and a half, a year of that where I had zero contact with family, even my kids, and I got two boys who are at an age they don't give a shit about anything but the fact the TV works and food is in the fridge. Considering they're boys, they'll probably never be at an age where they give a shit about anything but TV and food. Towels are not a priority and dishtowels are *definitely* not a priority."

My head tipped back to look at his shadowed jaw in the dark room. "You didn't see your kids or family for a year?"

His head tipped down and I felt his eyes on my face. "I didn't see it taking that long but it did, so another, bigger reason for my Statue of Liberty play with Darla."

"Oh," I whispered, thinking that now definitely made sense and it made sense before. It was just that now it made *more* sense. Then I asked, "Does that happen often?"

"I'd had to take undercover work before, not often but it happened, and it was another reason Olivia made my life a misery."

This, I had to admit, made sense too.

"She didn't like your job?"

"Olivia likes attention and if she doesn't get it, she wants other shit to make up for it and that other shit costs money, lots of it, far more than I made. She also isn't real big on bein' a mom so bearin' the brunt of raising two sons was not her favorite pastime and she regards it as a pastime, no joke. So she wasn't doin' cartwheels that she didn't have a man dancing attendance on her and she didn't have what she felt was restitution for being denied that."

Oh man. This didn't sound good. *Any* of it, but especially the part about Olivia not big on being a mom.

"But what you do is important," I stated.

"Yeah," he agreed.

"And dangerous," I added and his arm gave me a squeeze.

"Yeah," he repeated.

I tipped my head down and pressed my cheek against his chest processing the fact that he had a job that meant he might disappear. I was also wondering if I'd be like Olivia, not too happy about that, acting out when it happened, and thinking, uncomfortably, since I knew from experience I'd miss him if he was gone, I might.

"Lease is up on this place next month and I'm already lookin'," he announced into my thoughts and my head tipped back again.

"Sorry?"

"Things are hot for me here. Last job before the Heller gig exposed me to some folks I don't wanna know where I work but now they know where I work. This cripples what I do for the DEA, which means deskwork, which means, since I'm a field man and deskwork would be like certain death, I put in for a job with the DPD. I interviewed, got it, and resigned from the DEA three weeks ago. I start at the DPD in the homicide unit in a week. This means more stability, total exposure, and if some slimeball follows me home and home happens to be a decent place, they won't ask questions. So, I'm lookin' for a new place."

I was blinking and processing this new information but having difficulty with it.

Therefore, the only word I could force out was, "Really?"

His voice again held a smile when he replied, "Really. Which means, after years of livin' with one foot in the underbelly of Denver, I step outta that into a stable day-to-day with that underbelly leaking in in a controlled way, not being what I breathe 24/7. My woman hightailing her ass to Kentucky would not be good."

"I'm currently reconsidering my plans to hightail my ass to Kentucky," I informed him and received an arm squeeze and a chuckle then he capped it with his lips touching my forehead before he settled back into the pillows.

Then he said, "Tomorrow, before putting my towels outta their misery, job one for you is callin' your real estate agent and gettin' that fuckin' sign outta your front yard."

"Okay," I agreed instantly, got another arm squeeze and chuckle but, alas, no kiss on the forehead.

I pressed my cheek to his chest again thinking stupidly but hopefully and oh so pleasantly that Ellie would look cute in a pink flower girl dress.

"Sweetness?" he called into my replete gathering drowsiness.

"Mm?"

His hand slid from my head down my neck and farther, down the silk at my spine. "You got any more nighties like this?"

"Uh, no, and I have to sell a hundred and fifty cupcakes to afford another one."

"Jesus," he muttered.

"It was worth it," I muttered back.

"Damn straight," he agreed, still muttering.

I let out a soft giggle.

His hand kept sliding down, rounded my waist, and settled curled around my hip against the bed so he was holding me tucked super close to his warm, hard body.

Then he murmured, "Sleep, baby."

"All right, honey. 'Night."

"'Night, Tess."

I drew in a breath and let it go. Then I pressed my cheek deep and held tight to Brock.

My body relaxed and I fell asleep.

CHAPTER TEN

You Baked a Cake?

One month later...

"UH...AREN'T WE just gonna eat that?" Joel asked and I looked from piping a border of cream cheese frosting on the cinnamon carrot cake I was decorating to him and his brother sitting at their dad's bar.

Update: The last month had been busy.

First, Brock had made two moves.

The first was from his job at the DEA to his job at the DPD.

The second was from his shabby, somewhat scary, definitely taking your life in your hands to ascend the outside staircase apartment to a very *not* shabby, not at all scary, having no outside staircase rented condo. It was in a small, well-landscaped, quiet, L-shaped layout of condos. The only drawback was he had two parking spaces and the entire complex of twelve units had only three visitor spots, which were around the bend of the L from Brock's place. So, if his family were around, which was somewhat often, considering he was available, they were close-knit, and still in the throes of emotional turmoil, parking could become a problem.

The rest of it was awesome. A fenced-in front patio that was a sun trap and thus, if the sun was shining (as it had a tendency to do a lot in Denver) the minute you opened the wooden gate, you entered warmth even though it was November. Inside the front door was a big living room with fireplace and two-story slanted ceiling. Up a short-ish flight of stairs to the right was a humungous master bedroom with bath. In that was a new king-sized bed with new sheets and comforter.

The bed Brock bought. The sheets and comforter I picked out, *not* with Brock, who flatly refused to go shopping for sheets and bought the first bed he laid eyes on which, luckily, was a nice one. But instead I went with Elvira, Gwen, and Martha, the former two throwing themselves into this errand with scary abandon and the latter doing it under obvious protest, for she still was waiting for Brock to expose the dickhead within.

In his condo, next to the up flight was a down flight that led to a door that took you down to a full basement with laundry. The lower level above the basement had two smaller rooms separated by a full bath. Beyond the up and down staircase was another short staircase, this only five steps that led to an elevated kitchen that had a railing facing the living room, a small dining area, and a bar that separated a somewhat compact but modern and relatively luxurious (for a rental) kitchen.

As threatened, I had bought Brock new towels and dishtowels and when he moved I added more sets for the boys' bathroom.

As I would learn, considering they were more meddling,

nosy, and intrusive than even Elvira, without his knowledge and using the key he'd given his mother, Fern, Laura and Brock's other sister Jill commandeered his ratty-assed furniture and delivered it to places unknown that were so covert even a DEA agent couldn't track them down (and he tried). They then filled the space with a large fantastic, masculine, comfortable sectional, new square coffee table, a handsome upright chest that held his flat-screen TV, stereo, DVD player, PS3 (for the boys) and DVDs, shelves that held CDs and books, and a new dining room set.

Oh, and three new standing lamps and coasters for the living room as well as placemats and an unusual but appealing wrought-iron fat candleholder (with candles scented in "ocean") to sit on his dining room table.

Unfortunately, they were not finished illicitly rearranging Brock's new décor and even more unfortunately I was with him when he walked into his new space.

He took one look at it and the air in the room went abrasive as he lost his ever-lovin' mind.

Also unfortunately, all members of the Lucas family shared the trait of their mood invading the room. These three women had attitude, knew Brock since his life began (except Laura, who was five years younger than him), were not afraid of him, and gave back as good as they got.

Thus began a shouting match that was loud, long, surprising, intriguing, but also a little scary.

I could see that Brock was a man, *all man*, and his space was his space, his shit was his shit, and he did not appreciate the intrusion *and* that intrusion signifying a trio of women taking care of a forty-five-year-old man.

And that was all I could see because even though I kept my mouth shut and hung in the kitchen while they shouted it out (though his new furniture *was* awesome), I agreed with Brock that they were out of line.

This went on for a while and when I say that I mean a *long* while.

I had the sense they did this not because of new furniture and unwelcome intrusions but more deep-seated issues all of them were dancing around.

It got to the point where I feared things that could not be unsaid would be said. Therefore, I was going to have to step outside my status of new girlfriend, and thus person who really shouldn't get involved, and wade in when Fern pulled out the big (and arguably emotionally manipulative) guns, as it was my experience that mothers on the whole were wont to do.

"If we all haven't learned something with what's happening with Cob, Slim, then we're in trouble!" she shouted.

I watched with some despair as Brock's torso jerked like he'd been struck and the stony look he had frozen on his face as Fern went on.

"Life is too darned short. Too *darned* short. I'm a year younger than your father and it is not lost on me that I'm next. So, I've decided that my kids are gonna enjoy me and what I can give them while I can watch. Jill and Laura kicked in a little but most of this is from me. This means you won't get a big inheritance but you weren't going to get that anyway. It also means I can see my grandsons lazing around on nice furniture in a decent place and I know you don't think that's important, but I do. That's what I want and that's what I'm going to have."

She stopped speaking and when no one broke the silence she continued but did it quieter. However, the words she delivered next packed an even bigger punch.

"My girl endured a nightmare," she said.

My body got tense, Brock's eyes sliced to his sister, to me then back to his mother when she kept speaking.

"I know you pulled in every favor owed to you and I know you ended up owing more to make sure that man paid for what he did to my girl. I saw what that did to her and I saw it eat at you, you and my other babies. But you were the only one in the position to do something about it and you didn't rest until that was done for her. I watched my son exhaust himself to make it so his sister could have some peace after that nightmare. And if Laura and I want to say thank you for it then, Slim, you're damn well going to let us say thank you and keep your mouth shut about it."

These words, regrettably, had as profound an effect on me, learning this about Brock, as they had on the familial combatants in the living room.

I tried to pull myself together, promptly failed, began to lose it, and found my feet rushing out of the kitchen, down the short flight of stairs with my mouth mumbling a trembling, "Excuse me," as I raced to the other flight, up, into, and through Brock's bedroom to his bathroom where I closed the door.

I pressed my back against the wall, slid down, shoved my face in my knees, and burst into tears.

I would learn later that Brock had not shared my ordeal with his family. And considering my dramatic reaction, even though Brock was in that bathroom with me about a nanosecond after my ass hit the floor, his mom and sisters were so worried, they didn't leave until after Brock calmed me down and left me curled on his bed while he went down to explain and get them gone.

Luckily, thus ended the fight, though Brock didn't give up. He just quit shouting about it. However, when he couldn't find his furniture, he gave up and gave in.

Weirdly (or maybe not), this elevated my new girl-friend status, seeing as they'd found out I hadn't been with Brock for a few weeks like they thought but instead quite a bit longer. They sensed there was seriousness to our relationship. I shared a tragic circumstance the like of which had been visited on their family, which clearly moved them. And, although I couldn't explain how they did it or all the reasons why, I knew I'd been welcomed wholeheartedly into the family fold.

Brock, seeing as he missed little (or possibly nothing), couldn't have missed this and he had no reaction to it what-soever except for settling naturally and casually into it.

It was safe to say I really liked Brock but I'd also spent a number of years huddling in my own space as a defense mechanism and a big, loud, interfering family kind of freaked me out.

I kept this to myself, thinking that if Brock and I sur-vived for the long haul, I'd get used to it mainly because I wouldn't have a choice.

The other big thing that happened was I met Rex and Joel. In fact, the Friday after Brock and I got back together heralded his next weekend with them. He picked them up from school and three hours later I met them at Beau Jo's for pizza.

Brock was not wrong. His genes were dominant. I didn't know what Olivia looked like but both her boys looked like miniature Brocks. Joel had Fern's blue eyes;

Rex had someone else's nose but other than that, features, body shape, everything was so like Brock it was uncanny. It was different, unique to them but still somehow the same.

And he was also not wrong about something else. They were good kids. Polite. Soft spoken. Attentive. Well-behaved.

Maybe *too* much for kids their age, considering they weren't much older than Grady and they had none of the exuberant little kid-ness of their cousins.

I saw Brock every night (and therefore every morning) but when Brock had his boys, these were the only times he and I spent blocks of time being apart. He explained this to me as being an attempt to introduce me slowly into their lives rather than shove me in their faces and force them to spend time with someone they didn't know too well. So, after our first Friday night dinner together, I didn't see Brock until Sunday night. And the next time Brock had them I saw them again on Friday night and then didn't see Brock until Sunday.

But it was the next time I would get it about his boys' good behavior. Because we didn't meet for Beau Jo's for pizza. I brought cupcakes and Brock cooked spaghetti at his old pad, where we were going to eat dinner and watch a movie. But I was at his place when they got there in late afternoon and didn't leave until they were in their twin beds in Brock's second bedroom.

Spending more time with them, I noted on arrival they seemed wound up and when I say this I mean *tight*. Jumpy. Hyperattentive. Anxious. And Rex once actually looked fearful and this was when he spilled his glass of pop on the coffee table. His wide, terrified eyes shot to his father. His face paled right under my gaze and his body grew visibly solid.

I also saw this make Brock's mouth get tight. Not because of the spill but because of his son's reaction to doing it. He quickly hid his reaction and cautiously and gently dealt with the spill while assuring his son (who, with effort, allowed himself to be assured but clearly didn't commit to it) that it was in no way a big deal.

It didn't take a child psychologist to see, if Rex spilled pop at his mom's, the reaction he got from his dad was not even close to what he'd get at his mother's.

I had never been with a man with children and I decided to bide my time and let Brock discuss it with me when and if he wanted. This was not a game. This was me giving my man space. We were still getting to know each other and he didn't need me nosing into his business with his boys and his ex.

So I didn't.

But this weekend Brock decided would be different. He talked to me about it, asked me if I was comfortable with it. I wasn't (exactly) and told him so. But also told him I'd give it a shot.

So Friday night was his with his boys. So was Saturday. But Saturday night, I came over and made (at Brock's request, since he wolfed down three-quarters of it when I made it for him) my Mexican tortilla casserole (though, obviously, since Brock liked it so much, I doubled it). This was followed by hot fudge sundaes with my homemade hot fudge sauce.

After, I spent the night.

It was a compliment when the boys dug into my food with the same relish as their father.

And it was a relief when they took my spending the night in stride.

Now it was Sunday. The kids were being picked up by their mother at five and Brock told me that Olivia had long since informed him she wanted the kids returned to her fed and watered so we were going to have a big late lunch after which I was serving homemade carrot cake.

A cake I was decorating at that present moment even though it was just for us.

This was something I had to do. It was a compulsion. Every cake deserved to be pretty, even if the decoration was simple.

And considering the thousands of baked goods I'd decorated, it took me the same amount of time to decorate a cake as it did for most people simply to frost them, so it really didn't matter.

So I smiled into Joel's blue eyes and answered his question with, "Yeah."

He looked at his brother. Rex looked at him then they looked back at me.

Then Rex asked, "Do you do cakes like *The Cake Boss*?"

I shook my head and went back to piping while explaining, "My shop is small. I only have two girls who help me with the baking and decorating. I'm not set up for that kind of operation and my cake mission doesn't include extravagance, just the drive to make every cake I bake pretty."

"Cakes don't need to be pretty. They just need to taste good," Joel informed me as his dad moved up the steps.

My eyes went from Brock to his son, whereupon I shared, "In order to decorate a cake, you have to make more frosting, which means the cake has more frosting, which means the eater gets to eat more frosting. So, agreed, cakes need to taste good but decorated cakes, being decorated with loads of extra frosting, taste even better."

Brock circled Joel's chest with an arm, tugged him playful-rough back into his torso, and muttered, "Can't argue with that, Joey."

"Nope," Joel agreed, his eyes on the cake, and looking into their hungry depths I knew my work was done as clearly his horizons had been expanded.

At that point there came a knock on the door. I looked to Brock, saw his brows draw together and his head turn in that direction then he let his son go and sauntered away. I went back to piping.

"Carrot cake's my favorite," Rex shared, his voice not hiding his anticipation and the sound of it made me grin.

I knew this. It was his father's favorite too. This was why a homemade one was sitting on the counter.

"Good," I muttered.

"What the fuck?" I heard Brock growl.

My head went up and both boys' necks twisted to look toward the door.

"Nice," I heard a woman say, then go on, "I've got to get the boys early. Can you get their stuff together? I'll be waiting in the car."

"Come again?" Brock asked.

"I have to get the boys early," she repeated. "I'll be waiting in the car. Tell them to hurry."

"Olivia, you don't get them until five," Brock stated.

Already tense at the knowledge my mind was refusing to believe, that Brock's ex was at the door sounding like the bitch I suspected she was from what I'd learned from Brock (and Fern and Laura *and* Jill), I went tenser when this was irrevocably confirmed. It was then I noticed both the boys were frozen to the point of looking calcified on their stools.

"I know that, Slim, but today I need to pick them up early," she retorted.

"You need to pick them up early, you tell me you need to pick them up early. We discuss it and make plans. You don't show at my fuckin' door and tell me to get them packed."

"Oh for God's sake!" she snapped. "It isn't a big deal. Why do you make everything a big deal? It's only two hours. Just get them to get their shit packed and I'll be waiting in the car."

"Woman, I get four days a month with my boys, two hours shaved off that *is* a big deal," Brock returned on a dangerous rumble.

"There you go, making it a big deal," she shot back.

"They haven't eaten," Brock told her.

"Dade will take them out to get some burgers or something later," she replied.

"No, Dade won't. We got plans. You'll come back in two hours or I'll drop them at your house at five or whatever the fuck time you'll be home to look after your sons."

"You can do whatever you have planned next time you see them. I'm here now, I went out of my way to come and get them, and I don't have time to discuss this."

"You went out of your way to come and get your boys?" Brock asked, his dangerous rumble getting more dangerous.

"Jesus, Slim, just tell them to get packed."

"All right, you are not hearing me and you need to

listen. We have plans. The cake's baked and the boys are lookin' forward to it. They're gonna eat it and they'll go back when it's time for them to go back."

"The cake's baked?"

Uh-oh.

Brock didn't answer that question. Instead, he ordered, "Go, I'll bring the boys to your place at seven."

"What cake's baked?" she asked. "You baked a cake?" This was incredulous.

Apparently, Rex nor Joel had shared about me.

I looked back at the boys at the same time their heads in unison slowly turned to me.

They looked terrified.

Oh man.

"Olivia, Christ, step back," Brock growled.

Oh man!

"What cake, Slim?" she asked, her voice rising as well as getting closer, then on a shout, *"What cake?"*

There was a moment of silence, a muttered, "Fuck," from Brock and my eyes went to the living room half a second before a woman appeared at the foot of the stairs to the kitchen.

And one look at her was like a sock to the stomach.

She was utterly, top-to-toe, the definition of beautiful.

Shining, healthy, long blonde hair. Fabulous bone structure. Perfectly symmetrical features. Intriguingly shaped bedroom eyes. Cheekbones to die for. Tall and rake thin. Slim-fitting, stylish sweater, two-hundred-dollar jeans, seven-hundred-dollar boots and fifteen-hundred-dollar handbag.

And she had extraordinarily beautiful hands tipped with perfect, crimson fingernails.

She looked like she walked out of the pages of a celebrity magazine.

And she was Brock's ex-wife.

Her striking, angry, venom-spewing eyes leveled on me and she demanded to know, "Who are you?"

I opened my mouth to answer but Brock entered my vision and he spoke before me.

"This is Tess, Olivia, and seriously, this is not fuckin' cool," he snarled.

"Tess?" she asked, eyes on me then they cut to Brock. *"Tess?"*

"Maybe you'll do me a favor and go outside for your tantrum instead of havin' it in front of my boys and my woman."

Wrong, wrong, *wrong* thing to say.

I knew this when she hissed, *"Your woman?"*

"Jesus, Olivia, can we fuckin' go outside?" Brock asked.

"No we fucking can't!" she shrieked.

And that was it for me.

"Okay, boys," I said softly, putting down my pastry bag, "do me a favor and get your coats. Let's take a walk around the block."

"Don't *you* take my sons *anywhere*," Olivia lashed out, her arm coming up so she could jab a finger at me.

"Take them, Tess," Brock growled.

"Up boys, let's go," I whispered as they seemed planted to their stools.

"Don't you dare walk out of this house with my children!" Olivia shouted.

"Go, Tess," Brock barked.

"Guys," I called, rounding the counter, "up. Let's go."

"We have problems if that woman takes my sons out of this house," Olivia threatened Brock.

"You steppin' *into* my house, we already had problems, Olivia," Brock fired back.

"What's going on?" I heard and Olivia and Brock both looked to the door as I tried to place the voice that was vaguely familiar and couldn't until Joel spoke.

"Grandpa," he whispered.

Boy, Cob Lucas had interesting timing.

"What's going on, Cob, is that I'm here to pick up my sons and Slim won't release them," Olivia informed her ex-father-in-law at the same time she crossed her arms on her chest, hitched a hip, and put out a foot.

"Well, I'll be," the invisible Cob replied. "I musta got somethin' messed up. I thought you picked the boys up at five. That's why I stopped by, to see my grandsons. Did I lose two hours somewhere?"

I watched Rex look at his brother. Joel gave him a small grin then they both finally moved to jump off their stools and race down the steps.

"Hey, Grandpa!" I heard Joel shout.

"Hey, Gramps!" Rex shouted after him.

"Joey, Rex, come give your Granddad a hug," Cob ordered.

Olivia glared at proceedings I couldn't see. Brock scowled at his boots.

"Tess baked us a cake!" I heard Rex say excitedly. "Carrot. My favorite *and* Dad's!"

"And mine, boy," Cob added. "Is it someone's birthday?"

"Naw," Joel answered. "She does it all the time. We had cupcakes last time we visited Dad. She bakes cakes for a living."

"She bakes cakes for a living," Olivia whispered disdainfully.

I felt my back go straight but watched Brock's head snap up and neck twist, whereupon he aimed a look so vicious at his ex-wife that it made me, not even the recipient of the look, quake a little.

"You should see her decorate it, Gramps," Rex said. "She goes so fast, you can't see her hands move. It's like those people on TV."

That made me feel better, and when I say that I mean that made me feel downright smug. But I aimed my smug grin at my feet.

"This I gotta see," Cob muttered.

"You gotta hurry. She's almost done," Rex told him.

"All right then, how about me and my grandsons watch Tess decorate this cake and you two go on out to the parking lot and finish your talk," Cob suggested. "Does that sound like a plan?"

I looked from my feet to the living room to see Olivia glare at Cob. She transferred her glare to Brock then moved her eyes to shoot daggers at me.

Her eyes traveled the length of me and back and she asked me, "Why am I not surprised you bake cakes?"

"Maybe 'cause she's got a real woman's body that a real man enjoys"—pause, then a pointedly emphasized kill shot of—"*a lot,* rather than a body full of points and ridges that, newsflash, Olivia, really doesn't feel all that fuckin' good?"

Brock asked this as her gaze snapped to him and it was clear by his look, the mood that hadn't shifted out of the room, and the fact he didn't shut up that he wasn't done.

"You should watch Tess decorate her cake too. Probably

would be fascinating, seeing as having talent of any kind is
foreign to you."

He'd already delivered *ouch,* but with that he twisted
the knife deep. But he still wasn't done.

"I'll make sure the kids wrap a couple of pieces up to
take home. You taste it, you might learn life can be sweet
rather than bitter. Dade tastes it, he might remember that
there are women out there who know how to take care of
a man rather than expend all their energy suckin' the mar-
row out of his bones."

"Slim," Cob said softly, moving into my vision and
giving his son a gentle look that, albeit gentle, clearly said
that Brock had made his point. He moved up the stairs.
When his eyes hit me, he said softly, "Heya, Tess. Good to
see you again."

"Hey," I said softly back.

"Have the children at my house by five," I heard Olivia
hiss at Brock.

"I'll have them back at seven so Dad can have a good
visit,"

I moved back behind the counter but glanced at the
living room as Cob and the boys gathered at the bar and I
saw her pinched face now staring daggers at Brock.

And Ellie was not wrong. She *did* have a pinchy face.
After the initial impact of her looks, her words, attitude,
anger, and inappropriateness colored those looks and she
was not nearly as beautiful as I'd thought.

"Fine," she bit out, then started stomping to the door.

I picked up the pastry bag and went back to decorating
even as I listened hard.

Therefore, I heard Brock rumble low, "You cool down,
you reflect on this, Olivia. You do this shit one more time,

and I mean any of it, from you showin' two hours early to take my boys to you throwin' a shit fit in front of them and my woman, I warn you, I'll take action."

"Go fuck yourself, Slim," was her hissed retort.

"Jesus," was Brock's muttered reply.

My eyes slid to Cob to see his mouth tight, his jaw hard, and his eyes aimed at the counter. He must have felt my look because his head came up. His gaze caught mine, he schooled his features into a smile that did not reach his concerned yet angry eyes then he released my gaze and reached out to wrap a big hand around Rex's head and pull him into his side.

"That's a big cake, boy. So big I'm thinkin' I can talk Tess into lettin' me stay so I can bum a piece," Cob said to Rex.

"I don't know. We were all gonna take quarters," Rex said back and Cob grinned at him.

Brock showed, stalked to the end of the bar, and looked between his sons.

"You guys all right?" he asked.

Joel shrugged and kept his gaze steady on the cake so I went back to decorating it even though I knew this nonanswer actually meant a big fat hairy *no* to his father's question.

"Yeah, Dad," Rex mumbled.

"Right," Brock whispered disbelievingly but let it go. Then, "Tess?"

"I'm good, honey," I told the cake, then asked it, "You want me to get you a beer?"

"I'll get it." Pause, then, "Dad?"

"Sounds good, Slim."

"Boys?" Brock called.

"We can have a beer?" Joel asked.

My eyes went to him to see him looking beyond me to where Brock was at the fridge and I saw him grin at whatever look Brock was giving him.

Then he said, "Okay, I'll take a pop."

"Me too," Rex chimed in.

I went back to piping.

"Wow, Tess, the boys didn't lie. You can barely see your hands move," Cob noted.

"Practice," I muttered.

"I can see that," Cob muttered back.

Then he said something that made warm gushiness flood my belly and my hands freeze midsquirt.

"Could be he's my son but been around men as a whole a long time. Women who can pull off lookin' beautiful bein' barefoot in a kitchen wearin' a T-shirt and glasses and no makeup with their hair pulled back in a ponytail while they decorate a cake that makes your mouth water just lookin' at it, well..." My eyes had gone to him and he smiled gently at me. "Don't know a man alive or dead who I met in my sixty-eight years who wouldn't want that woman above all others in his kitchen."

He didn't need to reassure me after my first acid encounter with Olivia.

But it was still a nice thing to do.

"Thanks, Cob," I whispered.

"Don't thank me for tellin' the truth, sweetheart," he whispered back.

Brock's front hit my back and Cob's beer hit the counter as Brock set it there while he joked, "Quit flirtin' with my woman, Dad."

This made Rex and Joel emit boy snickers and Cob to mutter, "I'll try, Slim, but it'll be hard."

"Jesus," Brock muttered back and I felt him take a swig of his beer.

I went back to piping but I did it smiling.

*   *   *

"Here you go, Cob," I said, handing Brock's father a fresh beer.

Dinner (and cake) consumed, visit with Gramps (and Dad) over, Brock was off taking the boys back to Olivia and her husband Dade's house and I was hanging out with his dad at his place.

Why Cob was still there, I wasn't sure. I was still there because I was spending the night.

I curled in the seat across the sectional from him with my peppermint tea and tried not to be obvious as I studied him while he studied the fire Brock had built.

When silence stretched as we sipped at our beverages and Cob's look went from reflective to dark, I whispered, "Hey," and his eyes came to me. "You okay?" I asked quietly.

Cob didn't delay in letting me know what was on his mind.

"When he was datin' her, I felt joy," Cob stated and I stared at him. "We weren't close, still aren't close, but I was around. Looks like that and sugar sweet," he muttered, then went on to say, "Turns out saccharine."

Oh man.

He was talking about Olivia.

His eyes got intense and he said carefully, "Not my place, lost that place and I 'spect you know it but I'm gonna say it anyway and I hope you know I got my son's best interests at heart. But, like Olivia, you are far from hard on the eyes and, like Olivia, you're sugar sweet. I need you now, Tess, to promise me what's under all that frosting"—he jerked his chin at me—"tastes just as sweet."

I felt my heart melt at a question from a man who was facing sickness, pain, and possible death and wanted to face it knowing his son had good things in his life and I whispered, "What you see is what you get with me, Cob. I promise."

He studied me, nodded, and looked back at the fire.

Then he said to the fire, "Jill told me you're a survivor."

This unexpected blow caused me to pull in a breath, close my eyes, and look away. I opened them when he spoke again to see he was looking at me.

"My girls and me, always close. Always been better with females than males, 'cept Fern, but that's because I been a jackass for forty-odd years. I don't know where Slim stands but far's Jill's concerned, it's all in the family and what I want you to know is, where I stand, that's the God's honest truth."

"Okay," I whispered.

"A man hurt you?" he asked.

"Yes," I answered.

He stared at me. He did it long and he did it hard. Then I watched with some shock and a lot of other, stronger feelings as his eyes went bright.

Then he asked in a thick voice, "What possessed him?"

"I don't know," I answered in a thick voice.

"He pay?"

I shook my head.

To this he murmured, "Sweetheart."

"There are lots of different ways to survive, Cob," I defended.

"Well, honey, you stick with however you're doin' it. No judgment here. You get me?"

I nodded.

He pulled in a soft breath.

Then he shared, "Wish my boy Levi'd find a woman like you. Makes him look like Slim looks when he looks at you. Makes him feel however Slim feels that makes him get close to you anytime you're even a little near. Like any moment a lion's gonna come roarin' into the room and he's gotta be close enough to come between you and it so he can keep you safe. Can die knowin' my Laurie and Jill got men like that at home. Can die knowin' Slim feels like that about a woman. Wish I was dyin' knowin' that was warmin' Levi's bed at night."

His words warmed my heart, settled in my soul, and made that tight, coiled snake of poison in my belly shrink near to oblivion.

"Maybe you're not dying," I suggested.

"A man knows, Tess," he replied with resignation.

"Does it hurt to fight?" I asked and he smiled small.

"Oh sweetheart, don't you worry. I'll go down swingin'."

"Good." I smiled small back.

"Just hope I got it in me to fight back at the same time make peace with my family."

"I'm getting to know your family, Cob, and I don't want to get your hopes up but I see good things."

His eyes grew intense on me and he asked, "Slim?"

I tipped my head to the side, surprised he asked.

"You just ate dinner with him and his sons," I reminded him.

"There's him lettin' me in the door and lettin' his boys know their granddad while they got the chance. And there's him just lettin' me in. I didn't do right by Fern, and in doin' that, I didn't do right by all my kids. But Slim bore the brunt of it."

"I know," I whispered and pain shadowed his face.

"Right," he muttered, looking back at the fire.

"Cob," I called and he looked back at me. Then I told him, "Life is funny. And the funny part is, sometimes out of bad comes good. I don't like to see you conflicted and, no offense, but it's upsetting to know things were rough for Brock and Fern and your family growing up because of the choices you made. But because of those choices, Brock is the man he is today. If he wasn't, I honestly don't know where I'd be."

I leaned toward him and kept sharing but I did it quietly.

"That's because there's a lion in the room, Cob, and Brock's standing between that lion and me. If he wasn't, I don't know how long I'd survive. You created that, not in a good way, in a bad one but that doesn't mean it isn't done. No one can erase mistakes. But in the end, your actions brought them together. They're close. They love each other deeply. They're fiercely loyal. They look out for one another and the ones who mean something to them. You had a hand in that and that doesn't excuse what you did. But I hope that it brings you some peace to know the family you created, well, they're survivors too even if the thing they had to survive was you."

"That's the loopiest thing I ever heard, sweetheart," he replied. I shrugged and he went on, "But, I'll be damned if it isn't true."

That's when I laughed.

And after I was done, I told him, "Just FYI, where I

stand is, you're welcome at my bakery and my home any-time. And if you need anything, now or if it gets rough, I want you to know, honestly and I mean it, you can call on me."

He stared at me, and while he did his eyes got bright again.

Then he whispered, "Frosting all the way through."

I smiled and whispered back, "Nope, you eventually get moist, rich cake. Even so, that layer of frosting is more like a mountainous swirl."

"A mountainous swirl?"

"Yeah, lavender. Or sometimes pink. Occasionally baby blue or mint green or anything else I can dream up. But always with candy confetti and edible fairy dust."

His face cracked right before he burst out laughing.

When he did, Brock came through the front door.

We both looked to him as he examined the occupants of the sectional, shrugged off his leather jacket, and threw it on the back of the couch.

"Something funny?" he asked, moving around the couch making a beeline to me.

And as he moved toward me, I thought of Cob's words.

Makes him feel however Slim feels that makes him get close to you anytime you're even a little near. Like any moment a lion's gonna come roarin' into the room and he's gotta be close enough to come between you and it so he can keep you safe.

This life-altering thought was interrupted by Cob speaking.

"Tess here's a mountainous swirl of frosting with candy sprinkles and fairy dust," Cob told his son as Brock folded his long body next to mine on the couch, curled an arm around my shoulders, tucked me close, and rested his boots on the coffee table.

"Come again?" he asked and I giggled.

"Nuthin', Slim, you had to be there," Cob muttered and I tipped my head back to look at Brock.

"You want a beer?"

"You, or me, gettin' me a beer requires you, or me, gettin' up and walkin' across the room. It's fuckin' cold outside, my truck's heat went out on the way home, and you're warm so the answer to that question is . . . no."

"All right," I mumbled at the same time I leaned forward, put my tea mug on a coaster by his boot, and then went back and curled closer. Sliding my arm around his middle, I found that he was cold so I gave him a squeeze.

I looked to Cob to see he'd watched me do this. His face was thoughtful and then it turned guarded.

"Slim," Cob started hesitantly, "I know you won't thank me to point out the obvious but you got a little lady who bakes heavenly cakes and fries a mean beef cutlet. I'm not sure payback for that is makin' her freeze her ass off anytime she's in your truck."

I felt Brock's body get tight and it was at that moment I knew why Cob was hesitant and guarded and why he asked about where his son stood. Because his body getting tight told me Brock wanted his sons to know their granddad, he wanted peace in his family, he didn't like the idea of his father being sick or alone, but he had by no means let him in.

"Dad—" he started in a warning tone.

Cob cut him off to say softly, "Get a new truck, Slim."

Crackling electricity started invading the room and I got tense.

Cob felt it, but he thought he was dying so his next words showed he felt he had nothing to lose.

"You need to deal with that woman," he announced.

Brock's body went solid. "We are not—" he started.

"No," Cob interrupted again. "That bitch is...a... *bitch*. I heard her shoutin' all the way 'round the parkin' lot. Tellin' *my* boy to go fuck himself in front of my *grandsons*?" He shook his head, clipped out, "No." Then he sucked back beer.

"I'll deal with it," Brock growled.

"When, in a decade?" Cob shot back.

Uh-oh.

The voltage of the room ratcheted up to the red zone and Brock took his feet off the coffee table, leaning slightly forward, taking me with him, saying low, "Careful, Dad."

"Look at me, son, feel what you're feelin' right now and look at me, the man who's makin' you feel it," Cob invited, leaning toward Brock. "I spent my whole life puttin' off tomorrow what I shoulda done today and *you*"— he gestured with his bottle of beer—"felt the worst of it. Learn from me, do not make your sons feel what you're feelin' right now. I do not know what's happening in that bitch's house. What I do know is that seven years ago, I had two grandsons who felt just fine in their skin and now they look like they're about ready any second to jump out of it. It's either her or that man she married but it's somethin' and that somethin' is not you. You're done with that other job. You're available. Your life is steady. Now you got no excuses."

"I cannot believe you got the balls to sit on my couch and coach me on raisin' my boys," Brock ground out.

To that, Cob sucked back a huge swallow of beer as he stood. He bent and slammed his bottle on the table and looked down at his son.

"No, what I got is not enough time to hope you do not fuck up like your old man and instead do right by your family."

The air turned harsh, scratching at my skin, and Cob's eyes came to me.

"Nice dinner, Tess, beautiful cake. And honored you talked to me, sweetheart, swear that to my soul." At these words Brock's solid body grew rock hard and Cob looked to him. "I'm okay with you bein' pissed at me because I deserve it. But, Slim, once you stop bein' pissed you'll see I'm not wrong. You don't have to tell me. You just gotta get your shit sorted." He jerked up his chin, started to the door, and mumbled, "I'll see myself out."

Then he saw himself out.

I sat immobile and silent, still curled around an infuriated Brock, and I stayed this way because I didn't want to do anything to tip the edge on that fury.

I should have moved away.

"Honored you talked to him about what?"

I pulled away, removing my arm, tipped my head back, and looked at him. "Sorry?"

"Honored you talked to him about what?"

"We, uh . . ." I started cautiously, too cautiously.

"Spit it out, Tess. What did you and Father of the Year talk about?"

Oh man.

Seriously, the Lucas family needed to work through these issues and soon.

"He was worried that I was like Olivia and showing

you what you wanted to see but was something else under-neath," I said softly and Brock fell back against the couch.

He lifted both hands and rubbed his face but under them he bit out, "Jesus Christ."

"I wasn't offended," I told him. His hands dropped and his eyes cut to me.

"Well, babe, that's good but *I* am."

"Brock—"

"That it?"

"Uh…"

"Tess," he growled.

"He knows what happened to me," I whispered.

Brock scowled at me in a *very* scary way then he snarled, "Fucking, fucking, *fucking*." He stood, swiping his father's beer bottle off the table and sidearm throwing it across the room so it exploded against the wall, beer splattering everywhere as he finished, "*Hell!*"

At these actions, I crawled back into the corner of the sofa and curled my legs tight against my chest, wrapping my arms around them. I watched him standing there, shaking his head and tearing his fingers through his hair all the way to the back of his neck where he left them curved around still shaking his head.

Then he dropped his hand and turned to me.

"Which one?" he demanded to know.

"Which one what?" I asked quietly.

"Which sister? Jill or Laura?"

"Brock, I don't really mind," I told him cautiously.

"Bullshit," he fired back and I had to admit he was right. It was. "That man has no business knowin' that happened to you."

"Your family knows," I pointed out.

"Precisely," he clipped. "And that man isn't family."

"Brock," I whispered, "he's your Dad."

"He is?" he asked sarcastically and I decided that was a good time to quit talking.

Even furious, Brock didn't miss much. He saw me close down, decided to aim at a new target, and thus yanked his phone out of back pocket, hit some buttons, and put it to his ear.

He started pacing.

Then he said, "Yeah, Jill, it's me and, heads up, I'm fuckin' pissed."

Oh man.

He guessed.

He kept going. "Why? I'll tell you why. Because Tess didn't tell her fuckin' best friend she'd been raped, not for six fuckin' years. Martha found out a month ago. Her own goddamned mother and sister don't know but you know who does? *Dad*."

He paused, maybe to listen, but not for long before he continued.

"Do not pretend you know by association what that shit feels like. Laura knows. That's why Laura didn't fuckin' share. You had no fuckin' business spewing that shit to Dad. I left the house to take my boys home, left her with Dad, and he fuckin' *talked* to her about it. She's alone here with a man she barely fuckin' knows, and bein' Dad, he thinks it's his place to have a conversation with *my fuckin' woman* about her *bein' violated*."

Another pause that didn't last long.

Then, "Is she okay? What do you fuckin' think? She's curled in a ball in the corner of the goddamned sofa because I was so fuckin' pissed my sister is fuckin' screwy, the instant I learned, I threw a goddamned beer bottle across the room. And the reason I'm so fuckin' pissed, Jill, is because she is supposed to feel *safe with me*. And my own goddamned sister orchestrated a fuckin' scenario where, my back's turned for half a goddamned hour, she was sittin' on my own fuckin' couch and she was *not*."

Okay, weirdly, what Brock said made me feel less freaked out at his wild, angry, unrestrained behavior.

There was another short pause.

Then, "Jill, you had a different dad than me. You and Laura, you had a different dad than Levi and me. And now, for years, I've been takin' your back with this shit, even before he got sick. But you gotta get your head outta your ass, woman. No man, even Dad, deserves to die alone, thinking his son has abandoned him. But that's as far as it goes and you need to get that and you need to show me while I have your back, you have mine and I'll make this official right fuckin' now. You have my back, you have Tess's, and you can read what you want into that and my guess is what you read will be right. Are we clear?"

Oh my God.

Did he mean what I thought he meant?

"Jesus," Brock clipped. "Uh... *yeah*. Wake up, Jill. She's met my fuckin' boys. In seven years has one woman I've been with met my boys, or, for that matter, *you*?"

Oh God.

He meant what I thought he meant.

I was feeling warm and gushy again.

"No," he declared firmly. "Tess will tell you it's okay because Tess is sweet and she won't want you to feel bad

so, no. You aren't talkin' about this with her. You're lis-
tenin' to me tell you that shit you did wasn't right. And
you know"—his voice dropped—"you *know*, Jill, from
watchin' Austin, I gotta have this covered for a lifetime.
That ghost shadows her, just like Laura. I gotta have this
and I gotta know my family has it too. So this is the last
we'll speak of it but before we're done, I gotta know. Do
you have this?"

A lifetime?

"Right," he said quietly. Then, "I'm sorry too. It's done.
We're movin' on. Tell your daughters their uncle hasn't
dropped off the face of the earth. They both got cars. They
can drive them to my place. Tess will have a cupcake
waitin' for them." Pause, then, "Right." Another pause,
then, quietly, "Jill, we're cool. Aren't we always cool?"

A moment passed before I watched him tip his head
back to look at the ceiling.

I knew why he did this when he dropped his head to
look at his boots and said gently, "Babe, quit cryin'."

Oh man.

I pressed my lips together.

Then Brock said, "You fucked up. I called you on
it. You listened. It's done and we're cool, darlin'. Quit
fuckin' cryin'."

I was thinking for the first time in my life that I was
glad I didn't have a brother and at the same time contradictorily sadder than normal that I didn't.

And I was also thinking it was high time I Skyped my
sister.

Then Brock said, "Right. Me too." Pause, then, "Fuck,
right. I'll tell her." Another pause, then, "Me too, darlin'.
Later."

He snapped his phone shut and looked at me.

Then he announced, "Seein' as I now have a woman, I have assignments for Thanksgiving dinner, something, as a guy, I avoided for seven years and something, because my mother and sisters hated my wife, they never gave her the honor. But apparently you're in charge of dessert and when I say that I mean enough dessert that'll feed sixteen."

My "Okay" came out sounding strangled because I was trying really, really hard not to laugh.

Brock wasn't laughing. He was dropping the phone on the coffee table. It clattered but he ignored it because while doing it, his eyes didn't leave me.

I would know why when he told me, "I can get pissed and when I do, I've learned to let fly. I bury shit, it is not good. So I let fly. But you, Tess, no matter how close you are to me when I flare or what pisses me off, you are never in any danger. I may lose it but I will never lose it in a way that I'll hurt you. That's a promise. No man who is a decent man would ever put his hands on a woman or child in anger. And I'm not your average kind of man but I know, even so, I'm a decent man."

"I know," I whispered.

"If you do, why are you shoved in a corner?" he asked.

"Because you freaked me out," I answered.

He studied me. Then he sighed.

Then, softly, he said, "In future, sweetness, I'll do my best to check that."

I stared at him.

In seven years has one woman I've been with met my boys, or, for that matter, you?

I gotta have this covered for a lifetime.

In future, sweetness, I'll do my best to check that.

He was going to try to change . . . for me.

He introduced his sons . . . to me.

He took me on knowing, if we went the distance, he'd be helping me battle ghosts for a lifetime.

On these thoughts, I found my mouth whispering, "You like me."

His head jerked and he asked, "What?"

I didn't repeat myself. Instead, I said, "I don't want you to change who you are for me."

"Tess—" he started but I shook my head, sat straighter, and interrupted him.

"I can layer up so I don't get cold in your truck and I can deal when you get so pissed you throw a beer bottle. I don't want you to change for me."

His head dropped and he looked at his boots but not before I saw his eyes close slowly.

"You know," I told the top of his head. It came up and he looked at me. "You walked into my kitchen a month ago and I didn't want to have one thing to do with you. But when you told me you threw a chair in reaction to learning what happened to me, I knew somewhere I've never known with another man that you would never let anything harm me. And wherever that somewhere is, it's deep and it's real and after nearly a decade of not feeling safe, not for a day, in that moment in my kitchen I finally did. So now"—I gestured to the couch—"here I am. So if you throw a beer bottle or two or shout the house down, I'll deal."

His eyes held mine for long moments and then his long legs brought him to me in less than a second. I was plucked out of the sofa but right back in it and stretched on top of a Brock "Slim" Lucas who was kissing me harder than he ever kissed me, sweeter than he ever kissed me but unfortunately not longer.

When he released my lips, I lifted my head, fought for breath, and watched his warm, quicksilver eyes roam my face.

Then I asked breathily, "So, is this Thanksgiving gig traditional as in pumpkin, apple, and pecan pie or can I get creative?"

His eyes stopped roaming, locked on mine, and he grinned.

Then he said, "Do whatever the fuck you wanna do. They'll eat anything."

"Both then," I muttered musingly and I felt Brock's body start rocking with laughter under mine.

Then I felt Brock's body rocking with laughter *over* mine because he rolled me to my back while rolling on top of me.

Then my glasses were no longer on my nose but on the coffee table and I felt Brock's laughter in my mouth because he was kissing me.

Then I felt a lot of other things given to me from Brock but none of them had one thing to do with laughter.

CHAPTER ELEVEN

Thanksgiving

A week and a half later...

"YOU WANNA TELL me, sweetness, how dessert for seventeen people translates into seven pies and two cakes?" Brock asked.

I watched Rex give Joel a look as we all stood at the trunk of my car and Brock carefully handed out bags filled with cake boxes and stacked pie holders to his sons. Joel caught Rex's look and they both visibly struggled with quelling their laughter.

I answered Brock, "I did the calculations."

Brock straightened from the trunk with the last bags and slammed it shut.

Then he looked at me, saying, "You did the calculations."

"Yes," I answered, holding a bundle of flowers, a six pack of bottled Bud, and a bag filled with a tub of Cool Whip, canned whipped cream, a carton of the real stuff not yet whipped, and a gallon of gourmet vanilla bean ice cream

Brock continued not to move and also continued to stare at me.

So I asked, "What?"

"How many slices do you get out of a pie?" he asked back.

"That isn't the point," I informed him.

"What is?" he asked me.

"Well, it's Thanksgiving and people look forward to it and everyone has something they look forward to about it. So, say you're looking forward to a piece of pumpkin pie and I only made one pumpkin pie. One pumpkin pie isn't enough for seventeen people should, even though it's unlikely but it could happen, all seventeen people want a slice of pumpkin pie. Then, say, you didn't move fast enough so you didn't get your piece of pumpkin pie. Think of how disappointed you would be. So I made *two* pumpkin pies, *two* pecan pies, and *two* apple pies, the traditional pies of Thanksgiving. That way everyone can be sure to have what they're looking forward to."

Rex and Joel continued to quell their laughter, however not entirely successfully as I heard snickers.

Brock continued to stare at me but now he was doing it like he thought I may be a little crazy.

I kept talking.

"Then, just in case there are those who wish to venture out of the traditional, I made a maple buttermilk pie, which isn't traditional but it *is* autumnal so it fits with the occasion. And there might be those who want a little something different but a taste of traditional so I made a pumpkin cheesecake. And for those who just might be in the mood for cake, I made a crowd pleaser of chocolate with whipped cream frosting."

Brock continued to stare at me and now he was doing it like he didn't have any doubts about the fact that I was crazy.

"Jeez, Tess, how long did it take to make all this?" Joel asked and I looked to him.

"Honey, I own a bakery. I do this for a living. Even in my kitchen at home, I whipped all that up in about three hours."

This wasn't true. It took more like five.

"Awesome," Rex muttered. "She's like a cake baking superhero."

"And a pie baking one," Joel added.

I smiled at the boys, looked back at Brock, and suggested, "Maybe we should go in?"

"Yeah, and hopefully me and my boys can haul all this in without any of us getting a hernia," Brock muttered.

Both his sons lost their battle with their humor and burst out laughing. Eyes to his boys, Brock jerked his chin toward his mother's house and they started marching.

I fell in step beside Brock, following them, and heard him say under his breath, "Only I could find a woman who describes pies as 'autumnal.'"

"Well, how would you describe maple buttermilk pie?" I asked.

"Babe, I've never had maple buttermilk pie but there are only three adjectives to describe any pie and those are bad, okay, and fuckin' great."

"Then it's good you work in law enforcement and not as a food critic," I muttered.

"Yeah, that's good," he muttered back and I could hear the smile in his voice.

I watched Rex walk up his grandmother's front walk,

cautiously carrying the bag with the boxed chocolate cake well away from one side of his body and the one with the cheesecake well away from the other lest they bump into his legs and get jostled. Then my eyes moved to Joel, who had two bags, each with two carefully stacked pies in holders, and he was also cautiously holding his arms away from his body. Then I looked down at Brock's hands to see he had one bag with three carefully packed pies and another bag with two bottles of wine and a two liter of pop.

Then I considered the possibility that I might have gone overboard.

"Maybe I went overboard," I murmured as we neared the front door.

"Baby, *my* calculations say, just with the pies, there are fifty-six pieces open to seventeen people. That's more than three pieces of pie for each person. And that doesn't even take into account the cake. I think 'maybe' should be deleted from that sentence even if it is Thanksgiving and we can all expect to lapse into a food coma in about three hours."

Seeing as neither had free hands and they were treating their baked-goods-carrying responsibilities with paramount importance, neither Joel nor Rex braved knocking on the door, so Joel started shouting, "Grandma! Open up!"

At this, it hit me that Brock wasn't wrong.

Then I found my mouth whispering, "I didn't want to mess up."

To which I heard Brock say softly, "Hey," and I stopped watching Joel shout (with Rex now accompanying him) and looked up to Brock. His eyes moved over my face then captured mine before he leaned in deep, touched his mouth to mine, pulled back an inch, and murmured, "What am I gonna do with you?"

"Eat a lot of pie so it doesn't look ridiculous how many leftovers there are?" I murmured back and he grinned.

"Scout's honor, darlin'. I'll do my best to have your back."

I returned his grin and whispered, "Thanks."

The door opened and Jill was there.

A year and a half older than Brock, her hair had started to silver and she let it go at that. She got her mom's eyes, both her parents' height (like all her siblings), wasn't pleasantly rounded like Laura but fit in a sturdy way. She'd been with her partner, Fritz, for twenty years, they'd never married, and they had two daughters named Kalie and Kellie, aged, respectively, eighteen and sixteen.

I'd been around Jill three times because she came with Laura and/or Fern to my bakery but I had yet to meet Fritz, Kalie, or Kellie. To add to that, Austin, Laura's husband and Levi, Brock's brother, would be new additions to my ever-expanding Lucas social network.

In other words, regardless of the fact that I knew some of them, I didn't know others so I was more than a little bit nervous, thus my going overboard on dessert.

"Hey, guys. Welcome to the madhouse," she greeted, pushing open the storm door and holding it, whereupon Joel and Rex carefully scuttled in sideways, giving their aunt their greetings then disappeared into the house.

Jill's eyes went to her brother.

Then she asked quietly, "How'd you talk the Wicked Witch of the Rockies into relinquishing her offspring for a family holiday?"

"I didn't. Tess provided distraction for me in the front

while I penetrated the house through a basement window and the boys and I escaped out back. She still doesn't know they're gone."

Brock said this as we both slipped by her and into the house but I did it smiling because my man was funny.

Jill closed the door and looked at me muttering, "I wish."

Brock finally spoke the truth. "It was my turn, Jill."

"The other story is better," Jill said as she guided us toward the kitchen, and when we hit it, I noticed what a madhouse it was.

Fern lived in a two-bedroom bungalow with a finished basement in the out, out, outskirts of Washington Park. In other words, she was in my 'hood, though I lived close to Reiver's Bar and Grill so I was *officially* in the 'hood while Fern was *arguably* in it.

Brock had told me he and his family didn't grow up in this house but in a much bigger one situated in the Highlands. The house he grew up in was the house Cob had left his family in and he left his family in that house when his wife was a nurse's aide and didn't make a lot of money. And he left his wife, who was from Montana and all her family still lived there (to this day), and didn't provide either financial support or very much of his time to help his wife raise their children and pay the bills and she had no kin close to help her do it.

Cue Brock and Jill, at very young ages, growing up fast to assume heavy responsibilities as Fern took extra shifts as well as night classes to become an X-ray technician. Then they kept these responsibilities as Fern went on to take classes to become a radiology technician in order to make enough money to keep a roof over the heads and food on the table for her brood, which included two growing strong and tall boys. And always, Fern worked full-time hospital shifts, which meant Brock and Jill never lost these responsibilities but Brock, being the oldest boy, assumed more.

However, once the kids were out, Brock told me Fern put their big four-bedroom house on the market "two seconds after Laura's foot left the threshold" (Brock's words) and downsized.

Lucky for her, she'd been in that old house for decades. The real estate boom and regeneration in their old neighborhood meant she made a mint on it. This meant she owned outright this cozy, comfortable, easy-to-maintain bungalow that, even small, still managed to look and feel like the definition of Grandma's House.

And the big kitchen full of family on Thanksgiving Day screamed it when we walked in and were immediately accosted.

And I had to say, seeing it, I liked it.

For about ten minutes.

Laura swept forward and, with a kiss on her brother's cheek and a quick hug for me, she divested me of my flowers, the beer, and the bag and swept away at the same time Jill took Brock's burdens.

Dylan and Ellie (in another princess dress, this time with pink, sequined mary janes but she'd added a crown adorning her dark locks and I got that, seeing as Thanksgiving was a big occasion, royal headwear was an important accessory), both screeching, attacked Brock's legs. Grady hung back and played it cool when he greeted his awesome uncle.

I watched Brock's big hand give Dylan's neck a

squeeze but he swung Ellie up in his arms to kiss her neck and, this time, tickle her sides so the air rang with her peals of little girl giggles.

After he was done with that, she turned to me.

"Are we gonna watch *Tangled,* Aunt Tess?" she asked.

I got the title of "Aunt Tess" at the bakery the second time Laura brought the kids in.

I also liked it.

"Sure, honey, maybe after we eat."

"*Yay!*" she shrieked, arms straight up in the air, and Brock smiled down at her.

"Great, *Tangled,*" Dylan muttered.

"I'm watchin' football," Grady declared.

"So am I," Rex said, seconded that notion.

"And everyone knows Thanksgiving means football, not cartoons," Joel told Ellie.

"Boys can watch football in the basement while the girls have girl time with *Tangled* in my bedroom," Fern declared while unearthing my chocolate cake from a box. "Now, children out. Go play Wii. Go play football in the yard. Go play anything, just go *play.*"

Hmm. It seemed cooking for seventeen was putting Fern in a mood.

Joel, Rex, Grady, and Dylan raced out screaming, "*Football!*" and Brock put a confused-looking Ellie on her feet.

She watched the door where the boys disappeared, considering this dilemma and clearly wishing to play princess games though unsure how to convince her all-male older brothers and cousins this was what they'd prefer. Then, gamely, she raced out after them and I hoped they didn't damage her crown when tackling her.

"Hey, Uncle Slim," I heard and I looked up to see a very pretty, dark, curly-to-frizzy-haired girl come forward and give Brock a hug. She was dressed like she was at a costume party and she was a sixties hippie (without headband or funky sunglasses but the rest...all there).

"She lives," Brock teased, hugging her back and I scanned the room.

Those I knew were there, including Elvira, who was standing at the sink peeling potatoes liked she'd been to Thanksgiving at Brock's mom's house every year since she was born.

Yes, I said *Elvira*.

Although it was me who "asked" her (in quotes because she mostly invited herself), I wasn't entirely sure why she was there.

I'd since had cosmos with her and the girls (twice) and she was not afraid of texting or phoning to tell you anything that was on her mind (frequently). I still didn't know her very well.

What I did know was that she was currently in some drama with her sister and they weren't speaking. She detested (with a passion) her brother's new "skanky ho" of a girlfriend. And, wisely (I thought) to escape this discord, her parents had chosen Thanksgiving to vacation in Hawaii. Therefore, Elvira was at odds for a Thanksgiving meal and although she had tons of friends, she latched on to me.

I suspected undercover work for Martha but I knew what it was like to face a Thanksgiving alone and the lengths you'd go to avoid that so I'd let her make that play and, when I asked, Fern told me she felt the more the merrier.

Brock did not feel the same and nonverbally let this be

known (another time he looked at me like I was crazy) but
he didn't say word one.

Also in the room was a tall blond man with light-blue
eyes who was smiling at me like a madman (my correct
guess, Austin). A stocky salt-and-pepper close-cropped-
but-obviously-still-frizzy-haired man (another correct guess,
Fritz). A tall dark-haired girl who was for some reason
in late November wearing short-shorts and a thin drapey
T-shirt over a camisole (and that reason might be because
she was young, she was gorgeous, she had great legs, and
I was with her—if you had them, flaunt them) who had to
be Kellie (Jill and Fritz's youngest). And the girl hugging
Brock who had to be Kalie.

Lastly, a breathtakingly handsome man who, with his
tall, lean, powerful, fit body, thick dark hair, but strangely,
since no one else had them, hazel eyes, had to be Levi.

Hovering visibly nervously at Levi's side was a young
woman (another correct guess, in her late twenties) with
a fabulous figure, blonde hair in a pixie cut that suited her
very pretty features, and a carefully selected outfit that
said she wanted to impress but not show off. Levi's latest
squeeze.

Jill introduced me to Fritz as Kellie went in for her
snuggle with her uncle (and also got stick from him for
"disappearing into thin air," his words). Laura introduced
me to Austin, who smiled warmly at me while giving
me an equally warm hand squeeze. Elvira muttered, "Yo
bitch," at me, to which everyone chuckled even though
they all had just met her that day.

Then Levi came forward with his girl and I watched
him as he did it.

Oh man.

Suffice it to say, one look at him and I knew he trusted me a fair sight less than Cob did.

He clapped his brother's arm while shaking his hand, kissed my cheek, stepped back, and introduced his girl as Lenore before he launched in.

"Tess, been hearin' a lot about you."

"I'll bet," I replied.

"You been hearin' a lot, which makes me wonder why we haven't seen you a lot," Brock put in and Levi's eyes went to his brother.

"Been busy," he muttered.

"Not too busy to hear a lot about Tess," Brock remarked.

Levi decided to ignore that and he looked back at me.

"Got tight with Slim quick," he noted.

"Levi," Fern said in a warning tone.

"Oh boy," Elvira said to the potatoes in an undertone.

"Not exactly," Brock said in a rumbling tone and Levi looked back to his brother.

"Yeah, heard about that too."

I tensed at Brock's side. Brock felt it and his arm came around my shoulders.

"It's Thanksgiving. I got my boys. I got my family and I got my woman. What I don't wanna get is pissed off," Brock said low and Levi held his eyes.

Standoff, and I didn't think this was good. Levi was questioning his brother's judgment and it might be for protective reasons but Brock was the kind of man who wouldn't appreciate that. Brock had also both said and demonstrated that he intended to protect me, and a full-frontal assault to test me within ten minutes of arriving for Thanksgiving, if Levi didn't back down, was not going to go down well.

It was time to institute damage control and I did it by looking to Lenore, who was studying Levi with both concern and bafflement.

I took her in and then said, "Lenore, I really like your boots."

Her body jerked and her eyes came to me. Then she whispered, "Uh...thanks. I was, uh..."—her eyes shifted to Levi, then back to me—"thinking the same thing about yours. And that's a really nice sweater."

"I have a friend who works at Neiman's," I told her, and now I did, for with Elvira came Gwen, Tracy, and Cam, and Tracy was generous with her discount. My sweater cost a whack but, as all girls knew, I needed the perfect sweater for Thanksgiving dinner with Brock and his family so, like the nightie, I'd splurged. And, unfortunately, that wasn't the only thing I bought.

I really needed to sell more cupcakes.

"Employee discount," Elvira muttered over her potatoes.

Lenore gave another searching glance to Levi, then to me, "Cool."

I studied her and it hit me.

She liked Levi, a lot.

He was with his family and she was just his latest piece.

But to her, this was important. To her, this was meeting his family and she was reading this as a hopeful occasion when, with the way Levi was behaving with her, it was not. She was noting this and therefore understandably confused. And with the way Levi was behaving, in the not-too-distant future, she was going to be heartbroken.

I looked back at Levi to see him opening his mouth to say something but Fern got there first.

"Men, out. You're underfoot, you have no intention of helping, and if you tried, you'd mess it up. Go turn on a TV somewhere. Take those crackers and cheeseball with you. And the bowls of nuts. And the chips and dip."

Elvira looked over her shoulder at me and with her head she gestured to the kitchen table, which was covered in bowls and plates filled with pre-Thanksgiving nibbles that might defeat the purpose of Thanksgiving. She gave me an approving look that said Fern was not Ada and this clear plus was to be reported to Martha at her earliest opportunity.

"Tess! These pies are just *beautiful*!" Laura exclaimed and I looked to her.

She was right. My pies were gorgeous. I'd gone all out. The pumpkin ones had a border of egg-washed pumpkin cutouts I'd stamped out of pie crust and I'd even rolled out and arranged curly miniature vines that I'd attached to the pumpkin stems. The apple one had an apple cutout border. The maple buttermilk, maple leaves. And with the pecan, I'd painstakingly fashioned a decorative pie edge that was experimental but came out looking great.

It wasn't just cakes that deserved to be pretty.

"Jesus, fuck me, flashback," Levi muttered under his breath, eyeing the unveiled pies on his mother's kitchen counter. He looked to Brock. "Olivia used to make you cinnamon nut muffins. Granted, they didn't look that good *or* taste good, but she did it."

The air in the room went static as Laura snapped, "Levi!" Austin said low, "Dude, uncool." Fritz muttered under his breath, "Jesus." Elvira muttered under hers, "Oh boy." Kellie and Kalie whispered in unison, "Ohmigod." Brock's body went solid and Fern whirled on her son.

"Tell me you did not just say that," she demanded and Lenore slid closer to her man who was not her man.

"Am I wrong?" Levi asked his mother.

"What you're wrong about is thinking you're too old to get a slap across the mouth from your mother," Fern shot back.

"Outside," Brock growled and everyone looked to him but Brock only had eyes for his brother.

"Seriously?" Levi asked.

"Now," Brock rumbled.

Again, within ten minutes of arrival, it was time for damage control and I got close to him, curling my hands on his arm and tugging.

"Leave it," I whispered and his flashing, mercury eyes tipped down to me.

"Tess—"

I shook my head and gave his arm a squeeze. "The options available: have a brother who doesn't give a shit or have a brother who does. You're pissed now, honey, so you don't get, with those options, you lucked out."

Brock's jaw got hard and I looked to Levi.

"I get it. Your brother was fucked over, you care about him, and you're cautious. Thank you for being that way."

Levi blinked at me.

I let Brock go and moved to Fern, asking, "Now, what can I do?"

Fern didn't answer because she was committed to the act of glaring at her youngest son so Jill said, "You can help me lay the tables, Tess."

I ignored the family tension and followed Jill's lead setting the table.

On the way from dining table back to kitchen, I ran

into Fritz, smiled at him, but suddenly found my hand clasped in his and he got close.

When he did, he whispered, "Good play, Tess. This crew is tough to crack. Twenty years and I gave them my two girls and, sometimes, they get together, honest to God, I *still* feel like an outsider. But me and Austin, honey, we'll have your back."

Before I could say a word, he squeezed my hand and headed to the door that I guessed led to the basement.

I watched even after he disappeared and I did it feeling a whole lot better.

This again lasted ten minutes. In that ten minutes, the good news was, Jill and I set the tables (plural because there were folding ones set up in the living room for the overspill). The men disappeared to watch TV. Fern got the sweet potato casserole in the oven. Laura and Elvira tackled the mountain of potatoes and they were on the stove. Kalie and Kellie had arranged my plethora of desserts on the side table in the dining room and were currently arranging my bouquet of flowers in a vase. And Fern, Jill, and Laura clearly had a good deal of experience with Levi loving them and leaving them thus they were inclusive and gentle with Lenore even though it was probably the last time they would see her.

The bad news was, after ten minutes of relative harmony, Ellie came in shrieking, *"Grandpa's here!"*

The air in the room got thick as everyone in the room froze. Elvira and Lenore did it just because they felt the vibe and had no idea that Ellie's delighted shriek heralded Armageddon.

Then Elvira muttered a premonitory, "Oo lawdy, I'm thinkin' family drama is far from over."

"Uh…" Jill started, "Mom, we should have, um…Laura and I should have probably told you we invited Dad."

Oh *man!*

"We thought that…" Laura began then hesitated. "Well, it would be the kind of news better delivered at the last minute."

My eyes flew to Elvira, who had her hands full with shoving potato peels down the disposal. Her eyes hit mine and her eyebrows hit her hairline.

Fern didn't move. Fern was frozen. Fern was engaged in what fifteen seconds before was a thought she never thought she'd have and that was that she wanted to commit double homicide, with her victims being her daughters.

"Grandpa's here! Grandpa's here! *Grandpa's here!*" Ellie shouted from the doorway, then added, "Yippee!" She raced away, shouting, "Grandpa's here!" in what I was guessing was on her way to the TV room.

Dylan filled the doorway next and he did it tugging on Cob's hand. "Look!" he cried. "Grandpa! Isn't it *cool*? Grandpa hasn't *ever* been to Thanksgiving!"

"Heya, girls," Cob said carefully to Jill, Laura, and his granddaughters then his eyes came to me. "Heya, Tess, honey." Then they went to Lenore and Elvira in turn and he bowed his head slightly in greeting.

"Hey, Dad," Jill warily whispered.

That was when we heard, "What…the…*fuck?*"

My eyes got big and my lower lip stretched out in an *eek!* look at Elvira as everyone turned to the door.

"*What the fuck?*" This time it was shouted and I didn't know him very well but I knew it was Levi.

"Dylan, honey, go get your sister and go outside and

play," Laura said urgently to her bewildered and somewhat frightened-looking son who had his head tipped
back and was looking at someone in the hallway. "Now,
honey, all you kids stay outside." Dylan dazedly looked at
his mom and she repeated, "*Now,* baby."

He let his grandfather's hand go and dashed away.

Cob's gaze slid through Jill and Laura. He cottoned
onto the situation and he turned to look down the hall.

"Now, Levi—" he started.

"Get the fuck out." We heard.

"Levi—" Jill began, moving to the door.

"Get... *the fuck*... out!" Levi roared.

"Son—" Cob started again only to be cut off by Levi.

"I am not your son, you motherfucking asshole."

Cob winced.

Oh man.

"Levi!" Laura snapped, also moving to the door but
she didn't need to.

Levi shoved passed his father and entered the kitchen,
starting the wave that included Austin, Fritz, and Brock.
But Brock settled just inside the doorway close to his
father.

"Levi, cool it until the kids are outside," he rumbled.

Levi scowled at his brother, visibly counted to ten,
then fifteen (and I was right along with him), and we all
heard the door close and he let loose.

Turning to his sisters, he snarled, "You two are
un-fucking-believable."

"Careful, bud," Fritz growled.

Levi swung to Fritz and declared, "Fuck that."

This needed to play out but without the audience it had.

This was my decision. Therefore, I whispered, "Kalie,

Kellie, why don't you guys, Lenore, Elvira, and I go out and see what the kids are up to?"

"Good idea, Tess. This is a family situation," Levi gritted at me.

Bad move.

Really bad move.

I knew this when Brock took two long strides to his brother and got toe-to-toe and nose-to-nose with him and the thick atmosphere became suffocating.

"Tess talked me down earlier and now I'm seein' I shouldn't have let her. You need to *cool it* or, honest to fuckin' God, Levi, I'll see that you do."

"Do not bullshit me, Slim. You do not want that man here any more than I do," Levi shot back, throwing out an arm and pointing at his father.

"You don't know what I want," Brock replied and Levi's eyes narrowed.

"Fuck me, *you*? *You* are buyin' this bullshit? Pretty convenient he sees the error of his ways when he's got cancer eatin' out his insides," Levi returned scornfully.

I pressed my lips together. Laura made a noise like a whimper. Kalie moved so she was closer to Kellie. And Fern decided she was done. I knew this because she said so.

She did this with a whispered, "I'm done with this."

Brock disengaged from the angry-man stare down, turned, and stepped to his brother's side.

All eyes turned to Fern.

Fern looked to Cob.

"This is my house and I say who's welcome here. It's Thanksgiving, Cob, and I'm sorry for you that you don't know if you'll have another one. But I'm happy for you to sit at the table with your family for this one. You didn't give me much but you did give me the four most precious things in my life. For that, I can give you this."

Okay, well, I pretty much liked Fern before.

Now I knew I *really* liked her.

She looked to Levi and kept talking.

"I love you, sweetheart, but you have to get that hate out of your gut or it'll eat out your insides like the cancer is eating your father. And"—her eyes slid to Lenore then back to Levi—"I'll add it might be a good time for you to wake up."

I felt eyes, looked to Elvira, and saw her grinning at me.

Fern wasn't done.

"Now, we've got dinner to finish off so go and watch your game and, I'll tell you this"—her eyes honed in on Levi—"it might be Cob's last Thanksgiving with his family but that also means it might be his family's last Thanksgiving with him. And we all should do what we can to make it a damned good memory because, for my grandbabies out there, it's gonna need to last a while."

No one said anything and no one moved.

So Fern went on, "Levi, can you do that for your family?"

Levi didn't answer. Levi stared at his mother for long moments before his eyes sliced through his sisters, he turned on his boot and walked out.

Fern sighed.

Cob said quietly, "Appreciate it, Fern."

Her eyes went to him and she nodded.

Then she looked to her granddaughters and said softly, "That looks pretty, girls. Put it in the middle of the dining room table, would you?"

Then she went to the stove to check the potatoes.

I looked to Brock in time to see him jerk his chin up at his father, pass him, and turn in the same direction Levi went. Austin and Fritz guided Cob out.

Elvira came to me.

"Shoo, girl, big ole honkin' W...T...F? Your bad boy's family is *whacked*. Makes my brother with his skinny, skanky, natty-'fro ho and my sister with her inability to return that fabulous dress she borrowed *without* red wine stains seem tame."

I didn't think a ho in the family was good news but definitely Brock's family issues were more intense than a dress returned with wine stains.

"Um..." I mumbled. "Brock's family is working through some issues."

"Issues?" she asked, leaning back a bit and then again leaning in to confide, "I knew it. Got me a premonition. Woke up and it said, 'Thanksgivin' with Tess.' Tellin' you, girlfriend, this is better than TV."

Well, it was good someone was enjoying themselves.

"I can't wait to see what happens next," she muttered, then moved away and the away she moved was in the direction of the plethora of wine bottles on the counter.

I could. I could wait to see what would happen next.

And with what did, Elvira was probably not disappointed.

CHAPTER TWELVE

The Coolest Move Ever

AN HOUR AND a half later, I found that, upon calculating the need for dessert, I had not taken into account children who had bottomless stomachs, men who had high metabolisms so they didn't really need to worry about how much they shoved down their gullets, and women who were experiencing one of six days of the year they could let it all hang out (the others being Christmas, New Year's, Easter, the Fourth of July, and their birthday).

Let's just say, even though Fern provided a plentiful and delicious Thanksgiving spread, there weren't a lot of dessert leftovers.

For dinner, at the big table I was sandwiched between Fritz and Austin, who made it clear, after Levi's earlier show, that they cast themselves in the roles of my protectors. It was all for one and one for all when it came to being hooked to a member of the Lucas family.

It was also seriously cool and obviously very appreciated.

Brock sat at the head of our table, Fern sat at the foot, and Cob, Jill, Kalie, Laura, and Elvira rounded out our company. Cob being at the big table meant Levi, who Brock somehow talked into rejoining the family festivities, commandeered Lenore and he sat among the card tables set up across the way in the living room with Kellie and her younger cousins.

Although a fair amount of wine and beer were being consumed, the tense atmosphere had not lightened and the only person who seemed oblivious to it was Elvira.

Therefore, I engaged Elvira in conversation, knowing from experience that anytime Elvira spoke, interesting if somewhat surprising and possibly inappropriate things would come out. I did this in the hopes it would lighten the atmosphere.

It did.

Austin and Fritz clearly thought she was a hoot, Cob not far behind, Jill, Laura, and Kalie shortly joined in, and finally Fern melted. For his part, Brock mostly studied Elvira like she was an unknown creature he didn't know what to make of but I could sense he was relaxed and pleased his family was enjoying dinner. I could sense this because that was the mood he filled the room with.

Further making things seem almost festive was the fact that Uncle Levi, although having a short fuse, was clearly the funny uncle and much beloved by his siblings' progeny because laughter rang from the card tables across the way with a lot of giggled "*Uncle Levi!*" shrieked from Ellie.

Since we made it through dessert without another scene, I relaxed and unfortunately let my guard down.

Therefore, I wasn't prepared to feel the snap and crackle of Brock's mood hitting the room.

My head swiveled to him to see his back straight, his face like thunder, and his eyes pointed out the window.

Then I heard from the card tables, "You are fuckin' *shitting* me."

This was Levi.

Suddenly there was motion and that motion was Brock and Levi folding out of their chairs and the rest of us craning our necks to look out the window.

When we saw what we saw, I froze and stared.

Fern, Jill, and Laura didn't freeze.

Fern hissed, "Oh no, I do not *think* so."

Jill snapped, "I do not *believe* that woman."

And Laura bit off, "On *Thanksgiving*."

They jumped up and followed Brock and Levi, Cob going with them, and both Fritz and Austin scooted closer to me, with Fritz saying, "Kalie, honey, you and your sister get your cousins downstairs, yeah?"

Kalie turned her own angry face from her contemplation of the window. Kalie and Kellie, I had noted, much like their younger counterparts, had a close relationship with their Uncle Slim. They had also, it would appear, been old enough to have some dealings with Olivia. And, it would also appear, had not liked those dealings. She headed to the living room to do what she was told.

I hadn't moved.

That was because Olivia was outside.

What on earth?

"Uh...who's that?" Elvira asked the window, still looking out, and now Olivia was standing on the front walk confronting the full force of the Lucas Brigade.

"Brock's ex-wife," I whispered.

"Oo lawdy," Elvira whispered back.

She could say that again.

Half a second later, we heard Laura shriek, *"Bitch!"* and we saw her lunge at Olivia.

Elvira repeated a whispered, now emphasized, "Oo *lawdy*."

Austin muttered, "Fuck," at my side, pushed his chair back, and took off.

It was then I watched Brock plant a hand on his sister's chest. Cob wrapped his arm around his daughter's waist and pulled back. Olivia lifted both her extraordinary hands to her face and melted into beautiful woman tears, which every woman on the face of the earth knew held magical powers over any man who was breathing as long as that man wasn't blind.

Oh man.

"I'm just going to, uh…start to clear the dishes," I heard Lenore whisper.

Fritz muttered, "Good idea, Lenore. Elvira? Tess, honey, why don't you two help? I'm gonna go on outside."

And outside words were being exchanged while Brock was leading a still-sobbing Olivia down the walkway with a hand at the small of her back and I decided Lenore's idea was an excellent one.

So I nodded, got up, and started to help her as Fritz headed out.

"I got your back, sister. I'll keep an eye out," Elvira told me but I didn't answer. I started loading my hands with plates.

After trip two, when I was in the kitchen, I heard the reentry of the Lucas Brigade and this included Jill's "I do not, do not, do *not* believe that *bitch*."

"Jill, sweetheart, shush," Cob shushed her.

"She's a piece of work!" This was Laura and it wasn't shushed. It was loud.

"Laurie, quiet . . . Tess." This was, surprisingly, Levi.

I waited several seconds and walked into the hall. They were all standing at the front door and all their eyes came to me.

"It's okay," I told them when I got nearer. "I've met her. It's okay."

I went back to the table and started clearing, but try as I might, I couldn't keep my eyes from straying to the window. When I looked out I saw down the way that Brock and Olivia were standing by a silver Mercedes. Olivia was still sobbing but now she was doing it with her face planted in Brock's chest and his arms were around her.

Damn.

Damn.

Elvira got close and I tore my eyes away from the window.

"Why don't you take Ellie and watch the movie?"

"I'm okay," I whispered.

"I think that's a good idea." Fern was now also close. "Just go on up. I'll send Ellie up with the DVD."

"Really, I'm fine," I lied.

Fern looked at Elvira. I gathered plates and went to the kitchen.

The men disappeared and the women all hit clearing mode. When the tables were nearly empty and I was going back to gather napkins and bits and bobs, Brock came in.

His eyes came to me and I saw at once they were not angry, not impatient, but conflicted.

I'd seen him look conflicted before and it wasn't a good memory.

"Hey," I whispered as I moved to him.

"Hey," he replied, distracted.

Oh man.

"Everything okay?" I asked.

"We'll talk later," he muttered. "Where're the boys?"

"Downstairs."

He nodded, his eyes going down the hall. He lifted his hand to my neck and after a short, preoccupied squeeze he walked down the hall and disappeared through the door to the basement.

I watched.

And while I watched, it was not lost on me in any way that not once, not even in the beginning when he was Jake, he was undercover, and all sorts of shit was going down, had he ever been distracted and preoccupied with me. I always had his full attention. Always.

I helped the girls do the dishes. Then Elvira said goodbyes to everyone, gave her thanks, and I walked her to her car.

"Your bad boy is hot," she stated bizarrely, standing with me at her driver's-side door.

"What?" I asked, having walked with her while in my head and finally focusing on her.

"Your bad boy is hot," she repeated. "She instigated a play."

"Sorry?" I asked, feeling my brows draw together.

"Tess, hon, her ex-bad boy, ex-*hot* boy just hooked his star to a brand-new, bright and shiny moon. He's into his new moon. He traded up. He likes it. He's gonna stay awhile. She knows this probably from her boys. She don't like it. She instigated a play. Looks of her, she's got a big playbook. She may not want him but she doesn't want anyone else to have him. Or she thinks she's all that and never thought he'd move on and doesn't like it that he has. It shook her awake and she's finally lookin' around and sees what she's missin'. I'll give it to her. It was a good play, drama, tears, family as an audience. But if he got shot of her ass, he'll see through it. You just need to keep your chin up."

I stared at her, wondering if it was actually true that people did that kind of thing.

So I asked, "Do people actually do that kind of thing?"

"Uh . . . yeah," she answered.

"They have children," I told her.

"Right, Tess, and heads up. Right now, to her, whatever her game is, those two boys just stopped bein' boys and they became pawns."

Oh my God.

"She wouldn't," I whispered.

"Mark my words, girlfriend, that bitch has got *bitch* written *all over her*. You got your hands full, hon. Lucky for you, you got your posse and his family at your back. After she made that play, they were all whispering, worried about you. Not him. They know your boy sees it for what it is. They were worried about *you* 'cause they know her for what *she* is and they know this is play one and right now she's got her nose in her playbook, decidin' what to do for play two. Chin up. He'll see her play for what it is and he'll be on the lookout for her next one. You just gotta ride that wave."

Kentucky, for the first time in a while, was looking good again.

This time, though, I was packing up Brock, Joel, and Rex to take with me.

I said good-bye to Elvira, walked back to the house, and was struck by Ellie Lightning the minute I made it through the door.

"*Tangled*!" she screeched.

I pushed aside my thoughts and smiled down at her.

"*Tangled*," I agreed.

Thus I found myself up in Fern's bedroom lying across the foot of the bed with Ellie in her princess dress tucked in front of me.

Kalie and Kellie wandered up and camped out on the floor. Jill and Fern came as well and lay behind us in the bed. Lenore and Laura were with the boys watching football.

Tangled turned to *Beauty and the Beast*, which was one of my favorite movies ever, animated or not.

Still, I'd just had Thanksgiving dinner and it was Thanksgiving law to pass out shortly after consumption of said dinner and therefore I zonked out in the middle of the movie.

Therefore, when I heard Ellie whisper loudly, "Uncle Slim, she's *sleeping*," I woke up.

I blinked my eyes, surprised that I had drifted off, to see *Mulan* playing behind Brock, who was crouched by the bed. My eyes opened right before his hand curled warm around my neck.

"Time to go, sleepyhead," he said softly to me. "Gotta get the boys home."

Home. To Olivia's.

I nodded, pushed up from the bed after giving Ellie a brief snuggle, tried to pull myself together through hugs and farewells, and then found myself in the passenger seat of my own car, Brock driving, the boys in the back, the same arrangement as when we arrived.

They chatted about football.

I stared out the window.

We drove into the elegant drive of a big house in Cherry Hills Village, which meant that when Brock said Olivia's new husband was loaded, he actually meant *loaded*.

"Later, Tess," Joel said to me.

"Later, honey," I said to Joel, turning to the backseat.

"Later, Tess. Thanks for the pecan pie and the pumpkin pie and the cheesecake I ate during football," Rex shared his gratitude.

I smiled at him.

"I was in the mood for cake, so thanks for the three pieces I ate," Joel put in, so I smiled at him.

"Anytime, baby," I said softly. "See you guys later."

They waved and got out.

"I'll be back, babe," Brock muttered, waited for me to look at him and nod and he got out and followed his boys.

I watched.

Olivia met him on the front step.

I kept watching.

Joel and Rex gave their dad hugs and disappeared inside. Olivia didn't look once at the car as she engaged Brock in conversation. Brock started to look my way but didn't get his head fully turned when her hand came up and curled around his bicep. She stepped in closer so his head turned back to her.

I stopped watching.

I was staring out the side window when I heard Brock get in, put the idling car in gear, and reverse out of the drive. I kept staring out the side window as he pointed us home.

About ten seconds later, his fingers curled around mine and he pulled them to his thigh as he asked quietly, "You okay?"

"Just tired," I lied. "Too much food."

"Right," he muttered, giving my hand a squeeze and saying no more but not letting my hand go.

He took us to my house. We both got out, walked up, and I let us in. I shrugged off my coat and took it to the hall closet. Brock shrugged off his and threw it on the sofa.

He went to the fridge for beer.

I went to the island and looked at him.

"If you've got football to watch," I said. He turned from the fridge and his eyes came to me. "Go ahead. I'm going to read up here for a while."

He stood in the opened fridge door and held my eyes.

I knew why he did this.

Unless he was with his boys, we spent every night together and we woke up next to each other every morning.

And when we were together, we were *together*, watching TV, a movie, if he was watching a game. We were up together and when we went to bed, we went to bed together.

He did not go downstairs and watch a game while I stayed upstairs to read.

Perhaps, in future, this might change, but now, I liked it like this. I liked being with him. He was attentive, touchy, we cuddled or were close and it felt good.

The fact that Brock was attentive, touchy, and we cuddled meant he liked it too.

And, clearly, from what would happen next, Brock

was not ready for us to move on to a different kind of relationship.

I knew this when he closed the fridge and walked around the island. He came to me, grabbed my hand, pulled me into the living room, sat on the couch, and pulled me to sitting astride his lap.

Once he had me in position and his hands settled on my hips, he said, "All right, babe, what's up?"

"Nothing, I—" I started to lie, his fingers dug into my hips, and he interrupted me.

"I got a new job, a new house, new fuckin' furniture, and a new woman in my life. That woman comes with a motherfucker of an ex who's poising to strike—I know it in my gut and I gotta be prepared. My dad's sick, he may be dyin', and my family's fucked up about it. Somethin' is goin' on with my boys and I gotta look into that. And today, my bitch of an ex-wife shows up on Thanksgiving to inform me her husband is steppin' out on her, she doesn't care, and she knew it was a mistake before she signed the marriage certificate."

I gasped at this news but said nothing mostly because I didn't have a chance.

Brock kept talking.

"She went on to say she fucked up with him *and* me. She sees this clear now, feels that time is of the essence, considering our boys are growing up without a stable family unit, so, upon a great deal of reflection, her fuckin' words, regardless of the holiday, she felt it prudent she didn't delay in informing me she wants me and our family back. With all that, you gotta see I do not have it in me to play guessing games. All I got left in me for today is to have a beer with my woman, watch a game, take her to bed, let her fuck me sweet like she always fucks me then go to sleep."

I stared down at him thinking there was a lot there, a lot, a lot, but I honed in on one thing.

So I asked, "She told you she wants you back?"

"Yeah, if you can believe that shit."

I kept staring down at him.

Then I stated, not a question this time but still a question, "She told you she wants you back."

His fingers dug in again and he said, "Yeah."

"She walked up to your mother's house on Thanksgiving and told you she wanted you back," I, yet again but with some added detail, stated.

Brock didn't reply. He just watched me closely.

"I don't know what to say," I told him and I didn't. I buried my head in the sand, sure, but I knew people did crazy shit, case in point my own husband raping me. But *that*, that was *insane*.

"Nothin' to say," he told me.

"Do you want her back?" I asked and he did a slow blink.

Then he asked, "Come again?"

"Do you want her back?" I repeated.

"Do I want her back?"

"Yeah, do you want her back?"

His brows drew together and his fingers dug into my hips again before he asked, "Have you lost your mind?"

"No," I replied. "She's beautiful. She's the mother of your children. And you loved her once enough to marry her. I saw you outside holding her in your arms and I saw you when you got back into the house after that scene and you looked conflicted. Not annoyed, not angry, not frustrated, *conflicted*. So no, Brock, I haven't lost my mind."

His mouth got tight then he said low, "Babe, I was holding her in my arms 'cause when the mother of your sons cries crocodile tears, your best play is to give her that play and then, soon as you can, walk away. That's what I did. And when confronted, *again*, with the knowledge that my boys got a mom like they got, in other words, she's the kind of woman who would walk into my house, see another woman in my kitchen, and lose her mind when she sees someone playin' with what she considers *her* toy and scheme in preparation for makin' a play in my mother's motherfuckin' front yard on motherfuckin' Thanksgiving, that is gonna make me conflicted."

This, I had to admit, made sense.

Brock kept speaking and making more sense.

"And I'm conflicted because this means, with all that other shit I just laid out for you, I gotta look into attorneys and whatever else I gotta do to make certain my boys don't spend the vast majority of their time suckin' up whatever acid she leaks. Not to mention whatever-the-fuck her man is like, steppin' out on their mom, if that's even true, and at least try to give them somethin' good for more than four fuckin' days a month. Now, with this, I'll ask you, what's the priority? You and your motherfucker ex? My dad dyin' and my family at each other's throats? Or my boys in that viper's den?"

Hmm. This was a good question.

And I had the uncomfortable feeling I'd been a bad girlfriend to my hot guy.

Time to sort myself out.

"Your boys in that viper's den," I told him. He did a

slow blink again and I explained, "Damian does something, we'll deal. Your family are all adults. *They* need to deal. Your sons are powerless and they need *you* to deal."

He stared up at me and I kept talking.

"I'm sorry, my reaction was selfish. I should have thought of you and I'll work on it but I'm a woman and women have this thing when their men have had women in their lives who are better looking than them."

This got another slow blink coupled with a finger squeeze at my hips but I was on a roll so I ignored these and stayed on that roll.

"You're hot. I should have known she would be beautiful but just how beautiful she is took me by surprise. Like I said, I'll work on that and try to get over it. But, in my defense, it's my experience that not a lot of men say no to a woman like her and, even if it didn't work out in the end, at one time you were one of them."

"Tess—" he started but I talked over him.

"And, just to say, you were able to talk your brother back into the house and I know you have a full plate, but once some of this other stuff is sorted, you need to carve time out to have more words with him. Not about your dad or about me. He needs to sort himself out about your dad and I'll win him over eventually. So, if you're worried about that too, then you need to stop doing it. But about Lenore. She's in love with him. She's a good person. She's sweet. And if he isn't into her he needs to cut her loose. He also needs to get his head out of his ass because if he's breaking hearts like that all through Denver, that isn't cool."

When I stopped talking, Brock remained silent and stared up at me.

When the silence stretched for a while, he asked, "Are you done?"

"Well," I started, "yeah."

Then he asked, "You think Olivia is better looking than you?"

My brows drew together and I repeated, "Well... yeah."

He was silent again while staring at me.

"Brock—" I started but he cut me off.

"Jesus, you haven't, have you?"

"I haven't what?"

"Ever played games."

I thought about it. Then I answered, "No."

He shook his head while his lips tipped up and his hands slid up my sides, pulling me to him at the same time. I put my hands to his chest as I got closer and Brock wrapped his arms around me.

Then he spoke. When he did, he did it softly and I noticed the sweet hum in the room just as it hit me his eyes were amused.

"Okay, sweetness, it shits me to do it but I'm gonna have to educate you."

Uh-oh.

I tipped my head to the side as I felt my body tense and I asked cautiously, "About what?"

"About the games a woman like Olivia plays. Specifically *why* she instigates a play."

Oh, well. That didn't sound too bad. It actually sounded interesting.

I relaxed against him and said, "Okay."

His lips tipped up more and he began, "Now, a woman like Olivia walks into my place and sees a woman in my kitchen who isn't better lookin' than her, she does not throw a shit fit. She does not make bitchy comments. She has no reaction at all. She's content in the knowledge I've settled for somethin' less and falls asleep smilin', thinking *I'm* thinking I settled for second best."

I nodded when he quit speaking so he continued.

"If she sees a woman who's better lookin' than her, her hackles rise and she gets pissed. Right at that moment it's game on. Then she throws a shit fit and makes bitchy comments and she drives home thinkin' about nothin' but how to stake her claim. And she instigates a play to remind me of the Olivia she played me with, and, by the way, that was who was on my Mom's lawn today. It was the first time I saw her since the last time Olivia wanted somethin' from me. And she did this not because she wants me back. She did it in order to best you so she can go back to fallin' asleep smilin', content in the knowledge that she's top of the heap, she's taken you down, and she's still got what it takes to manipulate me."

I stared into his eyes.

Then I began, "I don't—"

His arms gave me a squeeze and he talked over me.

"Tess, no lie. Olivia is beautiful but she is not better looking than you. No fuckin' way. You think, she was, Levi would take one look at you and put you to the test?"

Hmm. Interesting point.

"But—" I started and got another arm squeeze.

"Babe, seriously. I'm committed to my job and there were a lot of things about Darla that were foul, most especially the shit she snorted, injected, and inhaled into her body, but she wasn't tough to look at. There were a lot of ways to make my play with you as a possible asset or suspect. The minute I saw you, it took me a split second to decide what play I was gonna make and"—another arm squeeze—"when I say the minute I saw you, I'm talkin' your pictures in a file. The minute I saw you in person, babe, cast your mind back. How long was I in your shop before you said yes to me askin' you out for a beer?"

I cast my mind back but I didn't have to. Meeting Brock slash Jake was burned in my brain.

I was filling the display with fresh cupcakes, the bell over the door went, I looked up, and his eyes were on me. Then he smiled as he walked straight to me, ignoring the two counter girls, asked for half a dozen snickerdoodles and if I'd meet him for a beer.

He was probably in my shop thirty seconds before he asked me out.

I thought it was the coolest move ever, no bullshit, cocky, confident, and self-assured.

Not to mention he was the most beautiful man I'd ever seen.

So it wasn't but five seconds later when I said yes (to my counter girls' disbelief and delight).

I stared at him.

Then it hit me and I blurted, "You think I'm more beautiful than Olivia?"

"Babe," he muttered, grinned, gave me an arm squeeze but that was it.

Whoa. He thought I was more beautiful than Olivia.

"I think I need to spend some time perusing myself in the mirror," I told him and his body started shaking with laughter as his arms separated. One went low, one went high so his hand could sift into my hair and pull my face closer to his.

"How 'bout you peruse yourself in the mirror later," he muttered, his eyes dropping to my lips.

"Later?" I whispered, knowing what his eyes dropping to my lips meant because that had happened before but also the hum in the room changed to warm and close and I knew what was on his mind.

"Yeah." His eyes came to mine then his hand pushed my head closer to his but veered it to the side, so at my ear, he whispered, "I had maple buttermilk pie at dinner and chocolate cake during football but I still have a taste for somethin' sweet. And the sweet I wanna eat right now is my Tess."

I felt tingles at my scalp, along my skin, and about three other places besides.

"Okay," I whispered, sliding my hands out from between us to wrap my arms around him and press my torso close to his.

His lips slid down my neck and back up, making me roll my hips in his lap involuntarily and, back at my ear, he growled, "Fuckin' love goin' down on you, baby."

I shivered and I did this because I loved it too but almost (not quite) better was him growling it in my ear.

"Brock," I whispered.

His arm slid up my back, wrapped around tight, and his fingers stroked light as a feather against the side of my breast as he went on. "Never had a sweeter cunt than yours, Tess. Not in my whole fuckin' life."

I made a noise in my throat and pressed my lips against his neck right where his hair curled as my hips rolled against his lap again.

"You wet for me?" he murmured against my neck.

Oh yeah. Definitely.

"Yes," I whispered.

"Good, then you're ready."

He moved his head and mine, crushed my lips down on his, invaded my mouth with his tongue, and surged off the couch, taking me with him.

I wrapped my legs around his hips, my arm around his shoulders and slid the fingers of my other hand in his hair as he kissed me while he carried me to my bedroom.

I gave Brock something sweet.

After, he gave me something sweeter.

Then we both gave each other something even sweeter.

Then he tugged his tee and jeans back on, I pulled on a nightie, warm socks, and dug in his exploded bag that now had a permanent place in the corner of my bedroom and pulled on one of his flannels. He got a beer and poured me some red wine while I took out my contacts and slipped on my glasses. We curled on my couch in the basement and watched football.

I zonked out with my head against his thigh and his fingers sifting through my hair.

I reawakened when he set me in bed and only stayed that way until he pulled me deep into his body and tangled his legs with mine.

My last thought before drifting back to sleep was that Thanksgiving, as with anything with Brock's family, was interesting, to say the least.

But Thanksgiving night with just Brock and me was fabulous.

The best Thanksgiving night I ever had.

Ever.

CHAPTER THIRTEEN

Errol Fucking Flynn

ONE ARM WRAPPED around my back, one hand on my ass, Brock surged out then back inside me. I stifled my moan against his neck as my fingers fisted in his hair and the nails of my other hand dragged down his back.

He growled in my ear because my man liked my nails on his back and then he surged out and thrust in again.

And again.

And again.

I lifted my head and yanked his up by his hair, maneuvering his mouth to mine. I kissed him hard as he pounded inside.

Then my nails dug in his back and my legs spasmed around his hips as my head jerked back and I whimpered, "Oh my God, honey, I'm gonna—"

I didn't finish. My eyes closed, my head fell back, he drove in faster and harder, and I gasped and held him tight as I came.

"Eyes," he growled and my eyes fluttered open and focused hazily on him. "I want your eyes when I come," he ordered.

"Okay, baby," I whispered and held his eyes, held him tense in three limbs as one hand roamed. Gliding across his skin, up his back, around his side, my thumb rubbing his nipple hard then down his chest, his abs until it was at our wet connection and I was feeling him taking me from outside as well as in. "God, that's beautiful."

"Tess," he groaned.

I touched my lips to his, held his eyes, and whispered, "Fucking beautiful, baby."

He slanted his head, took my mouth, and planted his cock, his grunt of release driving down my throat.

Yeah. Beautiful.

Since his mouth was on mine, when he recovered, he started gliding in and out as he kissed me, deep but soft and sweet and I wrapped him tight and kissed him back.

Then his mouth released mine. He buried himself to the root as his lips glided down my cheek to my ear.

His arms curved around me squeezed and he whispered in my ear as his hips pushed deep, "Sweetest fuckin' cunt I ever had."

I shivered in his arms.

Brock pulled out and pulled me off the vanity in his bathroom where he'd walked in when he heard me turn off the faucet after I brushed my teeth. He'd closed the door and instigated operation maximum physical contact in the only room in the house (possibly and hopefully) his sons couldn't hear us having sex in. Thus, me ending up with my ass to the vanity, my arms and legs wrapped around Brock, and my first-ever orgasm in a bathroom.

It was sublime.

But when he dropped me to my feet, he surprised me when he stayed close and turned me to face the mirror. He pressed forward and fenced me in against the vanity, his hands moving slowly around my ribs, my belly, crossing over to go down to my hips.

My surprised eyes went to the mirror and I saw his were already there, following the trail of his hands. I saw my hair was a mess, my cheeks pink, my eyes still hazy, and his hands were still moving over the amethyst-colored, simple, short silk nightie (another Neiman's purchase, not the splurge of the first I got at Nordstrom's, but also not cheap either) he'd fucked me in.

I could tell looking at his face he liked it.

Actually, I already knew this, considering I could tell by his face (and actions) last night when he first saw it that he liked it.

Suffice it to say we'd broken the seal on having sex with his sons in the house. Last night, it was late, the boys definitely asleep but Brock still took care to muffle my noises with his mouth and his own with mine or my neck.

This morning, the bathroom.

"How many cupcakes you gotta sell to give me this, darlin'?" he asked and my eyes shifted from his hands moving on me to his in the mirror.

"Less than the extravaganza I treated you to that first night at your apartment. More than the cotton-candy eyelet one," I answered.

He grinned at me. "Cotton-candy eyelet one?"

"The one I wore our first night together."

"The pink one?"

He remembered.

Damn.

He remembered.

"Cotton candy," I corrected softly.

His grin became a smile and for some reason that smile settled in my belly.

He thought I was funny. He thought I was beautiful. He got close anytime I was near. He wanted to stand between me and roaring lions. He wanted to help me battle my ghosts. He had two fantastic sons, a screwy but loving family, a great body, an affectionate manner, and he remembered the color of the nightie I wore our first night together in my bed.

I stared into his smiling, warm, quicksilver eyes in the mirror but I wasn't smiling.

I was searching.

But it was gone.

"It's gone," I whispered. His smile faded and his brows drew together as his arms convulsed tight around me in reaction to my tone.

"What's gone, baby?"

"That poisonous thing in my belly."

I felt his body still against mine as his eyes locked on mine in the mirror. Then I was turned from the mirror and lifted up. Automatically, my limbs wrapped around him as he walked us out of the bathroom, into the bedroom, and he put a knee to the bed, twisted, and I had my head in the pillows and my man on me.

He didn't say a word but his eyes searched my face and I let them.

My search was going to be multisensory.

So my fingers went to his face and moved over his skin, his stubbled jaw and chin, his lips, his temples, his thick eyebrows. Then both hands glided down and wrapped around the sides of his neck where it met his shoulders and my eyes went back to his.

"My wild man," I whispered. "My snake charmer."

He closed his eyes and shoved his face in my neck, groaning, "*Fuck, Tess.*"

I turned my head so my lips were at his ear and no lies, no masks, no bullshit, no games, I kept whispering when I told him, "I love you, Brock."

He growled against my skin then his head came up, his hands slid up the silk at my sides, over my armpits, forcing up my arms. They kept sliding up, up until his fingers laced with mine and he planted them in the pillow above my head.

Then he asked, "My sweet fuckin' Tess, what am I gonna do with you?"

"I'm yours so... anything," I answered.

His fingers clenched mine then his head slanted and he kissed me hard and deep and wet and sweet and, most importantly, un-fucking-believably *beautiful*.

I bucked my back. He let go of my hands, allowed me to roll him and we kept making out with him on bottom, me on top, his hands at my ass.

About that time, as was our luck, a loud knock came at the front door.

My head went up and his fingers dug into my ass as he snarled, "This is fuckin' unbelievable."

He had *that* right.

We waited, frozen in position, and then it came again.

"Fuck," he clipped. One hand left my ass, drove into my hair, and he positioned my face close to his. "Don't want whoever's there to get one of the boys or wake 'em. I'll be back."

I nodded. Brock lifted his head, touched his lips to mine, rolled me off of him, and rolled off the bed. Tagging his jeans off the floor, he pulled them on as another knock came at the door. He tagged his tee off the floor and prowled to the door, yanking it on, jeans still undone.

Damn but my man was hot.

The door closed and I pulled his pillow to me, hugging it close and smiling.

Then I smelled his hair on the pillow. His hair, not cologne, not aftershave, all Brock.

My smile got bigger.

I rolled off the bed, went to the bathroom, and cleaned up, thinking about our upcoming day.

No, thinking how much I was looking forward to our upcoming day.

It was Saturday after Thanksgiving. Brock got the boys yesterday at three. Why Olivia didn't let him have them all day Thursday and Friday considering they had both days off school, I did not know.

Upon asking Brock, his response was to ask back, "Why the fuck does that bitch do anything?"

I had no clue as to the answer to that question but also, at his response, I decided not to prod further.

Since our plans were what they were for that day, I came over last night, made dinner, and spent the night. We were going to see how it went with the boys as to whether I spent the night tonight.

And what we were going to do that day was go out and buy Christmas decorations, a tree, and decorate Brock's tree and house. *Then* we were going to go back out and buy *another* tree and take it to my house and decorate that.

With the boys.

I already had my Christmas decorations out and at the ready.

Double the Christmas.

Double the joy.

I couldn't fucking *wait*.

I rinsed out the washcloth and smoothed it around the edge of the basin. Then I stared at it.

Navy blue, like his sheets, both of which I bought.

My eyes went to my own personal toothbrush in the holder on the wall. Then they went to the shower where my shampoo, conditioner, and bath wash was. I'd noted Brock's brand and bought him shampoo so his was in my shower. He also had a toothbrush at my place.

I leaned forward and opened the medicine cabinet.

My face wash. My body lotion. My moisturizer. My contact lens solution. My deodorant next to Brock's.

I did the same thing with his deodorant, buying his brand and putting it in my medicine cabinet.

This all came about naturally, no words, no discussion. He came to my place and found the stuff then didn't say a word but didn't bother packing it again. He only brought over clothes and when he did, he brought enough to last awhile. I went to his place and saw a new toothbrush in its wrapping on the vanity. A statement. The next time I went over, I stocked his bathroom. He didn't say a word. Nor did he say a word when I brought a big workout bag filled with fashion selections, and as he did in my house, deposited it in a corner and that was where it stayed unless it was scheduled for rotation.

I smiled again.

Yeah, it was gone. That thing in my belly was long gone.

This different kind of wild was a good, safe place to be.

I closed the medicine cabinet, spied my undies on the floor, nabbed them, and slid them on.

I walked into the bedroom thinking Brock had been gone awhile. Maybe he was making coffee. Maybe one of the boys was up.

I considered this dilemma. Then I walked to the nightstand, slid my glasses on my nose, and walked to Brock's closet and selected one of his flannels. Soft, oft-worn, burgundy. I slipped it on and it engulfed me.

Okay, it wasn't a robe but it hid more than most robes and if I saw one of the boys, I could hightail it back to the bedroom and put on clothes.

I rolled back the cuffs and walked out to the landing.

I stopped dead when I heard Brock's clipped, "Jesus, she's in the next fuckin' room, brother."

To that I heard the whispered, but still loud angry words, "So?" Then, "Fuck, Slim, this is the same damned shit as with Bree."

Levi.

But who was Bree?

"Leave it," Brock growled.

"Honest to God you think I'm gonna leave it? You think I'm gonna stand aside, keep my fuckin' mouth shut, and watch you slide over the edge *again*, tied to another woman with a mountain of problems you think you can fix?"

I sucked in a silent breath and put my hand to the wall.

"Levi—"

"No, Slim, fuckin' *no*. You need me to spell it out? I will. Bree got raped. That was tough, man. You know *I know it*. It was ugly, it was brutal. Fuck, Slim, it was *me* who went with you to visit her in the hospital and I saw her, Slim, I fuckin' saw her messed up, jaw wired, teeth gone, eyes swollen shut, bones broken, same as you."

At these words, I closed my eyes but opened them again when Levi kept speaking and his next words also rocked me.

"Then you go gung ho, nearly losin' your job, I might add, pullin' out all the stops to take that motherfucker down. I get that too. Then she finds her way to deal and she does it usin' a needle. She checks *way* the fuck out before she injected too much of that poison and finally *checks out*. What do you do when your ex-fuckin'-girlfriend overdoses? You leave the force and take a job with the fucking Drug Enforcement Agency and no one fuckin' sees you. You're undercover, livin' with the scum of the earth on some wild-ass crusade to turn back time and bring Bree back. Well, man, you can't do that. It isn't *Bree's* ass hangin' out there, 'cause she's dead. It's *yours*. Mom, Jill, and Laura, and, I'll admit, *me*, we all lost sleep with you doin' that job, wonderin' when the call would come."

"Well, now you don't have to lose sleep, Levi," Brock said low.

"No, now we don't. 'Cause sweet Tess and her cakes are in your life now."

I moved closer to the wall of the landing and tried not to hyperventilate.

"Careful," Brock snarled.

"Careful?" Levi asked. "Not even for your own fuckin' *wife*, and I will give it to you, I wouldn't do shit for that bitch either, but not for your own fuckin' *boys* did you leave that job. But Tessa O'Hara with her haunted eyes walks into your life and what do you do?" A pause, then, "No, your answer will be bullshit so don't even say it because you told Laurie and Laurie told me that you knew before you even approached her to see if she'd accept you back in her life that you looked for a way out of the DEA so you could concentrate on her and give her what you didn't give Olivia and you *couldn't* give Bree, seein' as the bitch essentially killed herself and took her time doin' it."

My heart started thumping and my legs started trembling.

Levi kept talking.

"And not only that, you lived in your goddamned place since Olivia took your ass to the cleaners but all of a sudden"—another pause where I visualized him throwing out an arm—"here you are in a sweet condo that sweet Tessa of Tessa's Cakes would find more agreeable. So now you're a homicide detective with a middleclass condo and five months ago you were an agent for the DEA with a death wish but at least you had a fuckin' mission and all that is for *her*. Fuck, I'm lookin' at my brother in his fuckin' kitchen with new fuckin' dishtowels and I don't even know who the fuck he is because he's losin' all that he is, *again*, for another, lost, haunted soul with a great pair of tits."

That was when I moved because it came over me. I didn't know what it was because I'd never felt it before. Nothing like it. But it was there and I had no control of my actions.

I just moved.

And I did it quickly.

So I forged through the abrasive atmosphere of the Lucas brothers' mood and in the middle of Brock growling something low in response, I ran down the stairs, took three long strides, and then ran up the steps to the kitchen.

Brock's eyes came to me, his mouth snapped shut, and
Levi turned in the direction of his brother's stare.

I ignored Levi and launched right in.

"I don't *believe* you," I hissed at Brock.

"Tess—"

I shook my head and made it to him. Planting both
hands in his chest, I gave him a shove. He went back on
a foot, his head jerking in surprise as his hands came up
and clamped on my wrists.

I got close and went up on my toes to get in his face
and snap, "I *told* you I didn't want you to change for me."

His face went soft and he whispered, "Baby—"

"No." I shook my head again, tried to yank my wrists
out of his hold, failed, and gave up. "I don't need you to be
anything but what you are. Hell, when I fell in love with
you I didn't even know your…" I got closer to his face.
"Fucking…" I got even closer. "*Name.*"

He let my wrists go but only for his arms to fix around
me. I pulled at them but he held tight, murmuring, "Tess,
darlin'—"

"Unh-unh, no way, Brock. I don't need a nice apartment where I don't take my life in my hands walking up
the rusty, rickety staircase to get to it. Don't you *see*? I'd
walk through fire if you were what I was walking to."

"Fucking hell," Levi breathed and I watched Brock do
a slow blink but I was in another zone. Totally in pissed-
off la-la land and there was no going back.

"If you had a dangerous job that took you away from
me, it would suck and I'll admit, I would hate it because
I had three months without you and that was enough.
But if it meant something to you, I'd suck it up. I'd *deal*.
Because I'd know you were doing something you believed

in and you'd eventually come back to me so that would be enough for me."

His arms separated, grew tighter, gathering me closer, his eyes so warm they were liquid mercury, and he whispered, "Baby—"

"You can be Brock. You can be Jake. You could call yourself Errol fucking *Flynn* and I wouldn't care because, bottom line, you'd be the man for me. I know from knowing a bad one, the worst, I know a *good* man when I see him and it's important to me to let him be just who he is, not what he thinks I want him to be."

"Tess—"

"No, I—"

"Tess—" he growled.

"No, I'm not done—"

"Tess," he clipped, one arm leaving me so his hand could cover my mouth and his face got in mine. "*Shut it.*"

I glared at him.

He held my glare and stared at me.

Then his eyes started dancing and he asked, "Errol fucking Flynn?"

"This is not fucking funny," I said against his hand so it came out garbled.

He burst out laughing, his hand leaving my mouth to become an arm wrapped tightly around me again and he shoved his laughing face in my neck.

"I'm not finding anything funny, Brock," I told the wall behind him as my hands slid up and put pressure on his shoulders (to no avail).

He lifted his head still chuckling and gave me a squeeze.

Then he asked, "Can you shut up for two minutes so I can talk?"

"Yes, but I'll give you that answer with the warning that you better not say anything that pisses me off or I'm cancelling Christmas."

His body started rocking and his eyes were still dancing but he wisely didn't verbalize his still-obvious hilarity.

"Right," he muttered but it came out sounding choked.

"You have two minutes," I prompted him.

He grinned at me, repeated a muttered, "Right." Then said, "All right, baby, no games, no bullshit, no lies. You called the scene and I've been playin' by your rules. I told you, shit got hot for me with what I did at the DEA and I was facin' a desk. I didn't lie. What I didn't tell you is that I had an option. They were thinkin' of transferring me to LA."

My body grew tight at these words and his arms grew tight with it.

"Now, I got family in Denver. I got kids in Denver. And, yes, *you* are in Denver and my boys are gettin' older. Shit is not right there so I had a decision to make. Bail on all that, leavin' my boys, and yeah, *you* behind or takin' a job with the DPD, doin' something that has less of an opportunity for my dead body to be found in an alley. Or stay here, take care of my sons, and explore things with you. No lie, you know you meant something to me when I was going over my options so you were part of that decision. But I didn't do it to change into what I thought you would want. I did it because it was time."

"Oh, well then," I whispered and he grinned again.

Then he said, "I got that apartment because Olivia worked part time as a medical receptionist when we were married. She wasn't very good at it and doesn't have any other skills except whatever she did to get her bulldog attorney to wring me dry. I didn't fight that too hard because kids get caught up in that shit and I didn't want my boys in the middle of a dirty war between their parents. I also didn't fight because, bottom line, she needed the money to take care of my sons. I lived in a shithole so they wouldn't. I got on my feet since and two years ago she got herself a man where the extra she asked for and I gave her, I stopped givin' her. But I had no time or need to move outta that apartment. In fact, livin' there solidified the cover I was under at the same time it allowed me to set aside a whack. Not havin' that job or crippled by Olivia, I didn't need to live there anymore. It isn't a great place for me to take my woman, for my boys to stay in, but honest to God, babe, I didn't like it either. I got my shot, I moved out. End of story."

Hmm.

Maybe I overreacted.

I didn't share this. I just held his eyes.

His arms gave me another squeeze and his lips twitched.

He knew I knew I overreacted.

Crap.

Then he asked, "Now, I was gonna suggest tomorrow that you go with me and the boys to look at new trucks. My heat doesn't work, the tires need changing, winter's almost here, and any money spent on that truck is the same as burnin' it. So are you gonna have a shit hemorrhage if I buy a new truck?"

"I didn't have a shit hemorrhage," I denied.

His face dipped to mine. "Baby, you flew up here, put your hands on me, and lost your mind. I had to put my hand over your mouth to shut you up. If that isn't a shit hemorrhage, I don't know what is."

Oh man. I did that. I shoved him.

Not good.

"I…" I swallowed. "That wasn't cool, Brock. I don't know what came over me. I shouldn't have shoved you."

His body started rocking again and he shook his head like he didn't know what to do with me. But, luckily, he was shaking it like he thought I was so damned cute, he didn't know what he was going to do with me.

"Darlin'," he said low, "I love that body of yours, all soft, all curves, no way you could take me, even in the middle of one helluva shit hemorrhage and you know it. You didn't do that to hurt me because you know you can't. You did it because you were pissed and wanted my attention. There's a difference."

"It still wasn't good," I whispered.

"You make a habit of it, I agree. You do that often?"

I thought about it. Then I said, "Uh…not to my recollection."

He burst out laughing again.

I glared at him still not finding anything funny.

"Uh…hello," Levi called.

My body grew tight. Brock stopped laughing and his eyes went over my shoulder.

Damn. I totally forgot about Levi.

All humor was void in his tone when Brock announced, "You and me got problems, brother."

Uh-oh.

I turned in Brock's arms and he let one drop but the other one he used to tuck my front in his side and keep me close as I looked to a Levi who had his hands up and his thoughtful hazel eyes were on me.

Then they went to his brother as his hands dropped. "I'm seein' I might have got it wrong."

"You think?" Brock asked sarcastically.

"I was—"

"You were doin' what you do, Levi, mouthin' off without thinkin'. You gave me the two minutes Tess gave me, I woulda told you the same thing I told Tess."

Levi's lips twitched and he reminded his brother, "You had to put your hand over her mouth to get that in there, Slim."

"All right, next time you mouth off and piss me off, I'll let loose the urge to find a way to shut your mouth so I can have my say. Is that good for you?"

Hmm. It appeared even though Levi admitted he was wrong, Brock wasn't going to let it go.

It was time for me to intervene, mainly because we'd lucked out the boys hadn't shown in the middle of this drama and the longer we were at it, the more we courted it.

So I found my mouth saying, "Lenore is in love with you."

Levi had his mouth open to retort to his brother but his head jerked, his mouth snapped shut, and his eyes sliced to me.

Brock's arm around my back gave me a squeeze.

"What?" Levi asked.

"Jesus, fuck," Brock muttered.

I looked up at Brock to see him scanning the ceiling.

Oh well. It was out there.

I looked to Levi.

"Lenore is in love with you," I repeated.

He did a slow blink.

Uncanny, just like his brother.

Then he asked, "Did she tell you that?"

"A girl knows," I informed him.

"A girl knows," he repeated after me.

I shrugged.

He stared at me.

Damn. I had to keep going.

"Okay, well, you'll probably never notice shit like this but her outfit at Thanksgiving... very nice. It suited her. This is good for you if you're, uh..."—I paused, then forged on—"interested in her. She's young but she knows herself, what suits her. A lot of girls struggle with that through their twenties and into their thirties. She's already found her style. That's impressive."

Levi blinked again.

I kept talking.

"Anyway, what I mean to say is, it was very nice but not *too* nice. She wanted to make a good impression, not to be in your face about how pretty she is or what a great body she has. And she's pretty, don't you think?"

His eyes slid to his brother and I kept going.

"Well, of course you do."

His eyes slid back to me.

"You were with her," I went on. "My point is she wanted to make a good impression on your family. She thought Thanksgiving was a move forward in your relationship and it was important to her. But I think it wasn't only that. It was about being part of you, reflecting on you. She wanted your family to like her but she wanted to represent you in a good light to them too. No flashy clothes. No cleavage. Not overboard. Decent and respectable. She cares about you and what your choice of her says about you."

Levi stared at me again.

Then he asked, "You got all that from an outfit?"

"Well..." I hesitated. "Yeah."

Brock's body started rocking again and I looked at him to see he was now staring at his bare feet but he was doing it smiling.

"That doesn't say she's in love with me, Tess," Levi noted and my eyes went back to him.

"No," I agreed. "It says you mean something to her. I knew she was in love with you when you tested me, your whole family got pissed at you, and she closed in on you."

Levi's body went visibly still.

Quietly, I continued. "It was automatic. You were pissed, facing off against the force of the Lucas Brigade, and she didn't move away and leave you hanging and she wasn't afraid of or turned off by your anger. And she also didn't hesitate. She moved right in and had your back."

"Christ," Levi whispered, his eyes glued to me.

"She's sweet. She's thoughtful. She's polite. She has great style. And she's head over heels in love with you," I said softly. "So, if you can't feel that for her, it's not my place to tell you this and I don't mean to offend you, but I'm speaking on behalf of the sisterhood here. You need to let her go so she can find someone who feels about her the way she feels about you."

I held his eyes before he closed his and turned his head away.

Crap.

Well, I was out there so I might as well finish it.

"Levi," I called, waited a moment, then his eyes came back to me. "Again, speaking for the sisterhood, if you gave all that devotion and loyalty to a woman and she was a good woman, I swear, honey, you will live every day for the rest of your life until your dying breath never regretting it."

Brock's arm got super tight, curling me partially into his front while Levi held my gaze.

When he didn't speak, I whispered, "I'm sorry. It wasn't my place."

"No," Levi finally spoke. "You're wrong. Any member of this family has a right to say what they gotta say."

My lips parted, my belly warmed, and I melted into Brock.

"Brother," Brock murmured and Levi looked to him.

He pulled in a breath through his nose.

Then he remarked, "It's good you didn't piss off your little minx, would suck, Christmas getting cancelled."

I grinned.

"She wouldn't do it. Longest Tess has been able to remain pissed at me is five minutes and that was when I came back after she thought I played her when I worked her for the DEA," Brock shared.

"Bodes well for you, Slim," Levi returned.

"Fuck yeah," Brock muttered.

Oh for goodness sakes.

I cut in, asking Levi, "Are you staying for breakfast with the boys or what?"

He looked at me. "What are you making?"

"French toast with caramelized cinnamon apples."

Levi did another slow blink.

"Brock loves it," I informed him when he made no response and continued to stare at me with unconcealed disbelief.

"Uh ... *yeah*. He would," Levi stated, and he looked to Brock. "She cook like this all the time?"

"Man, she owns a bakery," Brock answered.

Levi looked at me. "I'm stayin'."

"Good," I muttered and pulled away from Brock, ordering, "Honey, go wake the boys. I'll start breakfast. The Christmas trees aren't going to march in our houses by themselves and we need to get there early. There's always a rush the weekend after Thanksgiving and we need *two* good trees."

"She always bossy?" Levi asked as I turned to the coffeepot.

"No, she's usually always sweet but Christmas does shit to people," Brock's departing voice replied.

I yanked out the coffeepot, turned to Levi, and rolled my eyes.

He took that in and, sounding just like his brother and nearly as beautiful as when Brock did it, he burst out laughing.

CHAPTER FOURTEEN

You're with Me

Nearly two weeks later...

I PARKED BEHIND Brock's brand-new huge dark-blue GMC, turned off the ignition, exited my car, and headed to the trunk, shivering the minute my body left my warm vehicle and hit the arctic air.

It was Denver. Tomorrow, it could be sixty degrees even in December. But that night it was freezing and the air felt like snow, not to mention the forecast said we were going to get a dump.

Good for the mountains and ski resorts. Bad for Tessa O'Hara.

I loved snow, playing in it, looking at it, making hot cocoa, and reading a book while it was falling outside.

Driving through it... not so much.

I opened the trunk and grabbed the handles of the plethora of parcels in the back, carefully arranging the bags in my grip, bags made awkward due to the copious rolls of Christmas wrap poking out.

I had a weakness for Christmas wrap. In fact, I had a

weakness for any kind of wrap including bows and ribbons.
I gave into this weakness often so I had an entire closet at my
house dedicated to wrapping paper and all its accoutrement.

No joke.

Juggling bags while avoiding poking myself with rolls
of paper, I slammed the trunk using my elbow and headed
to Brock's patio.

When my eyes went there, my brows drew together.

There was a Harley outside the gate. It wasn't Brock's.
It was a Dyna Glide. And anyway, when not in use, Brock
kept his Fat Boy on the patio under a sturdy, custom-made
cover.

Hmm. It appeared Brock had company.

Still juggling bags, I maneuvered myself through the
high, wood patio gate then through the storm door and
front door.

Before I could call a word of greeting, I heard Brock
say low, "Tess."

I knew instantly he wasn't greeting me. It was a warning to halt conversation.

Oh man.

"Hey!" I called, shut the door, and walked into the living room, eyes to the right.

Then I saw them. A Hispanic man and a Native American man on the stools in front of Brock's bar, Brock
standing behind the bar.

My first thought, seeing as I was female and these
thoughts usually took precedence above all others, was
that these guys were hot. Not hot, per se, if you were
talking the average sense of the word. Hot in the Brock
sense of the word, which was to say mouth-watering, off-
the-scales hot.

My second thought was they not only shared hotness quotients with Brock, but both of them in different ways also had the wild man, dangerous man aura.

For some reason, Brock was communing with his brethren and the serious vibe pulsing in the room said it wasn't over beers, war stories, and nostalgically reminiscing about the bitches they'd tagged.

This was something else.

"Hey, babe," Brock rumbled. "This is Hector Chavez and Vance Crowe, friends of mine."

"Hey guys," I greeted.

To this I got a "Yo," from Vance Crowe, the Native American man but the Hispanic man just gave me a chin lift.

Definitely Brock Brethren.

I hefted the bags up over the back of the couch and dumped them on the seat then turned to Brock, pulling off my knit cap, and immediately running my fingers through my hair in an effort to fix or hide any possible hat head. "You need me to find something to do in the bedroom?"

"No." He shook his head and said softly, "Come up here, darlin'."

Damn.

Just as I thought, that something else had to do with me and/or it was not good news.

My eyes did a sweep through the male talent in my man's kitchen and I found myself having the curious reaction that not a lot of females would have. That was that I would rather go out, get in my car, and track down Martha and Elvira to drink cosmos than take off my coat and join the three best looking men I'd seen in my life in my man's kitchen.

Regardless of that, I nodded, unbuttoned my coat, and took it to the hall closet that separated the downstairs to the boys' rooms with the upstairs to the kitchen. I hung it up and headed into the kitchen.

The moment I got near, as usual, Brock claimed me with an arm around my waist, pulling my front to his side, and I noted all the boys had bottles of Bud.

"You want a beer?" Brock asked and I looked from the counter to him.

"I was thinking hot cocoa."

He grinned but he didn't commit to it. I knew this because it didn't reach his eyes and it didn't hit the room.

Damn again.

"What's up?" I asked quietly.

"Some shit went down today, babe," he answered.

Crap.

"What shit?" I asked.

He looked to his brethren then back down at me. "Olivia got the letter from my lawyer."

I found this confusing or, more to the point, this reaction confusing.

Brock had contacted an attorney and, using his change of career circumstances as an excuse, he was approaching Olivia to see if they could agree a joint custody schedule. The boys with Brock one week, back with Olivia and Dade the next.

In my mind, there were two possible reactions to this from Olivia. Relief that she could continue with her spa visits and shopping and whatever else she did during her days unhindered by the responsibility of her boys being around most of the time. Or anger just because she was a bitch.

Brock, being Brock, had to have prepared for either eventuality.

"And?" I prompted.

"And she phoned me."

"Okay," I said when he said no more.

"And when she phoned me, she asked if we could meet, have dinner. She told me she's close to leavin' Dade and she's scared. She hasn't worked in over two years, she signed an iron-tight prenup, has no money of her own, isn't in a position to set up again and take care of the boys, and certainly not in the position to hire an attorney to deal with me. She reiterated she wants to discuss our situation, the boys' situation, our family situation, and the possibility of reconciliation."

I felt my mouth get tight. Then I felt Brock's arm give me a squeeze.

"I said no, babe," he told me. "I told her that wasn't a possibility. I've moved on, that move from her is permanent and at this juncture in our lives, we need to talk through our attorneys."

My mouth relaxed.

"Then I got a call from Rex," he went on and I blinked. He kept talking. "Rex was freaked, said his mom picked them up from school and she was a mess. Cryin', carryin' on, told them what I was doin'. Told them she was leavin' Dade. Told them she was scared. Told them me bein' with you meant we'd never have a family again. And told them she didn't know what she was gonna do. He called when they got home and told me, even after they got home she was still cryin' and carryin' on, and she was. I could hear her in the background."

My mouth again got tight.

Through stiff lips, I whispered, "You're kidding me."

"Nope."

"Damn." I was still whispering. Then I asked, "What'd you do?"

"What could I do?" he asked back. I read it as the warning sign it was when his arm got tight, his body turned slightly into mine, his eyes locked with mine, and I braced. "I hauled my ass over there and calmed her down by promising to have dinner with her."

Fuck! Fuck! *Fuck!*

I pressed my lips together and looked at the counter.

"Baby." Another arm squeeze and I looked back up at him. "This is a minefield. I gotta go slow and cautious. That's why Hector's here."

I stared up at him in confusion then looked to Hector, still in confusion. My gaze went back to Brock when he started speaking again.

"Hector worked with me at the DEA. He now works for Lee Nightingale. Lee's got an operation, bounty hunting, some security, private investigation. I got enough on my plate and Hector owes me a favor. I'm callin' it."

"You're calling it?"

"Yeah. I'm havin' dinner with Olivia and we'll talk. But this shit, it's the last straw. Draggin' the boys into this, cryin' and carryin' on, freaking out Rex, plantin' shit in their heads about you. And when I got there Joey was freaked too. Said she was drivin' crazy, flipped them both out, and it didn't get better when she continued her drama back at the house."

Mouth tight, he shook his head and continued speaking.

"I am not down with that shit. I'm so not down with it, I'm done with it. I'm not goin' for joint custody. I'm going

for full. And to go for full, I gotta have shit to back that
play. Hector'll find it. Somethin' on Dade, somethin' on
Olivia." He pulled in a breath and said, "Sorry, sweetness,
but in the meantime, I gotta play her game. I want my
move to be a surprise, I want her scrambling, and, bottom
line, I want my kids. I'm willin' to do just about anything
to see that happen and I'm gonna need to ask you to ride
that out with me."

Immediately, I nodded.

He took in my nod and smiled. This one reached his
eyes.

That smile died and he said softly, "Somethin' else
happened today."

Fuck!

"What?"

He hesitated, studying me.

"Brock, honey," I pressed into him, "what?"

"You remember I told you that I knew in my gut Heller
was poising to strike?"

Oh no.

"Yes," I whispered.

"He's poising to strike."

"Oh God," I breathed.

"Good news is, with my old job, got contacts, infor-
mants, friends, folks who owe me. Had a call from one
who says Heller's been askin' a lot about me. Diggin'
deep. So I made a few more calls and found out he's in my
business, financials, credit history, work history."

My brows drew together. "Why would he do that?"
Then I asked, "*How* could he do that? Isn't that stuff
confidential?"

"You want it bad enough and you got the money then

you got the means to do just about anything, find someone who can or buy someone who'll talk."

This made sense.

"Okay then, *why* would he do that?"

"That, I don't know. That's why Vance is here." I looked to Vance and back at Brock when he kept going. "He works for Lee too and he doesn't owe me. I'll owe him but he's gonna nose around and see what he can learn so I can prepare for whatever Heller's planning."

This should have pissed me off.

It didn't.

It scared me.

And it scared me because that night Brock threatened Damian, Damian decided to take Brock down a peg. He might be facing serious jail time but that wouldn't matter to him. Brock had not only threatened him; he'd shut the door in his face then he stood in my living room at my window and waited until Damian did what he was told, something Damian wouldn't take kindly in a serious way. And last, but not least, he stood between Damian and what Damian wanted.

I knew from experience that Damian could play dirty, mean, and as nasty as nasty could be to get what he wanted. He might be looking into Brock but if he didn't find anything, which he wouldn't, then he'd still find a way to fuck with Brock's life. And fucking with Brock was fucking with me, fucking with Rex and Joel at a time when that situation was tenuous at best, and fucking with Brock's family, who I'd come to care about and were in the throes of their own turmoil.

But, bottom line, first and foremost, he'd be fucking with Brock.

And I couldn't allow that.

So I made a decision.

"I need to make a statement to him," I announced.

"Come again?" Brock asked, and automatically my hand fisted in his flannel but I didn't notice it.

"Tomorrow," I whispered, "I'll go into the station with you and I'll press charges against Damian. Assault, battery, and rape."

The room filled with crackling electricity that snapped vicious against my skin.

And this wasn't coming from Brock.

It was then I remembered we had an audience and I looked to the men at his bar.

At what I read on their faces, I tensed.

Uh-oh.

"Sweet Tess," Brock murmured, but I couldn't tear my eyes away from the men at the bar and Brock kept talking, "I didn't share. They didn't know."

I closed my eyes tight, turned my head to face his chest, and clenched his shirt harder.

Damn, now *I* was blurting that shit out willy-nilly.

I felt Brock's big, warm hand over mine at his shirt, pushing in hard so I had no choice but to unclench and he pressed my hand flat to his chest as he whispered, "Hey."

I pressed my lips together and continued to scrunch my eyes closed.

He gave me an arm squeeze.

"Baby, hey."

I opened my eyes and tilted them up to him.

He looked into my eyes and a shadow passed through his.

"Look at me," he said gently.

"I am," I whispered.

"No, sweetness, *look at me.* What do you see?"

I felt my throat clog.

"Don't go there. Stay here with me," he urged softly. I swallowed and he pulled me closer, dipping his face lower. "I took that away, baby. You gave it to me. Don't go there. Don't take that weight back. Look at me, see me. Feel this," he demanded gently, his arm tightening further, pulling me even closer, his hand pressing mine into the warm, hard wall of his chest. "Where are you?"

"I'm with you," I said quietly.

"Yeah, Tess, you're with me."

I held his eyes for a moment then closed mine and did a face-plant in his chest.

The fingers of his hand at mine curled around tight.

"This is free," I heard growled. I opened my eyes and turned them in the direction the words came from and saw Vance's infuriated gaze locked on Brock. "No marker. This I do for your woman."

I felt my belly tighten with shock as my fingers wrapped hard around Brock's at his shirt.

"I work that angle too," Hector announced and my eyes shot to him to see he, too, had his furious, dark eyes locked on Brock.

"Uh..." I mumbled but they were on the move.

"You see to your woman and your boys," Vance declared. "We'll get to work."

Um.

Wow.

I didn't know them, like at all, outside of the fact they were hot. But I liked them.

"Appreciated," Brock muttered.

They tore their eyes from Brock and looked at me.

"Tess, next time, hope it's better circumstances," Vance said to me.

I did too.

"Thanks," I whispered.

Hector, who didn't know me either, wasn't done being pissed on my behalf and therefore he scowled at me. Then he jerked up his chin at Brock and they moved to the steps. Brock let me go to start moving with them.

"Uh..." I called. They stopped and looked back at me. "I, um...own Tessa's Cakes in Cherry Creek."

They just looked at me.

"Uh, well, you boys look like you aren't cupcake eaters"—more like rib eyes grilled blue—"but, you know, if you're ever in the mood, come in, anything you want on the house for, like, eternity."

It was lame but then again, my cakes were really good. Maybe they wouldn't think it was lame.

They didn't. Vance's handsome face split into a shit-eating grin. Hector's dark eyes melted, his lips twitched then he gave me a glamorous white smile.

Brock chuckled.

"And, uh..." I started to add, "whichever one of you is on that bike, that bike is hot but be careful. Snow's coming."

"Will do, Tess," Vance murmured.

I got more chin lifts and they headed back out.

Moving on!

I headed to the fridge and was perusing options for dinner when I heard and felt Brock come back.

Determinedly setting the mood that what had just passed had passed and now we were going to get back to regularly scheduled programming that did not include bitchy, manipulative ex-wives or vicious, nasty, territorial ex-husbands, I stated, "Dinner choices, steak and potatoes, pork chops and rice, or hamburgers."

I pulled my head out of his fridge, closed the door, and turned to Brock.

He was leaning his hips against the counter, hands to his sides, palms to its top, studying me.

Then he gave me my play and answered, "Pork chops and rice."

I nodded, opened the fridge, and pulled out the package of pork chops. I dropped it on the counter and opened the cupboard to pull out the box of seasoned rice.

"What's with the bags?" Brock asked as I tilted my head down to study the directions on the rice.

"Christmas presents," I answered. "The boys get here tomorrow and the area under the tree is a little barren. Tree skirts are not meant to be barren, especially in a house with two boys aged ten and twelve. So tonight I'm wrapping and tomorrow they'll get here and see presents under the tree."

"Babe, how much did you buy them? There's gotta be twenty rolls of wrapping paper there."

"Something to learn about me," I muttered to the box. "I have a weakness for wrapping paper and not just the Christmas kind."

This was met with silence.

Until, "Babe, forgot to tell you something."

I looked from reading the directions on the box of rice to Brock to see he had hauled himself up on the counter and was sitting on it.

"Yeah?" I asked hesitantly.

"Coupla weeks ago, you gave me a fuckin' sweet nightie and words I loved hearing."

I felt my entire body go still as I held his eyes.

"Forgot to mention I feel the same," he stated and my insides hollowed out.

"What?" I breathed.

"Put down the rice and come here, baby. I wanna tell you I love you when you're in my arms."

I didn't move. I stared at him, my internal organs gone, but still my body managed to produce tears that gathered in my eyes and promptly and silently slid down my cheeks.

Brock watched this for about two seconds then he whispered, "Tess, darlin', come here."

I went there. He opened his thighs and reached out to me when I got close. He pulled me between his legs, deep into him, one arm tight around me, one hand cupping my head and pressing my cheek against his chest. I wrapped my arms around his waist and held on.

He dipped his head so his lips were at the top of my hair and whispered, "I love you, my sweet Tess."

A soft sob hitched in my throat. I held on tighter and pressed deeper.

"Jesus, my girl, so fuckin' sweet," he murmured against my hair.

Another hitch and I tilted my head back, his came up, and I pulled an arm from around him, lifted it, curled my hand around his neck, and pulled his mouth down to mine.

Then I kissed him as hard as I could, trying to show him how much his words meant to me.

I was guessing this worked when he tore his lips from mine and muttered, "Maybe I don't love you. Maybe I just love your mouth."

I grinned up at him.

"And your cunt," he went on.

My grin got bigger.

"And your cupcakes," he added.

I started giggling and he smiled.

Then he whispered, "No, it's just you."

I stopped giggling, stared into his quicksilver eyes then dipped my chin and did another face-plant in his chest.

He held me close, arm around me, hand at my head becoming fingers sifting through my hair.

After a while, I sighed, lifted a hand to my face, swiped away the wet, and muttered, "Let me go, baby. I gotta feed my man."

His hand stopped sifting through my hair and both arms wrapped around me tight.

Then he let me go.

I moved away and got down to the business of feeding my man.

*   *   *

I sucked back the dregs of the hot cocoa and then moved on my hands and knees across the floor, dragging boxes with me to arrange the newly wrapped presents under the tree. Then I cleaned up paper scraps, put away scissors and tape, bunched up and folded bags and tucked them away, and stowed the rolls of Christmas wrap, ribbons, and bows in the hall closet.

Through this, Brock lay on his back on the couch, head to a pile of toss pillows, one hand behind his head, one resting on his abs, eyes on a game on television.

I approached the back of the couch, put my ass to it, turned, whipped my legs over while straightening, and, at the last minute, announced, "Incoming." Then I dropped full body on his.

He grunted and his body jerked on impact then his arms wrapped around me.

"Jesus, babe," he muttered, humor in his tone, that sweet hum filling the air.

I slid off, my back to the couch, my front pressed to his side. I rested a cheek to his chest, arm around his abs, and settled in.

Brock moved a hand back to his abs but his other arm stayed curved around my waist, hand at my hip.

I watched football I didn't give a shit about but I did it contentedly because it was late, I was tired, my mind needed to shut down, and the beautiful man who loved me who I loved back was stretched out beside me.

At a commercial, I heard and felt Brock rumble, "What'd you get 'em?"

Hmm. Apparently the game took all his attention, considering the fact that I spent the last forty-five minutes on the floor right in front of him wrapping presents that I did not in any way try to hide.

"Nerf stuff," I answered.

"Nerf stuff?" he asked.

"When you were out running before we went to look at trucks that last Sunday you had them, I asked them to write a letter to Santa and they did," I informed him.

"Babe, hate to break this to you but they're ten and twelve. They know there's no Santa Claus."

I lifted my head and looked down at him. "Yeah, I know. But they aren't stupid. They humored me because they know I have a credit card."

Brock's body shook slightly and pleasantly against mine with his chuckle and I smiled at him.

Then I settled back in.

"What do you usually do for your nieces and nephews?" I asked the TV screen.

"I give their moms fifty dollars for each kid and they put my name on a card."

My head jerked up as my eyes shot to him.

Then I asked a horrified, "What?"

"You think fifty dollars is too much?" he asked back.

"No. I think their uncle should buy them presents that he's put some thought into."

"Darlin', the last time I walked into a mall was two presidents ago."

I stared at him in shock.

Then I asked, "Is that even possible?"

"I got a dick and I was single so, yeah, it's possible."

"So how do you buy the boys presents?"

"Four options, give a wad of cash to Mom, Jill, Laura, or all three."

I stared again.

Then I asked, "Where do you buy clothes?"

"I don't. I got a mom and two sisters. I get them for Christmas and my birthday."

"T-shirts?"

"I don't get my tees at a mall, Tess. No decent tee can be bought at a fuckin' mall. A good tee is bought during an experience."

I had to admit, this was true. When I went the way of tee and jeans just months ago, I'd done copious research with Brock's tees as my guide and I'd found no tee in any store that was even close to the cool tees he owned.

"Boots?" I kept at him.

"Harley store, babe, doesn't count."

This was also true. The Harley-Davidson store was one of those rare and exceptional experiences where women and men could go and enjoy but in entirely different ways. Therefore, considering it was an experience, it was acceptable to buy tees there.

That and Harley tees were freaking awesome.

"And, Tess, sweetness," he went on, "before you get any ideas . . . you wanna shop for my family, have at it. But I'm not breakin' my streak."

Hmm. Dylan, Grady, and Ellie, no problem, especially Ellie. The adults, again, not a problem.

There were only two problems.

"I barely know Kalie and Kellie," I reminded him.

"Kalie, anything with fringe, a peace sign, or a fair trade logo. Kellie, don't bother with anything other than a gift certificate unless it's the absolute trendiest shit among teenagers," he advised.

Well, he didn't shop but that didn't mean he couldn't be thoughtful.

Brock continued, "Keep the receipts, put both our names on the card, and I'll pay you back."

"I—" I started and his arm gave me a squeeze.

"Receipts. Payback," he grunted.

It was in that moment I got what Elvira said weeks before about Vic at Ada's party.

Vic needed to man up.

If a man had a line you didn't cross, he told you. He did it straight out, honestly, and made his point clear, like Brock just did.

Clearly, Gwen and Cam had men like that and, now, I

had one. Brock wanted Christmas to come from us. He was fine with me buying it and wrapping it but he was going to pay for it. I knew by his tone that this was a point I didn't argue. For whatever reason, it meant something to him. And for that reason, whatever it was, it meant something to me to give it to him without mouthing off about something that, in the end, was a decent trade-off.

Therefore, I whispered, "All right."

He held my eyes. Then his went to the TV while his mouth twitched.

Whatever.

I settled back in.

Twenty minutes later, the game ended, Brock's arm tightened and he rolled us both. Stretching out an arm, he tagged the remote on the coffee table. The TV went blank, he dropped the remote then he settled back in but pulled me partially onto his front and up so my face was close to his.

Mm. It appeared we'd arrived at my favorite part of the day.

"You good?" he asked and I blinked.

"Sorry?"

"Earlier, all that shit, you good?"

Damn. It appeared we hadn't arrived at my favorite part of the day.

"Yeah," I told him.

"Okay, babe, no," he said, his face serious. "I get why you want to make that play and you were raw earlier so I let you make it then but you gotta know, I don't like that you're makin' *any* play. Olivia is gonna be in our lives and I don't like that for me, so I really don't like it for you. Not to mention, full custody is a fuckuva lot different than joint. That works out for me, it means you get me and two boys. I gotta know you're cool with that."

"Brock, I'm cool with it."

"Convince me," he ordered and I stared at him.

Here we go again. This was important (obviously) and he told me straight out. No game playing, no lies, no avoidance, no subterfuge. This meant something to him (again, obviously) and I had to share.

So I told him, "I wanted kids."

It was then he started staring at me.

Then I shared, "Around the time we were ready to go for it, Damian started hitting me."

Brock closed his eyes.

I kept speaking.

"He thought I went off The Pill. I hid it from him and kept taking it."

Brock opened his eyes.

"You've got two great sons," I said softly. "And I lost my shot. So I'm never going to be a mom. I came to terms with that a while ago. Not easy terms but I had no choice. Something else I allowed Damian to take away from me. But this keeps being as good as it is, I have the shot to be a damned good stepmom and if that comes with four days a month or every other week or every day, I don't really care."

I settled deeper into him and kept sharing.

"I had a good stepmom, honey, so I have a good role model. Donna was awesome. She and Dad didn't have any kids because he was sick. He never knew for sure where that disease would take them and he didn't want to leave Donna alone to raise a child and he didn't want to do that *to* a child because he watched my sister and me deal. So she poured the love she'd have had for her kids into my sister and me. I love her. We're still close. She means the world to me. So, if my life with you comes with them, since I love you and I'm falling in love with them, however that comes about, it makes me happy."

His hand slid into my hair, his eyes got soft, and his mouth murmured, "Tess."

"Convinced?" I asked.

One side of his lips tipped up. "Yeah."

"Good," I whispered.

I studied his relaxed face and took in a soft breath.

Okay, since we were having a serious conversation, I decided we might as well continue to have it and also address something Brock and I had not addressed since it happened.

In preparation, I slid my hand up his chest to his neck, wrapped my fingers around, and relaxed my body fully into his before I asked softly, "Will you tell me about Bree?"

His fingers tensed on my hip and he asked back, "How much did you hear?"

"Not sure, but at a guess?" He nodded. "Most of it."

He stared at me. Then he muttered, "Right."

"It wasn't cool to eavesdrop it was just—"

"Babe, with Levi, fuck, with my entire family, you'd hear it one way or the other and bein' with me, you'd learn it eventually, so it doesn't matter."

"I won't eavesdrop again," I promised and his hand gave me another squeeze.

"Darlin', we get to the point where we're keepin' anything from each other, we got problems. This is not me and Olivia, where she'd go shoppin', hide shit in the closet, and I wouldn't find out we were maxed on our credit cards until I got the statements and learned she was dedicated to the mission of memorizing every square foot of Cherry Creek Mall. And this is not you and that ass clown where you gotta protect yourself by hidin' somethin' as important as takin' birth control. This is you and me. Eavesdropping is not an available option 'cause to make this real and make that real rich, it's gotta all hang out."

I liked that. A whole lot.

So I whispered, "Okay."

"Okay," he whispered back, then said, "I asked Bree out the first day of her freshman year, my sophomore year of high school. She said yes and we were tight from that day on. She was tight with me and she was tight with my family."

I nodded.

Brock kept talking.

"I got a scholarship to U of A to play baseball. She followed me down there. But she was close with her family and mine and her friends up here. She didn't last. She hated Arizona, not because of Arizona, because she missed home. Her sophomore year, she transferred to UC. We thought it'd be cool. We survived the long distance thing my freshman year in Arizona; we figured we'd make it a couple more years. We didn't. By Christmas, I'd met someone else and realized I was not the kind of man who was not going to taste the variety of flavors life had on offer. Because of that, I also realized what I had with Bree was more about history and friendship than what it takes to make the long haul. I came home, talked to her about it, she was not in that place and wasn't happy about it but she had no choice. I was done."

Oh man. Harsh.

Honest, but harsh.

I pulled in a breath but kept quiet and Brock continued.

"I went back after Christmas and so did she. She got it about a month later." He grinned. "I got good taste and she was seriously fuckin' pretty. Available for the first time since she hit the dating game, she had 'em eatin' out of her hands. She enjoyed the fuck outta that. She connected with me in the summer when we were both home and told me she got it. I was pleased as fuck. She was a good friend and I missed her. Our relationship changed and it got better 'cause, like I said, she was a great friend and she was damn fun to be around. We had good times. We still had each other's families. It worked."

I nodded again.

Brock kept on with his story and I knew we were hitting the hard part when his eyes got dark.

"She had an older cousin and when I say that, he was a second cousin nearly old enough to be her father. Like my family, hers was close. I knew them all and I did not like this fuckin' guy's vibe, never did. Bree was immune to it. To her, family was family even if they were weird, nuts, or off. That was the kinda heart she had. She let everyone in and didn't ask questions."

Oh man.

"By this time, I was out of school, went to the Academy, and was an officer with the DPD workin' toward detective. She had graduated, workin' full time but still goin' to school at night to get her master's degree. One night, he shows outta the blue, and she lets him in."

"Brock," I whispered when that darkness in his eyes intensified and his fingers dug into my flesh and didn't loosen. "Maybe you should stop."

"Can you handle it?" he asked.

"If you need me to," I answered.

"That ain't a good answer, sweetness."

"Then, yes, I can handle it."

He examined my face. Then his fingers loosened.

He carried on. "He fucked her up, Tess. We're talkin' bad and that shit's bad anytime but hers was worse. Violated her and laid her out. Beat the fuckin' shit outta her before he raped her and he didn't do it once. He spent all night with her and did it repeatedly. She was so fucked up, she reported it took her half an hour to crawl to the phone after he was gone. She was in a hospital bed two weeks. This guy fucked her up and this guy was fuckin' *whacked*. When I got him and we finally got his DNA, it showed Bree was his fifth or at least she was the fifth who reported it."

"Oh my God," I whispered and he nodded.

"Compulsion," Brock told me. "Uncontrollable. That was why he fucked up and went after family. In interrogation, they broke him. He'd had his eye on her for fuckin' years, beat it back. That night, whatever broke in him broke and he couldn't beat it back anymore."

"So," I said hesitantly, "*you* got him?"

He nodded. "Wasn't my case 'cause I didn't have cases. I was still in uniform. Levi and I went to go see her, took some time 'cause her fuckin' jaw was wired shut, but she finally got out the basics of what went down and I took leave because he'd gone to ground and they couldn't find him. He knew he fucked up. He was in hiding, preparin' to bolt. I hunted him down and we'll just say when I found him, I did not exactly follow procedure."

Damn.

"You hurt him," I whispered.

"Remember what I said to you about what I wanted to do with Heller?"

I nodded.

"I did that to him and I did it in a way I know he still hasn't forgotten me. And the DPD frowned on that. I was suspended and it was investigated. I didn't fuckin' care. It was worth it to me then and it's worth more to me now, even though, then and now, I knew I fucked up."

"They didn't fire you," I noted.

"No, don't know why. They should have. What I did weakened their case. What I did made it so his case mighta been thrown out and it was iron tight with his DNA matching multiple samples and women making solid IDs. What I did fucked those cases too. But they didn't can my ass and the case didn't get tossed because it didn't go to trial. Family pressure, he confessed to all five. His confession swung good my way and since the case didn't get fucked, with me, they said extenuating circumstances. I had a good record, I was a good cop, and my captain had taken to me, saw in me that I'd have a good career so he took my back and so did some brothers on the force."

He took in a deep breath. I silently waited for him to release it and continue.

"Everyone knew who she was to me, they knew what he did to her, and, right or wrong, all of them, someplace inside them, knew the same thing happened to someone they gave a shit about, they'd either do what I did or consider it. They still gave me shit work, put me at a desk, and this is why I know desk work is not for me. I worked my way outta that shit and back on the beat. Then to detective."

His jaw went hard and I again silently waited for him to release it before he kept talking.

"Through this, Bree went off the rails and then she went down. Heroin. OD. Everyone, including me, tried to pull her outta that shit. We couldn't. Watchin' her descend into that world was like a form of torture, not only watchin' her but watchin' her mom and dad and sisters watch her while bustin' their asses and failin' to get her straight. Don't know how many times I was called in 'cause she was in a holding cell, strung out, dazed, not even knowin' where the fuck she was and that she was pulled in for solicitation on a sweep. Too fucked up even to be smart enough to avoid getting arrested no matter how many times it happened. Suckin' cock for twenty dollars so her pimp would keep her supplied. The last time I saw her breathing, I barely recognized her."

Oh God, *God*.

"Honey," I said gently.

"It was fucked, Tess."

"Yes, it was, baby," I whispered. "So you decided to do something about it and moved to the DEA?" I ventured cautiously.

He closed his eyes and drew a breath in his nose.

I waited.

Then he opened his eyes.

"She was my first," he said quietly, his voice thick and I pressed closer. "I still loved her, Tess. Not the same as when we started but she was a big part of my life. Does somethin' to a man to have that kind of person in his life, to be able to laugh with her about shit that went down when you were fifteen and have her end like that."

His fingers tensed deeper and his voice dipped lower.

"She was the first to go down on me, to take my cock, and to think she sold the beauty she had to give for dope burned out my insides. She was the first woman to tell me she loved me. She shared her dreams with me, Tess. What she wanted to do, where she wanted to go, how many kids she wanted to have. At one time in our lives, we talked about those things in a way we thought we'd be sharin' them. So, yeah, I was driven to do something about it. But Levi was wrong. He didn't see her in a holding cell. He didn't see all she turned out to be. I knew she was gone before she was gone. I let her go way before that and I did that for my own peace of mind because I already nearly lost my career and fucked over four other girls who needed justice gettin' too tied to what happened to her and not makin' smart decisions."

His fingers in my hair twisted gently but the clouds in his eyes didn't part as he went on.

"I didn't do what I did on a crusade to bring her back. I did what I did because Bree isn't the only girl out there with family who loves them and old boyfriends who give a shit facin' that life and someone had to help them. So I decided that someone would be me."

At that, it swelled inside me, so huge and so fast, I couldn't stop myself from blurting, "I love you."

"I know," he replied.

"No," I shook my head and got close. "I *love* you, Brock Lucas."

His eyes lost that darkness and his hand in my hair slid down and curled around my neck.

"Baby," he murmured.

"What you did, you saved a lot of girls," I whispered fiercely.

"I know."

"That's beautiful," I told him.

"Tess—"

"And that's her legacy as well as yours," I stated.

He stared at me.

I kept talking.

"You cared about her that much to do what you did for others. It was you doing it, putting yourself out there. But it was how you felt about her that pushed you to do it and she was the kind of person who made you feel that deeply so she gets that part. She died tragically but her death meant something to the futures of a lot of other people and that's beautiful."

"I never thought of it like that," he said quietly.

"Well, start," I ordered.

He looked into my eyes a moment, then started chuckling.

"Shit, babe, when'd you start gettin' bossy?"

"Christmas. It does shit to people," I answered and his chuckling got louder.

Then he asked, "We done pourin' out our hearts?"

"For now," I replied and he smiled again.

His smile faded, a warm, sultry feeling filled the room, his eyes dropped to my mouth and his fingers pressed into my neck.

Then he muttered, "All right, then let's go to bed."

I stared into quicksilver eyes that were staring at my mouth. The eyes of the man who loved me. The eyes of a wild, rough, beautiful man who I knew but the proof had just been laid out for me felt exceptionally deeply and had an endless capacity for loyalty. And I didn't protest.

Not that I was going to anyway.

CHAPTER FIFTEEN

Unexpected Company

One month later...

IT WAS SATURDAY and Brock had just gone out for a run, his weekend with his boys having been interrupted by them being invited to a party that they were at right this moment. He was set to return, shower then take off and get them and I wasn't going to see him again until Sunday night as he intended to have "a talk" with them (in quotes because it was going to be heavy) about all that was going down.

While he was gone, I was putzing around in my kitchen.

It was my first full day off since two weeks before Christmas because Tessa's Cakes had been a madhouse and it was all hands on deck.

The good news about this was, I could afford more nighties.

The other good news about this was, when I pulled myself out of bed every day and dragged my ass home every night arriving late, exhausted, only to face Christmas crap (cards, wrapping presents I ducked out from work to buy or ran around the malls to get on the way home—we'll just say my Christmas spirit took a hit), Brock didn't like it much and told his mother about it. So of course she told her daughters about it.

So I got a visit at the bakery from Jill with Kalie and Kellie in tow and both girls were looking for jobs (Kalie, to buy Christmas presents and also to aid her goals in helping to save the world as well as for college, Kellie to buy Christmas presents and then continue to work her way to top fashionista of the sophomore class) and they wanted to work at Tessa's Cakes.

I hired them on the spot.

They were still on the payroll working some evenings and weekends, and although business had slowed, it was not by much. They were godsends, considering they were punctual, understood customer service, were hard workers, didn't like to be bored, and were hilarious. Kellie was even learning how to decorate cakes.

In other words, they were two of the reasons I could finally have a day off.

The bad news about this was, I was overworked, exhausted, and my Christmas spirit had been drained out of me. Not to mention, I didn't have it in me to stay on the ball with all that was happening around me.

Therefore, I pretty much didn't know what was happening around me because Brock locked himself straight into protective mode and told me not to worry about that shit. Instead focus on the bakery and Christmas.

And I probably shouldn't have taken him up on that but I did.

It wasn't really true that I had no days off. I had Christmas and New Year's off. But neither of these were days off, as such, considering the activity levels.

First, Mom was taking a long visit, enjoying an Australian summer with my sister, there Thanksgiving through the New Year, so I had to be up at an ungodly hour to get their Skype.

Then Brock only got the boys for half a day on both days and half that time needed to be spent having Christmas lunch/New Year's dinner at his mother's house, the other half at his pad. Then they had to get back home. So we were running around most of the day and I was doing my damnedest to make them good days for the boys because Olivia was still filling their head with garbage about me. They were visibly confused, worried about the state of affairs, worried about their dad, and struggling with loyalty to their mom in how they dealt with me.

So, suffice it to say, even protected from that shit by Brock, it still leaked in and I had also descended from really not liking Olivia to pretty much hating her.

Brock had had two dinners with Olivia since the first drama (yes, *two*, the bitch). This did not fill me with joy but luckily I was too exhausted to build up any emotion about it because that emotion would probably not have been pleasant and Brock came home from both dinners looking like he wanted to rip someone's head off, so I needed to look after my man.

In other words, just like Elvira warned, Olivia was playing every game in the book, not listening to a word Brock said, and that situation had not gone away.

Though, that said, after dinner number two, Brock came home not only looking like he wanted to rip someone's head off but also declaring, "That's it, done with that shit," which I suspected meant dinner number three would happen when hell froze over.

This was also part of the reason for "the talk" with his boys this weekend.

I had no clue what Damian was doing and Brock didn't fill me in. I figured my man was honest enough with me that he would tell me if there was something I needed to know. So I kept my head down and did what he told me to do, focused on what I needed to be doing, and that was not lapsing into a coma.

So right then, due to pure habit, I was in my kitchen thinking for the first time in my life if I saw a cake I'd scream.

And thus I was also realizing that I hadn't had a vacation in over a year and I was wondering, since Brock hadn't been in his job too long, if he could get a week off and we could go to a beach somewhere.

When my mind skidded into this thought, it moved onto other thoughts of beaches, water, tropical drinks that tasted like liquid candy, and the fact that local fashion dictates would mean for the vast majority of time Brock would be in nothing but swim trunks.

This was what was pleasantly occupying my mind when a knock came at the door.

My pleasant thoughts evaporated, I looked at the door, and my first instinct was to run downstairs and hide in the guest room.

Another knock came and I heard Martha shout, "Tess! I know you're in there because I can see your car and *his* new fancy-ass truck! Open up!"

Oh man.

Martha was on a tear.

I sucked in a breath, reconsidering the guest room and instead considering escaping out the back.

Then, because it was Martha, I walked to the door.

I opened it to see Martha plus Elvira as well as another black woman with tawny eyes and an enormous afro that had to have its own zip code and they were all accompanied by a woman who, at first glance, I would have sworn was Dolly Parton.

After blinking, I saw she was younger but she still had the masses of fabulous platinum hair, enormous bosoms, and she was wearing skintight stonewash (yes, *stonewash*) from shoulders to toes (including platform boots made of stonewash). The entirety of this was adorned with what looked like a layer of glitter, not to mention a heavy array of rhinestones decorating the shoulders and down the front of her jeans jacket.

Whoa.

"You exist," Martha snapped and my eyes moved from Dolly to her.

"Hey," I said softly.

Suffice it to say, with my life as crazy as it was, I didn't have time for Martha except for some random texts and quick phone calls.

And suffice it to say, Martha wasn't down with that.

She pushed in and her posse pushed in with her, Elvira giving me a wide-eyed look that spoke volumes and those volumes were that I needed to brace because Martha was on a tear.

She didn't have to warn me. I'd known Martha a long time. I knew before I even opened the door.

Damn.

I closed the door behind them, turned, and trailed them

as Martha made a beeline to my kitchen, introducing, "This is Shirleen and Daisy. They're friends of Elvira and Gwen's. Gwen met Shirleen during her thingamabob and with Shirleen came Daisy and with Gwen came Elvira and with Elvira comes me and now we're all here."

I looked to Shirleen and Daisy and greeted, "Hi guys."

Daisy gave me a bright smile and I knew she was Daisy because she said, "Hey, I'm Daisy."

"You're Tessa of Tessa's Cakes," Shirleen (the black lady) announced like I didn't have that information.

"Yes," I confirmed.

"I been to your place, like, a lot. Too much. It's important for a black woman to have booty, but not a Tessa's Cakes booty. You owe me at least ten pounds. You get what I'm sayin'?" she stated.

"Uh...yeah," I replied because I did but even if I didn't, she was kind of scary of the Elvira variety so I still would have agreed.

"Only two things better in the whole world than your frosted sugar cookies with daisy sprinkles and those are pigs in a blanket and a man with a fine package. This I know as fact," she declared.

I blinked at this unusual compliment, Daisy emitted a little giggle that sounded like bells, Elvira grinned big at me, but Martha shouted.

"What the *frig*?"

We all turned to her to see her glaring at the empty, ornate, milky-green glass cake stand at the edge of my counter (I'd rotated).

"What?" I asked.

Her eyes cut to me and she jabbed a finger at the cake plate. "What's that?"

I looked to the cake plate and then I looked to her.

Then I answered, "That's my fabulous, ornate, green glass cake plate."

"It sure is fabulous," Daisy agreed, eyeing my cake plate. "I need to get me one of those."

But Martha's eyes narrowed, as in went squinty. I knew what that meant. So instead of thanking Daisy, I kept my focus on Martha.

"It's empty," she pointed out.

I looked at the cake plate, then at her.

"Yeah," I agreed unnecessarily.

She glared at me.

What on earth?

"Martha—" I started.

She cut me off to say, "We're going shopping, and after, we're hitting Club. We dropped by to see if you wanna go."

No way in hell. Not that I didn't want to spend time with her but I was shopped out. Buying presents for Brock, his boys, his family, and my personal list had beat even me, a seasoned shopper dedicated to remaining as such. I had vowed to myself (and shared with Brock, who not only approved, he also laughed his ass off when I shared it), that I had sworn off malls until March.

Therefore, I had to find a kickass nightie for his Valentine's present online (for I might have sworn off malls but I figured online shopping didn't count).

"I've sworn off malls," I announced, saw Martha's eyes get big, and heard Elvira *and* Daisy suck in shocked breaths. "Christmas did me in. The bakery was crazed and having to buy presents for Brock, his boys, his family, you, all my employees, Mom, my sis, and—"

"I know your network has expanded, Tess, *I know*," Martha cut me off to say.

Oh man.

There it was.

"Martha—"

"I also know *my* Tess never but *never* has an empty cake stand at her house. And *my* Tess could shop until she dropped as evidenced by you getting up with me at five o'clock in the morning when that traveling, discount designer shoe emporium opened up their tent at the flea market and we stood in line for four hours to get in and we tried on every single pair of shoes in our size even if we didn't like them just in case they looked hot on when they didn't in the box. And *my* Tess could get busy at the bakery but she'd pry herself away to meet for a quick lunch or pop by for a glass of wine or be home occasionally so I could pop by her place."

"I went to that emporium," Daisy whispered to Shirleen. "Found me three pairs of boots. *Three.* It was hot."

"Mm-hmm," Shirleen muttered back, not tearing her eyes off the action.

I said to my friend, "Martha, honey—"

She threw up her hands. "But *oh no,* not you. Not the *new* Tess. *Brock's* Tess. *Brock's* Tess barely has time to return a text because she's busy with him, his boys, his family, staying over at his house, having his fancy-ass new truck in front of hers—"

I interrupted to ask, "Are you still stalking me?"

"Am I Martha Shockley, your best friend since fifth grade?" she asked back.

"Martha, things have been busy," I snapped.

"Yeah, busy with you gettin' a little somethin' some-thin' from a bad boy"—she leaned in—"*liberally*. You don't have time for me but you have time to haul your kickboxing ass to his house on average three days a week seeing as your car isn't here or the bakery."

Jeez, she'd totally been stalking me.

"Oo, lawdy," Elvira muttered.

"You got *that* right, sugar," Daisy matched her mutter.

I glared at Martha.

"I'm in a new relationship," I reminded her. "It's always intense when it's new."

"You're in over your head is what you are," Martha shot back and my torso jerked back.

"Oo, lawdy," Elvira repeated.

"You got that right, sugar," Daisy whispered.

"You don't know what I'm in," I said softly to Martha.

"No, you're right, I don't," Martha agreed. "Because I never *see you* or *talk to you*." She shook her head and crossed her arms on her chest, saying, "I never thought you, you, Tessa O'Hara, my best friend since I could remember, would toss me aside for a guy. I don't care how hot he is."

"Depends on what he's packin'," Shirleen whispered to Daisy and Daisy audibly stifled another giggle.

I kept my gaze on Martha.

Then I announced, "I'm in love with him."

At that, *her* torso jerked back and she added her eyes getting big. The rest of the women shuffled their feet but kept silent.

I kept talking.

"I've shared this with him and Brock has shared he feels the same about me."

"Oh God," Martha whispered, sounding slightly horrified.

"I'm happy," I told her. "Happier than I've ever been in my life. Which makes it suck that his wife is playing games and using her sons as pawns to do it, filling their heads with crap about Brock being with me meaning they can't ever have a family again and making plays to get Brock back when he hates her only slightly more than I do."

"Oh God," Martha whispered, sounding definitely horrified.

I nodded. "She's a piece of work and a pain in the ass and the kids are totally confused because they like me but she's pretty much telling them they can't because if they do, that means they don't love her."

"Oh God," Martha repeated on a whisper, staring at me.

"*And*, if that wasn't enough, Brock's dad has cancer and might be dying from it. There's history there that's unpleasant and his possible future demise is stirring up stuff that has long since been buried. Brock's dealing with his own emotions with all that as well as his mom's, his sisters', *and* his brother's."

"Oh, Tess, I didn't know." Martha was still whispering.

"I did," Elvira mumbled to Daisy and Shirleen. "I had Thanksgiving with them and we'll just say his people are *not* the Waltons 'cause, far's I know, the Waltons never dropped the f-bomb *repeatedly*."

I ignored Elvira's commentary and replied to Martha.

"No, you're right. You didn't because I haven't had time to tell you because all that's happening on top of the bakery being busy. And if that wasn't enough, when

Brock came back into my life, Damian came over for reasons only Damian understands."

Martha's torso shot back again but this time her eyes got wide and she sucked in a breath.

"That's her ex. He's cornered the market on asshole," Elvira explained on a mutter to Shirleen and Daisy.

"Lotsa those," Shirleen muttered back.

"No, sister, I mean he's *cornered the market on asshole,*" Elvira stated firmly and Daisy and Shirleen stared at her with dawning understanding and then they looked at me.

"Why did he come over?" Martha asked softly.

"I don't know. Brock answered the door and wouldn't let him in. Then he threatened that if he ever saw Damian anywhere near me, he'd deal with him. Then he shut the door in Damian's face. Then he called his law enforcement buddy and told him to tell the DA to tell Damian's attorneys that he wouldn't only be facing drug charges but also harassment, assault, and sexual assault charges."

More air being sucked in all around as understanding fully dawned.

"This Damian Heller we're talkin' about?" Shirleen asked and I nodded to her. "Shit," she muttered.

"Unh-hunh," I agreed.

"Tess, I had no—" Martha started and I looked to her and cut her off.

"I know you didn't and you wouldn't because I didn't have time to tell you. But now I hope you understand why I didn't have time to tell you. And that's just that. I didn't get into the fact that Damian is poking around in Brock's life to find some way to make him miserable."

"Holy crap," Martha mumbled.

"No joke," I replied.

"Girl, I'm so sorry. This all sucks," she said quietly.

"Yeah, it does. Because he's a good guy, Martha. The best. I didn't even know they *made* guys like him but I can tell you I'm not only happy to know. I'm beside myself with glee that he's mine."

She held my eyes.

Then she whispered, "You *do* love him."

"Yeah," I replied. "He thinks I'm beautiful and told me so. He thinks I'm funny because I make him laugh all the time. He's fantastic in bed and when I say that not once, not even *once* have we been together where he hasn't taken care of me, and it's not unheard of he takes care of me *twice* in one go."

"Oh boy, TMI," Elvira muttered.

"Yowza," Daisy muttered.

"Holy crap," Martha muttered.

"Hold onto that one, girl," Shirleen muttered.

My voice dropped quiet when I kept laying it out for Martha.

"He gets close to me anytime I'm near. And his dad says he does it like he thinks there's a lion that's going to come charging into the room and Brock wants to be close enough to protect me. And he wasn't wrong, Martha. You know with Damian back, and *Brock* knows, that lion is prowling out there and Brock..." I swallowed as I felt tears sting my nose. "Even with all this stuff going down, Brock's positioning to make sure that lion doesn't get anywhere near me."

"Oo lawdy," Elvira whispered.

Martha continued to hold my eyes. Then tears filled hers.

Then she whispered, "You love him."

"Yeah," I replied.

"You love him," she repeated.

I grinned. "Yeah."

Then she threw both arms straight in the air and shouted, "My best friend's in love with a bad-boy hot guy!"

Elvira rolled her eyes. Shirleen stared at Martha like she had a screw loose. Daisy giggled her pretty bell laugh.

I smiled at Martha.

There you go. That was Martha. One drama fed into the next and all of them weren't bad.

I sighed a relieved sigh and a knock came at the door.

Well, relief didn't last long.

I looked toward the door and stared at it like on the other side was a dirty bomb.

"You two kiss and make up, I'll get the door," Elvira offered.

I opened my mouth to stop her when I felt Martha's arms close around me.

And what did you do when your best friend since fifth grade's arms closed around you?

Yours closed right back.

"I'm so happy for you, honey," she whispered.

"I am too," I whispered back, then added, "Outside the sinister threat of impending doom delivered by one, the other, or both of our exes and the cloud of possible terminal disease."

She pulled back but not out of my arms and she said softly, "This, too, shall pass."

I hoped she was right.

"Uh, girlfriend." Elvira was close. I let go of Martha

and looked to her then beyond her to a handsome but somewhat elderly man I'd never seen in my life who was standing just inside my door. "You got a visitor," she informed me of the obvious, then went on, "Says his name is Dade McManus."

I blinked at her then I looked at the handsome but somewhat elderly man standing just inside my door.

Whoa.

That was Olivia's husband?

He was handsome, yes. And I could see even a room away that his clothes were of very good quality, as in he was not a stranger to Neiman's good quality. And he wore them well on a still slim, fit body. And he had good style. And he was only *somewhat* elderly.

Still.

Maybe Brock was wrong. Maybe Olivia *did* want her bad-boy hot guy ex-husband back.

Damn.

And double damn because what the fuck was he doing here?

"Um…" I mumbled.

"I'll only take a moment of your time, Ms. O'Hara, but it's important," he called politely.

Damn!

"Who's that?" Martha, up on her toes and at my side, whispered in my ear.

"Brock's ex-wife's husband," I whispered back.

"Oo lawdy," Elvira muttered.

"You got *that* right, sugar," Daisy whispered.

"Fuckin' A," Shirleen mumbled.

"Holy crap," Martha murmured.

"Uh…I'll be right there," I called.

He cordially lifted his chin then moved to study the books on my inset shelves.

Crap.

I rolled my hands toward me to indicate the girls should huddle.

They didn't delay in huddling and I whispered low, "Okay, I don't want to go shopping but I'll meet you at Club later." I turned to Martha and ordered, "Text me." Then back to the group, "Have fun, and if you happen to see a sexy nightie that shouts, *'Happy Valentine's Day!'* there's a free cupcake in it for you."

"Make that a frosted sugar cookie with daisy sprinkles and I just found me a mission," Shirleen stated and I nodded to her.

"Two, if it's superhot," I said.

She nodded back, a determined look in her eye, and I guessed from that that Brock was going to have a happy Valentine's Day. I shuffled them to the door, called farewells, gave Martha another hug, and then they were gone.

And I was alone with Olivia's husband.

"Can I get you something? Coffee? Hot tea? Cocoa?" I offered and he turned from his polite perusal of my shelves to me.

"No, Ms. O'Hara. I won't take up much of your time."

"Tess," I said softly and his head tipped to the side. "Everyone calls me Tess."

"Tess," he said back.

I smiled at him and motioned to the seating area.

He took a seat in my armchair. I planted my ass in the couch.

"What can I do for you, Mr. McManus?"

"Dade," he corrected quietly and I nodded. Then he

studied me a moment, shifted uncomfortably in his chair, and said, "I actually don't know how to say this or even why I'm here."

This was a good question that had two parts. The second part being how he knew where I lived.

"Can I ask how you, um…found me? I mean, where I live."

"I asked Joey," he answered.

Right. This made sense. The kids had been to my place and clearly Joel was as observant as his father.

His eyes locked with mine and he stated, "I might as well just say it because you should know." He paused then declared, "I have reason to believe your, er…boyfriend and my wife are having an affair."

I blinked at him as my lungs contracted.

"What?" I whispered.

"I have…" He paused. "Had the occasion to…" Another pause. "Hire someone to follow my wife," he admitted. "And it's been reported to me that twice she's met your boyfriend for dinner."

I waited for more.

None came.

So I prompted, "And?"

His brows drew together. "And?"

"Yes, and?"

"What do you mean, and?"

Oh God.

Belatedly, it hit me. He didn't know his wife was meeting Brock for dinner to discuss custody. She hadn't told him.

Oh God.

"Dade," I said gently, "I know Brock has been meeting

Olivia for dinner. This is because, recently, Brock made a career move, which means his schedule is more stable. Therefore, a couple of weeks after Thanksgiving, Olivia received word from Brock's attorney that he wanted to negotiate a joint custody arrangement. Olivia for..." It was my turn to pause. "Her own reasons wanted to discuss uh..." Damn! "Various things with Brock, including this and she asked him to meet for dinner. She was, uh...somewhat, um...*discontent* when he refused and she was, um...*discontent* in front of the boys, so Brock agreed. However, after two dinners without a resolution, Brock will now only be communicating through his lawyer."

Dade's mouth had gotten tight right around the time I mentioned Olivia got word from Brock's lawyer and it was stretched taut by the time I was done.

He looked behind me, out my side window.

Oh man.

"She hasn't discussed this with you," I said softly.

"No," he clipped shortly.

I remained silent.

Then I asked, "Are you sure you don't want any coffee?"

His eyes cut back to me and he didn't answer my question.

Instead, he asked, "Discontent?"

I again remained silent.

"You mean she threw a tantrum in front of the boys to get her way."

I bit my lip. His eyes dropped to my mouth and his mouth again got so tight I thought his skin would split open.

"Let me go put some coffee on," I said softly.

His eyes shot to mine. "And my wife's reasons for wishing to see your boyfriend do not all revolve around discussing the boys seeing more of their father."

"No," I whispered.

He nodded and looked back out the window.

"I'll just go make some coffee," I whispered, got up, and hurried to the kitchen.

I set it to brew, put out a plate, and did the unheard of. I put store-bought cookies on a plate for company.

Sacrilege.

But I didn't think he wanted to hang while I whipped up one of my extravaganzas so that was going to have to do.

I did unearth my fancy-shmancy coffee service and the cups with saucers, filled up the sugar bowl and creamer, set it all on a tray, and carried it back.

By the time I arrived, he was still contemplating my landscaping with its thin but pretty layer of snow that sparkled in the sun. But he wasn't seeing snow sparkling in the sun. By the look on his face he was trying to figure out how to get away with murder.

"How do you take it?" I asked.

"Splash of milk, please," he answered, his eyes moving back to me.

I fixed his coffee and gave it to him then fixed my own and sat back in the sofa.

I barely got my back to the rest when he launched in.

"They're good boys," he declared.

"Rex and Joel?" I asked.

"Yes," he answered. "Fine boys. Very smart. They get good grades. Solicitous in their studies. Solicitous with practicing their sports. Solicitous in keeping their rooms clean. Solicitous to their mother. Solicitous *all the time*."

This was interesting.

I had, of course, noted this. It was just interesting that he did *and* that he obviously felt troubled by it.

I sipped coffee and held his gaze but kept my mouth shut.

Dade didn't.

"Tess, Olivia, she gets . . . *discontent* a great deal."

Oh man.

"Dade," I whispered.

"They're terrified of her," he announced. "Or, *for* her."

I closed my eyes and looked away.

Then I opened them and looked at him. "You need to speak to Brock."

This time he kept his mouth shut.

I leaned forward and put my elbows on my knees, holding the cup and saucer in front of me. "If you have concerns, their father should know."

"I have had concerns for some time, Tess. My concerns are one of the reasons I hired someone to watch my wife, outside of the fact that she's slept with her tennis instructor *and* her personal trainer *and* the massage therapist at her spa. She likes to collect men. This is her pastime outside of spending my money."

"Perhaps you've misunderstood these relationships. Perhaps she's just, um . . . friendly," I suggested lamely.

"I have pictures."

Eek!

"Okay," I gave in.

"She's a different woman than the woman I courted."

Jeez, he said "courted."

I nodded. "I've heard that before."

"I'm certain you have."

I had nothing to say to that so I didn't say anything.

"I have not spent decades being relatively successful in a boardroom only to get played by an out-of-the-bottle, forty-four-year-old blonde who doesn't know the difference of the uses 'their,' 'they're,' and 'there.'"

"I'm sorry," I said quietly.

"I am too," he replied.

I put my saucer down on the coffee table, picked up the plate with the cookies, and extended it to him.

"They're store bought and that would be 'they're,' with the apostrophe 're,'" I said in an attempt at a joke. He blinked and I smiled. "If I'd known I was going to have a heart-to-heart, I would have been certain to make a chocolate cake, the heart-to-heart kind with the whipped chocolate frosting between the layers and ganache on top. Unfortunately, I didn't know, so this is all I have."

He studied me and his face softened.

Then he said quietly, "I'll decline. But perhaps you'll send a slice of your chocolate heart-to-heart cake back with the boys sometime."

"I'll be certain to do that," I whispered, setting the plate down.

"I would advise you to hurry," he went on.

I got the hint and I smiled sadly at him.

"I'm so sorry, Dade."

"She speaks of you," he whispered back and I pulled in a breath. "To the boys *and* me. You're all that's on her mind." He smiled a small smile. "And that would be 'you're,' with an apostrophe 're.'"

I smiled, then sat back in the sofa, muttering, "I was afraid of that."

"She does not give up easily, Tess," he warned and I pulled in another breath. "After my wife died, I told myself, not again. Never again. My wife was a good woman, kind, generous. I did not wish to…" He paused. "But Olivia, she worked hard at it. Three years. I thought I was lucky to be a man who, in his lifetime, found two beautiful, kind-hearted women."

I bit my lip again.

Dade finished, "I was wrong."

I tilted my head to the side, about to say I was sorry again, when the front door opened.

Crap!

I turned to it to see my man in a black skintight long-sleeved running shirt with dark gray piping and matching (but loose) track pants. His hair was wet with sweat, as were the muscles of his neck, and you could see the dark stain of it on his shirt even though it was black wicking.

He took one look at Dade on my armchair, his brows snapped together over dangerously narrowed eyes, and he rumbled, "What the fuck?"

I jumped up and rushed to him.

"It's cool, honey. Joel told him where I live and Dade he's… well, coming to terms with some things and those things aren't the things that Olivia may have told you they are," I explained, then continued, "You need—"

"No shit?" he cut me off, eyes never leaving Dade. He slammed the door behind him, took two long strides into the room with me following and staying close then stated, "You got issues, you do not bring them to my woman's doorstep."

Dade straightened from his chair. "Lucas, I was under the false impression—"

"That I was fucking your wife," Brock finished for him. "Yeah, Dade, I know. Your PI sucks. I clocked him five minutes into my first nightmare meal with Olivia so I obviously clocked him five seconds into my second one. What you obviously don't get is that, in a healthy relationship, a man doesn't keep shit from his woman or vice versa."

Ouch!

"Lucas, I—" Dade started but Brock cut him off again.

"If you got something to say, say it to me. Do not land your shit on Tess's door."

"He's a little protective," I said, defending Brock to Dade and then I turned back to Brock. "Honey, I think you might want to get over being pissed and sit down and talk with Dade."

Brock's eyes narrowed on his ex-wife's husband.

Then he asked, "You gonna tell me why my boys are jumpy as shit?"

"Yes," Dade answered but said no more. Or at least he didn't speak fast enough.

"So…" Brock started, "spit it out."

"She's fragile," Dade stated.

Brock let out an entirely unamused, short bark of laughter before he declared, "Man, Olivia's made of stone, figuratively, and I assume you've fucked her so you know also literally."

Ouch again!

"Brock, honey," I whispered as Dade's mouth got tight again.

"No, Lucas," he bit out. "What I mean is, this is what she communicates to the boys."

Brock's entire body went still.

Then he asked softly, "She's *playin'* my *boys*?"

"With every breath she takes," Dade answered.

I froze and stared at Dade.

Oh my *God*.

"Why the fuck would she do that?" Brock asked what I thought was a very good question.

"I would assume, since you've known her longer than I, you understand that she's careful to acquire important allies. And I would assume, as you divorced her, that your reasons for this were at least partly what mine are going to be."

I heard Brock pull in a sharp breath through his nose at learning this news but Dade went on,

"And she simply is who she is. So, I would assume that you understand that her needing as much attention as possible is as necessary to her as breath. But she's forcing affection she's not capable of obtaining in natural ways in case she should, for instance, need to battle me or…"—his eyes slid to me, then back to Brock—"you."

"Fuckin' piece of work," Brock clipped under his breath, looking away while lifting a hand and tearing it through his wet hair.

"They're exceedingly cautious around her because she dissolves into tantrums or tears often and at random. They have no idea what will set her off so they're careful with everything," Dade continued sharing, and he looked at me. "She was not like this prior to us being married or, at least, not that I knew."

"Let me guess," Brock put in and Dade's eyes moved back to him. "It happened, what? An hour after she signed the marriage certificate?"

"Upon return from our honeymoon," Dade corrected.

"Terrific. At least you got the honeymoon," Brock returned and Dade's eyes widened.

"No," he said quietly.

"Uh...yeah," Brock replied.

"My Lord," Dade whispered.

"So you're divorcin' her ass?" Brock asked.

"Indeed," Dade answered.

"Shit, fuck, *fuck,*" Brock muttered harshly to the floor.

I would guess there were several reasons for Brock cursing at the floor. One of them would be that, without Dade, Olivia would be on her own again to drain him dry financially. The other was that she would have the time to put more effort into making him miserable.

Damn.

Dade looked at him. Then he looked at me.

He looked back to Brock and said softly, "Whatever move you're going to make"—Brock's head came up and his eyes locked with Dade's—"make it soon. I will delay for a few weeks so the boys will have some stability, a roof over their heads, familiar things around them. But only a few weeks, Lucas. I cannot take much more."

I felt my heart beating hard and I felt Brock's body still beside mine.

"And," he went on, studying Brock closely, "if it comes to that, I will do what I can to help you." He paused. "For Joey and Rex."

Wow.

Whatever they said about a woman scorned, when a man was...*whoa.*

When Brock said not a word and continued staring at Dade, I waded in.

"Dade, that...that's very kind. *Very* kind. The boys

may never understand but if they did, they'd appreciate it and, um…"—my head jerked to Brock and I
finished—"we do too."

Dade nodded, then said quietly, "This gives you only
weeks to make that heart-to-heart cake, Tess."

"I miss the deadline, I'll bring a full one by your house
and leave it on the doorstep," I offered.

"My dear," he replied, moving toward us and stopping in
front of me, "ring the bell anytime." He turned his head and
his eyes went up to Brock before he said softly, "I started
with a good one. Lucky for you that you're ending with one."

Wow. That was sweet.

He nodded to me and muttered, "Pleasure, Tess. Thank
you for the coffee. I'll let myself out."

He waited for my smile, skirted us, and let himself out.

I turned to Brock.

"If you want, I'll gather all the things I don't mind you
smashing and put them on the coffee table, or an alternate
option, I can go grab you a bottle of beer," I offered.

He looked down at me. Then he stalked to my armchair, sat down, bent forward, put his elbows to his knees
and both hands to the back of his head.

I hurried to him and crouched down beside him, my
fingers curling around his thigh.

"Seriously, Brock, let this out," I whispered.

"Fucked up," he muttered to his knees.

"Brock—"

"Knew I shouldn't've but left them to her for a year. A
fuckin' *year*," he bit off.

"Honey—"

"She's playin' my boys," he said, still talking to his
knees.

I squeezed his thigh. "Honey—"

"With every breath she takes."

I squeezed his thigh again but kept my fingers tensed into his flesh and also kept silent.

"*Fuck!*" he exploded, then threw himself back against the chair.

I straightened, moved, and climbed in, putting a knee in the seat on either side of his hips so I was astride him. I leaned forward, hands on the fast-drying material of his running shirt, and put my face in his face, feeling his hands curve around my hips.

"This, too, shall pass," I whispered.

"Yeah, babe, but it needed to pass yesterday or, say, two fuckin' years ago," Brock responded.

"Okay, it didn't. You can't turn back time, honey. Just talk to them."

"And say what, Tess? That their mom is a miserable, scheming cunt and their dad is an asshole who put his job before them and left them to that bullshit?" Brock asked angrily.

"I would shy away from the c-word," I advised on a whisper, sliding my hands up to his neck and holding tight. "And, also, maybe the a-word too."

He sucked in a breath through his nose and looked over my shoulder as his fingers dug into my hips.

Then his eyes came back to mine. "I want you over tonight."

I shook my head and squeezed his neck. "You should be with your boys and Martha came by earlier. I'm meeting her and some friends at Club."

"You didn't hear me, Tess. I want you over tonight."

"Brock, they need their dad and me being around is

just confusing them and making them feel torn and maybe even guilt."

"Babe, you are not gonna disappear every time I have them *especially* when I have full custody of them. Eventually, this two-house bullshit we got goin' is gonna be done, we're gonna be livin' together, and they're gonna be with us."

My fingers spasmed on his neck at this news. News it appeared Brock took for granted. News that was news to me.

Happy news.

He kept talking, cutting into the tingles I was experiencing due to receiving this happy news.

"They gotta learn her games just like the rest of us and they also gotta learn that a woman who'll work twelve-hour days and still break her neck to give them a fuckin' good Christmas, smilin' bright even though she's got fatigue in her eyes, is not someone they need to feel torn and guilty about likin'."

Okay, he wasn't wrong about that.

"Okay, honey, but I have to go out with Martha. She came over and had a drama about how she never sees me. I need to give her some time."

He stared at me and I could tell this wasn't going over very well.

I leaned closer. "You have your talk with your boys, dinner, guy time. I'll have my girl time and come over later. And tomorrow, I'll make something fabulous for breakfast."

"Tess—"

"Payback, Brock," I cut him off and his eyebrows shot together. "They asked me to go to the mall with them.

I declined but traded free baked goods if they found a nightie that a bad-boy hot guy would appreciate being given for Valentine's Day. I'm sworn off the mall until March. For you to have a happy Valentine's Day, you owe them."

He stared at me again for a few seconds then his lips twitched and he shook his head.

"My sweet Tess," he muttered before he leaned in and touched his mouth to mine.

When he leaned back, I whispered, "It's all gonna be okay."

"Yeah," he whispered back.

I smiled at him then informed him, "You need a shower."

"So do you," he replied.

"I took one this morning," I reminded him.

"Well you're gonna take another one," he told me.

The tingles came back.

"Okay," I whispered and he grinned.

Then he stood up, taking me with him and putting me on my feet, saying, "We gotta be quick, babe. I gotta get the boys."

We'd done quick before. I preferred not quick.

But quick would do in a pinch.

CHAPTER SIXTEEN

When Exes Attack

I HAD MY head thrown back, Brock's hand was lifting my breast to his mouth, his mouth pulling hard on my nipple, his other hand was curved around my other breast, thumb circling the nipple, my fingers were in his hair, and I was grinding into him hard.

I'd accepted a lift from Daisy (who was my new best friend seeing as she had a limo *and* a driver *and* she was sweet *and* she was hilarious) to get to Brock's from Club.

I'd done this because I was more than slightly inebriated.

I'd also attacked my drowsy hot guy bad boy the minute I hit his bedroom and I'd done this because, as I said, I was more than slightly inebriated.

Obviously, he didn't mind.

I started to make noises that Brock had heard many a time thus he did not misinterpret.

His mouth left my nipple, his thumb stopped circling the other one only to be joined by a finger and start rolling, and he growled his order of, "Mouth."

I stopped grinding and started to ride him, whimpering

deep, too caught up in what was happening between my legs to respond immediately.

"Tess, *mouth*," he growled again.

My head tipped down, his hand slid up my spine, my neck, fingers in my hair. My whimpers became gasps as the sensations grew brilliantly desperate. He pressed my mouth down so my lips were against his, my noises filling his mouth. I was *this close* when we heard the knock on the door.

We both froze, me doing it after a downward glide so I was full of Brock.

Then both our heads turned to the door when we heard Joel call, "Dad? Mom's on the phone. She says it's urgent."

Oh.

My.

God.

"Tell me this isn't happening," Brock whispered, his voice super low but vibrating with fury.

I wanted to tell him it wasn't happening. I really, *really* wanted to tell him that. But I couldn't tell him it wasn't happening because it was.

My eyes went beyond Brock to the alarm clock on his nightstand to see it was two thirty-four in the morning.

A nanosecond later, Brock's hands were at my waist. He pulled me swiftly but gently off him, twisted, and then I had my back to the bed, head to the pillows.

He quickly bent and kissed my belly, rolled out of bed, and tossed the covers over me as he called, "Just a sec, Joey."

I pulled the covers all the way up to my neck and watched Brock tag his pajama bottoms from the floor, tug them on, and stalk to the door. Then I watched him put his hand to the doorknob, take in a deep breath, and open the door a wide crack while crouching at the same time.

At this point, I heard a Joey I couldn't see say a trembling, "Sorry, Dad, but she sounds scared."

I felt my mouth get tight as I watched by the hall light Joel had turned on as Brock's did the same then I saw him reach out a hand.

I watched him put a cell phone to his ear and my brows drew together.

Since when did Joel have a cell phone? The kid was twelve, for goodness sakes.

"Olivia?" I heard Brock ask as I turned and shoved my hand under my pillow to grab my nightie. "Intruders?" Brock enquired as I struggled to get it on under the bedclothes, then, "Where's Dade?" Pause, then, "Have you called the cops?" Another pause, then, "Yeah, I'm the cops, Olivia, but I'm not available for personalized 24/7 callouts. Call the cops." He paused while I got the nightgown down then rolled, put a hand to the floor, and stretched an arm out to nab my panties. "You won't. I will, Olivia. If someone's there their ETA will be a fuckuva lot shorter than mine. Stay put and I'll call dispatch."

I was not having an easy time pulling my panties on under the sheets as I heard Brock snap the cell closed, then, "Wait here, buddy, I'll be right back."

I got my panties up and watched Brock prowl, face set in stone, to the nightstand. He turned on the light, grabbed his cell off the nightstand, and I rolled off the bed.

Then I went to the door.

I got to it and opened it farther to see a pale-faced, scared-looking Joel standing in the hall. The bad news was, Joey looked scared. The good news was, Joey didn't look psychologically damaged at possibly hearing his father having sex with his girlfriend.

Immediately, I put my hand to his neck and whispered, "It's gonna be all right, baby. Come on in," and I guided him in as Brock spoke.

"Yeah, this is Detective Lucas, homicide. My ex-wife just called, worried there's an intruder at her home. Can you send a unit…?"

He gave the address as I guided Joel to the bed and sat him on the edge of it, me sitting close to his side and wrapping an arm around his waist.

His eyes were glued to his dad.

"Appreciate it," Brock stated. "Can you give me a call-back? Let me know the state of play?" He nodded. "Thanks."

He flipped his phone shut, opened it again, hit buttons, and put it to his ear.

Then he said, "Just called dispatch, a unit is gonna swing by. Hold tight. They should be there in around five."

He didn't wait for an answer and flipped his phone closed.

Finally, his eyes went to his son, "Everything's gonna be all right, Joey. Unit will be there soon."

Joel nodded.

"Your brother sleepin'?" Brock asked.

Joel shrugged. "I guess."

"Well, if he is, don't wake him but go down, be quiet, find his cell, and bring it up to me, yeah?"

Joel nodded again, then jumped from the bed and took off.

The minute he left, the room filled with the harsh sandpaper of Brock's extremely pissed-off mood.

"Cells?" I asked cautiously.

"Found out durin' our talk that Olivia bought them both

cells yesterday. Said they were New Year's sales treats. What it was was preparation for a middle of the night stealth attack."

I bit my lip and nodded.

Still cautious, I queried, "Um...why didn't she call the cops?"

"Said if it wasn't an intruder, she didn't want to look like an idiot or waste their time."

Hmm. Seems she didn't mind wasting Brock's time. Or waking him up. Or Joel for that matter.

Again cautious, I asked, "Did she honestly think you were going to get up in the middle of the night, go to her house, and check?"

He gave me a look. That look told me exactly how Olivia had made Brock's life miserable in the years they were divorced but she was not married to Dade.

I decided to stop asking questions.

Brock opened Joel's new phone, hit some buttons, which I suspected powered it down, closed it, opened his nightstand drawer, dropped it in with a clatter then shoved the drawer closed so violently his lamp wobbled on top.

Oh man.

"Honey," I whispered.

"I got it in check, babe," he rumbled and I shut up because he did but I could tell only barely.

Joel came back and the instant he hit the room, the atmosphere changed, though it only became nonabrasive. The spark and flash of electricity still filled the air. Joel gave his dad his brother's phone, Brock did a repeat of the power down, drawer thing but without the lamp wobble and Joel watched him do it.

Then his eyes lifted to his father's.

"Dad—"

"Benefit of the doubt, Joey," Brock cut him off to say. "Yeah?"

I didn't get this but Joel did because he nodded. Then he shuffled his feet and his eyes moved to glue themselves to the cell in his father's hand.

It came to me in that moment that I should have asked my drowsy bad boy about the important talk he had with his sons rather than jumped his bones.

Alas, I did not.

Very long seconds ticked by in silence before I broke it with, "Joey, honey, you want me to make you some hot cocoa?"

Joel tore his eyes from his father's phone and looked at me.

"No, thanks, Tess," he mumbled.

"You want to come over here and sit down with me?" I asked.

"I..." He hesitated, looked to his dad then walked over to me and sat down, but not close.

I pulled in a light breath, looked to Brock, and saw his eyes on his son and his jaw so hard, a muscle was jumping in his cheek.

Then he started pacing.

I got up, went to the bathroom, and belatedly took out contacts that had been in way too long. I left the bathroom and grabbed one of Brock's flannels, pulling it on to cover my nightie, thinking I might need either to break my vow not to go to the mall or hit a computer to buy a robe to leave at Brock's since the only one I owned at home was warm, fluffy, and I'd had it since before Damian and therefore it was ratty-assed.

I needed a Brock's Place Robe.

I dashed downstairs, dug my glasses out of my purse, slid them on my nose, ran back upstairs, and sat down on the bed closer to Joel than he sat by me and I let out a silent sigh when he didn't move away.

Then we waited for a decade (slight exaggeration) while Brock paced, or, more aptly, *prowled* the room, his pissed-off energy filling the air.

Joel and I both jumped when Brock's cell rang.

Instantly, he flipped it open and put it to his ear.

"Detective Lucas," he answered, then, "Yeah." A pause before another "Yeah." Then more listening and scarily a "No shit, this is my life." Another pause, then, "Yeah, cryin' wolf, won't happen again." Finally, "Yeah, thanks," and he flipped his phone shut.

He turned to Joel.

"No sign of intruders, buddy. Your mother is perfectly fine and the officer reports Dade answered the door. Dade reported his alarm system is comprehensive, inside and out, and it was set. Anyone gets within two feet of the perimeter of an entry into the house, including a window, a signal sounds inside the house, goes to the security company, and if one of the windows or doors are breached, a message is sent direct to police dispatch. Did you know that?"

Head tipped back to look at his dad, Joel shook it slowly while his lip trembled.

God, God, *God,* I fucking *hated* Olivia McManus-soon-to-be-whatever-the-fuck.

"The alarm did not signal," Brock told him.

Joel nodded, lip still trembling.

Brock held his son's eyes. Then he sucked in a heavy breath.

Finally, he held out an arm and said gently, "Come on, buddy, I'll walk you to your room."

Joel nodded again, got up, muttered a "'Night, Tess, sorry," without looking at me and scurried out of the room.

Brock followed him without looking at me either.

I scooted into the bed, arranged the pillows behind my back, rested against them, legs crossed, and I pulled the covers up to my waist. I noticed that my happy-cosmopolitans-with-the-girls buzz was long gone and my other happier-having-fun-with-Brock buzz was *way* gone.

Yep, totally fucking hated Olivia McManus-soon-to-be-whatever-the-fuck.

Brock returned some time later. I straightened my back from the headboard where I was resting while contemplating vacation spots, which graduated to me contemplating getaway options when I took Brock, Joel, and Rex on the run, and I watched him close the door. Then I watched him walk in the room, stop, flip the phone he still held open, and hit some buttons.

He put it to his ear and waited while I bit my lip and braced.

This was a good idea.

Olivia obviously picked up, for Brock growled low, "Even for you, that was low. FYI for future, the bullshit with the phones is done. They can have 'em during the day but the minute they enter this house, they're turned off and confiscated. *You* do not enter this house. *Ever.* Any fuckin' way you can do it. And warning, Olivia, you can kiss your sons good-bye, which means you can kiss any support you think you can drain outta me good-bye. You don't get them and you don't get a dime. You just declared war and mark this, woman, I'll stop at nothin' to win. You . . . are . . . *fucked*."

He closed his phone but stood there staring at it and I knew he did this because he was struggling with the urge to throw it.

"Baby," I called softly and his head came up.

"Just got finished explainin' to my twelve-year-old boy that it is highly unlikely that his mother has lived in that house with Dade for over two years and doesn't realize they have top-notch security. Then I told him, should she be worried about intruders anyway, she should call nine-one-one, as everyone knows to call nine-one-one. They even got dogs trained to dial nine fuckin' one fuckin *one*."

Oh man.

Brock kept talking.

"Then I told him, if she's freaked, she should go to her husband. If they're not gettin' along and she's freaked and forgets what to do, she should call me direct. What she should not do, under any circumstances, is call a twelve-year-old kid in the middle of the fuckin' night and scare the shit outta him. And then I had to explain *why* she called him, which was, essentially, so she could scare the shit outta him and yank my chain. Then my kid started cryin'."

Yep, totally hated her.

"Honey, come here," I whispered.

He held my eyes. I watched with despair as his eyes grew conflicted, then he dropped his head and looked at his feet as he lifted a hand and curled his fingers around the back of his neck.

Okay, I was wrong.

Before, I just disliked her intensely.

Now, I totally *fucking* hated her.

"Brock, baby, *come here,*" I urged.

His hand dropped and his head came up.

"I did not want this for them," he whispered and I felt my throat clog.

"Come here," I repeated huskily.

"Did everything I could to protect them from this shit," he went on. "I should never have taken that cover that took me outta their lives for a whole fuckin' year."

I gave up, threw the covers back, and went to him. I got close, wrapped my arms around him, and pressed deep.

I tipped my head back when his arms curved around me and my eyes locked with his.

"She is who she is," I said quietly. "And because she is, even if you didn't take that cover, they would eventually learn who she is *because* she is who she is. You have no responsibility for her actions. You were doing your job. Your job was important but it required sacrifices. There are a lot of important jobs men and women take that require them to make that kind of sacrifice. Soldiers for one. And undercover DEA agents for another."

"Yeah, Tess, but—"

I interrupted him. "You have to be who you are. If you're doing something important and you believe in it, you have to do it even if that means sacrifices. You have to do it because that's how you teach them to do the same."

"Tess—"

I cut him off this time by giving him a squeeze.

"She's doing this to herself. Do you think they live in fear of whatever reaction she'll have, whatever tantrum she'll throw, and they'll not cotton on eventually?" I asked but didn't wait for his answer. I shook my head and gave him another squeeze. "No way, Brock. Those are *your* boys and they are far from stupid."

One of his arms left me so he could curl his fingers around my neck as he whispered, "Baby."

"It's your duty to teach them to be good men. You learned because you had a good mother, and despite a bad father. They've got the opposite. You're obligated to do this anyway but in this situation you're all they've got. There is no escaping it and it wouldn't matter what they faced in their lives, you'd still have to do it. And part of being a good man is being a strong one, doing what you believe in, standing up for yourself and the ones you love, protecting them from harm, and you're doing that. Think about what happened when you were growing up. I'm sure Fern wanted to protect you but she couldn't. That was your life. You can't protect them from this because it's a part of their life. What you *can* do is help them understand what's happening around them and teach them how to cope. It sucks that you had to explain to your son that his mother scared him on purpose just to fuck with you but you were right to do it."

His fingers dug hard into my neck and his eyes flared.

Then his fingers relaxed and his head dropped so he could touch his mouth to mine.

When he lifted his head, I told him softly, "We need to talk about your talk."

He nodded but said, "That was only a little less painful than this shit tonight."

Not good news.

I licked my lips, then pressed them together.

Then I gave him a gentle tug toward the bed and whispered, "All right, come to bed and tell me."

Brock studied me for a minute before his fingers left my neck to slide up into my hair then down through the back of it.

Then we went to bed and he told me.

He turned out the light, held me, and I held him back until he fell asleep in my arms but I lay awake in his.

And only then did I let the silent tears of frustration and powerlessness fall.

But luckily there were only a few.

Then I burrowed into my man and fell asleep.

CHAPTER SEVENTEEN

The Nuggets Won

"THOSE LOOK FREAKING fantastic!" I exclaimed and I was not lying.

Kellie was at a stainless-steel table in the back of my bakery (where the magic happened) and she was adorning chocolate cupcakes with mountainous swirls of mocha frosting. She'd already finished a tray and they were lightly dusted with cocoa powder and showered with orange-flavored sugar and chocolate sprinkles.

They looked awesome.

Her eyes went from her pastry bag to me.

Then the tip of her tongue, which had been poking out the side of her mouth disappeared, and she asked, "Do you think?"

I looked at the cupcakes then back to her. "Uh... *yeah*."

She grinned at me.

We'd had a busy day and stocks were low by the time she got there after school, so I set her to work alongside me, seeing as business was picking up due to the after-work crowd swinging by to get goodies for home. I'd just returned from refilling cookie jars (fat, yummy peanut butter with those crisscross fork indents in them and oatmeal with dried cranberries and white chocolate chips).

It was the first time Kellie had been let loose unsupervised and unaided. And by the looks of it, she'd done great.

I walked to her, gave her a sideways hug, and kissed her temple before letting her go and telling her softly, "Honey, you're a natural."

"So, they're Tessa's Cakes Worthy?" she asked.

"Absolutely," I answered.

"Cool," she whispered, eyes shining bright.

I smiled at her. Then I swiped a cupcake.

I started to walk away, peeling back the brown paper as I told her, "I'm off. When you're done with those, take them out and unleash them on the world."

"Okay, Tess, and tell Uncle Slim I said hello," she called after me.

"Tell him yourself." I stopped at the office door, turned, and looked at her. "Now he's blaming *me* that you're never stopping around at his place."

"Well, then tell him he doesn't pay me to be around and he doesn't have huge bowls of homemade frosting at his house," she returned.

This was true.

I grinned at her and disappeared into my tiny office, taking a bite of her as delicious as it looked cupcake.

Totally Tessa's Cakes.

Once I got over the orgasmic taste sensation of chocolate cake and whipped mocha frosting with a hint of orange, I took in my tiny office.

My life was a mess because of outside factions. My

home was never a mess. And this now meant that Brock's home was never a mess.

I had to admit to one drawback. Having Brock meant having two houses to clean.

Brock didn't clean. In fact, Brock didn't like it when *I* cleaned.

When I asked, Brock informed me that, in the past, he kept his pad clean mostly by not living in it and therefore it wasn't really clean. It was just that he wasn't around to see the dust accumulating. Things occasionally got cleaned when his mother popped by. This, I'd realized, was something she did that was essentially taking care of a forty-five-year-old man that he didn't mind. Then again, he didn't care if his place was clean and he also didn't care if his mother spent her time with him cleaning.

He did mind with me. He thought we had better things to do when we were together, like eat, watch sports on television while cuddled together, and have lots of sex.

We'd had words, not heated, just words. Several of them.

Unusually, I won.

Then I wondered why I fought for the right to clean his house. This was not fun. But it had to be done because I was not able to live in unclean and not tidy and it had to be said, Brock and I were living together. It was just that we were doing it in two houses that both had to be cleaned.

But the one thing in my life that was not tidy was my office. In the beginning, when I was busting my hump to make a go of my bakery, it got out of hand and I never got it back into hand. Now it was organized disarray. Although it looked like a cyclone hit it, I knew precisely where everything was.

I had few rules for my employees. Those being excellent hygiene, smiling faces, not being afraid to show personality, for personality was Tessa's Cakes, and there was never an excuse to be bored.

And last, never touch anything in my office upon threat of death (or not getting to take any of the end-of-the-night-not-sold cakes home).

I grabbed my purse and the minute I did I heard my phone ring in it. I dug it out of the side pocket, looked at the display, and saw it said *Slim Calling.*

I touched the screen and put it to my ear. "Hey, honey."

"Hey, darlin'. Change of plans."

It was Monday after Olivia phoned in the middle of the night on Saturday (or, more precisely, way early Sunday morning). The boys were back with Olivia and Brock's attorney and Hector had been informed first thing that morning that plans had not only changed but had been shifted into overdrive. I'd had to come into the bakery for a few hours on Sunday, which gave Brock more alone time with his boys. But I'd met him at his place yesterday evening, when we pretty much zonked out because he'd had about four hours of sleep and I'd had about two.

Tonight, it was my place and I was leaving early to go home and make dinner.

"What change of plans?"

"My house, not yours. Game's on," he informed me.

"What game?" I asked.

"Nuggets," he answered.

Hmm. This was interesting. Nuggets beat out Monday Night Football.

"And?" I asked.

"My set is better than yours," he stated.

"Your set is better than mine?"

"Babe, your TV should have been retired about six years ago."

"It's only three years old."

"Okay, then your set should have been retired about two and a half years ago."

I blinked at my desk.

Then I asked, "What?"

"You trade up every year."

I blinked at my desk again.

Then I asked, "Your truck was twenty years old but you trade up TVs every year?"

"Uh...yeah," he said like, "Uh...duh."

This was gearing up to be a milk jug discussion, I could feel it.

Therefore, my decision about the future of the discussion was...whatever.

Moving on.

"I haven't stocked your fridge in a while," I reminded him.

Another thing to note, two houses with one woman meant one woman cleaning two houses *and* stocking two fridges. Brock, I had learned, was not clean *or* tidy. Brock, I had also learned, had lived his life since divorcing Olivia (who, he informed me, was not a master chef or even close) on pizza, Chinese, fast food, and takeaway Mexican.

Considering this, it was beginning to dawn that Brock's body was a minor miracle even with all that running and gym time.

"We'll order pizza," he decided.

That I could do.

"Cool," I agreed.

"And I'm tied up, gonna be half an hour later, maybe an hour," he said. "I'll text you when I'm on my way home and you can order the pizza."

"Does that mean someone died?" I asked.

His voice held restrained humor when he answered, "Yeah, sweetness. Part of the gig of homicide is someone dying."

I turned and looked out into the bakery, smelling cake smells.

When my phone rang at the bakery, this usually meant someone wanted to order a birthday cake. When Brock's rang at the station, this usually meant someone had a cap busted in their ass.

My job was *way* better.

Thus, I didn't mind (too much) cleaning two houses and stocking two fridges.

"Okay, baby, text me and I'll order the pizza," I said softly.

There was a moment's pause before I got a "My sweet Tess," and then I got a disconnect.

I allowed myself some time to feel the tingle Brock calling me his sweet Tess sent shimmering through me. I shoved the rest of the cupcake into my mouth and allowed myself some more time to feel a different kind of tingle.

Then I shoved my phone in my purse, pulled on my coat, and headed out.

I hit the public area of my bakery and, as it always did and I hoped it always would, that gave me a tingle too.

Three robin's-egg-blue walls, one of them with a huge stenciled pattern in lavender of hibiscus blossoms attended by hummingbirds with the back wall behind

the display case painted lavender with "Tessa's Cakes" in
flowery script painted in robin's-egg-blue surrounded by
hibiscus and hummingbirds. This was positioned just a
few inches from where the wall met the ceiling so people
could see it clearly from the wide front windows facing
the street.

I still had no idea where I got the theme, outside those
colors being my favorite. Flowers and birds didn't scream
bakery! But the colors were warm and beautiful, the flowers and birds delicate and striking. I'd paid a whack for
the look and the customized stenciling. With my constant
changes and obsession with getting it *just right* I'd driven
the artist who created it and my logo bonkers, but it had
been worth it.

In fact, I'd paid a whack for everything that had to do
with the look or feel of my bakery.

Upon copious consumption of wine with Martha as
I planned the rest of my life post-Damian, we had both
decided if I was going to go for it, I might as well go whole
hog. So when I launched Tessa's Cakes, I didn't fuck
around. I planned everything to the minutest detail, hired
my staff with careful consideration that went beyond
them arriving on time and being able to punch buttons on
a cash register, and I launched the entire concept. Beautiful cakes that tasted really freaking good bought from
friendly personnel who didn't have vacant looks but easily apparent personalities in a bakery where you either
wanted to come back or you wanted to stay awhile.

The floors were wood, as was the frame of the old-
fashioned display case that was filled with beautiful
cakes, cupcakes, and delectable-looking cookies, this
topped with mismatching but very cool covered cake

stands and glass cookie jars. There were battered wooden counters on either side of the display case that also held cookie jars and cake stands and there were shelves on the wall behind the case and counters with even more. Two big blackboards were on the walls on either side of the shelves with the day's ever-changing goodies scrolled artfully on them in lavender and blue chalk, hibiscus and hummingbirds decorating the corners.

There were tables out front if you wanted to hang and eat your treats. These again all wood, again all mismatched. The only thing each of the chairs shared was being wide seated, sturdy, and comfortable. Each table was topped with a tiny steel bucket with a poufy display of flowers and there was a much bigger bucket filled with a spray of them on one of the counters. These were rotated twice a week by a local florist who gave me a killer discount because I had a small sign that advertised they were hers.

I served coffee, tea, and different flavored milk but no espresso drinks because my place was about baked goods, not coffee drinks, and I wanted the hum of the place not to include the blast of steam every five seconds nor the look of it marred by a behemoth espresso machine. I also didn't want my kids spending their time sweating over making lattes. I wanted them to spend their time selling cakes.

As Brock was dealing with a dead person and this, in my mind, required cake to expunge any residual mental unpleasantness, I headed to the stacks of flat-packed boxes (piled alternate blue and lavender, all with my Tessa's Cakes logo stamped on top). I grabbed a six-cupcake one, folded it, selected some treats for Brock then closed it and tied it with bakery string (again, two colors, blue on lavender, which was what I had, and then there was lavender string for the blue boxes).

I held the box by the string, called my good-byes, headed outside, and after the warmth of my bakery, the arctic blast was a physical hit.

We were having a harsh winter, lots of cold, bursts of snow. It was after five, full-on dark, and the air was crisp. As I disliked driving in snow, I checked the weather every morning with an obsession that was slightly scary (however, I never thought this. I only thought this after Brock told me he thought this but luckily he did it while chuckling).

Today they said forty percent chance of snow flurries. Considering my snow-o-meter was finely tuned, I thought the air said more like a one hundred percent chance.

I got in my car, stowed the box and my purse, and fired it up then pulled out my cell to call Martha to see if she was home for me to come by and hang for a quick glass of wine before heading to Brock's. But it rang as my finger hovered to slide it on.

It said *Cob Calling*.

My brows drew together.

Cob and I had exchanged phone numbers but he'd never phoned me. I'd, of course, seen him on occasion, considering we'd just finished holiday season, and during it, he'd popped over to see his boys and give them presents.

And when I'd seen him I'd noted the obvious and that was that he was not looking good. His treatments had started in earnest, his weight was dropping at an alarming rate, his eyes were sinking into his head, and his skin appeared sallow. He did not complain and acted his usual self but the physical manifestations of the treatments were impossible to miss.

My heart skipped a beat. I took the call and put my phone to my ear.

"Hey, Cob."

"Sweetheart," he replied and he sounded about five times worse than he looked the last time I saw him, so my heart skipped another beat.

"You okay?" I asked.

"I had . . ." He stopped.

"Cob?" I called. "You there?" I asked when he didn't say anything more.

"Honey, I had an accident. Jill brought me home and she and Laurie . . ." He paused. "They've been doin' so much. I can't—"

Damn.

I quickly cut him off with, "Where do you live?"

"I wouldn't ask. It's just—"

"Cob, where do you live?"

He didn't say anything until right before I opened my mouth to repeat my question.

"This shits me," he whispered. "It shits me, Tess. So damned embarra—"

"Cob," I broke in quietly. "Honey, where do you live?"

He hesitated and then gave me his address and I knew where it was.

"I'll be there in fifteen minutes," I promised.

"Thanks, sweetheart," he whispered.

"Hang tight," I said, disconnected, tossed my phone on my purse, backed out, and headed to Cob's.

Cob lived in Baker Historical District, not far from where Brock used to live. Baker was a great 'hood, a mishmash of houses, personality, and most folks took care of their homes.

Cob's was tiny with a chain-link fence, an overabundance of tall trees planted close to the house, which would, in summer, totally block out any light, and a look that said he didn't spend much time keeping up with the Joneses even when he wasn't being treated for cancer.

I knocked on the door and entered when I heard him call weakly, "It's open."

When I entered, I was assaulted immediately with the hideous smell of vomit.

Oh God.

Cob was on the couch, the TV on. I noticed at once he'd lost more weight. His eyes were more sunken in his head and his skin seemed to hang on his face. Even though he was reclining, I could see his clothes were loose on him and there was a vomit bucket he'd missed on the floor beside him.

His eyes came to mine.

"I can't...I can't..." He shook his head. "I don't have it in me to clean it up, sweetheart," he finished on a whisper.

"Of course not," I whispered back, closed the door, and rushed forward, dropping my bag on an armchair that made Brock's old furniture look like it belonged in an interior design magazine. "I'll get this sorted, don't worry," I said softly as I pulled off my coat and dropped it on the chair.

"It's also..." He pressed his lips together. "I also couldn't make it to the bathroom when I was lyin' in bed."

Great. More vomit.

I nodded, buried my distaste for my upcoming chore as well as the smell hanging in the house, and smiled. "Okay, honey."

I went to work, clearing his immediate space first and scrounging in the kitchen for a big bowl to give him just in case another wave came on. Then I set about dealing with the mess on the bedroom carpet. Then I realized that even with the cleanup, the smell lingered.

I needed to do something about that. The smell was making *me* sick and I wasn't having chemotherapy.

I walked back to the living room and said, "Okay, cleanup done but I'm heading to the store to get some stuff to deal with this smell. Do you need anything else?"

He shook his head. "Laurie and Jill keep me pretty well stocked."

I nodded but replied, "I'll just go look. And, I know this doesn't sound great right now, but if you can keep it down, you need dinner so we'll get you set up when I get back."

"Thanks, sweetheart," he said quietly.

I studied him a second and then, gently, I queried, "Cob, don't they give you something for the nausea?"

His face shut down almost to stubborn but he was too weak to manage even that.

Then he stated, "So many damned pills."

"I can imagine, but you need to keep your strength up," I advised.

"For what?" he asked, his eyes never leaving mine.

"To fight," I answered, again gently.

He continued to hold my eyes, then his moved to the TV.

Damn.

I gave up, hit the kitchen, did an inventory, found a piece of paper to make a list, and headed out, stopping to lean down and kiss Cob's cheek on my way out.

The good news was, the flurries were holding off so I felt a little better as I made the five-minute drive to the Albertson's on Alameda.

The bad news was, I was so involved in what I was doing, I was standing in line at the checkout when my phone rang. I yanked it out, saw it said *Slim Calling,* and realized I forgot to call him.

Crap.

I engaged it, put it to my ear, and said, "Hey, honey."

"Where are you?" was Brock's terse reply.

"I—"

"I'm standin' in my livin' room, you're not here, and you didn't reply to my text."

With all the fun I was having cleaning up puke, I must have missed it.

Crap again.

"I'm—"

He cut me off again. "You also didn't call."

"Brock, give me a second to speak," I said softly, pushing my cart toward the conveyor belt and starting to unload.

"So, speak," Brock ordered.

"I'm at Albertson's on Alameda," I told him but got no more out when Brock spoke again.

"Babe, we're doin' pizza, remember?" he asked, and didn't give me a chance to answer before he went on to query, "And what the fuck are you doin' at Albertson's on Alameda?"

This was a good question, considering the fact that for

his place or mine I shopped either at Wild Oats or King Soopers, both on Colorado Boulevard.

I kept unloading the cart as I answered, "I'm here because your dad phoned. He had a treatment today, got sick, didn't make it to the bathroom, and he needed someone to help him out. Jill and Laura are taking him to and from treatments and helping out at his house. Jill had dropped him off and he didn't want to ask her to do more. I told him a while ago, if he needed to call on me, he could, so he called on me."

This was met with silence.

I had the cart unloaded, and I shifted and commandeered the handle, pushing it through as I smiled at the checkout clerk and settled in to watch the bag boy bag my purchases.

When he didn't speak, I did.

"So I went by his place, got it cleaned up but it still doesn't smell that good. I'm buying some stuff to help with that then I'm going to make him some dinner, see to it that he eats it and keeps it down, and then I'll be over." I paused, then said, "Do pizza without me, honey. I'll eat with Cob."

Again, silence but this didn't last as long.

Brock broke it when he said, "Your plans change, the shit goin' down around us, you fuckin' phone."

Then he hung up.

I blinked at the bags.

Then I slid my phone in the side pocket on my purse, a variety of feelings battling it out in my head.

Brock had never hung up on me.

Sure, I didn't call and it was obvious he was worried but it wasn't like I was currently at one of the biker bars he'd introduced me to, on a bender, standing on the bar, and teaching all the bikers in attendance how to dance like Axl Rose (something I had done once while on a mini-bender—that was to say, it lasted a few hours— while I was with Brock when he was Jake though I didn't do it on the bar, I did it on the stage while the band was playing "Paradise City" and Brock was standing just off the dance floor laughing his ass off).

I was taking care of *his* dad.

It hit me that the surprise at his hanging up on me and fear of his being angry with me were mingled quite liberally with me being somewhat pissed off. Then being pissed off started winning out and I realized I was getting more pissed off. Then I wasn't scared Brock was angry with me or surprised he'd hung up on me, I was just pissed he'd hung up on me.

I managed to pay, get the stuff to my car, and get to Cob's house without calling Brock back and giving him an earful. I got the stuff in and battled the smell first with air freshener and then with rug shampoo. I didn't want to overwhelm Cob with a warring combination of intense smells that were worse than just vomit and luckily I managed this feat. The vomit smell was gone, the air freshener evaporated, and the shampoo didn't stink.

I set a soothingly scented candle I bought at Albertson's to burning in the bedroom, I got Cob an iced lemon-lime, and then I set about making dinner.

The chicken noodle soup was warming in the pan and I was setting out bowls on plates with buttered saltine crackers around the edges (what my Mom used to serve when my sister or I got sick), hoping the butter wouldn't be too rich for Cob, when I heard the front door open.

Then I heard Cob surprised greeting of, "Heya, Slim."

I sucked in a breath through my nose.

Then I heard Brock ask, "How you feelin'?"

"Better," Cob answered, then offered, "Tess is in the kitchen."

"Right," I heard Brock mutter, then, "Be back, Dad."

"Okay, son."

I grabbed the spoon, started to stir the soup, and braced.

I felt his mood hit the room before I saw him do it. It wasn't sparking and pissed off. It wasn't abrasive and angry. It was something I'd never felt before. Something heavy. Weighted. Soft but not warm. And when I saw him, that heavy look was in his eyes, the soft on his face.

He stopped by the stove but not too close.

He held my eyes and said, "Hey."

"Hey," I replied.

He studied me.

Then he noted quietly, "You're pissed."

"I don't like to get hung up on anytime but especially not when I'm buying carpet cleaner to eradicate puke smells," I returned, also quietly.

He continued to hold my eyes.

Then he nodded once and murmured, "Right."

"I've got this, you didn't need to come," I told him, still quietly so Cob wouldn't hear.

"He's *my* dad, Tess," Brock replied.

I tipped my head to the side and asked, "He is?"

I watched his mouth get tight.

Then he warned low, "Don't go there, babe."

I turned off the burner and grabbed the saucepan, moving to the bowls.

While I poured, I whispered, "It's go time, Brock. You need to jump off that fence and land on one side or the other. You don't miss much so I'm guessing you can take one look at your father and know where this is heading. The destination is uncertain but the path is not and it's an ugly one. You no longer have the luxury to sit on that fence. You need to make a decision."

I put the saucepan back on the burner and my eyes went to his.

"Is he in or is he not? You've got ten seconds to decide while I take him his food. You walk out the door, that's your decision and I'll support you on that but you need to know my support will not include me not kicking in to help Jill and Laura with Cob. If you don't walk out the door, I'll make you a bowl and we're hanging with your father to make sure he keeps his dinner down."

I grabbed a spoon, put it in Cob's bowl, took the plate, and walked into the living room.

By the time I got back, Brock had moved. He wasn't standing at the stove. He was standing at the kitchen window, his weight leaning heavily into one hand set high on the window frame. His eyes aimed at the flurries now falling outside. His mood filling the room now, the weight so heavy, it was suffocating.

His jaw was clenched.

But I knew his decision was made.

And the decision he made made me love him all the more.

I pulled in a breath and walked to him.

Then I wrapped my arms around his waist and pressed my front into his back.

I held him for a while then whispered, "Snow keeps

up, will you take me to your place and bring me back to my car tomorrow morning? I don't like driving in it."

He didn't answer for several long seconds.

Then he said to the window, "Yeah, babe."

I pressed my forehead into his back.

Then I lifted my head away but pressed my body closer and carefully said, "He's not taking his nausea medication. You need to talk to him about that."

I looked over his shoulder at his profile and saw a muscle in his jaw jump. He made no verbal reply but I knew he heard me and he'd do what he could.

Then I gave him a squeeze and kept whispering. "Take that plate, honey, and go sit with your dad. He's got the game on. I'll make another one for me and be out in a minute."

He nodded to the window.

Then his body moved. I let him go and he walked to the bowl. He looked at it and walked back to me. Then he lifted both hands, cupped my jaw, and tilted my face up to his so he could touch his mouth to mine.

When he lifted his head, I whispered, "He loves you."

He closed his eyes, that suffocating feeling suffused the room before he opened them and whispered, "I know."

"I love you too."

His eyes got soft, the weight in the room lifted and, he repeated his whispered, "I know."

"We'll get through this," I promised.

He didn't look like he believed me and he didn't repeat himself again.

"Go eat. It's getting cold," I ordered.

His eyes held mine a moment before he let me go and walked back to his plate.

I made my own, took it out, and watched the Nuggets game with Brock and his father.

Cob held down the soup, crackers, and one of the cupcakes his granddaughter baked that I ran out to my car to bring in.

The Nuggets won.

CHAPTER EIGHTEEN

Somewhat Good for Now

"GONNA SWING BY Dad's with this TV then I'll be over."

I had the phone to my ear, Brock on the line, and I was sliding a chicken into the oven.

It was Thursday and it was a Thursday after Brock called his sisters to get them to put him and me on the Cob rotation. It was also a Thursday after Brock found out that Cob had only one TV and it was in his living room. So, lastly, it was a Thursday after Brock swung by Best Buy to get his dad a TV for his bedroom so he had something to do when he was feeling double extra shit and didn't want to leave his bed. Brock had even called the cable company to add an additional set and he'd laid it on thick about his father's illness, which meant the wait was not seventy-two hours but twenty-four. They were showing tomorrow and they'd thrown in a couple of months of free premium channels just because.

Brock did not mess around when it came to TVs *or* cable. He pulled out all the stops and got results.

So, nothing new.

"All right, honey," I answered. "Dinner'll be done in an hour and a half but it'll keep warm if you aren't home."

"I'll aim for that," Brock told me, then, "Later, babe."

"Later."

Then he was gone.

I hit end call then sent a text to Martha in return to hers. She was planning a girls' night in at her place for the weekend after this one, being cool about planning it when Brock had his boys so I could finagle some time for the boys alone with their dad without Brock (hopefully) cottoning on.

And I was at odds, as I usually was, with how I felt about Martha's girls' night in. This was not a new concept for Martha but it was a crapshoot what you'd encounter when you arrived. She would either be in the mood to experiment with a variety of recipes she'd totally made up, none of them successful, all of them you at least had to try. Or she'd fill her house with junk food and unearth all her vast collection of romantic comedies.

I was hoping for the latter.

My text to Martha started a flurry of texts that included Elvira, Gwen, Camille, Tracy, and even Shirleen getting in on the act. I fielded them all while dealing with the rest of dinner and felt great relief when Elvira firmly took charge of food preparation and stated in a way even Martha couldn't protest she was making her "boards."

I didn't know what Elvira's boards were but whatever they were they had to be better than fried celery.

Celery as celery was bad. Celery fried was the work of Satan.

The texting frenzy died down and I was basting the chicken for the last time when another text came through right when my landline rang.

I glanced at the screen on my cell to see it was Brock

saying "on my way" then I went to my landline, grabbed it out of the receiver, hit the on button, and put it to my ear.

"Hello," I greeted.

Nothing.

"Hello?" I repeated.

More nothing.

I was about to take the phone from my ear when I heard a man ask, "This Tessa O'Hara?"

A shiver shot down my spine. I didn't know why, it just did.

And it wasn't pleasant.

"Uh..." I started.

"Tessa O'Hara who's seein' Brock Lucas?"

Ice filled my veins.

"Who's this?" I asked.

"It is," the voice whispered then I had a dead line.

Fuck. Fuck. *Fuck!*

I put the phone in the receiver and moved to my cell, making quick work of calling Brock.

A ring, then, "Babe."

"I just got a creepy call."

A small hesitation, then, "What kind of creepy?"

"Creepy creepy. Creepy *wrong* creepy. It came in on my landline."

"You listed?" he asked.

Heck no, I wasn't listed. First, I was a single female. Second, my ex-husband was a whack job who raped me and eventually turned out to be a drug lord.

I didn't give Brock this answer.

Instead, I answered, "No."

"Fuck," he muttered, then, "What'd they say?"

I sucked in a breath, then told him, "He asked if I was

Tessa O'Hara. Then he asked if I was seeing you. I didn't answer either but I asked him who he was and he said, 'It is,' meaning he knew he got me and I was seeing you and then he hung up on me."

"Doors locked?" Brock asked instantly and I felt another shiver.

"I don't..." I paused. "I don't know," I told him, moving directly toward the backdoor.

"Check. Lock," he ordered.

Backdoor secure, I headed toward the front, saying a shaky, "Okay." Then I asked, "Is this the kind of thing Olivia would do, you know, to play with me?"

"Never played this dirty but wouldn't put it past her," he answered.

Freaking great.

"I'll be there in ten minutes," he said softly.

"Okay," I replied, locking the front door and then I told him, "I'm all locked."

"Good, baby. See you soon."

"Okay."

He ended the call, and I moved back to the kitchen, my eyes going to the microwave to note the time. Then I tried to control the fear that was mixing with the anger should this be Olivia as I dealt with the final preparations for dinner.

Eight minutes had elapsed when it happened. I knew this because I had just checked the microwave for the fiftieth time.

And what happened was I heard gunshots, six of them, one after another sounding like they were right in front of my house.

I stared at the window a nanosecond before I crouched

down behind the island as more gunfire sounded and it penetrated my frozen-with-terror mind that it sounded like return fire.

As the gunfight continued, I came to my senses, scuttled in a crouch to the landline phone, reached up, grabbed it, hit the on button, then dialed 911.

"Nine-one-one, what's your emergency?"

"Gunshots outside my house," I whispered.

"Where are you, ma'am?"

I started to give my address as I heard noise at my front door and I stopped, staring through my house at it, paralyzed with fear.

"Ma'am," the operator called, "please confirm you're safe and your address."

"Someone's—"

The door opened and Brock walked in, his overcoat on one side dusted with snow. He turned, slammed the door, locked it, and prowled to me, holding his gun in his hand.

I didn't, as I usually did, admire him in his work clothes. Today, a nice, thick black turtleneck (one, incidentally, I bought him for Christmas and I say one because I bought him three). Jeans that weren't nearly as faded as his normal jeans. A great black belt that the sweater was tucked behind (and that was the only part of the sweater tucked, I didn't know if he did it on purpose or what but for some reason I thought it looked awesome). And a handsome, tailored, black wool overcoat (which, also incidentally, Laura and Jill got together to buy him for Christmas and on him it was the bomb).

Although his work attire was only a nuance away from his nonwork attire, when he got home, after greeting me, he never hesitated in taking it off, putting on faded jeans, no belt, and, now that we were in the dead of winter, either a faded long-sleeved tee or a thermal.

Now he prowled through the house toward me and I didn't notice how hot he looked in his work clothes. I only noticed the dusting of snow on his overcoat and the gun in his hand.

How did he get that dusting of snow?

"Ma'am?" I heard the 911 operator call. "Are you with me?"

"That emergency?" Brock growled when he got to me, staring down at me still crouched by my kitchen counter.

I didn't respond. He bent and pulled the phone out of my hand and put it to his ear.

"This is Detective Brock Lucas. I was just fired on and exchanged fire with an unidentified male . . ."

He kept talking but my mind blanked of everything but his words repeating in my head.

I was just fired on and exchanged fire . . .
I was just fired on and exchanged fire . . .
I was just fired on and exchanged fire . . .

I straightened as he continued to growl into the phone, his eyes on me, but my thoughts were still elsewhere.

He had that snow on him because he'd thrown himself to the ground to dodge bullets aimed at him in front of my house.

My *man* had thrown his beautiful *body* to the snow to dodge fucking *bullets* aimed at him in front of my *fucking* house.

And he had his gun in his hand because he'd had to return fire.

And I knew *exactly* who ordered that unidentified male to aim bullets at my man.

No.

Oh no.

I did not *fucking think so.*

Just like I lost it when Levi was at Brock's house, I didn't think.

I just moved.

And what I moved to do was snatch my keys off the counter and I ran out of the house.

"Tess!" Brock shouted, but I was gone.

Down the walk and in my car.

"Goddamn it! Tess!" I heard Brock shout from somewhere outside the car.

Car on, I didn't even look and put the pedal to the floor.

I didn't know how I got there and it was a miracle I made it without killing myself or anyone else. But I hit University, then turned right, then turned left on Yale, then I drove like a demon through Donald Heller's established, tidy neighborhood with its big houses on big lots. A path I had taken frequently for twelve years while dating and married to my shit-heel of an ex but had not taken once in the last six and a half.

And I went there because I had no idea where Damian lived.

But I sure as fuck was going to find out.

I screeched to a halt at the curb, shot out of my car, and raced through the snow in the yard to the front door, not noticing the headlights of the truck that followed me go out as it parked behind my car.

I banged on the door loudly, not letting up as I shouted, "Don, open the fucking door!"

A hand came from behind me, fingers wrapping around my wrist, halting my pounding as I felt warmth hit my back and heard whispered in my ear, "Tess, Jesus, baby, calm—"

Brock didn't finish because the door opened and Donald was standing there.

His eyes flashed quickly back and forth and again between Brock and me then a tentative smile hit his mouth as his eyes started to light and he whispered, "Tess, honey, my—"

He didn't finish because I shouted, "Where is he?"

Donald blinked, his gaze moving between Brock, who now had my wrist and arm wrapped around my belly, his with it, and me, then he asked, "Who?"

"Your *fucking* scum of the earth shithead *asshole* of a son, that's who!" I shrieked.

He blinked again then I heard, "Tess?" and looked beyond Donald to see fucking, fucking, *fucking* Damian standing several feet behind him in his father's foyer.

That was when I lost it again.

Tearing free of Brock, I shoved straight past Donald and launched myself at Damian, arms raised, nails bared, ready to scratch his motherfucking eyes out.

His hands came up to defend himself and he took a step back but I didn't get there.

A steel arm clamped around my waist. I let out an "oof!" and was hauled back against Brock, who then clamped another steel arm around my shoulders and chest at the front.

At my ear, he whispered, "Cool it, sweetness."

"*Fuck cool!*" I screeched and struggled against his hold at the same time planting my feet as he tried to pull me back. Through this my eyes stayed glued to Damian. "You fucking *dick*!" I kept screeching.

"What on—?" Donald asked with soft shock at my side but I shouted over him.

"It wasn't enough hitting me?" I asked and Brock froze at the same time I sensed Donald doing the same. "It wasn't enough raping me?" I kept shouting and disregarded the noise that came from Donald that sounded like someone landed a blow to his stomach. "Then you call me out of the blue, *fucking lie to me* a-fucking-*gain* after you lied to me so many *fucking, fucking* times I lost count with the women you screwed who were *not me*, and told me your father was sick as a ploy to get me to meet you."

"My God," Donald whispered but I kept yelling.

"Then you keep contacting me when I asked you over and over and fucking *over again* not to call me and you drag me into your shit with the DEA and the FBI and the police and *now* you send someone to *shoot at my boyfriend in front of my house!*"

Damian kept his eyes glued on me too and when I quit shrieking, he said softly, "Tess—"

"*Fuck you!*" I spat. "Fuck you, Damian. What did I do? What did I do but fall in love with you? What did I do to deserve you treating me like a piece of garbage and then...then...*finally* when I have something good in my life, something beautiful...finally when I feel fucking *safe,* you move to destroy that too?"

"Honey, I didn't do—" Damian started but I cut him off.

Screaming at the top of my lungs, the sound so shrill it pierced the space like a dart, I shouted, "*Don't you dare call me honey!*"

Damian held my eyes. Brock held me close. I glared at Damian, heat boiling through my veins, through my brain, so fucking hot, it was burning me alive.

Then Damian pulled his eyes from mine, turned his head to the side, his face grew concerned, and he started to move that way, saying, "Dad."

"Don't," Donald ordered and I tore my eyes from Damian to see Donald standing at the wall of the foyer, hand pressed against it, that hand clearly holding him up. His face was pale, his eyes on his son wounded, and I hadn't seen him for a while but he'd always seemed younger than his years, his humor and love of life making him that way. But in that moment he looked beyond his seventy-two years and well into his nineties.

At the sight of him, a wave of pain rolled through me. My hands went to Brock's arms, my fingers curling around, one at my chest, one at my belly and Brock's arms got tighter.

"That's why," Donald whispered to his son.

"Dad," Damian whispered back.

"That's why we lost Tess."

I felt tears fill my eyes.

Donald didn't look away from Damian when he whispered a tortured, "You *raped* her?"

"It wasn't—" Damian started. My body straightened, the tears vanished, and I interrupted him.

"It was," I snapped and Damian looked at me.

"Tess"—he shook his head and started to lift a hand—"things just got out of hand."

Oh.

My.

God.

Brock made a noise low in his throat, his arms going super-tight around me but I didn't read these warning signs because I lost it again.

"*Out of hand?*" I shrieked.

"Tess—" Damian started again, his eyes darting back and forth between me and Brock and, honest to God, it looked like he was weighing the decision to approach.

"Don't you get near me, you motherfucking asshole," I clipped. "And, newsflash, Damian. A woman is fighting you tooth and nail, screaming, 'No!' at the top of her lungs, crying uncontrollably, and begging you to stop and you *still* fuck her that…is…*rape* even if she *is* your goddamned wife."

Brock's super-tight arms convulsed twice through this speech but I only had concentration enough for Damian, who winced.

Then he said softly, "You left the next day, Tess. You never gave me a chance to explain."

I felt my eyebrows hit my hairline.

"Explain?" I asked. "Explain?" I repeated my question. "Are you fucking *high*?"

"Tess, I was—"

"Clawing your way up a drug cartel," I finished for him then leaned forward, taking Brock's arms with me, thus taking Brock with me. "I know," I hissed and leaned back. "Stressful, hunh?" I asked. "So stressful you suddenly lose your ability to be a decent human being and when your patience snaps because your wife is asking you simple questions like, 'Honey, what's stressing you out?' you take your hands to her. And when she says no to sex, you lose your mind and rape her. It must have been tough for you dealing with all that stress as you climbed to the highest heights of the criminal underworld, Damian. I feel bad for you that you didn't have a different woman in your life who'd eat your shit. Sorry I was such a crap wife."

"You weren't a crap wife," he whispered.

"I know," I bit out. "I was being sarcastic, you moron."

"I made some bad decisions and let my emotions get the better of me, Tess. I'll admit that," Damian said.

"Big of you," I retorted. "Though bad decisions and emotions getting the better of you don't entirely destroy lives, Damian, something you've been doing to people you care about and people you don't even fucking know for over a decade now."

"I—" he started. His jaw clenched and he looked away, tearing both his hands through his hair and I noticed belatedly he looked good.

Like his father, age barely touched him. And like the asshole he was, impending incarceration didn't faze him. Fit frame at least three inches shorter than Brock and probably more than thirty pounds lighter. Light brown hair. Dark brown eyes. A sharp crease in his well-tailored dark blue trousers. A light blue shirt that I knew had been made specifically for him because he always spent a whack on his clothes. Polished, dark brown, Italian leather shoes.

Even now, he had it. Even now, even as detached as I was, I sensed his magnetism. Decent looks, great clothes he wore well, undercurrent of charisma never switching off.

Toxic charisma.

Poison.

He dropped his hands and leveled his eyes on mine.

Then he stated, "If you gave me a moment to explain at lunch before you took off, I got in touch with you because I was trying to make it up to you."

Make it up to me?

Maybe he *was* high.

He kept talking.

"I asked you to lunch to explain"—his eyes moved to Brock then back to me and he carried on—"about the money. To go over the bank documents with you. I wanted you to have"—again he looked to Brock, then back to me—"if something happened to me, I wanted you covered."

"You wanted me covered?" I asked, my voice filled with derision mixed with shock.

"Yes," he clipped.

"Why?" I queried.

"Because you were my wife. Because I still love you. Because I fucked up. And because I wanted to make it up to you."

"You thought..." I whispered but stopped, momentarily unable to go on then I went on. "You thought that you could make it up to me by infiltrating my life and saddling me with your ill-gotten gains. And when I didn't hang around long enough to say yes to this super-generous offer, you forged my name on the documents anyway so you could be certain to continue infiltrating my life at the same time fucking it up when the best thing you could do, bar building a time machine so that you could go back and make sure you never met me, would be to leave me... *the fuck*...alone?"

He pressed his lips together and said not a word.

I turned to his father.

It killed me to see this was killing him.

But I could not help that. I couldn't. I had enough on my plate.

So I wasn't even going to try.

"I love you," I said softly. "I always will. I think of you often, so often…" I sucked in a breath and decided to leave that because I couldn't go there. "Your son took a lot from me. All of it hurt, so much you wouldn't believe me even if I described the pain. And losing you was part of that pain."

Tears filled his eyes. I watched them as I felt the same happen in mine.

"Honey," he whispered, taking his hand from the wall and turning away from his son to face me.

"I love you and miss you but I'm not coming back, never, no matter what happens to Damian. I can't have anything that reminds me of him in my life. It's toxic. I just released it and I can't take it back. I can't have it poisoning me anymore. Not anymore. He took eighteen years of my life. He can't have any more."

I watched him swallow.

"This man holding me is the man of my dreams, Don," I told him quietly. "Tonight, someone shot at him. It doesn't take Sherlock Holmes to follow that trail to Damian. He has family. He has children. And he has *me*. Talk to your son. Make him stay out of my life and leave me and everyone I love alone. Please. Please do that for me."

He sniffed, his eyes still wet and getting wetter and then he nodded.

I looked back at Damian and stated in a firm voice that still shook, "I never want to see you again. If you can, for once, listen to what I say rather than what you want to hear then hear this. I never, *never* want to see you again. Never. No matter what. I don't want your money. I don't want your guilt. You cannot make up to me what you tore from me or the years I lost because your poison infected me. Do not call me. Do not come to my house. Do not fuck with my life. Do not fuck with people I care about. Go away and stay away."

"Tess," Damian whispered and it was there, right in his eyes, pain and regret.

Pain and fucking regret.

The motherfucking asshole.

"Go away and stay away," I whispered back.

Without looking at Don again, I moved my body toward the door. Brock felt my movement and let me go. But he grabbed my hand, led me out, through the yard, and to the passenger side of his truck that was parked behind my car.

He bleeped the locks and opened the passenger door before I noticed what he was about.

I locked my body and looked up at him, saying softly, "I'm okay to drive."

He shook his head, gently pushing me toward the seat, saying, "Get in, baby."

"I don't want to leave my car here," I told him.

"Get in, don't worry about it. I'll deal with it."

"Brock—"

He closed in on me and I had to tip my head way back, he was that close.

"Up into the truck, Tess," he said softly.

I bit my lip and nodded. He moved back and I climbed up.

He rounded the hood, swung up beside me, his truck rumbled to life, and off we went.

And when we hit Yale it came to me that of the many awesome powers my man held, clairvoyance was one of them, for the adrenalin surge fled and the emotions rushed in on its tail. I lost it again, this time melting into deep, body-rocking, uncontrollable sobs.

I was so far gone I didn't notice us getting home. I didn't know how I got in. I didn't even know how I got myself curled on the bed. I was just suddenly there and I just kept crying.

I vaguely heard snatches of Brock saying, "She's bad, Martha. I need to deal with the police and she needs you so I need you over here soon as you can come." And also what might have been just minutes later or longer, I was too far gone to tell, "My woman lost it after it went down. I can't come to the station. The boys are outside investigating the area. You need to come here."

But that was all I noticed until I felt Martha crawl into bed with me, curve her body into the back of mine, her arm wrapping around and holding me tight.

I heard the voices in the living room then.

"Who's here?" I asked through a sniffle.

"Cops, honey," she whispered. "Brock has some business he needs to tend to after what went down tonight."

Of course.

I shut my eyes tight and pressed out more tears. Finding her hand with mine at my belly, I pulled it up to my chest, held it tight with my fingers as I pressed it deep into my chest.

I opened my eyes and whispered, "He got shot at tonight."

"I know," she whispered back.

My hand clutched hers and new tears stung my eyes and nose. "I can't lose him."

"I know, honey."

"His boys can't lose him."

"I know."

"His family—"

"Shh, Tess."

I sucked in a broken breath.

Then I stated a trembling, "I hate Damian."

Her arm gave me a squeeze and her hand twisted to hold mine.

"I do too."

I fell quiet. So did Martha.

Then I sucked in another broken breath and told her, "There's a chicken in the oven."

"I know. I sorted it," she told me. "Are you hungry? Do you want me to get you something?"

"No, but Brock—"

"He's a big boy, honey. He can take care of himself."

"I know, but—"

"Tess, honey, trust me," she said while squeezing my hand. "Right now, he's not hungry. Right now that man out there is concentrating on making a statement to his colleagues and trying not to rip your living room apart. He pulls his shit together, I don't think the first thing on his mind is going to be dinner."

I nodded, then said, "I should go to him."

"No." She held me closer. "He wants you here and safe with me while he deals with that shit. Let him have that. You do what he needs you to do and get *your* shit together."

She was right.

Therefore, I nodded again and settled.

She held me for a long time. The voices in the living room silenced. Brock didn't come in.

Then Martha sensed I'd gotten my shit together (and she was right). I knew this because she gave me a squeeze and said, "The chicken is burned so I'm gonna go rustle up dinner. Time you two ate."

She pulled away and I rolled to my back to look at her.

She hadn't even taken off her coat.

She came right to me and didn't take off her coat.

Fresh tears hit my eyes but I beat them back and started to suggest, "Maybe you shouldn't—"

"I'm not going to cook, Tess. Riviera."

Well that was a relief.

"Chile rellenos," I ordered and she grinned.

That was to say she grinned before she muttered, "Like I don't know that," as she rolled off the bed, rounded it, shot me another grin, and then she disappeared.

She would know I liked the Riviera's chile rellenos, considering I'd eaten approximately seven hundred and twenty-two plates filled with them while sitting across from her.

I gave it a while before I got up, went to the bathroom, took my contacts out, washed my face, and went back to the bedroom to grab my glasses.

I moved out to the living room to see Brock standing just inside the front door talking to Levi and Lenore.

This was interesting.

Quick update: Lenore had not gone away. Lenore was around for Christmas lunch and New Year's dinner with the Lucas clan. When I quizzed Brock about this, he told me he had no clue and when I pressed him to get the dirt, he told me had no intention of giving his brother the third degree about his love life. He said this firmly. Therefore, I let it go reluctantly.

But I was thinking good thoughts.

"Hey, Tess," Levi called, his hazel eyes gentle on me in a way that was sweetly familiar mostly because his brother often looked at me the same way.

"Hey, Levi." My eyes went to Lenore. "Hey, Lenore."

"Hey, honey," she said softly.

I got close and Brock claimed me, arm around the shoulders, tucking my front to his side.

I tipped my head back to look up at him and he informed me, "They went and got your car. It's all good."

It wasn't all good. It wouldn't be all good for a while.

But at least it was somewhat good for now.

I looked to Levi and Lenore. "Thanks, guys."

"Not a problem," Levi rumbled.

"Are you staying for Mexican?" I asked.

"No, we already ate, Tess, and we gotta go. But thanks," Levi answered.

I nodded.

Lenore smiled at me.

Levi looked to his brother and gave him a chin lift.

"I'll walk you out," Brock muttered then looked down at me. "Stay here, babe, yeah?"

I nodded, gave out cheek kisses, hugs, and more words of gratitude and Brock walked out behind his brother and his brother's girl.

I closed the door behind them but stared out the little window, exhausted from my terror-filled, adrenalin-surge, tantrum-throwing, crying-jag evening but not so exhausted I couldn't be nosy about Lenore and Levi.

And I saw that I was right to think good thoughts. As they walked down my walk, Levi slid his arm around her shoulders and Lenore slid hers around his waist. Bonus was, when they stopped at Levi's SUV to talk with Brock, Levi kept her close and Lenore rested the side of her head on his shoulder and when she did, it appeared Levi held her even closer.

Excellent.

After playing busybody, I walked to the kitchen. I had two cold ones popped open by the time Brock got back and I was taking a huge freaking swallow from mine.

Brock walked right to me and I had to jerk my arms to the side because when he walked to me, he didn't stop. He folded his arms around me and pulled me in deep.

Then, against the top of my hair, he asked, "You good?"

"I think that was cathartic," I said to his chest, my arms snaking around him.

"Good," he muttered into my hair.

"I still feel the need to get drunk," I went on and he chuckled. "Blotto." I changed my mind as to the state of drunkenness I aimed to achieve and Brock kept chuckling. Then I changed my mind again, "No, shitfaced. Totally."

His arms gave me a squeeze before one of them released me and my head went back just as his hand wrapped around my neck, his thumb stroking my jaw.

"Have at it, sweetness," he said quietly.

I sucked in a breath.

Then I asked, "Are you okay?"

"Yeah," he answered immediately.

"Brock—" I started warningly but stopped when he shook his head, his thumb stopped stroking, and his fingers grew tight.

"I could be wrong, babe, but you got through. I don't know if he was behind the shit that went down in front of your house tonight but if he was, it won't happen again. You wounded him. No, you crushed him. Whatever fucked-up shit that's in his head that makes him tick, it unscrambled and he focused long enough for your message to get through. Even if I miss my guess and he still intends to dick with you, I suspect his father will move mountains to try and make him stop."

"Well, that's good news"—and it was—"but I was talking about your getting shot at."

At that, I felt and saw his casual shrug before, "Not my favorite pastime, baby, not even in the top hundred and fifty, but it's happened and you deal."

Okay, well...

Yikes!

I'd pulled my shit together but frankly I'd dealt with enough that night and enough the last however many years. I would deal with the fact that my man was a man who got shot at later.

Like, in my next life.

Moving on.

"You said *if* that was Damian, do you not think it is?"

"He'd be my prime suspect. Or he was until I saw him with you. Probably not his brightest move to admit to calling a hit on a cop ever but definitely not right in front of the cop he called the hit on. But when you were shoutin' at him, he seemed genuinely surprised and started to deny it, though he didn't get to finish considering you were still shoutin'."

"I had things to get off my chest," I told him and he grinned as his hand at my neck as well as his arm around my back gave me a squeeze.

Then he dipped his head, touched his mouth to mine,

and the lifted it away before he whispered, "Yeah, and I'm fuckin' glad you did. You were magnificent, sweetness. Fuckin' *phenomenal*."

It was nice he thought that and all.

But...

"I lost it again," I whispered, pressing in closer.

"No, you're finding it," he contradicted.

"What?"

"Babe, he took your power. Tonight, you took it back. And it"—his arm gave me a squeeze—"was"—his hand gave me a squeeze—"fuckin' "—his forehead dropped to rest on mine—"*beautiful*."

I closed my eyes and pulled in a deep breath.

Then I opened them and said, "You had my back."

"I always have your back."

Warm gushiness flooded through me. One of my hands slid from around his back, up his chest, his neck to cup his cheek.

"Thank you," I whispered.

"You're welcome, Tess," he whispered back.

He lifted his forehead and his thumb swept my jaw as my fingers slid from his cheek into his hair.

Then he declared, "Shit that went down tonight, get it outta your head."

I blinked.

Then I asked, "Sorry?"

"It happened, it's reported, the phone call prior is bein' looked into. You live your life. You bake your cakes. You spend time with your friends. You already tell me where you are and where you're goin', you intensify that. I'll send someone to look at the security at your bakery and also look into setting something up here."

"Brock—"

"Vance is good at that shit. Stellar. I'll talk to him."

"Brock—"

"Units are gonna drive by regular, keep a look out. And your bakery is now on radar."

"Hon—"

"They got shell casings. Those might have prints. Guy was wearin' a ski mask but I got his build, make and model on the car, a partial plate, and he wasn't wearin' gloves so we know he's white."

"Can I—?"

His thumb stopped stroking and his fingers gave me a squeeze.

"You be smart, you be vigilant, but I have your back, Tess. I always do. You do not need to worry about this."

I stared at him, thinking now maybe *Brock* was high.

Then I reminded him, "You got shot at tonight."

"Yeah, babe, and it's happened before. I hope it won't happen again but in my line of work that's a possibility. I deal and you bein' my woman, you deal."

"But—"

His hand shifted so his thumb could press on my lips.

"This is the job you have now, Tess. You're with me, you deal. And you're with me. And the woman I saw tonight shrieking in the face of the monster who violated her, she won't have a problem with that. The only way you beat motherfuckers who try to fuck with you is not to let them beat *you*. So you deal."

Damn, I freaking *hated* it when he made sense.

"Yeah?" he prompted when I said nothing.

I didn't answer. Instead, I asked, "Did Martha ask your Riviera order?"

"Yeah, she did. Now did you get me?"

It also bugged me that you couldn't pull shit over on him.

I rolled my eyes.

Then I said, "I got you."

He grinned. Then he dipped his head to touch his lips to mine again. He lifted it and looked at the counter of the island.

Then he looked back at me. "That for me or you double-fisting it?"

"For you," I answered, though double-fisting it sounded like a plan. Until one of my fists was wrapped around a fork and shoveling in chile rellenos that was.

He let me go with one arm and grabbed his beer. I moved my hand in his hair to around his waist and lifted my beer to take another slug.

Then I remarked, "Well, silver lining, toxic exes, middle of the night phone calls interrupting great sex and imminent orgasms, gunfights in the front yard, our lives aren't boring."

Brock finished taking his pull, dropped his beer hand, and agreed, "Nope."

"That said, I'm investigating vacation spots. Requirements include beachfront hotel, therefore a beach, a bar that serves cocktails that taste like liquid candy, and that's pretty much it. If you can't get off work, I'm selling cupcakes on street corners to make up the dough so you can take leave without pay. And we're kidnapping Rex and Joel if we have to because I am *not* waiting two months for spring break and we'll answer to the charges when we get back."

He stared down at me.

"It'll be worth it, I promise," I assured him.

He continued to stare down at me.

"We'll get Rex and Joel their own room. Adjoining. Locks on our side."

He looked away, muttered, "Now you're talkin'," and took another pull of beer.

I grinned and took another pull at mine.

A knock came at the front door.

Martha and Mexican.

No, my best friend Martha who dropped everything to be with me during a serious drama and really freaking good Mexican.

And, as ever, the ride continues.

But at this present time, that ride was on an up.

So I was going to take advantage.

And clearly Brock was too for he didn't hesitate to let me go and move to the door.

Or maybe he was just hungry.

Still, the ride was on an up. I knew this because, as I stood in my fabulous kitchen with a beer in my hand and my man heading toward the door, my best friend and really freaking good Mexican, I was watching his ass.

Definitely an up.

Absolutely.

CHAPTER NINETEEN

A Day at Tessa's Cakes

"TESS! YOUR HOT guy is here!" Nora, one of my kids, called from the front of the bakery. "And he's got two mini hot guys with him."

I looked up from the birthday cake I was decorating and toward the swinging half doors that separated the bakery part of the bakery from the public part of the bakery. Within seconds I saw an amused Brock push through, followed by his two smirking sons, who it was plain to see liked being referred to as mini hot guys, especially when a pretty, perky young thing like Nora called them that.

I was happy to see them but surprised.

It was more than a week after the Damian drama. It was Saturday and business was still booming. I'd been in the shop since seven because I had six birthday cakes to decorate by noon and an anniversary cake to decorate by three. I also had two appointments with blushing soon-to-be brides to discuss their wedding cakes.

It was now just after eleven and again (mostly) all hands on deck. Kalie was out on the floor with Nora and Suni. Kellie was back with me and my two other bakers and decorators extraordinaire and the place was humming.

"Hey, Uncle Slim!" Kellie called, hands busy with rolling snickerdoodle balls of dough in cinnamon and sugar. "Yo, Joey, Rex."

"Hey, Kellie," Joel called back.

"Hey," Rex said distractedly, his eyes big and taking in the sights and smells of magic happening all around and his face registered exactly that—magic.

I giggled at Rex and my eyes went to Brock, who'd greeted his niece verbally but came to me and greeted my physically by getting close to my side and kissing my neck.

Then his mouth moved to my ear and he whispered, "Sweetness."

I shivered and my head turned, my eyes finding his.

"Hey, honey," I whispered back. His eyes danced, I got another shiver, and then I looked to the boys. "Hey, guys."

"Hey, Tess," Joey replied.

"Hey," Rex mumbled, staring at the huge cake in front of me.

"Poppy seed with raspberry and cream filling and vanilla bean frosting," I told him.

He blinked at the cake, his eyes lifted to mine, he blinked at me, and then his eyes dropped back to the cake and he licked his lips.

I giggled again.

Then I shouted to the swinging doors, "Guys! Anything they want, on the house for my two boys!"

"You got it, Tess!" Suni shouted back.

Joel muttered, "Awesome," and took off on a dash into the front.

Rex was already gone.

I giggled again.

Then I looked at Brock and asked, "What're you guys doing here?"

I asked this because our plans for the day were set. Considering my schedule and the fact it was girls' night in and Brock had the boys, I was working all day then hoofing it to Martha's. Depending on my level of inebriation and the lateness of the festivities, I was either going to go to Brock's later, call him to get me if I was hammered, or crashing at Martha's.

A visit to the bakery wasn't on the agenda thus a surprise though a good one.

"You got a minute?" Brock asked in return and that was when I wondered if this surprise was a good one.

I looked down at the cake, which was almost done. I'd baked them all the day before and only had to decorate them. This was the last birthday cake and next up was the anniversary cake. My appointments weren't until after three. Therefore, I had time.

So I nodded, put down the pastry bag, and muttered, "Let's go to my office."

We went and when I closed the door behind me and saw Brock looking around with unconcealed surprise, I realized he'd never been back here. Not when we were seeing each other when he was Jake and not when we got back together when he was mine.

He looked at the chaos then at me and said simply, "Babe."

"I know where everything is," I defended myself.

He looked around again, then back at me. "That's impossible."

"No, really."

He grinned.

Then he tipped his head toward the door, crossed his arms on his chest, and remarked, "Madhouse."

I nodded. "I need to consider more hires, decorators for the back, staff for the front. It isn't lightening up even on weekdays and special orders are getting out of hand, so I don't have time to help the girls keep the front stocked."

"You need to consider opening new locations," Brock returned and I blinked at him. "It's a madhouse out there 'cause this is the only place in Denver they can get your stuff so they descend en masse here. You open shops in LoDo, Park Meadows, considering additional foot traffic and convenience to locals, you'll clean up."

I had, of course, thought of this after I'd learned Brock was not Jake, we were apart for those three months, and I was hell-bent on doing anything that might take my mind off being played but mostly losing him (an effort that, incidentally, failed).

I'd even looked at locations for expanding, including one in LoDo or what lower downtown Denver was known as. However, these activities clashed with my half-baked plans to sell my house and move to Kentucky so I didn't fully investigate them.

But also, I didn't fully investigate them because already the success of my shop was cutting into the time I got to do the fun stuff. I had an accountant and outsourced payroll but that was it. All the hires, scheduling of personnel, ordering, inventory, my calendar, and the rest of it I did. The idea of adding another shop to that load, or worse, two, didn't fill me with glee.

"I'm uncertain of my desire to be the 'cake guru' of

Denver. I like baking and decorating. I'm not champing at
the bit to build and oversee a cake empire."

He grinned then decided he was done with our distance,
which, considering my office was tiny was only two feet so
the distance wasn't *that* distant but still, he obviously didn't
like it. I knew this because his arms uncrossed and one shot
out. He grabbed my hand, tugged on it hard so I was forced
to take a big step forward, and I fell into his body. Then both
his arms wrapped around me and I tilted my head back to
look up at him as my arms slid around his waist.

Then he gave me no time to make a comment or react
to this change of physical circumstances. He casually
continued the conversation, like yanking me into his arms
in the middle of one was a totally normal thing to do.

Which, I realized in that nanosecond, for Brock it was.

"So hire a business manager to oversee the shit you
don't wanna do at your different locations and spend your
time baking and decorating," he suggested.

This idea held merit but I still shook my head and
explained, "Sometimes, when folks expand, things get
out of hand. You lose quality. You lose personality. It
starts to be about money, not about soul. I put a lot of work
into what's happening out there and my name is on these
cakes." I gave his waist a squeeze and said quietly, "To me,
baby, this isn't just cakes. It's my vision. It's *me*. And I need
to control it."

And it *was* my vision; it *was* me. I'd not that long ago
finally discovered who I was and what was inside me and
that didn't only include a mountainous swirl of frosting
under which was rich, moist cake. It also included robin's
egg blue and lavender and hibiscus blossoms and hummingbirds and smiling clerks and kids who walked in

with looks on their faces like Rex and walked out with smiles on their faces like pretty much everybody.

"All right, darlin'," Brock said softly and my focus went back to him. "You'd had a tough night so you might have missed it but over Mexican, your girl bitched...at length...about her job. She's in a bad place, hates what she's doin', and she's been lookin' around now for months and findin' nothin'. You told me your income quadrupled over Christmas, and that isn't slowing. Right now, you got the means to do this and you got someone you trust. Someone who knows you *and* your vision and understands the importance of it to you. Talk to Martha. Maybe she'll be open to takin' on a new gig. Even if you don't expand, with how it is out there, you still could use someone doin' what you do in here so you can get outta here and do what you prefer to do out there."

Again, this idea held merit but this one held more. Like a lot more. *Doable* more.

"That's a great idea, honey," I whispered.

"It's a selfish idea, baby," he whispered back. "The more money you make, the more sexy nighties I get, and if you get help, I'll maybe see you sometimes when you're not flat out exhausted and trying to hide it."

See? Totally could not pull shit over on Brock.

"I'll talk to her tonight," I told him.

"Good," he said on an arm squeeze.

"So"—I tipped my head to the side—"did you come here to advise me on the future of my bakery?"

He shook his head and answered, "Nope, gotta go to work. Mom's got plans to go see a movie with friends. Laura's got a gaggle of girls over because Ellie had a slumber party last night. Jill and Fritz are up in the mountains snowshoeing. I don't think dad's up to it. Levi isn't answering his phone and Kalie and Kellie are out there. 'Cause of that, I need to ask you to look after the boys. If I can get hold of Levi, I'll give you a call and send him 'round to pick them up."

It was then I noticed he wasn't in a thermal, his leather jacket, and faded jeans but in a navy blue turtleneck (again, one I bought him for Christmas), his nice jeans, and his black overcoat.

Work attire.

"Someone get a cap busted in their ass?" I asked.

He grinned, shook his head in that way he did (that way I liked) when I knew he thought I was cute, and answered, "Yeah, and that someone was done exactly the way another someone who hit my desk last week was done. I gotta get to the crime scene and I gotta look into that shit."

Not fun.

"Okay," I agreed readily and his arms gave me another squeeze.

"They'll be cool," he told me.

"I know they will," I told him.

"If they can help out, put them to work," he suggested.

"They just got KP duties," I decided.

He smiled again. Then he dipped his head to touch his lips to mine.

He lifted his head and murmured, "Thanks, baby."

"Anytime, honey," I murmured back but even at a murmur I meant it and he knew it.

Therefore, he smiled then that smile faded as a shadow drifted through his eyes telling me he wanted to spend a Saturday when he should be with his sons going to a crime scene and "looking into that shit" about as much as he wanted to get a tooth pulled without Novocain.

Then he muttered, "I gotta go."

I pressed into him and whispered, "Yeah."

I got another squeeze, another lip touch (this one on my forehead), and he let me go but lifted a hand to cup my jaw before he murmured, "Later."

Then he was gone.

I followed him out, moved through the back and front telling the girls we had two new helpers, approached Joel and Rex at their table where they were finishing up devouring a slice of carrot cake (Rex) and a red velvet cupcake (Joel), told them what they were going to do to earn their keep, and at this news their eyes lit.

Only kids would think clearing tables and washing up coffee cups, plates, and forks in a bakery was cool.

Or maybe it was only Brock's kids.

And lucky for me they did because I could use the help.

*   *   *

"Aunt Tess!" I heard someone shriek.

I turned from loading a cake stand on the back shelves with cupcakes just in time to see Ellie darting through the shop, heading for the opening at the end of the counter, and rounding it.

Luckily, although her speed was akin to an Olympian who, with great dedication, trained daily and maintained an athlete's lifestyle 24/7, I had time to brace before she hit my legs, arms wrapped around them.

My hand not holding the cupcake tray settled on her head and then dropped as she arched her back at an impossible angle without releasing her hold and grinned up at me.

"Mom's buyin' us pink cupcakes!" she screeched, jumped back, and clapped. "I can't *wait!*"

I smiled at her and was surprised to see she'd ditched the princess attire and was now a mermaid, complete with a flashy green iridescent tail and flat lilac shells as bodice. However, this ensemble was marred by a winter coat and a cute, fluffy wool hat with a bobble on the top, both of which didn't exactly say "under the sea."

"Ellie, come out from behind that counter right now," Laura snapped, standing at the end of it. "What did I tell you about when your Aunt Tess is working? You don't go behind the counter when Aunt Tess is working."

This wasn't true. Ellie *always* came behind the counter when she visited Tessa's Cakes. That was, she came behind the counter if Aunt Tess was there in order to do what she just did.

"She doesn't care," Ellie shot back and this was true but Laura instantly got a "mom face" that clearly stated without words that she was not in the mood for backtalk.

Ellie read her mother's face, she scrunched *her* face, looked up at me, unscrunched her face, gave me a toothy grin, and then skipped out from behind the counter.

"Go, sit down with your friends," Laura ordered. "I'll be there with cupcakes and milk in a second but I *won't* be there with cupcakes and milk if you don't behave."

I could tell by Ellie's face she took this seriously and I could also tell it by her ensuing actions for she did not delay in rounding up her three also mermaid-attired friends (obviously this slumber party had a theme) and herding them to an open table at the window.

Suni took my tray of cupcakes. I shot her a grateful

smile and moved to Laura and the minute I arrived she started bitching in an undertone.

"Remind me never but *never* to do this again. I knew it. I've done it before but, like childbirth, you forget how freaking painful it is in between times and therefore convince yourself you're good for another go. And Ellie gets invited to slumber parties all the time and it was our turn. I shouldn't care. Turns don't matter. Peace of mind matters. Not losing your hearing due to the constant shrieking of little girls matters. Sanity matters. If those girls' mothers are fool enough to take on that energy and noise level, great, fine, more power to them. But I...am...*not*."

I nodded like I understood (when I actually didn't) and opened my mouth to say something soothing but she kept bitching.

"And Austin abandoned me. He had four hours with the girls last night and he took off first thing this morning leaving me *a note*."

Oh man. Not a smooth move on Austin's part. I had a feeling Austin was in the doghouse.

Laura kept right on going.

"Okay, so, he took the boys out to breakfast and then to a movie so I don't also have Grady and Dylan to deal with but Grady and Dylan are a piece of cake compared to four four-year-old little girls. Ellie told them all about you and your cupcakes and that's all they've been talking about. So, to shut them up, I had to bring them here. But I have to tell you, Tess, I'm uncertain about injecting even a teaspoon of sugar into those four. They're bouncing off the walls now. With sugar in them, they might explode through like four-year-old little girl Hulks in mermaid outfits."

I bit my lip and waited for her to continue complaining

so she could get it all off her chest but she didn't. Her eyes suddenly wandered to a blackboard but she wasn't reading it. They'd glazed over and I knew she was on a mental deserted island with a very strong mai tai and a romance novel.

I waited a moment to allow her to experience her fantasy before I was going to lift my hand and wave it in front of her face but I didn't get the chance.

"Aunt Laurie," Rex called, moving through the swinging doors followed by Joel.

Laura's body jerked, her mouth tilted up into a smile, and she said, "Hey, kiddo," and accepted a hug around her hips as she ruffled his hair then her eyes went to Joel and she said, "Hey there, Joey."

"Hey, Aunt Laurie," Joel replied, two years older than his brother and those two years were the two years you grew out of giving your Aunt a hug around her hips.

At the arrival of the boys, I took charge.

"All right, guys, I've got a big job for you. Your Aunt Laura needs a breather so I want you to go over to Ellie's table, get cupcake and milk flavor orders from those girls, put the cupcakes on plates, get the milk, and get Kalie to make your aunt a coffee. And also, find out what treat your aunt wants and sort that out. Then I want you to hang with the girls and make sure they're good. Can you do that?"

"Sure," Joel said.

"Cool," Rex said, then asked, "Like, we're waiters?"

I smiled at him. "Yeah, like that."

"Awesome," he muttered, his eyes alight.

Jeez, kids.

"You do the girls. I'll do Aunt Laurie," Joel ordered, all bossy big brother.

Rex nodded, all used to being bossed little brother, and took off.

Joel headed to his cousin Kalie.

I looked to Laura. "Do you want to take a moment of sanity in my office or do you want your coffee to go and Joey, Rex, and I can watch the girls while you take a much longer moment of sanity walking through the shops of Cherry Creek?" I asked. "With Kalie and Kellie here as well as the boys, I'm sure we'll be good with the girls and you can nip away for half an hour, forty-five minutes."

She grinned and stated, "Now I know why Slim loves you. I always thought it was your, um…endowments." She tipped her head to my chest then explained, "He's my brother. I know it's gross but you can't help but notice that stuff and he's totally a boob man."

I pressed my lips together to stop myself from laughing *and* to stop myself from informing her that she was not correct.

Yes, Brock liked breasts and it had to be said he liked them a lot but it was a tossup if he went for the rack or the ass since he showered attention on both. Then again, there were other, *better* areas he showered attention on so who knew? I only knew I was not going to share any of this knowledge with his sister.

Even so, Laura didn't give me a chance because she kept speaking.

"Olivia, she was busty too. Then she got her ball and chain on him and lost twenty-five pounds she didn't have to lose, which was not looked on favorably by Slim. But all the rest of his chicks"—she grinned—"totally. Now I'm seeing things more clearly. This place is crazed and you still offer a moment of sanity to a mother on the verge of breakdown. Very cool."

"Well...thanks, I think," I said to her.

"You're welcome," she said back and then, I didn't know why, but something moved my eyes from Laura to the front window and at what they saw I got a chill down my back when I discovered I had a superhero power and it wasn't super-cake-baking.

It was bitch radar.

I discovered this because Olivia was standing in the window, glossy Cherry Creek North bags dangling from her fingers, eyes staring at a Rex who had clearly taken orders from a gaggle of mermaids because he was heading back to Laura and me.

Her eyes moved from Rex through the shop and locked on me. Then her entire face got tight and she moved toward the door.

"Uh-oh," I muttered, my eyes glued to her closing in on the door, my body experiencing an omen of doom, and I knew when Laura clocked her because she muttered, "Oh my freaking God."

Olivia opened the door and took two long strides in, did another scan of the shop, and her eyes narrowed on Joel when she caught sight of him, and then, if you can believe this, *from across the room,* she snapped loudly, "Where's Slim?"

I quickly looked between the boys, who both were close to me and were now frozen to the spot and staring at their mother.

"I got this," Laura muttered and panic seized me because I was afraid she would "get this" and how she would get it was not so good, considering the fact that the last time she was near Olivia, she attacked, nails bared. But before I could stop her, she headed toward Olivia.

"You stay away from me," Olivia snapped, again loudly, her hand raised with finger pointed at Laura. And all my customers, and I had many, were starting to stare. Then her eyes came to me. "Where's Slim?"

"He's working and you need to go," Laura told her.

"Boys," I said quietly to Joey and Rex. "Why don't you go in the back?"

"No!" Olivia flared, getting louder, moving forward, skirting Laura, and coming toward Joel, Rex and me. Then, if you can believe *this,* she announced, "Boys, come with me. We're going home."

I blinked in shock.

Then I asked, "What?"

This was at the same time Laura, who was following her, snapped (loudly), "What?"

Olivia ignored both of us and said to Brock's sons, "Get your coats, let's go."

Damn! What did I do about *this*?

Both boys stared up at her, Rex with an open mouth, Joel with indecision warring clear as day on his mini-hot-guy face.

Okay, I didn't know what to do about this but I did know I had to do something and whatever it was wasn't going to be in front of the boys *or* my customers.

"Olivia," I said, taking a step toward her, "how about you come into the back and we can talk?"

She totally ignored me and snapped at her sons, "What'd I say?"

"It's Slim's weekend," Laura told her, sidling close

to her side and Olivia's head turned sharply to her ex-sister-in-law.

"It is? Then where is he?"

"Like I said, he's working," Laura answered.

"Well, if he's working then he's working and that's his problem but my sons are not with that"—she jabbed a finger at me—"bitch." And at this there were a number of audible gasps.

Okay, now hang on a minute.

I was not a bitch and I was not about to be called one, but definitely not in front of Rex and Joey *and* my staff *and* my customers.

"I cannot believe you," Laura hissed, anger turning to fury as the attention around us went from curious to avid.

"That is *way* uncool," Kalie stated from behind the counter.

"*Totally* uncool," Nora chimed in.

"Like, off-the-charts uncool," Suni put in her opinion.

"How about we take this to my office," I suggested again, holding tight to my control on my temper. "Or, if that doesn't work for you, outside."

Olivia's angry eyes slashed to me and she declared, "You do not exist."

I ignored that idiotic comment and replied, "For Rex and Joel, please, Olivia, let's discuss this elsewhere."

She ignored me again and looked to her sons. "Right now. What did I say? Let's go!" Then she started marching to the door.

"Kalie, go get your phone, call your uncle," Laura ordered. "Rex and Joey, you stay put."

Olivia stopped marching and turned to Laura. "Don't you tell my sons what to do."

"I'll do what I like, and stop making a scene," Laura snapped. "This is where Tess works."

"Do I care?" Olivia retorted.

"No, but I do and so does Uncle Slim and everybody else." Kalie entered the fray.

"What's going on?" Kellie asked from behind me. I turned to her, saw her eyes on Olivia, her face scrunched, and she muttered, "Oh, I know what's going on."

"Mommy, what's happening?" Ellie called, her voice shaky, her eyes and all the eyes of her mermaid friends riveted to the activity and not in a good way.

"It's okay, baby," Laura called back. "Mommy's just talking with Olivia."

"Please, please," I cut in, sensing the situation was deteriorating and, getting desperate, my eyes moving to Olivia. "Can we talk about this in the back?"

Olivia ignored me yet again, her face going stone cold and her voice dripping with ice when she clipped loudly, "Joel! Rex! Now!"

I moved closer to her (though not that close, she had nails and I was afraid she'd use them) and said softly, "I'll ask again, Olivia, because you're distressing the boys, Ellie, and her friends, can we talk about this in the back? When we get back there, I'll call Brock and you can discuss this with him."

"Fuck *Brock* and fuck *you*!" she suddenly shouted.

My torso jerked back like she'd hit me. Laura's pissed-off energy snapped through the air. I sensed movement behind the counter so I knew Kalie and/or Kellie were on the go and I opened my mouth to speak but someone beat me.

And that someone was Joel.

"That's not nice," he whispered, his voice trembling. I stepped aside and turned to see his face pale and his hands clenched in fists at his sides. "You shouldn't talk to Tess that way. She's a nice lady. She's nice to everyone and that's not nice."

Taking him in and hearing his words, my hatred for his mother achieved new heights.

"Joey, honey, get your brother and go into the back," I ordered quietly.

But as I was speaking, Olivia moved quickly.

Closing in on Joel, she wrapped her fingers around his shoulder and gave it a yank, snapping, "When I tell you to do something, you do it!"

More gasps filled the air, including my own, and both Laura and I moved in on her and Rex shrank back.

But Joel ripped his shoulder from his mother's hold and stepped back and at the same time stood firm so I stopped and so did Laura.

"It's Dad's weekend," he declared.

"If it's your father's weekend, where is he?" Olivia returned.

"He has to *work*, Mom. He's got a *job*. Somethin' bad happened to someone and he's gotta find out who did it. With Dad comes Tess and if Dad has to work then we get to be with Tess. We're havin' fun here. We like it here. We'll see you tomorrow."

"You'll see me now and I'll talk to your father later about who he allows to spend time with his children," Olivia retorted.

Joel stared at her and I saw him battling. My heart went out to him but I was completely at a loss of what to do. He needed his father but his father was working. My phone was in the back and I didn't want to leave the boys with Olivia to go get it and call him. And if I did and he knew this was happening, he'd lose his mind.

Fortunately or unfortunately, Laura's phone was in her purse and she started digging into it.

Joel spoke again, quiet, soft, scared, but determined. "We don't wanna see you now."

Oh man.

"Well I don't care. I'm your mother and you mind me," Olivia shot back.

"We're havin' fun," Joel told her.

"I don't care about that either," Olivia returned.

"I know," Joel whispered. My heart clenched and I'd had enough.

But even so, I couldn't do what I wanted to do, which was, I was ashamed to admit, get in a bitch-slapping fight with her. I didn't think that would be good, although it would *feel* good. So instead, I had to try and play it cool, for Joey, for Rex, and for Brock.

"Please," I said softly, "can we talk about this in the back?"

Joel ignored me and told his mother, "You need to go."

She blinked, her shock apparent, then she asked, "What?"

He didn't answer his mother. He turned to his brother and ordered, "Go to the back with Kalie and Kellie."

I noticed then that Rex was watching this with wide eyes and he wasn't about to move but he wasn't given a choice. Kalie rushed forward, bent to grab his hand, and gently pulled him through the swinging doors, Kellie following them.

Okay, one down, one to go.

"Joel, honey, why don't you go with them?" I suggested.

Joel turned to me, shook his head then his eyes went back to his tight-lipped mother and he repeated, "You need to go."

"I'll say it one more time, Joel. Go get your brother, get your coats, and come with me."

"No," Joel replied instantly.

"Slim?" Laura said and all eyes moved to her. "I'm sorry, I know you're busy but I have to tell you that Olivia is at Tess's bakery, she's making a scene, and she put her hands on Joey."

Oh no.

That was the wrong thing to say. Not that it wasn't true or that there were any right things to say, but that was the *wrong* thing to say.

Laura kept talking. "He rightly refuses to go. They're in a showdown and all five hundred of Tess's customers are bystanders. She won't leave even though Joey has asked her to and she won't go to the back to discuss the situation even though Tess has asked her to . . . *repeatedly*. I'm sorry, Slim, but I think you're gonna have to deal with this."

To my shock, Olivia haughtily held out her hand to Laura and demanded, "Let me talk to him."

But Laura snapped her phone shut and informed Olivia, "Too late. He's angry. He's hung up. And I'm guessing he's on his way."

Oh no!

Time for emergency maneuvering. I didn't need Brock to show being pissed off and filling my magical, happy bakery with his pissed-off vibes *or* him entering the showdown with Olivia, considering he didn't shy away from the f-word either, or the c-word, m-word, b-word, a-word, and a variety of other words. Things were crazy busy but I didn't need my customers avoiding Tessa's Cakes for fear of witnessing a tense, combative, foul-mouthed domestic scene. Or, as the case was, a *worse* one.

"I think," I said quietly, "it might be a good idea if you aren't here when Brock shows."

"And *I* think it might be a good idea for you not to tell me what to do," Olivia retorted.

I studied her, my heart beating hard.

Then I realized she was going to have her scene no matter what. She wanted it especially now, considering that scene earned her Brock's attention, which was what she wanted most of all.

So I shrugged.

My customers were just going to have to deal and I'd barricade myself, the boys, Ellie, her little mermaids, and my staff in my office if it was going to be a blowout.

Then I said, "Suit yourself."

I turned to Joel and ordered gently, "Sort out Ellie and her friends, yeah? Then go in the back with your brother and wait for your dad. You cool with that?"

He looked up at me, nodded, his eyes moved through his mother, and then he dashed into the back to get the orders from Rex.

I looked to Laura, ignoring Olivia, who had dropped her bags at her feet, crossed her arms on her chest, hitched her hip with a foot out, and had a face like thunder.

I was right. She was in for the long haul.

Whatever. Her funeral.

So I told Laura, "I'll get you a coffee. How do you take it and do you want a cake?"

Laura fell into the ignoring Olivia tactic, placed her order, and then went to her daughter and her girlfriends.

I made her coffee and got her a humongous chocolate cookie with peanut butter chips. Joel took care of the girls and disappeared into the back. Through all this, Olivia stood in her bitch stance, glowering at us.

I was delivering Laura's stuff at her table when two uniformed officers walked in.

Olivia tensed. Laura grinned. I stared.

"We've had a report of a disturbance?" one of the officers asked the room at large, then his eyes honed in on Olivia. "A blonde woman. Late forties?"

"Late forties, hysterical," Laura mumbled gleefully.

"Her," a random customer pointed at Olivia before I could say a word. "She came in being loud and nasty, used foul language, and wouldn't leave when she was asked, like seven *thousand* times."

"Yeah, it was her," another random customer unnecessarily confirmed. "And she did all this *in front of little kids*." Then she added further unnecessary detail, saying, "Kids in mermaid outfits."

"And she put her hand on one and not in a nice way," another random customer added. "From what I could tell, he was her son but still. That ain't right." Then he went on to mutter, "Though, he wasn't in a mermaid outfit."

"You come into a bakery thinkin' to get a good cookie or a purple cupcake with sprinkles," another random customer piped up. "Then, all of a sudden, some uppity chick storms in droppin' the f-bomb *and* the b-bomb. I mean, what is *up* with *that*?"

Clearly this was enough evidence for them. After receiving these reports, one of the officers opened the front door and, eyes on Olivia, he requested, "Ma'am, can you come with me?"

Her jaw set, her chin lifted, and her eyes narrowed but otherwise she didn't move. This was surprising evidence that she was stubborn and stupid as well as manipulative and a screaming bitch.

I had not been in trouble with the law, as in *ever*, except, of course, when Damian dragged me into his business, but I was an innocent swept up in that. So I didn't really have any experience with dealing with police officers. But still, I was smart enough to know when a cop asked you to do something, if he did it politely or even if he didn't, you should probably do it.

I found in short order I was not in error and I knew this when the officer explained things further.

"If you're waitin' for Detective Lucas, he's tied up and we can't have you disturbin' this establishment so you got two choices. You can come outside and talk to us or we can take you to our squad car, take you to the station, and you can explain things there. But you should know, the second option, you'll be cuffed mostly because you'll be arrested. Which way we gonna go?"

Olivia sucked in an audible breath.

Then she bent, snatched up her abundance of glossy Cherry Creek North shopping bags, and stomped to and through the door.

The minute her feet moved over the threshold, the entire bakery erupted into loud cheers.

I bit my lip to fight back my smile and looked at a smiling-like-a-madwoman Laura. Then her phone rang as one of the officers followed Olivia and the other one came to me.

"I'm Officer Petri," he told me.

"Tess O'Hara," I told him. "I, um"—I swung an arm toward the big sign confirming my next statement—"own this place."

He nodded, his lips twitching, and then he said, "I know. I know Slim so I know who you are. What I gotta know now is what you want us to do here, Ms. O'Hara."

I opened my mouth to tell him I just wanted Olivia gone but suddenly Laura was there, arm extended, phone in hand.

I looked to her and she said, "Slim."

Great.

I nodded, smiled a "give me a minute" smile at the officer, took the phone, pulled in a calming breath, put it to my ear, and greeted with a soft, "Hey."

"Make a complaint," he growled at the same time he managed a new feat and that was filling the atmosphere with abrasive anger and he wasn't even there.

"Honey," I said quietly.

"Make a complaint, Tess. I want this shit on record."

Oh. Right. That would probably be good for the cause.

"Okay," I agreed.

"Too pissed right now to discuss this. We'll talk about it later."

Goodie. Something *not* to look forward to.

"Okay," I repeated.

"Later, babe," then he was gone, which meant he *was* pissed. Very pissed. But I didn't need that confirmed. I was pretty sure a layer of skin had been sanded off my ear from just having a twenty-second conversation with him on the phone.

I snapped the phone shut, handed it to Laura, and said to Officer Petri. "I'd like to make a complaint."

"Dig it," Laura muttered happily under her breath.

"It okay I talk to some of your customers?" Officer Petri asked and it wasn't. I didn't like that at all but they'd witnessed Olivia being Olivia, they showed they didn't mind speaking up, and their statements might help Brock get his sons with him and safe from any more of these nightmares.

Therefore, I said, "Yes."

He nodded, then told me, "I'll come to you last. Gotta get to 'em before I lose 'em."

I nodded.

He moved.

I looked to Laura.

"Happy days," she whispered gleefully. "That bitch is finally gonna get what's coming to her."

Indeed.

"I need to go see Joey and Rex," I told her.

Her eyes slid to the swinging doors and they weren't dancing anymore when they slid back to me.

"Yeah," she replied. "Send Kalie or Kellie out to look after the girls and I'll help."

I nodded, whispered, "Thanks," then moved.

I hit the back room and found with the boys that there were no tears but there was fear.

Luckily, we were in a bakery and surrounded by baked goods.

And baked goods soothed a lot of ragged emotions.

It was a Band-Aid.

But it worked in a pinch.

*   *   *

The cops were gone, Laura and the girls were gone, and the boys were back to KP duties, albeit doing it with far less enthusiasm and this was because their minds were filled with their mother's antics. This was also because wiping down tables and cleaning dishes had lost its luster (as it had a tendency to do, no matter what age you were). I was in the back icing sugar cookies when my phone on the stainless-steel table rang.

The display said *Slim Calling*.

I pulled in a breath, my eyes moving to the swinging doors to see if I could spot Joel or Rex and do a visual check on their state of mind as I reached for the phone. I took the call and didn't see either before I put the phone to my ear.

"Hey," I answered.

"Boys okay?" he asked as greeting.

"The bloom has gone off the rose of KP duty."

"Right," he muttered and I knew he got what I was saying. Then he told me, "Levi was at the gym when I called earlier. I finally got him and he and Lenore are gonna be around in the next half an hour. They're gonna take them to a movie and get them somethin' to eat. I should be done by then so I can get 'em and they'll be good."

There it was. Lenore again. Hmm.

"Lenore?" I asked curiously.

"Babe," Brock answered, not going to go there.

"All right," I murmured, giving up.

"Laura called me and filled me in," he informed me. I held my breath and he went on. "I called my lawyer at home and filled him in. She put her hand on Joel. He's gonna go with that and see if he can find a judge who'll hurry this shit along. She fucked up today. She fucked up two weeks ago when she cried wolf about intruders and the cops got involved. This is not the behavior of a stable woman who can look out for two boys."

After today's scene, I was thinking the same thing. Today's behavior was beyond just being bitchy and manipulative. It was way out of line to the point of being scary.

I didn't share this.

Instead, quietly, I told him, "Baby, you should have seen Joey. He stood up for me, for himself, and he took care of his brother. It took a lot of courage but you would have been proud."

There was a moment of silence, then, "Yeah, Laura told me."

"He was great."

"I'm glad he was great, darlin', just wish he wasn't in the position to have to *be* great."

This was, unfortunately, true.

"That sucks, but silver lining, Brock, he *was* in that position and he *was* great. He didn't back down and he looked after his brother. You should hold onto that because that means, like his dad and his dad's family, he's strong, smart, and loyal."

This was met with another moment of silence.

Then a soft, "Yeah."

I assured him, saying, "She put her hand on him, baby, and it wasn't nice but she didn't hurt him."

"Your mother ever put her hand on you when she's pissed or throwin' a tantrum?" he asked.

"No," I whispered.

"Mine either so I don't know but I 'spect that doesn't feel too good."

This was also unfortunately true.

"Right." I was still whispering.

"Right." Now Brock was whispering.

We both held those unhappy thoughts for a while and then Brock broke into them.

"No matter how drunk you get or how late you call, I want you in my bed tonight."

"Brock, I—"

He cut me off. "I want you in my bed because I want you in my bed but I also want you in my kitchen makin' my boys breakfast tomorrow. They need a good breakfast and they need to be around a woman who makes 'em laugh and feel safe. Tomorrow is their last day with me. It's a short one and then they gotta go back to her. I wanna make it as good as it can get. Can you help me do that?"

"Yes," I answered instantly.

Another moment of silence, then, "Yeah, I know you can," he replied quietly. I heard him sigh and say, "I gotta go."

"Okay, I'll tell the boys that Levi and Lenore are going to be here soon."

"Great, babe. See you later."

"Later, honey."

Then I had dead air.

*　　*　　*

Twenty minutes later, Joel pushed the swinging doors open, held them open, caught my eyes, and announced, "Uncle Levi's here."

"Right, honey, be right out," I said.

He disappeared and I stopped piping mountainous swirls of frosting on cupcakes, wiped my hands on a damp towel, and headed out.

Sure enough, standing in front of my display case looking like beautiful, glamorous movie stars was my man's gorgeous brother and his equally gorgeous girl-friend (or, I hoped she was his girlfriend).

"Hey, guys," I called.

"Wow, Tess, I've never been in here," Lenore stated, smiling at me. "Everything looks awesome and I *love* the hibiscus and hummingbirds. They're so *pretty*."

I totally knew I liked her.

"Thanks, babe," I replied, giving her a quick hug and touch of the cheek. I did the same with an amused-looking Levi. Then I stepped back and turned to the hovering Rex and Joel. "Guys, go get your coats. Time for a movie and dinner," and they dashed off, clearly very, *very* done with KP duty.

After the boys took off, Levi's smile faded and his eyes got serious.

"Scale of one to ten, how bad was it with the bitch this time?" he asked in a low voice and I knew he'd been briefed by Laura, Brock, both, or perhaps the entirety of the Lucas family, considering time enough had gone by for news to spread.

"Um...I've only been around her once before and that was unpleasant but considering what I heard about her I'm guessing that was around a five so this was a fifteen."

His mouth got tight.

Seeing that, to get his mind off it, I said quickly, "They're looking forward to spending time with you and, um...of course, their Aunt Lenore."

Lenore's lips tipped up in surprised happiness at receiving the Aunt title and I saw this happen before she tilted her head demurely to the side and therefore she missed Levi giving me a look and shaking his head.

"They love their Aunt Lenore," I added and Levi's eyes

moved to the ceiling. "Like, *loads,*" I continued. Lenore's gaze came to me and Levi's eyes tipped back. I looked to Lenore and informed her, "I'm only ahead of you because I own a bakery. But I think I lost ground today because they've been clearing tables and doing dishes for four hours. You like football and your little brother plays for Notre Dame. After today, you might have taken the lead."

She grinned but stated, "Not sure I can ever compete with your cupcakes and what I've heard are your totally awesome breakfasts."

"I don't know," I replied. "They like their football and they're their father's sons so I haven't hidden the catatonia I lapse into when I'm forced to watch it."

Her grin got bigger and I looked to Levi.

"Sooooo," I drew it out, "off to the movies and dinner with your girl and your nephews. How domestic."

He shook his head again but his eyes crinkled and his arm slid around Lenore's waist at about the same time the boys raced back.

Then he confirmed, "Yeah," as Lenore melted into his side and her grin became dreamy. And when she melted into his side, Levi not only took her weight but also his arm got visibly tighter.

Yes. Oh yes.

I knew where this was going. Someone had finally woken up and focused on the sweet, beautiful, stylish young woman who was in his life, who also adored him and had his back.

"Yeah," I whispered, smiling at him because I was happy for him (and Lenore). I then released him from his brief (but deserved) torture and bent to Brock's sons, kissing the tops of their heads in turn, which they endured with shuffling feet and I ordered, "Have fun."

"Right Tess," Rex said.

"We will," Joel said.

"Good," I whispered. Then I couldn't stop it but also didn't try, I lifted my hand and cupped Joel's cheek lightly and repeated a whispered, "Good."

I watched a shadow pass through his eyes that broke my heart before warmth that was close to the kind that I often saw in his father's suffused them and my heart instantly mended.

I let him go, turned back to Levi and Lenore, and announced, "Okay, I'm officially releasing them from duty."

"Good, we gotta go. Movie starts in thirty minutes. It's at the mall but we gotta get popcorn and shit," Levi declared, moving Lenore toward the door with his arm still around her waist and the boys and I followed.

"Maybe we can do dinner, you guys and Brock and me, sometime soon," I said to their backs.

Lenore threw a dazzling smile over her shoulder and Levi sent me a beleaguered look over his.

"That would be *awesome*," Lenore breathed.

"We'll set it up," I told her.

Levi turned back forward but I heard him sigh.

I giggled silently to myself and followed them out into the cold. The boys raced to their uncle's SUV. Lenore gave me a brief hug and followed them.

Levi moved in and did the same but stayed close to murmur in my ear, "You smell like cake but you're still a pain in the ass, you know that?"

"I've never had a brother," I murmured back. "I've got forty-three years of older sister pent up in me so watch out."

"Fuckin' great," he muttered and pulled away. I caught his eyes and grinned.

He shook his head but his lips twitched.

Then he turned and bleeped the locks on the SUV. Lenore opened her door. So did Rex. So did Joel. Levi headed to the driver's side. Lenore, Levi, and Rex got in but Joey hesitated.

Then he turned, dashed back to me, gave my waist a quick, tight hug then he dashed back, jumped in, closed the door, and instantly became absorbed in the complicated procedure of buckling his seatbelt.

I looked to the front of the SUV to see Lenore grinning wildly and mouthing, *I told you so.* Then I saw Levi and the look on his face made the tears already stinging my nose start to sting my eyes.

Suffice it to say, Uncle Levi loved his nephews and Uncle Levi was glad his brother had a decent woman in his life who would also be a woman his twelve-year-old nephew would take a hit to his reputation in order to hug.

Then I waved and rushed back into my bakery.

Luckily I succeeded in making it to my office before the first of the tears fell. Then I let the others fall.

Then I wiped my face and got back to work.

*   *   *

"You got sugar cookies with daisy sprinkles on the menu tomorrow?" Shirleen asked in my ear.

It was seven thirty. I was locking up the shop. Everyone was gone. I was exhausted from working a twelve-and-a-half-hour day and I wanted to go to girls' night in like I wanted someone to drill a hole in my head. I would have begged off if I didn't think Martha would send the

National Guard to collect me and bring me in restraints to her place.

"Uh..." I muttered into the phone, turning out lights in the front. "They can be."

"Good, 'cause I'm bringin' you three nighties tonight. All of them do not say 'good time with a bad boy.' They *scream* it."

I didn't know Shirleen. Although she'd been given my cell number by someone and I'd received and returned a variety of texts from her, mostly about sugar cookies, nightie requirements, and the upcoming girls' night in, I didn't know her very well mainly because we'd conversed solely about sugar cookies, nightie requirements, and girls' night in. This could be cool. It could also be scary. But with Shirleen, I was guessing I was in no position to argue.

Therefore, I told her, "Okay, then they are."

"Okay, then you take your pick or take all three and I'm in your bakery tomorrow to collect the debt."

"You got it."

"See you soon."

"Right, later."

"Later."

Then she ended the call.

I slid my phone in my purse and started to pay attention. No one had been shot at for over a week, which was good, and I hoped this luck continued but that didn't mean I was going to fall down on Brock's order to be vigilant.

I scanned the darkness outside and saw my car under a streetlamp. The coast appeared clear so I pulled out my keys, got them ready in my fingers, set the alarm, exited, locked the doors, and quickly moved to my car, arm out bleeping the locks.

I had my hand on the door handle when vigilance was foiled.

I knew this when I heard Damian say from behind me, "Tess."

I closed my eyes as my stomach clenched.

I opened them and said to the roof of my car, "You have got to be kidding."

Then I decided to use the Olivia tactic and ignore him so I opened the door and started to move to enter but I was foiled with that too when he put his hand to my forearm, gently pulled me back, and my door was shut in front of me.

But as he did this, I whirled. Twisting my arm to jerk it out of his hold, I took a step back and lifted a hand, palm out.

"Don't touch me."

He lifted his hand too, palm up and placating. "Listen to me, Tess. Please."

"Why would I do that when your being here means *you* don't listen to *me*?" I asked, dropping my hand.

Before he could answer a voice came out of the shadows.

And it said, "You need to get gone, Heller."

My eyes went in its direction and Vance Crowe, Brock's friend from the Hot-Guy Club, formed out of the darkness.

Hallelujah.

"Who are you?" Damian asked Vance.

"A friend of Tess's," Vance answered. "Now you need to move away from her vehicle and get gone."

Damian stared at him. Then he looked to me.

Then he announced, "He's dangerous."

"Who? Vance?" I asked disbelievingly, not that I didn't think Vance *could* be dangerous. Just that I knew instinctively Vance would never be dangerous to me.

"No," Damian bit off. "Lucas."

My body got tight and it got tight not because I believed him. Just that I didn't believe he showed up at my bakery after a very *bad*, very *long* day to trash talk my boyfriend.

"Man, not gonna tell you again," Vance warned, getting close. "Step away from her vehicle."

Damian had looked to Vance while he was speaking but he looked back at me and pleaded, "Please, Tess, you have to listen to me. I'm not here to start something. I'm not here to hurt you. I'm not here to get you back. I'm only here to help you. I'm here to stop you from making a grave mistake."

To help me. Right.

Asshole.

I sighed and said, "Go away, Damian."

"You don't understand," he said, leaning into me. I reared back and Vance was suddenly between Damian and me.

"Seriously, Heller, move *the fuck* on," Vance growled, audibly and visually losing patience in a very scary way.

"I need to speak to her," Damian clipped, ignoring Vance's scariness.

"I see that, man, but she doesn't wanna speak to you," Vance pointed out. "Now, I don't wanna get physical but I will, no fuckin' joke, so get the fuck outta here."

Damian glared at Vance and then, being Damian, his eyes moved beyond him to me standing behind him.

"He put a man in the hospital," he declared. "Was nearly suspended permanently from the police force because of it. Beat the hell out of him. He's known to be—"

I cut him off. "I know, Damian, yeesh. You don't think Brock would share that with me?"

Damian blinked. "You know?"

"Uh...*yeah*. The guy beat the crap out of his ex-girl-friend, raped her repeatedly and put her in the hospital for two weeks. Brock wasn't down with that and I don't blame him."

I heard Vance chuckle, his scariness evaporating (kind of) and I saw Damian's eyes narrow.

Then he stated, "He's had sexual intercourse with sus-pects he was investigating."

"I know that too, seeing as I was one of them," I informed him.

Vance chuckled again and Damian's narrow-eyed look turned into a scowl.

Then he shared, "You weren't the only one."

"Yeah, her name was Darla and he had his reasons. He shared them with me but I will not be sharing them with you. What I *will* be doing is hunkering behind hot-guy Vance while I call the police and inform them you're harassing me *again* if you don't *go away*."

Damian ignored me too and stated, "He's not a good man, Tess."

At that, I burst out laughing so hard, I bent forward and had to wrap my arms around my belly because my sides were hurting.

I did this for a long time and then straightened, wiped tears of hilarity from my cold cheeks, and focused on a Vance and Damian, who were both looking at me like I was more than a little crazy.

Then my eyes turned to Damian and I declared, "That was hilarious."

"I'm not being funny," he whispered.

"You wouldn't know a good man if he walked up and tapped you on the shoulder," I whispered back, suddenly deadly serious. "Brock Lucas is wild and he's rough and he's driven but he's loving and affectionate and so fucking loyal it isn't funny. He takes care of me. He makes me feel safe. He's good through and through and that is the first and last fucking time I'll listen to you talk shit about him. I'm done speaking to you or seeing you. I'm reporting this incident to the police immediately and any future ones will also be reported. I'm done with you Damian, and since you won't listen to me, maybe the Denver Police Department can make you listen."

Then I dug out my phone, dialed 911, and put it to my ear.

Vance stayed close and Damian stared at me.

"Nine-one-one, what's your emergency?"

"This is Tessa O'Hara and I'm standing outside Tessa's Cakes in Cherry Creek North. My ex-husband is harassing me and he won't allow me to get in my vehicle. Can someone come help me?"

"I'm trying to help, Tess. With this guy, you're in danger," Damian told me as the 911 operator informed me she was sending a unit to the scene.

I ignored his idiocy and told him, "They're sending a unit to the scene."

He stared at me. Then he looked at Vance Crowe, who was standing close to me, grinning his shit-eating grin, arms crossed on his chest.

Damian looked at me one last time, moved away and disappeared into the shadows.

Vance uncrossed his arms and dug his phone out of

his back jeans pocket. "You stay on with the operator. I'll call Slim."

I nodded. Then I told the operator Damian took off but I'd like to make a complaint as Vance told Brock what went down and Brock told Vance he was on his way.

The operator released me after telling me to get safe and stay put. I called Martha and begged off girls' night in, thankful I had an excuse but not thankful as to what that excuse was. Martha, surprisingly, agreed that after a visit from Damian I should relax at home with my boys. But she wasn't allowed to let me go until Shirleen confirmed I would be at the bakery the next day to peruse my nightie options and for her to collect on her debt.

I confirmed this through Martha and then Vance and I waited for the police.

"Good news is, he's dropped his shit with Slim," Vance said into the night and I looked up at his profile. "He isn't diggin' anymore. He found the only things he could find, laid those out for you tonight, and his activities on that have ground to a halt."

I turned my head and replied into the night, "That *is* good news."

And it was.

"The bad news is, he isn't done fuckin' with you," Vance went on.

I sighed.

"I know," I whispered.

"Advice," Vance said softly and I looked up to him to see his eyes tipped down to me. "No more conversation. You see him, you pull out your phone immediately and you dial nine-one-one. Even if he's near but hasn't tried to engage you, you make note of it, keep the card of the officer assigned to your case, you call him or her and you report it. Yeah?"

This sounded like good advice and Vance Crowe looked like a man who knew what he was talking about so I nodded.

"You want more good news?" he asked.

"Uh...yeah, more good news is always good."

He nodded.

Then he stated, "His shit is comin' to trial. Word on the street is they got a fuckin' great case. Word also on the street is, he's scramblin'. This means he's either gonna rat on factions higher than him, which makes him a marked man, and with the scum he worked for, they'll make certain he won't live to see trial. Or it means he's gonna go down and when he does, that'll be for a while. You gotta live with this a little while longer, Tess. But, one way or another, it'll be done. It just depends on how permanent that done'll be."

Hmm.

"Which way do you think he's leaning?" I asked.

"Man moved up fast. He isn't dumb. No way he's stupid enough to rat."

Conflicting news.

I didn't want to think I was the kind of person who wanted to see her ex-husband dead regardless of how hideously he'd treated me. But I was bone tired, standing outside my bakery, waiting for the police in the dark cold of the night. And this was the *second* official complaint I would make in a day when many people lived their whole lives without making even one.

Granted, a seriously hot guy was standing beside me

but he didn't happen to be mine. Mine was arriving immi-
nently and he was probably going to show pissed.

Therefore, although I couldn't exactly say I wanted
Damian dead, I could say, when this was done, I wanted it
to be done the *permanent* kind of permanently.

"That conflict you got workin' on your face," Vance
said quietly and I focused on him, "we all got that inside
us. Either way it goes down for Heller, he bought that trouble. That's on him and it's outta your hands. What I want
you to take away is, soon this shit is done for you and it's
done for Slim. Hold onto that, be smart, and stay strong."

I nodded again.

Then I looked down at his hand and saw a wide, shiny,
gold wedding band proudly displayed.

I looked back into his eyes. "You're married?"

"Yeah," he confirmed.

"She's lucky," I whispered and he grinned his shit-
eating grin again.

"Sorry, Tess, that's me."

Great freaking response.

So great, I felt my face go soft and I smiled. "Bet she
thinks differently."

His face went soft too and he replied, "Yeah, she does.
One of the many reasons she makes me lucky."

I heard the sirens and I suspected he was a man on the
move and wouldn't hang around long enough for me to
offer him gratitude cupcakes.

So, quickly, I said, "Thanks for stepping in tonight."

"Slim wanted you on radar, you're on radar. You got
eyes on you often but definitely anytime you lock up
alone. He called and told us tonight you were lockin' up
alone."

I didn't know this but I liked it.

"Well, thanks."

He jerked up his chin. Then he grinned. I smiled back. Then the cop car showed.

Ten minutes later Brock showed and I was right. The boys were in the truck looking freaked and Brock was in it looking pissed. I was also right about Vance. He made his statement, gave his card, and took off.

Ten minutes after that, Brock and the boys followed behind my car as we drove to his house.

Ten seconds after I arrived, I turned on the taps in the bath.

* * *

"Babe," I heard but didn't move. "Tess," I heard from closer and I still didn't move.

But a noise escaped my lips and it was, "Mm?"

"How long you gonna stay in the tub?" Brock asked and I couldn't see him, seeing as I had a wet washcloth on my face, but I knew from his voice he was crouched right by the tub.

"Infinity," I muttered.

I heard a chuckle then I heard water splash and I heard Brock again. "Water isn't even warm anymore."

"If I don't move," I told the washcloth, "I can pretend it's still steaming."

"Tess, darlin', get out. You need dinner. It's nearly nine."

"I'm too tired to eat."

"You still gotta do it."

"If I leave this tub, I enter the world. Damian doesn't exist in here. Olivia doesn't exist in here." Reluctantly,

I lifted a hand, removed the cloth from my face, looked
into his silver eyes, and suggested, "Let's move in here.
We can buy a mini-fridge, a tiny microwave, and a camp
stove and we'll be set."

He grinned. "I think, even for you, it'd be a challenge
to make a carrot cake on a camp stove."

"Yes," I muttered, looking to my toes at the end of the
tub, "that would be a drawback."

His hand moved to cup my jaw and force my face
back to looking at his, where I saw his eyes had melted
mercury.

"My sweet Tess has had a bad day," he murmured.

"Yes, officially it becomes a bad day when you make
a complaint to the police about your boyfriend's ex-wife.
Then it becomes a *very* bad day when you make another
one about *your* ex-husband."

He held my eyes as his hand moved, his fingertips
gliding along my neck and down as he said, "Get outta
the tub, get some food in you, and then I'll make the day
go away."

His fingertips were still moving down. Now at my
chest, they kept going. Into the water, they slid between
my breasts and kept going down as I felt my heartbeat
escalate.

"You'll make the day go away?" I breathed.

"Yeah," he whispered, his hand gliding through the
water at my belly, down, and automatically I shifted my
legs to give him access.

He grinned then his hand went *down*.

My eyes closed slowly and my lips parted.

"You want the day to go away, baby?" he asked quietly, his fingers moving magically.

"Yeah," I whispered.

Suddenly his hand was gone but his arms were around me and water splashed everywhere as he pulled me straight out of the tub. He put me on my feet in front of him, my wet body tight to his, his arms wrapped around.

"Brock!" I cried, fingers curved around his biceps.

"Food, rest, hang with the boys until they go to sleep then I'll make your day go away."

"Okay, fine but you got the bathroom all wet and *you* all wet," I informed him.

"I got dry clothes and the floor's tile, sweetness. It's not a big deal. What *is* a big deal is I can't keep an eye on you *and* a finger on the pulse of your state of mind *and* my boys with you hidin' in the bathroom, turnin' yourself into a prune."

"I'm fine."

"You had a shit day."

"I know but I'll survive."

He shook his head. "My job is not to help you survive, Tess. It's to make it safe *and* sweet when you walk through my door. Now, my woman is not goin' to bed hungry because my ex-wife is a cunt and her ex-husband is a motherfucking dickhead. She's gonna eat. She's gonna curl close to me. She's gonna show my boys she's okay. And then we're gonna go to bed and I'm gonna make her day go away. Yeah?"

That sounded like a good plan. Actually a great plan. Actually, I should have thought of it myself.

So, of course, I agreed and I did that by saying, "Yeah."

He smiled, dropped his head, and kissed me lightly.

Then he said, "See you downstairs."

He was at the bathroom door and I had a towel held

up in front of me when I called his name and he turned back.

"Vance said you were the reason he was there tonight."

"Yeah," he confirmed.

"You didn't tell me you'd—" I started but he interrupted me, his brows drawing together.

"Yeah, I did, Tess. I said the bakery is on radar."

I stared at him.

Then I told him, "I thought you meant by the cops."

"Cops. Lee's boys. Fuck, I even called Hawk fuckin' Delgado and asked him to keep his ear to the ground and his eyes open."

To that, I blinked. This was because I knew Brock was not the still unknown (even though he was Gwen's man) Hawk Delgado's favorite person. This was also because Brock had told me Hawk was not his favorite person either, mainly because he screwed the pooch on the Darla deal. Both of them were not over that situation, as in *way* not over it, and now knowing the details, I got why on both sides.

"Really?" I whispered.

He crossed his arms on his chest and stated, "Babe, you think I found the woman of my dreams at forty-five years old and I'm gonna let anything happen to her, think again. That's a long fuckin' time to wait for what you want. I waited. I found it. I'm pullin' out all the stops to take care of it. I know you feel the same for me so I'm doin' the same to keep me safe for you. So yeah, really, I called Delgado. I made peace and asked a favor. His woman is in your posse so she wouldn't be doin' cartwheels, he said no and something went down with you or, for you, me. And he isn't dumb. He's a man who knows to collect favors and he's a man whose business means he often has the need to call markers. So his ear's to the ground and his eyes are open. So if a cop isn't cruisin' by your house or bakery, one of Lee's boys or one of Hawk's commandos are. Smart people pay attention to who's cruisin' around people they want to fuck with and smart people will see cops, Nightingale's men, and Delgado's crazy motherfuckers, and my hope is, they'll steer clear. So, there you go. Now you got a full explanation of what I mean when I say you're on radar."

I heard all he said. I really did.

But I was stuck at the beginning part where he told me I was the woman of his dreams.

And that made me feel so warm and gushy, I was mostly incapacitated.

So the best I could do was force out an "Okay."

"Okay," he replied.

Then I forced out, "I'll be down in a minute."

He jerked his chin up.

Then he walked out.

I stared at the door. Then I did it a little while longer as I heard him moving around in the bedroom changing out of wet clothes. I did it for even longer after he'd left the bedroom. Then I toweled off, got dressed in loose-fitting drawstring lounge pants, a camisole, and a light hoodie and I went downstairs.

Brock fed me grilled cheese and oven-baked tater tots. It was really good. Brock grilled a mean cheese sandwich and the tater tots were baked perfectly, crispy on the outside, soft in the middle.

I hung out in front of the TV curled into Brock until he sent the kids to bed at ten. Then I hung out longer, curled into Brock.

Finally, Brock took me to bed and spent more than a fair amount of effort in taking my day away.

He succeeded magnificently, and seconds after he curled me into his arms when he was done expending this effort, I fell into a peaceful sleep filled with really, *really* good dreams.

CHAPTER TWENTY

I Take It I'm Movin' In

"I'm TELLING YOU girl, I think it's perfect," Martha declared from beside me in my car and she was right. It *was* perfect. Terrifyingly so.

We'd just come from viewing some space in Writer Square in LoDo. It was fabulous, great foot traffic, sandwiched between 16th Street Mall and Larimer Square, visibility from 15th Street and Larimer, sidewalk seating opportunity.

But the rent was *a whack*.

I was six months from paying off the business loan I got to open my first location so I knew how much it cost to set up a bakery. Location and setup costs were close to crippling.

One and one were equaling *thousands*.

It was just under three weeks since Brock suggested Martha be brought in to take the load off. I'd called her and discussed it the next day. She'd jumped at it, no hesitation. She loved the idea. And I knew she loved the idea for, upon sharing it with her, she screamed in my ear, "*I frickin' love that idea!*"

She had a good job and her pay was excellent, no way I could match it. But she said she'd take the hit for peace of mind and the opportunity to work close to my cakes. I promised a pay hike once the second location was up and going and turning a profit.

Oh, and of course, free cakes.

Martha put in notice and enrolled in accountancy classes the next day. I bought payroll software. I was going to save on outsourcing those and my business account was super healthy. Therefore, with both, I could easily absorb her additional salary. Not to mention, that freed me up to make more cakes.

Still, my account balance wasn't so healthy I could start a new location without additional capital, though this wouldn't be a problem because my bank contacted me approximately one point seven times a month asking if I wanted a further loan. Then again, my loan manager had four kids, a husband, six brothers and sisters, and the offspring they created and they all got birthday cakes from me so she knew I was a viable risk.

But I still needed a getaway with Brock and the boys. I had decided all-inclusive, five-star just because we deserved it. I had also decided I was going to pay for it just because Brock had lawyer bills and a cop's salary and, unfortunately, he *and* both of his sons had birthdays all sandwiched in the same week of the same month, *this* month—February. This was a cruel twist of fate for anyone who had their names on their present list. This was also a perfect excuse for me to take them all on vacation without Brock going macho ape-shit (hopefully).

"And I'm telling you, Martha, I don't know. The rent is pretty steep," I told her (again) as I wended my way through Cherry Creek North toward my shop. "Maybe we should look into something on The Mall or lower LoDo around My Brother's Bar?"

"I get where you're coming from but that location *is* Tessa's Cakes," she replied. "Already, you're in Cherry Creek and that isn't exactly shantytown."

This was true. My rent for my current bakery was also a whack.

Martha kept going. "The Mall is out. It's cool but it's not Tessa's Cakes. And lower LoDo is awesome but it isn't established awesome like Writer Square, unless you're talking about Brother's or Paris on the Platte, which are only established because they've been there yonks. Not to mention, foot traffic is *way* less. Practically every shop in Writer Square is fabulous and they've all been there for years. And they have flair. You'll fit right in."

She was right about that, all of it.

Eek!

"Tessa," she went on and I could tell by her voice she was facing me. I could also tell by her voice she'd hit her "listen to me, I'm being deadly serious" mode. "Your cakes don't say 16th Street Mall and they don't say lower LoDo. They say Larimer Square but you've nixed that because of the rent so the next best thing is Writer Square. This is perfect, honey. This is *you*."

She was right about that too. All of it.

Yikes.

Maybe it wasn't a good idea to hire someone who knew me and understood my vision. Maybe it was scary.

Damn.

Oh well. Nighties and sanity were on the line. And I didn't hire Martha to do payroll and create schedules. I hired Martha to help me expand and then to look after my vision when I did.

There was nothing for it.

"Okay, call them and tell them we want it."

"*Yee ha!*" she shrieked.

Dear God.

I pulled into the parking lot beside my bakery and parked in the spot that had the sign "Reserved for Tessa, you park here, you don't get cake" on the building in front of it. I switched off the ignition and my phone rang.

Martha, holding my purse in her lap, dug through it, nosily looked at it, and mumbled, "Bad-boy hot guy," then handed me the phone and started to exit the car, finishing, "I'm gonna go make the call now."

Then she was gone.

I took Brock's call.

"Hey."

"Well?"

He knew I was viewing the location.

"It's fabulous," I answered his mostly unasked question.

"And?"

I grinned at my dash.

"My guess is, even though she was exiting my car with great haste while the phone was ringing with this call from you, still, Martha's right now on the phone in the office with the landlord saying we'll take it."

Silence, then, "Good, baby."

"I'm scared out of my mind, Brock," I admitted.

"Be stupid not to be, Tess," he replied, and I pulled in a breath. "It's a risk but it's a risk worth taking. And it's a lot of work but it's work worth doing. It'll pay off, it'll pay off soon, and then it's all about the nighties."

I started laughing softly and then I stopped laughing softly and said quietly, "Yeah."

"We'll go out tonight, celebrate."

Well. There you go. This decision was seeming like the right one already.

"Sounds good."

"Not Lincoln's Road House meatloaf sandwiches celebrating. You in sexy heels and a short skirt celebrating," he clarified and I blinked at the dash because I'd never had sexy heels and short skirt fun with Brock. I'd had beer and pool table and plethora of neon signs on the walls fun with Brock plenty of times but never heels and short skirts.

Then I asked, "Really?"

To which he answered, "Absolutely."

"Okay," I whispered.

"I'll make a reservation and call you with the time."

"Okay," I repeated.

"Later, sweetness."

"Later, honey."

We disconnected and I tucked my phone into my purse, thinking about which heels I was going to wear with which short skirt, doing an about-face on my earlier thoughts, and congratulating myself on taking good advice from Brock because, since Martha started on Monday, already my time had been freed up. No schedules to do. No inventory to keep. No phone calls to pick up. And she helped out in front of the bakery too so I didn't have to rush up there when things got busy.

This meant I could leave early and concentrate on getting dolled up.

I was grinning to myself because I knew *exactly* what

I was going to wear: a dress and high-heeled strappy sandals I'd owned for over a year and had never worn. Martha talked me into buying them and I'd let her, for reasons unknown, because they were extremely sexy and thus something (at the time) I had no use for.

Now I had a use for them.

I walked through the front door smiling. I aimed my smile at Suni and Toby behind the counter.

They smiled back through the pack of people and Toby called, "Tess, a gentleman's here for you. He's waiting over there."

Toby tipped his chin toward the tables, my head turned that way, and my smile froze on my face.

This was because Dade McManus was sitting at a table by the window, cleaned plate in front of him, fingers through the handle of a coffee mug also in front of him, and lastly, a big manila envelope and folder also in front of him.

I tried to warm up my smile because he was a nice man.

I feared I failed because, even though he was a nice man, I wasn't fired up as to why he might be there.

Still, I approached him smiling.

"Dade," I greeted, and like the gentleman he was, he stood and bent to touch his lips to my cheek.

He leaned back, caught my eyes, and murmured, "Tess."

"This is a pleasant surprise," I lied.

His head tipped slightly to the side and his smile was small and solemn when he called me on it with a gentle, "I wish that were true, my dear."

I pulled in a breath.

He gestured to the chair opposite his, asking, "Please, can you sit with me for a while?"

I nodded and he waited until I was seated before he sat.

I looked at his plate and with years of experience my eyes moved from it to him and I asked, "Devil's food with dark chocolate buttercream?"

His brows went up in surprise and he answered, "Why, yes."

"Practice," I explained.

He nodded, then stated, "It was delicious." I smiled my gratitude for the compliment then he queried, "Would you like me to buy you a cake and coffee?"

"Honey," I said quietly, leaning in a little, "I own the joint. I don't have to pay for the goods."

"Every penny counts, Tess, and it would be my pleasure."

I sat back thinking, God, Olivia was so totally dumb. First, she had Brock and killed that dead. Then she had Dade and did the same.

Complete idiot.

"That's very nice but I'm good," I told him and he nodded again.

Then he announced, "Although the subject matter I've come to discuss is unpleasant, my reason for coming to discuss it with you is not. I see you're uncertain about our chat but I wish you to know that, before I leave, you'll be happy I came." He paused before he finished. "I hope."

"So you're saying I shouldn't play poker," I joked and he smiled.

"Definitely not."

"Okay then, sock it to me," I invited.

He sat back and rested a hand on the manila-ensconced mystery items beside his plate. I looked down at them then up at him when he started talking.

"I've been in contact with my attorneys. They're poised

to file divorce papers and will be doing so this next week. Once they're filed, I'll be giving Olivia two weeks to find alternate accommodation."

Oh man. Time had run out. And although Brock's lawyer was pushing Olivia, as well as doing what he could do at the courthouse to get something done, and soon, about custody, as they do, the wheels were grinding slowly. Brock's attorneys had learned that Olivia had just hired her own attorney two days ago and the first thing he did was pour cement on the proceedings. Fast-drying cement. Guardian ad litem cement. She wasn't going to sit down and discuss it. She was going to drag it out as long as possible. Which figured, since she was a bitch and didn't give a shit about her kids. It also sucked just because she was a bitch and didn't give a shit about her kids.

He continued. "I have a prenuptial agreement with Olivia. If we were to dissolve the marriage for anything other than infidelity, she would have walked away a very wealthy woman. Unfortunately, we will be dissolving the marriage due to a variety of reasons and one of those is infidelity. The clause in the prenuptial is that, if she were to be unfaithful to me, she would walk away with nothing and this, my attorneys assure me, is ironclad so this, my attorneys assure me, she will do."

Well, good.

Kind of.

"Okay," I said when Dade said no more.

He looked at me then he looked out the window then he looked at the manila folder and envelope under his hand and he sighed.

He looked back at me and said quietly, "I've known Joey and Rex now for nearly four years."

My heart started beating harder.

"Yes?" I prompted.

"They're good boys."

"Yes," I whispered, "they are."

"After what happened here a few weeks ago and, I'll say now, I'm sorry that happened to you and the boys. Although I heard it from her perspective, I know what most likely happened and I'm certain it was unpleasant."

"Unpleasant is one word you could use," I told him.

He gave me his solemn smile again and went on. "Well, after that, she has been doing nothing but ranting about you, about Lucas, and she does not hide this from the boys."

"I know," I said. "They tell their dad."

And they did, or at least Joel did. That cell Olivia bought him was in overdrive. Brock had been fielding calls from an alternately anxious and fed-up Joey since it happened. Surprisingly, Brock was keeping cool about this but he really had no choice. Joel needed patience, understanding, and a listening ear, not more intense emotion.

It was me who dealt with the sandpaper atmosphere after Brock hung up with his son. And my tactics were sometimes beer, sometimes bourbon, and sometimes blowjobs.

All, luckily, worked a charm.

So far.

Dade nodded before he remarked, "I do not see good things for their immediate future."

"You and me both," I agreed.

"I do not want that for them."

I held my breath and nodded.

He leaned forward, and as he did, he slid the manila envelope and folder toward me. Then he leaned back, leaving it in front of me.

"My private investigator's reports and photos," he stated. I blinked and let out a heavy breath then sucked in a heavier one. "Copies, of course."

"Dade," I whispered.

"Also, I've made a sworn affidavit as to her behavior subsequent to our marriage, specifically her behavior around the boys and also the escalation of it once your relationship with Lucas became known to her. That's what's in the envelope."

Oh my *God*.

"Dade," I repeated on a whisper.

"She is not a fit mother for a variety of reasons and those documents explain them all. I'll have my attorneys call Lucas's attorneys to let them know, if the affidavit is not enough, I will stand as a witness should this go to trial."

I said not a word, just stared at him.

"I believe, with what I've given you, there will be enough that this doesn't see a courtroom. However, I will also be doing my utmost for Joey and Rex to try, if it does, to make this happen quickly. Joel, I can see, is learning to stand up for himself and his brother. This is difficult to witness no matter how proud I am of him for doing it. And I *am* proud and have found quiet moments to tell him so. But it's difficult because Olivia is not taking kindly to it. That will likely continue and also escalate. Something must be done and I have..." He hesitated then said, "*Contacts*."

When he said no more, I asked, "Contacts?"

"Friends," he replied.

"Friends?" I was still not getting it.

"Friends, Tess, friends who wear robes and command gavels."

Oh.

My.

God.

Dade kept speaking. "Once I leave here, I'll be making calls."

I felt tears fill my eyes and, yet again, I whispered, "Dade."

"If Lucas provides this information to his attorneys and her attorneys do not see the wisdom of moving forward quickly to grant your boyfriend sole physical custody then I will see what I can do to get the ball rolling so this can be done quickly, for Joey and Rex."

I blinked away the tears in my eyes, momentarily speechless. Then that moment passed but, although no longer speechless, I still couldn't find the right words.

"I don't..." I shook my head and started again. "I don't know what to say."

"There is nothing *to* say, Tess. This business is distasteful for all concerned and there is no reason to drag it out for the innocents caught up in it and, as I'm sure you know, Olivia will do her best to drag it out. The others of us who genuinely care for those boys need to do what we can." He leaned forward and said softly, "And I genuinely care for them, so I'm doing what I can."

He leaned back and held my eyes so I said the only thing I could say. "Free cake for life."

Instantly, his face split into a smile that was not solemn and took ten years off his age. He was not difficult to look at normally but he was extremely handsome when he smiled.

So I told him so. "You have a very nice smile, Dade."

"Thank you, Tess, and hopefully in the not too distant future, I'll be doing it more often."

I nodded. "I hope so too," I said quietly. "I'm sorry this is happening to you."

His smile turned small again before he used my words to reply, "You and me both."

Then I shared, "Evidence is suggesting that I may be in the boys' lives for a while, and if I am, I'd like for us to work together to find ways for you to stay in their lives too."

The light died in his eyes but they got bright in another way.

He swallowed, controlling his emotions, and his smooth voice was rough when he said, "I would appreciate that, my dear."

"I'll talk to Brock," I whispered, reaching out and grabbing his hand.

He turned it in mine and gave me a squeeze.

Then he let me go, started to stand, and I went up with him.

"Take care of yourself, Tess," he said and I moved toward him, put my hands on his shoulders, and touched my cheek to his.

Leaving it there, in his ear I whispered, "You too, Dade. Anything you need, I'm here."

His fingers curled around my upper arms, gave them a squeeze, and I moved back. He again let me go, smiled his solemn smile, and walked out of the shop.

I snatched up the folder and envelope, hoofed it to my

office (which was now Martha's office, really), and found her on the computer.

"Can you give me two shakes?" I asked. "I need to talk to Brock. Private. Good news. I'll fill you in in a sec, but he gets the news first."

She studied my face, nodded, and didn't delay in dashing out and closing the door behind her.

I pulled out my phone, called Brock and held it to my ear as I dumped my purse and the folder and envelope on my desk.

"Babe," he answered as I opened the folder.

"I got a surprise visitor at the shop today," I told him and didn't make him wait. "Dade came by."

"Shit," he clipped.

"No," I said quickly, turned over some papers, and went mute at seeing a photo of Olivia doing it doggie style with a very muscled young man at least twenty years her junior. I also noted that repeated commentary from Brock was proved irrevocably correct through photo evidence. She was beautiful but she was *bony*.

Ick.

"Tess?" Brock called, his voice terse.

I slapped the folder closed and grunted, "Ugh."

"Babe, what the fuck?"

"Um . . . wait a sec while my retinas recover from being seared."

"Tess," he growled.

Crap. Time to pull it together.

"Honey, Dade just gave me copies of his private investigator's reports and photos as well as a sworn affidavit as to Olivia's behavior after their marriage as it pertains to the boys. He's going to be contacting your attorneys to tell them he will stand as a witness to her unsuitability to parent. And, if what I just saw does not set her attorneys scrambling to give you everything you want, he's going to talk to some of his buds who 'wear robes and command gavels,' his words, to see that this nightmare is sorted out sooner not later."

Brock was silent.

Then he asked, "What did you just see?"

"Let's just say what I saw means you aren't getting one of your favorite positions for a *long time* because it might take eternity for the image of her getting boinked, by what appeared to be her boy toy, to heal, considering it's burned like acid on my brain."

More silence then, "No shit?"

"Would I shit about that?" I asked and then I answered before he could. "No."

"Fuckin' hell," he muttered, sounding shocked but also pleased.

I sucked in a breath.

Then I told him softly, "He cares a great deal about Joey and Rex."

A pause, and then, "Yeah. The boys think he's the shit too."

This was good.

"Do you want me to bring these to you at the station or do you want me to drop them by your attorney's office?" I offered.

"You got the time, take them to Smith. If you don't, I'll try to get away and take them myself."

"I'll carve out the time."

Another pause, then, "Thanks, sweetness."

"My pleasure," I said with feeling, then asked, "Do you drink champagne?"

"If I have to," he answered and I started laughing.

Through my laughter I told him, "Well, tonight, you have to. We have things to celebrate, baby."

"Fuckin' finally."

"Yeah," I whispered.

Then he commenced in rocking my world.

"You got a lot on your plate and on your mind but I hope to God what McManus gave you means there's no time to waste. So, if my boys make a move it's probably best for them that they make a permanent one, not one that leads to two. A buddy of mine in the unit just left his wife, moved in with his brother and sister-in-law. He's not a big fan of his sister-in-law and only a slightly bigger fan of his brother. He's lookin' and he'd sublet from me. He left with nothin' but suitcases so he'll sublet furnished, which'll give us time to sort out two houses full of stuff. And it's time we put this two house bullshit to rest, babe. It's gonna happen eventually, it might as well happen now."

My heart started hammering in my chest and I whispered, "Now?"

"Now," he stated firmly.

I stared at my desk.

"Tess?"

I kept staring at my desk.

"Baby, you there?"

I kept right on staring at my desk.

"Tess, baby, talk to me."

The joyful sob hitched audibly in my throat before I declared, "You better drink champagne tonight."

Brock was silent for a moment before he said gently, "I take it I'm movin' in."

"Fuck yes!" I cried and another happy sob hitched audibly in my throat.

Brock expressed his happiness through a deep chuckle.

I swiped at my wet cheeks and told him, "I wish this wasn't happening over the phone so I could kiss you."

"You can kiss me tonight."

"Hard," I clarified.

"Hard," he rumbled through another chuckle.

I sucked in a calming breath. Then I whispered, "I love you."

"Yeah, sweetness, me too."

"I'll get this over to your attorneys."

"Appreciate it."

"See you tonight."

"Absolutely."

"Bye, honey."

"Later, babe."

We disconnected.

I stared at the envelope and folder.

Then I put my phone on the desk, looked to the door, and shouted, "Martha!"

*   *   *

"Brock," I breathed then his mouth went away.

I whimpered my protest but his hands went to my hips, rolled me to my belly. They went back to my hips and he hauled me up to my knees.

Then he was between them. Instead of his tongue darting inside me, his cock thrust there.

My head flew back and I went up to my hands, totally in the zone, totally loving this, totally not thinking of Olivia *at all*.

He kept thrusting as his hands slid from my hips, up my waist, in, over my ribs to cup my breasts then he tugged on my nipples and that felt fucking *great* so I moaned.

"Love your tits," he grunted, still pounding hard and deep.

"Baby," I whispered.

His hands slid back to my hips, clenched my flesh, and pulled them in to meet his thrusts.

"Love this cunt," he growled.

"Oh my God," I gasped.

"Hurry, sweetness," he urged, voice thick.

"Yeah," I whispered.

The pounding got faster, harder, his hands jerking my hips back to meet each one.

"Hurry, baby," he semirepeated, his voice now hoarse but he didn't have to say it. I was hurrying, so much, I'd hurried and it was on me.

"Brock," I breathed, then gasped, then moaned, back arching to the bed, ass to the ceiling as it thundered through me.

"Fuck yeah," he grunted, going deeper, harder, faster, five thrusts then he was there, joining me.

When we were coming down, silently and gently, he moved in and out and, silently and happily, I let him and enjoyed every stroke.

After a while, he pulled out. His hands glided down my sides and in, pulling me up in front of him until I was on my knees, my back pressed to his front. His fingers fisted in the little, slinky, sexy dress that Brock liked, like, *a lot*, that was bunched at my waist and he pulled it up. I lifted my arms for him. He yanked it free and tossed it to the side of the bed.

His face went into my neck as his hands roamed my body and, against my skin, he murmured, "Love you, baby."

I lifted an arm to glide my fingers in his hair and whispered back, "Love you too, Brock."

Carefully, he turned me and deposited me on my back in the bed and then turned his attention to the strappy, high-heeled sandals I still wore. One by one, he unbuckled them and they joined my dress on the floor. But after each one he kissed the inside of my ankle.

Once he was done, he moved his body to cover mine and I moved my legs to surround him, one around his ass, one I curved around the back of his thigh and I did this as my arms circled him, holding tight.

Brock put some weight into his forearm but his other hand came to my face and he traced it with his fingertips while I traced his with my eyes.

"You know," I whispered and his silvery-gray eyes came to mine. "The first time we were together, after you made me come, I looked at you and my first thought was how beautiful you were."

His fingers stopped moving, his eyes closed, and his forehead came to mine and when he groaned, "Tess," I knew it came from his gut because I felt it in mine.

My fingers slid into his hair and my lips went to his cheek. I moved them across, lifting my head and, in his ear, I kept whispering.

"And the way you were looking at me, I knew in my blood you were mine."

"You were right, sweetness," he whispered back.

Then he kissed my neck, lifted his head again. I dropped mine and both my arms gave him a squeeze.

"Thanks for drinking champagne with me."

"Thanks for makin' me drink only a glass so I could move on to beer."

I smiled at him and his eyes dropped to my mouth.

They came back to mine and I felt my body still at what I saw.

Then he spoke words that described the feeling I saw in his eyes.

"My dad was a dick. I grew up fast. I lost Bree the way I did and lost all our history with her. And I found Olivia and she made my life shit. Then I had a job where you wouldn't believe the shit I saw, the shit I did, and I hope to God, baby, you never get to a place you do. But all that was worth it, all of it, since my reward is you."

"Shut up," I whispered. I didn't know why, it just came out of my mouth but what he said meant so much, it filled me so full, it felt like I was going to burst.

A beautiful pain.

But he didn't shut up.

Instead, he went on. "McManus said he started with a good one and I was lucky I was ending with one and he was not fuckin' wrong."

Both my hands moved to either side of his face and I begged, "Please, Brock, be quiet."

"No fuckin' way, baby," he whispered. "Today, I been thinkin' a lot about McManus and he lost his good one and there is no way I'm gonna find mine and not know right to my fuckin' bones she doesn't understand *precisely* what she means to me."

I felt the tears well then slide out the sides of my eyes as my thumbs moved over his cheeks and I told him, "Well, I'm lucky too. I had it shit for a while and I found you."

He shook his head and his hand captured mine. He turned his head and pressed my palm to his lips where he kissed me and then his fingers curled around mine and he held my hand to his shoulder.

"It isn't the same. You're made of sugar, Tess, and it's a given you'd eventually get it good because people like you, sweet to the core, they deserve it. What I'm sayin' is I'm glad I'm the one who gets to give it to you."

Oh *God*. I loved this man.

"You're sweet too."

He grinned.

Then he muttered, "I see, all this time, you still don't know me."

I didn't grin. My hand tensed on his face as the other one clenched in his.

"You're a manly, macho, rough, wild, hot guy kind of sweet but you're sweet. I'm a mountainous swirl of frosting with a moist, rich cake as my core but you're smooth, delicious dark chocolate that tastes good from the second it hits your tongue and makes you want more the minute it melts away."

His grin got bigger. "Shit, Tess, you're makin' me hard again."

I took my hand from his face and slapped his shoulder, snapping, "I'm being serious."

His grin faded clean away and his mercury eyes locked with mine.

Then he whispered, "I know."

I stared in his eyes and what Vance said hit me as truth so pure and undiluted, it felt like I was touched by a rainbow.

Vance thought he was the lucky one that he had his

wife, and one of the reasons he thought that was because he knew she felt like she was the lucky one.

And I was lucky and so was Brock.

"We should go to Vegas," I announced. "We're on a streak."

His brows drew together. "Babe, not sure you're payin' attention, but shit that's flyin' around us does not say 'winning streak.'"

"I've got a naked hot-guy bad boy on top of me who proves you wrong."

At that, his brows relaxed and he smiled.

Then I informed him, "You and your boys' birthdays are next week and I'm telling you now I'm giving you and the boys an all-inclusive, five-star beach getaway for spring break for all your birthdays and I'm not taking any lip *and* I don't care the shit that's swirling. We're going no matter what."

His smile didn't die when he said, "We'll talk about it later."

"We won't. I'm doing this."

That's when his smile faded. "Babe, you're not payin' for me and my boys to go on vacation."

"Honey, *I* need a vacation, *you* need a vacation, and *the boys* freaking need a vacation. So much, it's got to be a really, *really* good one. And I don't bust my hump baking cakes not to live the good life and give it to those I love. So I'm going to give it to those I love."

"You got a bakery to launch."

"I got a vacation to take."

He held my eyes and I held his right back.

Then he decreed, "I'll buy the plane tickets."

"Brock—" I started to protest but he talked over me.

"Tess, I'll...buy...the plane tickets."

He was being firm in that way of his I knew he was taking charge of his woman so that firm was unyielding.

"Oh, all right," I gave in and he grinned again.

His head dipped so his mouth was at my ear. "Now, let's go back to me bein' like chocolate that melts in your mouth."

"That isn't exactly what I meant," I told him. His arms went around me and he rolled to his back, taking me with him.

Then his hand sifted into my hair, fisted gently, and my head came up.

"I would hope not, darlin', seein' as every time you take me in your mouth, the last thing I do is melt."

Hmm.

This was very true.

"This is true."

And, again, he grinned.

And, it must be said, I liked it when my man grinned.

Then he brought my mouth down to his. He kissed me hard and I kissed him harder.

Then I took my time kissing other parts of him.

And when I did, those parts did *not* melt.

CHAPTER TWENTY-ONE

Quiet Like

"THANK YOU," I mouthed to the clerk at Dillard's in Park Meadows Mall who was handing me my bag, which held six pairs of boys swim trunks. This purchase was made because, in two days, Brock, Joey, Rex, and I were boarding a plane headed for Aruba and I'd found upon asking them to check that the boys were growing so fast none of their old swim trunks fit.

The clerk smiled at me as I turned away and I smiled back. I had my phone to my ear and a man named Raul was talking to me through it.

"It's going to take another week," he said.

"Um…" I started, moving through the store and already feeling Brock getting pissed even though he wasn't there. In fact, he was nowhere near and he didn't know that the contractor we hired to renovate my basement in order to build another bedroom downstairs was delaying even further.

However, since we contacted Raul the last week in February, this was the third delay, taking us to the last week in March. Brock was not happy with the first delay.

He was unhappier with the second and I had a feeling his unhappiness would significantly escalate with this one.

We needed this room because Olivia had caved, or, at least her attorneys had talked her into doing so mostly because, with Dade out of the picture, if she racked up a huge bill fighting a case she had no hope of winning, there was no one around to pay it.

The stuff Dade gave Brock was useful but even without it, Hector had dug up so much dirt on her, Brock was sure to win. Hector had found they were often late to school and they were often hanging around after school because she was late picking them up.

Furthermore, Olivia had not made loads of friends among the other mothers and therefore these mothers had happily chitchatted with hot-guy Hector, telling tales of Olivia dropping the boys off late and then not staying at the boys' junior football and little league games or calling random moms at the last minute *during* the game to ask another mom to take the boys home and she'd pick them up later and her later meant *later*. Sometimes, the boys would be asleep at their friends' houses before Olivia would show, which meant she left them for hours.

And when she did all this, she was not at the soup kitchen spreading her benevolence among those less fortunate, but shopping or getting laid by her bevy of boy toys.

Of this, Hector, too, had photographic proof.

Luckily, I did not see Hector's proof. Unluckily, Hector had to, considering he took the photos, and his face upon handing over the evidence to a Brock, who was even unhappier to learn that his ex was less of a mother than he thought, shared the knowledge that Hector was of the same opinion as his bad-boy brethren that bony wasn't beautiful.

So, the papers had been drawn up, everyone signed them, a judge stamped his approval, and the boys' custody flip-flopped. Olivia had them every other weekend. Brock and I had them the rest of the time. Therefore, he wanted them settled in what would be their permanent rooms.

The first delay on the renovation meant that when they moved in with us, Rex had moved into my office upstairs that we converted to a bedroom and Joel into the guest bedroom (now his bedroom) downstairs.

This was something Brock did not like because it didn't say to Rex, "You're home and settled." He also didn't like it because Rex was right next door to our room. The walls weren't paper thin but they weren't soundproof either and the reasons he didn't like that were obvious. But there Rex was—a bathroom and hallway away.

Olivia was also coping with a move but hers would have been more settled if she was less, well...*her*. Dade had paid six months advance rent on a furnished, two-bedroom apartment for her. When he came into my bakery a few days after Olivia had left, he told me he'd done this for Joel and Rex and I figured this was true. But I knew it was also because he was a good man and if he tried to do something pure asshole, like kick her out on her ass without any support (even if she did deserve it), he'd probably spontaneously combust or something.

He had not given her any money, however.

"She was very fond of John Atencio," he said to me as he forked into a piece of my soured chocolate cake (to die for) with milk chocolate buttercream icing. Dade, I'd learned since Olivia left and he became a regular at

Tessa's Cakes, was a chocolate cake man. "I'm certain she can make her frequent trips to that store work for her."

John Atencio was a fabulous, exclusive jewelry store and I figured Dade meant that Olivia was going to be spending some time in a pawn shop, or perhaps learning how to sell things on on-line auctions.

Needless to say, although things had worked out for Brock and the boys, and the boys, to my surprise (and delight, and it must be said, Brock's too), had settled in quickly and easily, relaxing in my house and making themselves at home within days (or more like hours, since I made a carrot cake for Rex and a chocolate cake for Joel and this obviously screamed "You're home!" to now eleven- and thirteen-year-old boys), this did not mean our nightmare was over.

No.

Not at all.

Because Olivia was a bitch, and I was learning, when none of the games bitches could play were swinging their way, they scrambled.

Therefore, Olivia was a regular at the station and her name was on the display of Brock's phone so often, it was a wonder it hadn't etched itself into the screen.

When she phoned or visited him at work, she did not want to talk to or about the boys. No. She needed Brock to hang shelves. She needed Brock to look over legal documents Dade was sending her. She needed Brock to look at a sink that had a drip (even though she was in a freaking *apartment complex* with a freaking *maintenance man*). She was selling her Mercedes (something Dade allowed her to have) and she needed him to help her. She was buying a new car and she needed him to go with her so she didn't get screwed.

She told him (and Brock told me) that she was turning to him as the mother of his children to help her out in a bad situation.

And, also by Brock's report, she'd gone saccharine sweet.

"She's got her nose so far up my ass, babe, I swear I feel that bitch in my throat," Brock, unfortunately, gave me a rather disgusting visual while we were lying in bed one night, his head to the pillows, his hands rubbing his face, his tone frustrated, his mood heavy in the air.

Brock was a good man too, the best, but he was a different kind of good man than Dade. Or perhaps, he just had more of a history with Olivia. Therefore, he said no. Then he said no again. Then he said it again. Then he stopped taking her calls when her name came on his display. Then, without even a word, he started to flip his phone shut and turn off the ringer when she called him from other phones. And luckily his colleagues had learned to spot her when she arrived at the station. They started to give Brock the heads up so he could disappear before she made it to his desk whereupon his badge-wielding brothers told her he was out.

He was done. He was not going to hang shelves, look over legal documents, or help her buy a car.

The problem was, weeks had passed and she wasn't giving up.

While his frustration filled the room, in bed, I'd pressed into him and whispered, "She'll eventually give up and go away."

Brock's fingers had scored into his hair, his palms at his forehead and just his silver eyes tipped to me. But they told the tale. They told the tale that this was an example of her five years of her making him miserable until Dade came into her life. And now Dade was going out of her life. And Brock was facing five-plus years more. And he didn't like this either.

Since we were in bed and I was comfortable, I didn't want to go get him a beer or a bourbon. So, to make him feel better, I settled on a blowjob.

As usual, that did the trick.

"I'm not sure Brock's going to like that," I said to Raul.

I mean, I didn't understand what the big deal was. It was, essentially, a wall and a door. How hard could that be?

"Only another week," Raul said in my ear.

"We were kinda hoping you'd have it done by the time we got back from vacation," I told him.

"I don't see that happening," Raul told me.

Damn.

"Maybe you should talk to Brock about this," I suggested.

"No," he said quickly and I pulled in an annoyed breath, knowing his avoiding the wrath of Brock was why he phoned me in the first place. He never phoned me. This was Brock's deal. He'd made that very clear in his firm, unyielding, "I deal with things that require drywall, two-by-fours, hammers, and men with work belts" macho man way and I gave in. This was mostly because I had no desire to deal with *more* things that required drywall, two-by-fours, hammers, and men with work belts considering I had enough to deal with with my new bakery. "If you could do the favor of passin' it on, I'll schedule it in, for sure, when you guys get back."

"Actually, I think you need to speak to Brock," I said.

"Things're just pilin' up. I'll sort them when you're gone and I'll definitely get you on the schedule week after next."

"Raul, you need to tell this to Brock," I semirepeated.

He ignored me. "That's a promise, Tess."

I walked out of Dillard's and into the mall but stepped to the side, out of pedestrian traffic, and stopped.

Then I said, "I'll tell Brock, Raul, but I wouldn't waste your busy time scheduling us because, if I tell Brock you're delaying again, he'll phone and fire you. I know this for a fact. We needed this done weeks ago, when you promised you could get it done, and you aren't the only contractor in Denver. If you don't start work Monday while we're on holiday, he'll find someone who will. Now, I'll be happy to tell him you're delaying again but that's the same as your telling me you cannot do the job. There are two options here: either we go our separate ways or you find a way to get to the house on Monday and start work. And, if you pick door number two, I would advise you to actually keep your promise. I think you get you shouldn't rile Brock and I think you get that because you're on the phone with me, not Brock. You're right. You shouldn't rile Brock. He wants a room for his son and he's going to get it and not in June. Yes?"

"I do understand where you're comin' from, Tess, but if I could do it I would and you could go with another contractor but you couldn't get the guaranteed quality you'll get from me," Raul replied, and I sucked in another annoyed breath because I had hoped to save Brock from another frustration right before vacation.

And I failed.

Crap.

"Fine," I stated. "Prepare to be fired. Take care, Raul."

I disconnected and as my thumb found Brock's contact info on my phone, I headed to Mrs. Field's Cookies because Mrs. Field could bake a mean cookie and I knew I needed a cookie to soothe the abrasions I'd endure after talking to Brock.

I put my order in as it was ringing and Brock answered on ring two.

"Babe."

"Hi, honey, do you have any cookies nearby?"

Silence, then, "Shit. Olivia, Raul, or Tess Two?"

He was guessing as to the variety of annoyances in our lives that was making me ask if he had soothing cookies nearby.

"Tess Two" referred to my new bakery, which was not so much an annoyance as a huge time suckage. Martha was still getting her feet and she knew me, she understood my vision, she'd spent a lot of time in Tessa's Cakes, she'd been there when the concept was developed, but she loved me and she didn't want to mess up. Therefore, she involved me with everything that had anything to do with "Tess Two," even though I agreed with her on practically everything she'd asked for confirmation on.

And Martha didn't shut down at five o'clock. She didn't even shut down at seven. Martha was on a mission to get Tessa's Cakes in LoDo off and running and therefore it wasn't unheard of for Martha to phone whenever Martha needed to phone. This included once (and only once) Martha calling at eleven thirty at night, a time when both the boys were in bed asleep and Brock and I were busy.

This happened only once because Brock snatched up the phone, looked at the display, touched the screen, and growled, "Not a good time, *never* a good time, unless you're dyin' or you killed someone. We're in bed. When we're in bed, no one is in this bed but me and Tess. *Ever.* Now, are you dyin' or have you killed someone?" He paused, then, "Right."

Then he touched the screen, turned off the ringer, tossed it back on the nightstand, and came back to me. I thought it was prudent not to request details but I knew who the caller was and when Brock came back to me, he immediately resumed our interrupted activities, activities I had been thoroughly enjoying and wanted to recommence. Therefore, I made the decision to concentrate on said activities and explain things to Martha the next day.

So I did (though, she'd already guessed).

She never called late again and she also didn't get mad. She'd done an about-face with Brock, learning I loved him, he loved me and made me happy, so now she thought he was the bomb (and told me so).

And she adored his sons.

"Raul," I answered Brock.

"Fuckin' shit," he muttered.

"He said he has to push it back another week. I told him, essentially, he was fired though I have to admit he's waiting for your call to confirm that," I went on. "I'm at a mall, you're dealing with homicides. Do you want me to call him back and confirm that so you don't have to?"

"You call him, darlin', that'll deprive me the opportunity to tear him a new asshole. So, no, I don't want you to call him back."

Hmm. I kind of felt sorry for Raul.

"Okay," I said softly. I took my cookies and set them aside as I dropped my Dillard's bag to rummage in my purse for my wallet. "When I get home, do you want me to search for a new contractor?"

"I'll deal with it when we get back from the island," he surprised me by saying. "Rex is set for now. He isn't complaining. It's working so it can wait."

"Okay, honey." I was still talking softly. Then I offered, "I'm at Mrs. Field's. If you don't have cookies handy, do you want me to buy some for medicinal purposes later?"

"Mrs. Field's are sweet, baby, but nothin' beats your kind of sweet."

That was nice, *very* nice but I wasn't entirely certain if he meant cookies from my bakery or a different kind of sweet that I could give him for medicinal (and other) purposes.

I decided that I'd pop by the bakery, just in case. Cover all the bases.

"Okay," I said yet again.

Having paid for my cookies, I smiled at the clerk, shoved my wallet back in my purse, grabbed my stuff, and took off.

"All set?" he asked.

"Yep. The boys have a bevy of swim trunk selections. I'm leaving the mall now, on my way to get them from school. When we get home, I'll supervise packing."

"Babe, we got two days."

"And tomorrow we have *one* day. We don't want to rush. When you rush, you forget stuff. We need to be prepared. There are four of us and the boys need supervision. And I need a whole evening to sort myself out. Not to mention, I need to concoct dinner from whatever is in the kitchen so we don't leave stuff that will spoil."

"Tess, we're goin' to Aruba, not a jungle in Paraguay.

We forget stuff, we buy it. We come home, stuff spoils, we throw it out."

Hmm. This was true. Except the "we throw it out" part. Brock, Joel, and Rex would undoubtedly come home and continue to utilize the fridge as they normally did. That was, standing in its open door, staring inside like doing so could form whatever they wished to have (if it wasn't already there), and they would ignore anything with mold on it that had gone bad. Therefore, the "we" part actually meant "you."

Brock went on before I could remind him of this fact. "And, far's I can tell, you can take a carry-on because all you need is a bikini."

I continued to dodge fellow shoppers on my way to the exit as I explained, "Brock, first, I don't wear bikinis. Second, I need more than *one* bathing suit for a week. That requires at least three but I'm going with four, which is how many I bought when I was out shopping with Martha, Elvira, and the girls last week."

By the way, my ban on the mall was up and I made a vow to myself that, next year, post-Christmas, no matter how frenzied Christmas could get, I was lifting the ban in February because I'd gone gonzo when I hit a mall for the first time in over two months. I bought practically an entirely new vacation wardrobe. Some of it was *hot* but all of it was *awesome* and none of it I needed (really), especially not after paying for four to be accommodated at a five-star hotel and while setting up a new bakery.

"Third," I carried on talking to Brock, "although I intend to relax I also intend to shop and you can't shop in a swimsuit. And last, evening will require me in something other than a bikini and who knows what we'll be up to? We could be going to nice restaurants or local dive restaurants or family restaurants. I've never been to Aruba. Maybe we'll go to all of those kinds of restaurants and each kind requires a different kind of vacation outfit, not just for me, for *all of us*. Therefore, we *all* have to be prepared."

To this long-winded, multipoint explanation, Brock asked, "You don't wear bikinis?"

I rolled my eyes and headed to the exit doors, outside of which my car was parked. "No."

"Why not?"

"I just don't."

"Why?"

I pushed through the doors, asking, "Do I actually need to explain?"

He didn't answer. Instead, he asked his own question of, "Do you own a bikini?"

I answered his question. "No."

"Babe, you're at a mall," he told me something I knew.

"Actually, I'm outside walking to my car."

"Turn around and buy yourself a bikini"—he paused—"or four."

"Brock."

"Sweetness," his said, his voice had dipped low, "you got a great body. Fuckin' beautiful. Since you told me about this trip, I've been imagining you on the beach in a bikini. I've also been imagining you other places in a bikini. I've also been imagining *taking off* your bikini. All this imagining has lasted four weeks. I only got two days left to wait. Don't take that away from me."

Mm. I liked that. All of it. So much, I started imagining too.

My imagining took all my attention so I stopped behind a car and studied the tips of my high-heeled boots.

Then something else hit me and I asked, "Do you think it's okay to be in a bikini around the boys?"

I could actually envision Brock's eyebrows snapping together before he said, "Uh...yeah." Then, "Why?"

"I don't know," I mumbled.

There was a moment of silence then, softly, "Baby, you just became stepmom to two boys. That doesn't mean you gotta go June Cleaver." He ended on a muttered, "Or Christ, at least I hope you don't."

I thought about it.

Then I informed him, "Donna never wore a bikini."

"Did Donna have a great fuckin' body like you do?"

"Donna was five foot two and liked carrot cake more than Rex and chocolate cake *way* more than Joel. How do you think I learned how to make them?"

I listened to my man chuckle and then he said, "Turn around and buy me some bikinis."

"I already bought you three nighties."

More silence, then low, "Fuck. Make my year, sweetness, turn around and add bikinis."

I grinned.

He went on. "I'll swing by, get the boys, bring 'em into the station. Can you pick them up here?"

His question and the casual way he asked it made warm gushiness saturate my belly.

This was an addition to my life that I liked. Since Martha started and my load was less but Brock's hadn't changed, Brock dropped the boys off at school (on time) and I left the bakery to get them in the afternoons. Usually, they hung out with me at the bakery after school.

Sometimes, I had to take them to baseball practice, which had just started, and I'd hang while they practiced. Sometimes, I called it quits early and we all hung out at home.

I liked this. All of it. Meeting, even fleetingly, the other moms and dads I'd see during school runs, getting to know the boys' friends and their parents, having chats with the boys about how their day went. I never thought I'd have that, asking two beings I loved if they had their homework done, listening to them chatter in the car while I drove, hearing their voices drifting up the stairs while they fought in front of the television about what they were going to watch, going to the grocery store and buying food enough for a family, not just myself or not just myself and a partner.

I loved being with Brock. He made me feel safe. He made me feel beautiful. He made me feel loved. I loved all he'd given me, more than I could say.

But the best thing he'd given me was a family.

And since he gave me a family, I could give him bikinis.

Therefore, I turned back toward the mall, answering, "Sure."

"Text me when you're on your way."

"All right, honey."

"Later, babe."

"Later, Brock, love you."

"Me too, darlin'."

I sighed happily.

He disconnected.

I put my phone in my purse.

Then I saw the middle of a man in front of me. I started to scoot by him and say, "Excuse me," but I didn't get the "Excuse me" part out.

This was because the middle of that man scooted the direction I scooted.

My head came up and I caught his eye.

"Sorry," I said on a small smile and scooted the other way.

He again scooted the way I scooted.

Uh-oh.

"Uh..." I started.

"Mr. Heller wants to see you."

Damn!

I looked beyond him to the doors to the mall. I was four car lengths and a thoroughfare away. I was in high-heeled boots. He was big and brawny. Maybe this meant he'd be slow if I made a run for it.

There was a black sedan that was crawling along our lane and I heard a car also coming from behind.

I sighed in relief that we had company and scooted again, turning to the side to slide by, saying, "I don't want to talk to Mr. Heller."

"I'm afraid that isn't an option," he told me.

Great.

Damian.

God, I hated him. There I was thinking of bikinis and family and Brock loving me and *boom*! Damian rears his ugly head and sends a goon after me and all my happy thoughts evaporate.

I scooted faster. The black sedan stopped and the backdoor opened.

Damian was in the backseat.

Fuck!

The big brawny guy cut me off from scooting and the car was cutting me off in the other direction so I had to stop. Therefore, I juggled my bags to dig in my purse to grab my phone and call 911 so I could report Damian for harassing me.

"Tess, get in the car," Damian ordered. "It's urgent."

I didn't answer. Vance told me not to engage him and I wasn't going to. I was going to phone 911. I tried to push through big brawny guy but big brawny guy just put a firm hand on my arm to stop this.

I tried to twist away at the same time activating my phone.

"Tess, there isn't a lot of time," I heard Damian say. "Please, for your own good, get in the car."

Surprisingly, big brawny guy wasn't taking my phone away. I dialed 911 (which, at this rate, could be added to my favorites) and put it to my ear.

"Tess, *please,*" Damian entreated, sounding like it was, indeed, urgent (the jerk) but I kept my eyes on the pavement.

The big brawny guy, weirdly gently, started to pull me to the car and the 911 operator said in my ear, "Nine-one-one, what's your emer—?"

Then it happened.

Gunshots.

Right there.

Gunshots *right there*.

So loud. Unbelievably loud. Making my ears ring.

I stood frozen as the big brawny man's hand left my arm and it left my arm because he'd fallen to the ground, blood oozing from his chest.

In a fog of horror, I tipped my head down and stared at big brawny man, who was wheezing with blood oozing from his chest.

Oh my *God!*

Stupidly, in shock, I turned to look left and saw an older man I'd never seen in my life advancing, smoking gun drawn.

"Tess!" Damian shouted, jumping out of the car before I could do anything, say, like *flee. "Get in my fucking car!"*

Then he had a hand on me and he yanked me to the car as more gunshots were fired. Damian grunted in pain as I felt his body jerk but he still shoved me into his car, coming in after me, slamming the door.

"Drive!" he yelled. The older man was still firing at the car, bullets thudding into the metal even as Damian's driver put his foot down and the car shot forward, straight at the old, crazy, shooting man.

A bullet penetrated the windshield and the car veered crazily right and slammed into some parked cars, tossing both Damian and me to the side, skidding along them for a while, and coming to a stop when the driver slumped to the right.

And it came to a stop in a way that my door was wedged against cars. No escape except over Damian.

But I didn't even get that chance and I didn't because it all happened quickly. In the beat of a heart, the flash of an eye.

Damian pulled a gun out of his jacket just as the door was pulled open and old crazy shooting man leaned in, aimed at Damian, and shot him right in the face.

Right.

In.

The.

Face!

I screamed in sheer terror as Damian collapsed on me and then rolled to the floor.

I stopped screaming and looked at the old crazy shooting man who had the gun aimed at me and my heart and lungs stopped. My heart and lungs stopped but my blood was coursing through my veins. I felt hot everywhere. My scalp was tingling, my palms went instantly wet, my knees were quaking, and I stared right at him and his gun.

"Tessa O'Hara," he said and I didn't move, didn't speak, didn't even fucking blink. Nothing entered my mind, not his knowing my name, not blood, murder, and mayhem in the parking lot at Park Meadows Mall, nothing except him and his gun. "Brock Lucas's Tessa O'Hara," he whispered and that was when I knew him. I knew him. He was the man who called forever ago, the night someone had shot at Brock.

I still didn't speak. I just kept staring.

"You wanna keep breathing, you'll come quiet like."

I wanted to keep breathing.

So in the car with two dead men, I left my phone, my purse, my Mrs. Field's cookies and the Dillard's bag with my boys' swim trunks, and I went quiet like.

*   *   *

Brock

"Need a second in Cap's office," Brock Lucas heard. His eyes went from the computer he was shutting down before going to get his boys to the man standing beside his desk.

Or, that was to say, the *men* standing by his desk.

Hank Nightingale, Eddie Chavez, and Jimmy Marker, the first two men he'd known awhile, since they worked vice. Their relationship had been strained due to Brock's second-to-last job going bad and both of them having a strong negative opinion about the plays Brock had made during that job. Now, considering Hank was Lee Nightingale's brother, Lee was Chavez's best friend, and Brock was working with Hector and Vance, two of Lee's boys, not to mention he'd moved from the DEA to the DPD and paths were crossing, they'd come to an uneasy détente. As the days turned to weeks and then months, this détente improved as they got to know each other's histories, personalities, and work ethics. He couldn't say they were best buds but he respected them.

Jimmy Marker was a veteran cop, highly decorated, intensely dedicated to the job, and close to retirement. There wasn't a cop in the department who didn't respect him, including Brock.

It was Jimmy who had spoken.

"What's up?" Brock asked.

"In Cap's office," Jimmy returned.

That was when he knew it. He felt it. He saw it in their guarded eyes, their alert stances.

Something was wrong. Something big was wrong. And that something big was very big and it was also very wrong.

Fuck.

He said not another word, folded out of his chair, and moved to the captain's office, Jimmy, Eddie, and Hank following him.

The minute it came into view, Brock saw the captain had eyes to the window of his office.

Waiting.

Fuck.

He walked in, the men walked in with him, and the door closed instantly.

"Have a seat, Lucas," the Captain ordered, his eyes not having left him.

Brock didn't move nor take his eyes off Cap.

"Tell me," he ordered.

Cap held his eyes.

Then he stated, "You know Josiah Burkett was released on parole four months ago."

Bile crawled up Brock's throat.

Josiah Burkett was Bree's cousin who raped her. Brock had paid attention to Josiah Burkett and he knew exactly when that motherfucking monster was released. Brock also knew Burkett had kept steady with his meetings with his parole officer, the halfway house that asshole was in and hadn't moved out of yet, and that he managed to land himself a job working the line of an automotive parts factory off 6th Avenue.

What he did not know was why Cap was leading with Burkett.

This was not starting good.

"Yeah," he replied.

The captain held his eyes.

"Jesus, Cap, just—" Brock growled and Cap interrupted him.

Speaking quickly, he said, "A call came into nine-one-one twenty minutes ago. The caller didn't get the chance to explain what was happening. Shots were heard over the phone. Not a minute later, multiple calls came from Park Meadows Mall..."

Hearing the location, a location Tess was at twenty minutes ago, and he knew this because *he* was on the *fucking* phone with her twenty *fucking* minutes ago, every cell in Brock Lucas's body stopped moving.

The captain kept speaking, "...reporting an elderly man had opened fire on a black sedan. When units hit the scene, the shooter was gone, there was a man down, still alive outside the car, and two men dead in the car. Damian Heller was one of those men."

Brock didn't move, didn't speak, didn't even fucking blink.

"I'm sorry, son, but Tessa O'Hara's phone and purse were found in the back of that sedan."

Brock closed his eyes.

The captain kept going. "Witnesses report she went with the elderly man, who was holding her at gunpoint."

Brock opened his eyes.

The captain finished, saying quietly, "The descriptions of the shooter match Josiah Burkett."

Instantly, he turned on his boot, heading for the door.

Nightingale and Chavez were already there, prepared, and if he had any room for anything else in his brain, anything other than his sweet Tess in the hands of a whacked, sick lunatic who *he* had set on this path to revenge, making it *him* who'd made his Tess unsafe, he would have cottoned onto why those two were chosen. Not a lot of men could lock Brock down but those two could.

"Lucas, you need to stay calm and listen to me," Cap ordered urgently.

Brock stopped in front of Nightingale and Chavez.

"Outta my fuckin' way," he growled, his eyes moving direct to both of theirs.

They didn't move a muscle. If anything was on his mind other than the putrid garbage that was filling it, he would have seen understanding in their eyes, concern.

But nothing was on his mind but his Tess in the sick, twisted hands of Josiah fucking Burkett.

"Lucas," Cap called. "Son, calm down and listen to me. You don't, we'll lock you down. And you don't need that, you don't want that. I know you don't. Not now. Be smart, turn around, and listen to me."

Brock looked over his shoulder. "Get them outta my way."

"We'll find her," Cap promised.

"When?" Brock asked, turning. "After he beats the shit outta her? After he plays his sick fuckin' games with her? *Jesus fuckin' Christ!*" He said the last on a roar. "She's been through this before."

"I know, son, listen to—"

Brock turned his back on the captain and lifted a finger in Nightingale's face. "I want your brother on this, fuckin' *now*."

"He is, Slim. I already called him," Hank said quietly. "All his boys are on the hunt."

"Delgado," Brock snarled, his eyes moving to Chavez. "He needs to mobilize."

"That call's been made too," Eddie told him. "He's got his team in play."

Brock glared at them, that bile still eating away at his throat. Visions of Bree in her hospital bed filling his head, visions that morphed into Tess, jaw wired, teeth missing, eyes swollen shut, dark bruises at her neck.

Fuck.

Fuck!

He turned back to the captain. "My boys need to be picked up from school. I need to make some calls."

"You do it from in here," Cap replied.

Brock shook his head. "I gotta be out there. I know where he hides. I know where he creeps."

"You give that info to Jimmy, Hank, and Eddie. They'll follow it up."

"She's my woman, Cap," Brock reminded him.

"We'll find her," Cap promised again.

That bile in his throat was swelling, threatening to choke him. "My job to keep her safe," he spoke around the bile, this making his voice thick.

"We'll find her, son," Cap promised yet again and his eyes went intense. "Goes against the grain, man like you, I know it. Goes against the grain. But the smartest thing you can do right now is sit your ass down, brief Jimmy, Hank, and Eddie so they can work this, then call someone to take care 'a your boys. When we get her, you need to have your shit together 'cause she's gonna need you. So, you gotta keep your shit together, Brock, do the smart thing, help us help her."

After the captain stopped speaking, Brock "Slim" Lucas didn't delay.

He walked to the chairs in front of Cap's desk, sat his ass down, and looked to Jimmy Marker who was seating himself beside him. Then he ran down everything he remembered about Josiah Burkett, which was everything he knew about Josiah Burkett. He didn't forget anything. Not anything.

Eddie Chavez left first to disburse the first wave of intel.

Hank Nightingale left second.

Jimmy Marker waited until the end.

Then Brock called his mother to go pick up his boys.

And after that, standing at the window in the captain's

office, eyes staring unseeing outside, that bile still choking him, his brain torturing him, his instincts screaming for him to move, his palms itching, his teeth clenched, it took everything he had to lock himself down and not do, again, what he'd done years ago. Something that was wild and stupid and fucked up then and something that he could have no way of knowing would put his Tess in jeopardy now. And, for the first time in fucking years, he prayed.

My wild man, he heard her sweet words whisper in his head. *My snake charmer.*

Brock Lucas closed his eyes and prayed harder.

CHAPTER TWENTY-TWO

Tell Slim

"Do you know what he did to me?"

"You're the one who hurt Bree."

"Do you know what he did to me?"

I went silent when he started screaming.

He had the gun and his eyes on me. He was wrong. All wrong. And all that wrong came from his eyes.

As Brock would say, he was whacked. It shone out of his eyes. Clear as day. It shone straight from his eyes.

How could Bree not see that?

Or maybe he hid it from her.

But he wasn't hiding it from me.

And it scared me nearly senseless.

Not senseless enough not to pay attention. Not senseless enough not to note exactly where we were, in Englewood, in an old cracker box house on a big lot that was mostly muddy earth from the snow melt, dead weeds, lots of big trees. I thought it was a weird place to take me. It was a neighborhood, populated, and as the afternoon wore on, it would be more populated.

People could hear me scream.

But I didn't scream.

He did.

He was *whacked*.

He'd killed Damian, shot him right in the face. He'd shot two other men, one I knew was dead, the other might be. He hated Brock.

So he'd shoot me.

But he wanted to play with me first. I knew this. I knew he wanted Brock to live with that for the rest of his life. He might leave me breathing after or he might not.

But he wasn't going to play with me for long. I knew this too. He was an old guy, for one. He couldn't have that in him anymore. And also, he didn't care if he was caught. He'd shot three men in the parking lot of Park Meadows Mall. People had to see, to hear. He was going to do what he was going to do to make Brock pay and he wasn't going to waste any time.

When I didn't answer, his voice calmed and he ordered, "Take off your clothes."

I went still.

No, he wasn't going to waste any time.

This couldn't happen to me again. It couldn't. It couldn't happen to me again. I wasn't sure I could survive it. Not even with Brock at my back when it was done, if I was left breathing. I wasn't even sure *we* could survive it, not from what I knew of Brock, his capacity for loyalty and love, knowing he'd brought this down on me. It would undo him. So even if I survived, he might not.

"Take off...your fuckin'...*clothes*," he semirepeated and I stared at him.

He moved the gun an inch to the side and squeezed the trigger.

I screamed and jumped as the gunshot sounded loud in the room, the bullet embedding in the wall behind me.

God, please God, someone hear that.

"Take off your clothes," he again repeated.

I shook my head.

"No," I whispered and he blinked.

"What?" he asked.

I knew it then. I knew I couldn't take it. I knew Brock couldn't take it.

I knew I had to stop this.

And if I got hurt doing it, so be it.

But no one was going to hurt me like that, not again. And they weren't going to hurt Brock either.

Not again.

We'd had enough. We'd both had e-fucking-*nough*.

"You got what you deserved," I told him quietly and he stared at me. "No." I shook my head again. "You didn't. You didn't get what you deserved. If you got what you deserved you wouldn't be breathing."

He moved closer to me, gun pointed at me, but I kept my eyes steady on his and moved back as he moved toward me.

"You hurt her. You destroyed her," I told him, still moving back as he moved forward, his crazy-as-shit eyes riveted to me. "You ended her. This world isn't right because you're breathing and she isn't."

I hit the wall and had to stop and he stopped with me.

"Take off your clothes," he said yet again.

"No. No way. You aren't going to touch me. No way."

"Take off your clothes."

"Shoot me. Do it. I'd rather die than have your filthy hands on me."

"Take off . . . your . . . *clothes*."

I shook my head and kept my eyes on him.

Then I whispered, "No."

Then I moved.

Bending double, I went right at him as the next gun-shot sounded loud in the room and I didn't know where it went. I just knew it didn't go into me.

I hit him in the middle with the top of my head.

This was not a bright move. I should have paid more attention to all the football my boys forced me to watch. I should have caught him with my shoulder. Hitting him with my head sent my head into my neck and pain jolted through my neck and down my spine.

But I kept going, shoving him back. I felt his hand clenching in my jacket as my hand went out to his gun arm. Another shot was fired but it went wide because I was pushing his arm away. He hit the wall and another jolt of pain rammed down my neck and spine. He squeezed off another round accidentally but I had my hand on his wrist and the gun was still pointed away.

I righted and started grappling for the gun.

It sucked. He was old but he still was a match for me. Shit. I needed to do more kickboxing.

Our fight forced off another round, the gun pointed up with our arms as I pushed with all my weight and strength to keep him in the wall while at the same time keeping the gun pointed away.

Then I realized I wasn't making any noise.

So I started shouting, screaming, *shrieking*. I didn't even know what I was shrieking. It might not have been words. It might have been nothing but noise but no one could mistake the fear in it. No one could. Anyone hearing it would call the cops.

I hoped.

"Shut up," he demanded.

"*Fuck you!*" I screeched.

"*Shut up!*" he screamed and that was when I realized I should have paid attention to his left hand as well as his right for he clocked me right on the jaw.

Pain radiated from my jaw up through my skull and my head and body jerked to the side but luckily I kept hold of his gun arm.

Then I started shrieking again but I learned quickly. When he tried to punch me again, I ducked and he missed. His momentum took him sideways and I pushed forward, wedging him at an awkward position, both arms to the side.

"*Fuckin' bitch! Fuckin' cunt!*" he yelled, struggling, trying to right his body.

I kept pressing my weight into him as hard as I could, having trouble keeping him turned to the side, still screeching as loud as I could. I moved my hand down toward the gun, curling it around his, shoving my finger into the trigger.

"*Fuckin' bitch! Fuckin', fuckin' cunt!*" he shouted, his struggles intensifying.

I wasn't going to be able to hold him long.

I pressed the trigger.

Bam!

Bam!

Bam!

Over and over as I pushed him into the wall and he fought back until the clip was spent. No more bullets.

Thank God.

I instantly let him go, turned, and started to run.

He caught me by my hair, yanking me back. Pain. God, so much fucking pain exuding from my scalp. My neck wrenched and I cried out in agony.

He got close, his leg swiping both mine out from under me and I fell hard to my hip.

Then he was on me.

I started shrieking again, shrieking and fighting, pushing, kicking out with my legs, scratching. My fingernails scored down his face, blood oozing instantly from the three wounds I cut in his flesh. He reared back reflexively and I shot up with him. Planting a foot, I rolled him to his back.

At this point, maybe I should have got up and run.

But I didn't.

I sat up to straddling him and hit him hard, as hard as I could. Fist balled, I punched him in the face.

He grunted in pain and his head shot to the side when I did.

And he didn't right it before I punched him again.

And again.

And again.

And again.

And *again*.

Then I wrapped my hands around his neck and squeezed.

"You fucking dick," I whispered as I squeezed. His hands at my wrists trying to pull mine away, I put my entire body weight into my arms. Everything I had in me I transferred to my fingers and I...squeezed...*hard*. "You fucking, fucking *dick*." His body bucked, his feet kicked out, trying to push me off but I kept my focus, kept my place, and kept squeezing. "You took Bree's beautiful future. You are *not* gonna take *mine*."

I squeezed harder.

He started gagging.

I kept squeezing.

I watched his face turn purple as his mouth started opening and closing. His body stopped bucking and started jerking.

I kept squeezing.

I didn't hear the front door crash open and I didn't hear the pounding boots of men's feet on floorboards.

I just kept squeezing.

Then I wasn't straddling him anymore. I was up and my back was plastered to a hard male body. My wrists captured and wrapped around the front of me and lips came to my ear as I watched my attacker suck in air, hands to his throat as a tall, dark-haired man with a badge at his belt stood pointing a gun down at him.

"You're safe," those lips whispered in my ear. "I'm Hawk, Gwen's man, and you're safe, Tess."

My body, tense and wired, stayed that way for long moments and then it sagged in his arms, my legs going clean out from under me but he held me up and he held me close against his solid warmth.

"You're safe, Tess," he whispered again in my ear.

I nodded mutely, my eyes on the dark-haired man who was using his boot to kick my attacker to his stomach. He crouched down, knee in his back, pulling cuffs out of a holder on the belt of his jeans, yanking my attacker's hands behind him and cuffing them.

I started trembling.

Hawk, Gwen's man, arms went tighter.

The dark-haired man muttered a harsh, "Do not fuckin' move," to the man on the floor. He stood, pulled a phone out of his back pocket, hit buttons, and put it to his ear. Then his warm but intense and alert dark brown eyes came to me. He did a top-to-toe. They shifted up to Hawk, then back to me. Then he said into his phone, "Yeah, it's Lawson. We got her. She's unharmed. Tell Slim."

We got her. She's unharmed. Tell Slim.

That's when I started crying.

EPILOGUE

He Got His Wish

THE ALARM WENT off.

It was music, Tim McGraw, and Brock heard Tess murmur sleepily, "What on earth?"

He grinned before he even opened his eyes.

She shifted away from him but before she could touch the button to turn off the music, he opened his eyes, caught her about the waist, and pulled her back into his body.

She rolled in his arm and tipped her green eyes up to him, her light brown hair with its blonde highlights tousled and partly in her face.

"Who's that?" she asked, lifting a hand to shift the soft tendrils out of her eyes.

"Tim McGraw," he answered, understanding her question and knowing she had no fucking clue who Tim McGraw was. He'd spent more than a year introducing her to his music and she spent more than a year mostly ignoring these efforts.

The music started to get louder.

He watched her eyes narrow and it wasn't because she didn't have her glasses.

"How'd that get on my player?"

"I put it there."

"You—" she began, but he rolled into her so his body was on her soft, sweet one and he dipped his face close to hers.

"Baby," he whispered, "it's my birthday. I'm not wakin' up to Fiona Apple."

"Fiona wasn't in the scheduled mix," she informed him.

"Or Tori Amos," he added.

"She wasn't either."

"Or Sarah McLachlan."

"Her either."

"Or Paula Cole."

She snapped her mouth shut.

Yeah, there it was, and Paula fucking Cole was definitely not scheduled for his birthday.

He felt his body start shaking and he heard Tim McGraw start to get louder.

He controlled his humor, dipped his face closer, and again reminded her, "It's my birthday."

"I need to turn off the music."

"Yeah, you can do that after you start my birthday right."

"It's getting louder."

She wasn't wrong. It was getting louder.

"Tess," he growled as he pressed his body into hers. She bit her lip and then the door flew open.

His head jerked back and he watched Joel and Rex walk in just as they had last year, just as Tess organized for him, her, and Joel to walk into Rex's room two days later with his cake and for them with Rex to walk into Joel's room four days after that with his.

Joel was carrying a beautifully decorated birthday cake, undoubtedly carrot, his favorite, that held an abundance of tall, thin, blue candles, all of them lit.

They were sing-shouting "Happy Birthday to You" over Tim McGraw and smiling like idiots.

He looked down at Tess who was grinning up at him, not like an idiot. Her eyes were warm, her face was soft, and her smile was sweet.

All Tess.

He grinned back, bent his neck, and touched his mouth to hers then he rolled off his wife onto a forearm in the bed. She rolled to the alarm, turning off Tim McGraw at around the time Rex and Joey were standing by the bed and drawing out "Happy Birthday dear Daaaaaaaad," to which Tess sat up in the bed and joined them for the last four words.

Joel shoved the cake forward and demanded, "Blow out the candles and make a wish."

Brock "Slim" Lucas looked at his oldest son, his eyes moved to his youngest son, and then they slid to his wife.

And when his eyes hit her shining ones he realized he had not one thing to wish for. Not one. There was nothing he wanted.

He had it all right there.

Except one thing.

So he leaned over Tess, silently made his wish, and blew out the candles.

She hooted and clapped.

Rex stated, "So *freaking* cool! Just like last year! Cake for breakfast three days this week!"

Joel, having shot up in the last year, now well taller than Tess and definitely a boy-man only a week away from his fourteenth birthday, turned on his bare foot and started marching to the door, declaring, "I'll get plates."

Rex, also having grown, though nowhere near as much as his brother, still he was taller than Tess and nearly twelve, therefore maintaining boy status but only just, followed him, announcing, "I'll get the milk."

Tess threw back the covers and decreed, "I'll start the coffee."

He let her feet hit the floor before his arm curled around her waist again. He pulled her back into the bed and rolled over her.

Before she could say a word, he took his birthday kiss. He made it long, he did it hard, and it was wet.

When he lifted his head and saw her eyes slightly dazed but mostly happy and still shining, he got his wish.

*   *   *

Brock walked up to the door that was opening before he got there. When he arrived, he jerked up his chin to the older man. The man tipped his down and stepped aside.

Brock stepped in.

The man closed the door and turned to him.

"Would you like coffee?" he asked, like he always asked.

Brock shook his head like he always shook his head, shoved his hand in his overcoat, pulled the envelope out of the inside pocket, and handed it to the man.

Donald Heller took it. He didn't even try to hide his eagerness when he instantly opened the folded-in flap and pulled out the pictures.

He never tried to hide his eagerness.

Head bent, he studied the snapshots of Tess with Joey, Rex, and his family at Christmas. Tess decorating a cake in the back of her new bakery. Tess standing in their kitchen, phone to her ear, laughing at something Elvira was saying. Tess in an ass-to-heels, knees-to-chest squat, her arm around Ellie's waist, her head bent to listen to what Ellie was whispering in her ear, her body hidden by Ellie's exceptionally girlie, pink flower girl dress.

And he stopped at the last and studied it for a long time.

It was a picture of Tess standing next to him in a classy ivory dress that hugged her rounded figure and skimmed her knees. Her hair was twisted in a sophisticated knot at the back of her head. Her feet were encased in a pair of high-heeled, fuck-me shoes, one hand holding a bouquet which was a mixture of bloodred and bright pink roses, the other arm wrapped around his back. Rex was to her back left, Ellie standing to her front left. Joel was to Brock's back right, Levi at Joey's side with Dylan and Grady in front of them. Martha was standing at Rex and Tess's sides. Family and friends were scrunched all around behind the front crew.

The best part about the picture, to Brock's way of thinking, was the twinkling diamond you could only just see on Tess's ring finger, which was curled around the ivory-ribbon-wrapped long stems of her bouquet. That huge-ass diamond sitting on top of a very wide, very brilliant gold band that, only minutes before, Brock had slid on her finger. A band that matched a wider, no less brilliant one that Brock now wore that, that day, she had slid on his.

And, of course, another best part were those fuck-me shoes. An invitation he'd accepted approximately five hours after the picture was taken.

And, lastly, the fact that her smile was wide, her beautiful white teeth showing, her eyes shining because she was laughing.

Donald Heller studied that photo for a long time.

Then, head still bent to the photo, he whispered, "She looks happy."

"She is," Brock confirmed and Heller's head came up.

Brock didn't come often but he came regularly. He did this because the man in front of him loved Tess. He also did it because the man in front of him sired an asshole but the last act his asshole son perpetrated on this earth was trying to keep Brock's Tess from harm.

Damian Heller had picked apart the bones of Brock Lucas's life and in doing so, Damian Heller had learned about Josiah Burkett. And Damian Heller had had the means to keep an eye on Burkett *and* an ear. He knew Burkett was planning revenge. He should have told Brock and, if not Brock, then the cops. But if he did, he couldn't play out his knight-in-shining-armor act.

Even so, he went down so Tess wouldn't. He was an asshole, his play was foolish, and he could have caused Tess the harm he wanted to shield her from, but Brock couldn't deny his going down was worth something.

There was no way he was going to try and talk Tess into letting this man and the demons he didn't want to hold for her but couldn't avoid back into her life. A life Brock took pains to keep demon free, an effort that had, for nearly a year, succeeded and he'd do just about anything to make certain that streak continued.

But he owed this man the knowledge those pictures shared.

"Vegas?" Donald Heller asked.

"Yep," Brock answered.

"When?"

"Late last month."

He looked down again at the photo and then up at Brock.

"Her mother and sister made it," he noted.

"Everyone did," Brock replied.

And everyone did. It had been a fucking blast, wild, two days of family fun during the day and then Kalie, Kellie, Joel, and Rex looked after the kids and it was two days of drunken adult fun at night. Then they had the wedding, after which they ate, drank, danced, and laughed themselves sick and the next morning everyone left. Brock's mom had looked after Joey and Rex while Brock and Tess stayed in Vegas and had four days of adult one-on-one fun, the first two of which they had without leaving their hotel room.

Definitely wild. Definitely a blast.

Perfect.

Heller looked back down at the photo and then again at Brock.

"You have good-looking sons," he remarked.

Brock didn't thank him for telling him something he knew.

Instead, he informed him, "They love her."

"Hard not to love Tess," he whispered.

That was the damned truth.

Then he asked the last question he always asked before Brock left.

"Can I keep these?"

And Brock gave him the answer he always gave.

"Yeah."

He nodded.

Brock nodded back.

He opened the door and Brock went through it, turning as Donald Heller murmured, "Until next time."

Brock jerked up his chin and walked to his truck.

*   *   *

Brock crouched in the wet grass. They'd had a relatively warm winter, a couple of snows, nothing that really stuck and when it did it didn't stay for too long.

Tess loved it.

The boys hated it.

Brock didn't care either way.

He shoved his hand into his inside overcoat pocket and pulled out the photo, another copy of the one that fascinated Donald Heller. A photo that, blown up, was framed and sitting pride of place on the shelves in their family's living room.

He reached out and set it at the base of the gravestone.

"Shoulda been there, Dad," he whispered to the gleaming marble.

The marble had no reply.

*   *   *

"Shit," he heard Mitch Lawson say and his head came up to look across their desks to his partner.

If someone told Brock two years ago that he'd be partnered with Mitch Lawson, he would have laughed, or possibly growled.

Lawson was involved in the situation with Hawk Delgado and his now-wife Gwen. Lawson had a thing for Gwen then. He had another thing going now, a much better thing, a thing that had been a pain in his ass to win, but then again, most things worth winning were worth a pain in the ass to win them. But back then, Lawson had also not been happy with the plays Brock made that put him into contact with Hawk and Gwen Delgado.

But, like many cops, Mitch heard that Brock's woman was in the hands of a sick, dangerous man bent on revenge and, like many cops, he'd dropped everything to hunt for her.

Sharp as a tack, something that was good to have in a partner, Mitch contacted Delgado, a man who had more money and more resources but less strictures than the DPD, and they searched together. It was intel that Brock had handed over that took them to her.

Burkett wasn't stupid. It was not where Brock had found him years ago after what he did to Bree. But it was information Brock found when he was hunting him. A house kept in the family but for some reason unused. Bree's great-aunt's house, Burkett's mother's house where he grew up.

Luck or good instinct, it didn't matter which, sent Delgado and Lawson there first when the information Brock gave started making the rounds. This meant they got to her quick. This meant she'd only been in the hands of a madman for less than an hour before she was safe.

After it was done, Lawson told him Tess had taken care of the situation herself before they arrived. Although Burkett was old, this surprised Brock but not as much as it alarmed him. This was because Burkett was armed and very willing to use his weapon and he'd demonstrated this to Tess. Still, somehow she did it and outside of getting clocked on the jaw, which caused her a few days of pain and brought up some swelling and minor bruising, she miraculously did it without getting hurt.

In other words, that day, Brock Lucas learned the power of prayer and he still didn't utilize it often but that didn't mean God didn't hear from him more than He used to.

These days, though, sweet days, his messages were a lot different.

And Tess had told him Delgado and Lawson had been gentle with her. Tess told him that within minutes of their arrival she felt safe, and more important, within minutes of their arrival they got word to him that she *was* safe.

That last part was what had done it for her. When he made it to her fifteen minutes later, she was more worried about his state of mind than herself. When he arrived, she'd been in tears in Delgado's arms, Hawk had turned her into Brock's, and it didn't take long before she pulled herself together and turned her attention to him.

She'd witnessed three men get shot, two of them shot dead, but this didn't faze her, not at all. She slept like a baby in his arms that night, all through, and he knew this because he didn't sleep a fucking wink. And they'd gone to Aruba as planned and she'd enjoyed the fuck out of that vacation. His boys did too.

After he watched her closely for days and ascertained she wasn't burying anything, she was actually all right, putting it behind her, moving on, Brock enjoyed it too.

And this was because, he realized, she felt safe. Shit happened, she survived, and even though it wasn't him who made her safe, men he'd connected with did it for him, not to mention she did her part. To Tess, this incident was a blip and the next morning she was up and making breakfast for his sons like she did every morning, drinking coffee, being a smartass to him, and making his sons laugh.

But Delgado and Lawson got to her. They made her feel safe and they were gentle with her.

Therefore, he owed them too.

And he had no problem being Lawson's partner. Mitch was younger than Brock but smart, diligent, a good cop who had since become a good friend, and not just because they were partners.

Now he was looking beyond Brock like he'd just learned the world was going to end.

Brock looked over his shoulder and saw what Mitch saw.

Fucking great.

On his fucking birthday no less.

Olivia.

"Slim," she muttered when she came to a stop by his desk, her eyes shifting to Mitch then back to Brock.

"Olivia, for fuck's sake, it's my birthday."

"Yes, well, for some of us, this isn't a special day. For some of us, this day is just like any other day."

He made no reply. Just sat back, looked up at her, and waited for her to be done.

In the last year, Olivia had made short work of getting her talons in another man. Therefore, obviously, she'd stopped being saccharine sweet and gone back to her true self. In other words, a complete bitch.

Though, the good news was, with her claws in another man, she had stopped fucking with him.

When he said nothing, she announced, "Jordan's being transferred to Portland, Maine."

Holy fuck.

He felt his gut start to get light.

"And?" he asked.

"He wants me to go with him."

Holy fuck!

He felt his gut start to get lighter.

"And?" Brock repeated.

"I'm going."

Brock said nothing more but he did this because he was expending a great deal of effort not to smile.

She waited for a response.

Brock still said nothing.

She sighed, then stated, "Obviously, I'll expect the boys out for a couple of weeks during the summer and alternating Christmases."

Brock fought back another grin.

Losing the boys alternating Christmases would suck. Having them the vast majority of the time and losing Olivia three-quarters of a continent away would not.

"Have your attorney contact my attorney," he told her.

"No, have *your* attorney contact *my* attorney."

Whatever.

"You got it," he told her and she blinked.

Then she asked, "Will you tell them?"

Christ. Fucking bitch.

"No," he answered.

"Slim—" she started.

Brock sat up in his chair but did not get up, just kept his eyes on her, saying, "Olivia, honest to God, don't. Nothing you could say will make me do your dirty work. They're your sons. You're movin' most a country away from them. This is your decision, this is your consequence. Listen to me, serious to God, for once in your life, listen to me. I am done dealin' with your consequences, I am done dealin' with your shit, and I am done dealin' with you. You're my kids' mom, that's all you are, nothin' more. I do you no favors. You are not in my life at all except when I have to deal with you through them. Please, God, give me one thing in our miserable history and get that through your fuckin' head."

She turned her eyes to Mitch and remarked, "Always so charming."

Lawson strangled down a bark of laughter and this was because Lawson was around before she'd got her talons in another man and let him loose so Lawson knew all about Olivia and Lawson, being sharp as a tack, didn't like her much. That was to say, not at all. And Mitch Lawson was a good guy but not good enough not to advise his partner, repeatedly, to be a lot less charming than he was to Olivia, which was not charming at all, so that was saying something.

Brock sighed.

Olivia's eyes cut back to him. "Fine," she snapped. "I'll tell them." And she said this like she was doing him a favor.

Brock didn't reply.

She crossed her arms on her chest and held his eyes.

Brock said not a word.

She tapped her foot.

Brock finally spoke. "We done?"

"Don't you have anything to say?" she asked, flipping out a hand.

"Like what?"

"I don't know," she answered. "Something. I'm moving to Maine, for God's sake."

"And?" he asked.

"And?" she asked back.

Brock sighed again.

"Slim, we were married and in each other's lives for over a decade and you've got nothing to say after I just told you I'm moving away?"

"Bon voyage," Brock muttered.

Mitch tried to strangle down another bark of laughter, failed, quickly knifed out of his chair, and headed toward the hall.

Olivia's face got red.

"Nice," she hissed, gave him a long glare, turned on her high heel, and marched her bony ass out.

He didn't watch.

He turned to his desk, instantly grabbed his phone, flipped it open, and hit buttons without looking at them because he'd memorized them.

She answered on the second ring.

"Sweetness," he said the minute Tess finished her greeting, "you are not gonna believe the surprise birthday present I just got."

*   *   *

"Brock, honey?" Tess said in his ear as he walked through the backdoor into their kitchen.

After they finally got Rex's room sorted, he sorted the one-car garage in the back that was old, had no garage door opener, and thus Tess didn't use it and parked on the street. And he sorted it as in he had it scrapped and a massive two-car garage built in its place.

He did this because he was not a big fan of scraping ice off his windshield.

He also did this because he was less of a fan of Tess doing it so he did it for her and since he didn't like doing it on his own fucking truck, he didn't like adding her car.

And, lastly, he did it because it was a fuck of a lot safer for her to drive into a garage that had a door to a fenced backyard that had motion-sensor lights that lit up the backyard from both garage and house the instant she exited the garage. Something else he installed.

This took up a fair amount of the backyard.

Tess didn't say a word. Somehow, she sensed when something was important to him and she didn't argue. Ever.

He liked this. He also liked that she didn't make a big fucking deal about stupid shit like him (or his boys) drinking from the milk jug. If it mattered to her, she had a quiet word with him (or his boys). If she could find a fix without having her quiet word, she did. Case in point, they each got their own milk jug. She wrote their names on them in magic marker before putting them in the fridge.

This way, she could give him (and his boys) sweet mostly all the time.

And she did.

It made for a beautiful life.

For him.

And his boys.

"Babe, I'm in the house. You don't have to call me," he said into the phone, smiling because she had to be there somewhere too. He was meeting her and the boys there and they were going out to dinner with his family at The Spaghetti Factory.

"Um... well, I'm *not* in the house, I'm at the hospital."

Brock stopped dead, his eyes, unseeing, on a fancy-ass

cake stand on the corner of the counter that held the remains of his birthday cake that had been nearly decimated by him and his boys that morning.

She went on quickly. "I'm okay. The boys are okay. It's just Lenore. She's kind of..." She paused. "*Not* okay. She went into labor about three hours ago. Levi got her to the hospital and was separated from her because he was told both mother and child are in distress."

Fuck.

Fuck!

He did the calculations in his head and came up with an unhappy number.

Lenore, who became his sister-in-law three weeks before Christmas and not because she was pregnant but because Levi loved her—the baby was just good news on top of good news—was only six months pregnant.

"Which hospital?" he asked.

"St. Joe's," she answered.

"I'm on my way," he stated, turning back to the door. "The boys with you?"

"No, I called Dade. He went to get them at school. They're at his house helping him with Grady, Dylan, and Ellie."

Even though many would think it was fucked, Dade McManus had slid into their lives naturally and this was because Tess made that happen. He was a good addition because he was a good man, he loved Brock's boys, and he adored Tess. Brock grew to like him, grew to respect him, and he'd earned that back from McManus. This worked. How, he had no clue. But it did and Brock was glad that it did. As far as he was concerned, anyone who loved his boys and adored his wife was welcome in their lives, so

Brock welcomed him. And, just then, he was happier than usual that he did.

"Right." He was out the door and locking it.

"Baby," she whispered in his ear.

"Yeah?"

"Hurry."

Fuck.

*   *   *

When Brock arrived in the waiting room at St. Joe's, Levi was sitting with his elbows to his knees, his torso bent double, his fingers laced at the back of his head.

Brock's eyes slid through his wife, his sisters, his mother, and his brothers-in-law as he walked to Levi.

None of their faces were happy birthday faces.

He crouched down in front of his brother.

"Brother," he murmured. Levi's hands unlaced and just his head came up.

"Slim," Levi whispered. "Fuck, Slim."

Brock's arm moved out, his hand curling around the back of his brother's head.

"Keep it together," he whispered.

"Fucked it up with her. She was in and outta my life for three years before—"

"Get that out of your head."

"Never made it official. Never made it permanent. She came to Thanksgiving on a fucking *rotation*. Had a girl at Easter, a different one at Fourth of July, she was due up." He paused then the next two words came out tortured. "Due...*up*."

Brock squeezed his brother's neck. "Levi, get it outta your fuckin' head."

Levi held his eyes.

Then he whispered, "Under my nose, at the tips of my fingers, never saw her, never felt her, what she was givin' me. Not until Tess pointed it out and I opened my fuckin' eyes."

"Brother, keep it together."

Again, Levi held his eyes.

Brock returned the gesture, keeping his hand on his brother's neck.

Then he said, "She's in there. I'm out here. Nothin' I can do. She's battlin' and there's not one fuckin' thing I can do." He swallowed, then asked, "This what you felt like when Tess was taken?"

Brock had told Levi what had happened and where he had to force himself to be in order not to fuck up and do something stupid. For once, his brother kept that knowledge to himself. The only people who knew the full penance he was forced to pay for fucking up with Josiah Burkett were his colleagues, Levi, and Tess, the last being brutal penance in itself.

"In a way, I reckon...yeah," Brock answered.

"Brother," Levi whispered, that one word saying one hundred more.

Brock didn't reply.

Levi sucked in a breath.

Then he sat up, Brock's hand dropped, and he straightened out of his crouch. His eyes went to Tess. Hers were bright at the rims with tears. She sucked in her lips before she let them go and gave him a trembling smile.

He tipped his chin up at his wife and sat down next to his brother.

Half an hour later, a woman in a white doctor's coat walked in.

"Levi Lucas?" she called, but Levi was already up and walking across the small room, Brock at his back, his family behind him.

"She okay?" Levi asked.

"She's fine, baby's fine. We'll have to discuss curtailing activity for a while to see this through, but right now, both are safe and healthy."

"Thank God," Fern whispered and Brock heard Jill's shuddering breath and Laura's choked whimper.

"Can I see her?" Levi asked.

"I'll take you to her."

Levi didn't look back at his family as he walked away.

Brock watched his brother then felt Tess burrow under his arm.

He curled it around her shoulders and looked down into her eyes.

She caught his for a second before she did a face-plant in his chest, her arms moving around him, her body giving his her weight.

He held her.

Then he sucked in a breath.

An hour and a half later, in his truck while Tess was in her car on the way to get the boys from Dade's, he ordered a Famous pizza for his birthday meal.

*   *   *

In the middle of studying his face, the tips of her fingers moving over it, Tess started giggling.

This was unusual. Not her studying his face after he made her come, after he came, and when he was still buried inside her. She did that often and he let her because he liked to see what was working behind her eyes as they moved over his features. He liked it a fuck of a lot.

Her giggling in the middle of doing it, now *that* was unusual.

He found instantly he liked that too. Then again, he liked it anytime Tess laughed.

"What's funny?" he asked, getting the question in over her escalating laughter.

"Ma...Ma...Martha," she stammered, lifting her head to shove it in his neck, her hands sliding around his shoulders so both her arms and legs could convulse around him.

"Martha?" he asked her pillow.

She sucked in a breath and dropped her head back down, her eyes coming to his as she nodded.

There was a lot that was funny about Martha. The bitch was a scream. She hadn't toned down the drama, and likely at her age she never would. But she loved Tess and she'd cottoned onto the fact that Brock would accept her drama in Tess's life as long as it had no negative effects and she saw to it that that was so. She also loved his boys and didn't hide it. They thought she was a scream too. So, since her drama was mostly humorous and not annoying, Brock liked her and she made no bones about liking him, and he had to admit, he liked that too.

He figured his wife's sudden onset of humor had something to do with the fact that Calhoun had come into Tess's bakery about five months ago. When he did, Tess had gone direct into matchmaking mode and hooked him up with Martha. Calhoun took the bait and was still hooked. Martha didn't hide *any* of her drama from Calhoun, and surprising the fuck out of Brock, Calhoun apparently got off on it.

WILD MAN   481

Whatever. To each their own.

And anyway, the crazy dance between DEA Agent Calhoun and Martha Shockley provided his wife with a variety of things to giggle over when she told him about them. And he was happy with that.

She released her legs from around him, planted her feet in the bed, and bucked her hips slightly, telling him what she wanted.

He gave it to her. Sliding out gently, he watched her lips part, her eyelids get soft, that sexy-as-hell look that communicated both pleasure and disappointment at losing him being the second best part of fucking her (or the third, maybe the fourth, though it could be the fifth). Then he gave her what she wanted and rolled them so he was on his back and she was on top.

She placed a forearm in his chest, her other hand at his neck under his jaw, and suddenly her face got serious.

"What?" he whispered. Her eyes slid from her hand at his jaw to his, she tipped her head to the side, and she gave him more of her weight, her soft flesh pressing into his.

"When you came back," she started, her voice soft, "after what went down with you and me with you investigating Damian..." She trailed off, then started again, "When you came back, later, when I was at the shower and I confessed to Martha about everything that went down, well, you know, honey, she wasn't your biggest fan back then."

His hands, which were spanning her hips, slid down to cup her ass.

"I know."

Her lips tipped up in a small grin. "Well, she said I had my head in the sand. She said most women would take one look at you and know you were fun to play with but you weren't the one for the long haul. But me, she said I took one look at you and had visions of white picket fences and making you birthday cakes until the day you die."

She swallowed, the smile died, and her eyes grew bright.

Brock held his breath, his fingers clenching into her ass and he waited.

"She was wrong," Tess whispered. "I was right." She drew in a breath through her nose, dipped her face closer, and the pads of her fingers dug into his neck when she finished. "We don't have a white picket fence, baby, but I'm going to bake you birthday cakes until the day you die."

He let out the breath he was holding, the burn in his lungs moving to become warmth in his gut.

His hands sliding from her ass up her back, one arm curving around, the other one going up her spine, her neck so he could sift his fingers in her hair as he whispered, "Sweetness."

"I'm glad it's me who gets to bake your birthday cakes."

He was happy she was glad but he reckoned he was a fuck of a lot happier he had Tess making his cakes and not just because they were the best fucking things he'd ever tasted.

He closed his eyes, shoved his face in her neck, and rolled her to back, groaning, "Tess."

"My Brock," she whispered, her lips at his ear, her limbs moving to grow tight around him. "He's not so wild."

He lifted his head and brought it close, locking his eyes with hers.

"You're wrong, darlin'. I got wild in me. And I'll never lose it. It's just that my wild is a safe place for you and it always will be."

Her eyes got soft and one of her hands slid from around him to cup his cheek as she nodded.

Then her thumb moved to trace his lower lip as she asked, "Did you have a good birthday, Slim?"

He grinned against her thumb and answered, "I started it in bed with you wearin' a sweet nightie and I ended it in bed with you wearin' an even sweeter nightie. So, yeah. Outside the drama at the hospital, I had a great birthday, Tess."

She grinned back and asked, "So you liked your birthday present?"

His hand glided down the emerald-green silk at her side as he dropped his mouth to hers and muttered, "Fuck yeah."

Her fingers slid from his cheek and into his hair as she muttered back, "Good."

Brock was done talking and he shared this with his wife when he slanted his head. Tess read him loud and clear and tilted hers. He put pressure on her lips, she opened hers, his tongue slid inside, and she welcomed it.

And, with that, his sweet Tess made a great birthday even fucking better.

The following is an excerpt from

Law Man

CHAPTER ONE

Doohickey

"HELLO, THIS IS Mara Hanover in unit 6C. I've called three times today and I really need someone to come over and look at my bathroom tap. It won't turn off. Can you please have the maintenance guy come around? Thanks."

I shut down my cell after leaving my voicemail message and stared at my bathroom faucet, which hadn't turned off after I was finished with it that morning. I had called the management office of the complex before going to work and left a message. When I didn't get a call back, I called at lunch (leaving another message). Now I was home after work and it was past office hours, but someone was supposed to be on call all the time. I should have had a callback. I needed a callback. What I didn't need was a water bill out the roof or to try to go to sleep listening to running water while thinking of my money flowing down the drain.

I sighed and kept staring at the water running full blast out of my faucet.

I was a woman who had lived alone her entire adult life. I'd once had a long-term relationship with a Five

Point Five that got nowhere near living together. This was because I was a Two Point Five and he was a Five Point Five who wanted a Nine Point Five. Therefore, we were both destined for broken hearts. He gave me mine. He later found a Six Point Five that wanted a Nine Point Five. She got herself a breast enhancement and nose job, which made her a firm Seven (if you didn't count the fact that she thought she was a Ten point Five and acted like it, which really knocked her down to a Six) who broke his heart.

Regardless of the fact that I was now thirty-one and had lived alone since I was eighteen, I knew nothing about plumbing or cars. Every time something happened with my plumbing or my car, I vowed to myself that I would learn something about plumbing or cars. I would get that said something fixed and I'd totally forget my vow. Then I'd lament forgetting my vow in times like I was experiencing right now.

I walked out of my master bath, through my bedroom, down the hall into my open-plan living-slash-kitchen-slash-dining area and out the front door. I crossed the breezeway and knocked on Derek and LaTanya's door.

Derek knew something about plumbing. I knew this because of two things. First, he was a man and men had a sixth plumbing sense. Second, I knew this because he was a plumber.

LaTanya opened the door, and her big, dark eyes widened with LaTanya Delight.

LaTanya Delight was different than anyone else's delight and therefore deserved a capital letter. It was louder, brasher, brighter and cheerier. The look on her face communicated her joy at seeing me like she and I had been separated at birth and were right then being blissfully reunited. Not like she'd just seen me the night before when she came over to watch *Glee* with me.

"Hey girl!" she squealed through a big smile. "Perfect timing. I'm about to mix a batch of mojitos. Get your ass in here and I'll pour us some cocktails!"

I smiled at her but shook my head. "Can't," I told her. "Something's up with my faucet, the office hasn't returned my calls, and I really need Derek to look at it. Is he around?"

I sensed movement at my side and LaTanya did too. We both looked that way to see Detective Mitch Lawson walking up the stairs carrying four plastic grocery bags.

If I were a Seven to Ten and in his zone, which meant I could be in his life, I would lecture him about plastic grocery bags. Considering the state of the environment, no one should use plastic grocery bags, not even hot guys who could get away with practically anything. Since I was not in his zone and I didn't know him and *couldn't* know him for fear of expiring from pleasure should he, say, speak more than a few words to me, I'd never get the chance to lecture him about plastic grocery bags.

"Yo Mitch!" LaTanya greeted him loudly with Delight.

"Hey LaTanya," Mitch greeted back, then his beautiful eyes skimmed to me and his lips tipped up further, "Hey."

"Hey," I replied, locked my legs, ignored the whoosh I felt in my belly and looked back at LaTanya. She was checking out Detective Mitch Lawson—as any woman should or she would be immediately reported to then thrown out of the Woman Club. I heard the rustling of bags, but I ignored it and called her name to get her attention. When I got it, I repeated, "Is Derek around? I wouldn't bother him but my faucet won't turn off and I really need someone to look at it."

"He's not here, Mara, sorry, babe," LaTanya replied. "You said the office hasn't called you back?"

"No," I told her and was about to ask her if she would send Derek over when he got home when I heard from my side:

"You want me to look at it?"

This came from Detective Mitch Lawson, and I sucked in breath and turned my head to look at him. He was standing outside his open apartment door still carrying his bags and his eyes were on me.

My mind went blank. I lost the lock on my legs and my knees wobbled.

God, he was beautiful.

"Mara," I heard from far away, and even though I heard it and it was my name, I didn't respond. "Mara!" I heard again. This time louder and sharper, my body jolted and I turned to LaTanya.

"What?" I asked.

"Mitch'll look at it, that cool with you?" she asked me.

I blinked at her.

No. No it was *not* cool with me.

What did I do?

I couldn't have him in my apartment walking through my *bedroom* to look at my faucet. That would mean he'd be in my apartment. That would mean he'd walk through my *bedroom*. And that would mean I'd have to speak more than one word to him.

Crap!

I looked to Detective Mitch Lawson and said the only thing I could say.

"That would be really kind."

He stared at me a second then lifted the bags an inch and muttered, "Let me get rid of these and I'll be over."

I swallowed then called, "Okay," to his closing door.

I watched his door close and then I kept watching his closed door wondering if the weird feeling I was having was just panic or a precursor to a heart attack. Then La-Tanya called my name again, so I looked at her.

"You okay?" she asked, studying me closely.

I had not, incidentally, shared my love for Detective Mitch Lawson with LaTanya, Derek, Brent, Bradon or anyone. This was because I thought they'd think I was a little insane (or a stalker). They often invited him to parties and such, and if he came, I would usually make my excuses and leave. They'd never cottoned on. I figured mostly because he didn't often attend their parties due to his being a police officer with long hours, but also because he had his buds over for games and his babes over for other things. He wasn't the type of man who went to gay men's parties or LaTanya's cocktail extravaganzas. The ones he went to I suspected he did just to be neighborly. Though Derek, more often than not, went to his place to watch games. Usually in order to escape LaTanya's cocktail extravaganzas, which were frequent occasions.

"Yeah, I'm fine," I lied to her. "Just had a tough day at work," I continued lying. "And I'm not happy the management office didn't call me back. They don't pay my water bill." I wasn't lying about that.

"I hear you," LaTanya agreed. "Service around here has taken a turn for the worse even though they upped our rent three months ago. You remember our fridge went out last month?"

I remembered. I also remembered it took three weeks to get it replaced. Derek had been none too happy, and LaTanya had been loudly none too happy.

"Yeah, I remember. That sucked."

"It sure did. Buyin' ice all the time and livin' outta coolers. I don't pay rent for that shit. Fuck that."

Fuck that indeed.

Detective Mitch Lawson's door opened, and I realized my mistake instantly. I should have run to my house and done something. I didn't know what. Nothing needed tidying because I was freakishly tidy. There was nothing I could do with my appearance, but I figured I should have tried to do *something*.

He started walking our way asking, "Now a good time?"

No, no time was a good time for the Ten Point Five I was secretly in love with to be in my apartment.

I nodded and said, "Sure." Then I looked at LaTanya and said, "Later, babe."

"Later. Remember, a mojito is waitin' for you, when Mitch gets your faucet sorted out."

"Thanks," I muttered, smiled and then glanced at Detective Mitch Lawson before looking down at my feet, turning and walking the short distance to my door. I opened it, walked through, and held it open for him to come inside.

He did and I tried not to hyperventilate.

"Which one is it?" he asked as I closed the door behind him.

I turned, stood at the door and looked up at him. He was closer than I expected and he was taller than he seemed from afar, and he seemed pretty tall from afar. I'd never been this close to him and I felt his closeness tingle pleasantly all across my skin. I was wearing heels and I felt his tallness in the depth of the tip of my head, which didn't tip back that often to look at someone seeing as I was tall.

"Pardon?" I asked.

"Faucet," he said. "Which one? Hall or master?"

I didn't have any clue what he was talking about. It was like he was speaking in a foreign language. All I could focus on were his eyes, which I was also seeing closer than I'd ever seen before. He had great eyelashes.

Those lashes moved when his eyes narrowed.

"You okay?" he asked.

Oh God. I had to get a hold on myself.

"Yeah, fine, um…the faucet's in my master bath," I told him.

He stood there staring at me. I stood there staring at him. Then his lips twitched and he lifted his arm slightly in the direction of my hall.

"You wanna lead the way?" he asked.

Ohmigod! I was *such* an idiot!

"Right," I muttered, looked down at my feet and led the way.

When we were both in my bathroom, which, with him in it, went from a normal-sized master bath to a teeny-tiny, suffocating space, I pointed to the faucet and then pointed out the obvious.

"It won't turn off."

"I see that," he murmured. Then I stood frozen with mortification as he crouched and opened the doors to my vanity.

Why was he opening the doors to my vanity? I kept

my tampons down there! He could see them! They were right at the front for easy accessibility!

Ohmigod!

He reached in, I closed my eyes in despair and wished the floor would gobble me up and suddenly the water turned off.

I opened my eyes, stared at the faucet and exclaimed, "Holy cow! You fixed it!"

He tipped his head back to look at me then he straightened out of his crouch to look down at me.

Then he said, "No, I just turned the water off."

I blinked up at him. Then I asked, "Pardon?"

"You can turn the water off."

"You can?"

"Yeah."

"Oh," I whispered then went on stupidly, "I should probably have done that before I left for work this morning."

His mouth twitched again and he said, "Probably. Though you can't do somethin' you don't know you can do."

I looked to the basin and muttered, "This is true."

"There's a valve under the sink. I'll show it to you after I take a look at the faucet," he said, and I forced my eyes to his. "You probably just need a new washer. Where are your tools?"

I blinked again. "Tools?"

His stared at me and then his lips twitched again. "Yeah. Tools. Like a wrench. You got one of those?"

"I have a hammer," I offered.

One side of his mouth hitched up in a half smile. "I'm not sure a hammer is gonna help."

It took a lot of effort but I only glanced at the half smile before my eyes went back to his. This didn't do a thing to decelerate my rapidly accelerating heartbeat.

"Then no, I don't have tools," I told him, not adding that I wasn't entirely certain what a wrench *was*.

He nodded and turned to the door. "I'll go get mine."

Then he was gone, and I didn't know what to do, so I hurried after him.

I should have stayed where I was. I'd seen him move, of course, I just hadn't seen him moving around in my apartment. He had an athlete's grace, which I had noticed before. But it was more. He had a natural confidence with the way he held his body *and* the way he moved. It was immensely attractive all the time, but seeing it in my apartment was not going to be conducive to peace of mind. Something it was difficult for me to find on a good day, much less a day when my faucet didn't turn off and I was forced to endure an evening that included Detective Mitch Lawson having to be in my apartment.

He stopped at the door and turned to me. "I'll be right back."

I nodded, and he disappeared out the door.

I stood in my living area in my heels, skirt and blouse from work. Then I wondered if I had time to change before he got back. Then I wondered if he'd notice it if I'd spritzed on perfume when he got back. Then I wondered if I should do a shot or two of vodka before he got back. Then he knocked on my door, which meant he was back.

I ran to the door, looked through the peephole (you couldn't be too careful) and saw him looking to the side. I sucked in a calming breath then opened the door.

"Hey," I said, "welcome back."

I was such a dork!

He grinned. I stepped aside, and he came through carrying a toolbox. Learning from my mistakes, I immediately led him through the living area, down the hall, through my bedroom and to the bathroom. He put the toolbox on the basin counter and opened it. He pulled out what I figured was a wrench and went right to work.

I watched his hands, which I'd never really noticed before. They were a man's hands. There were veins that stood out that were appealing. His fingers were long and strong looking. He had great hands.

"So your name is Mara." His deep voice came at me. My body jolted and I looked to his head, which was bent so he could watch what he was doing.

"Yeah," I replied, and my voice sounded kind of high so I cleared my throat and stated, "And you're Mitch."

"Yeah," he said to the faucet.

"Hi, Mitch," I said to his dark brown-haired head, thinking his hair looked soft and thick and was long enough to run your fingers through.

That head twisted so I was looking into dark brown eyes whose depths were so deep you could lose yourself in them for eternity.

Those eyes were also smiling.

"Hi, Mara," he said softly, and my nipples started tingling.

Oh God.

I scanned my memory banks to pull up what underwear I'd put on that morning. I thanked my lucky stars that my bra had light padding, all the while thinking maybe I should leave him to it.

Before I could make good an escape, his head bent

back to the tap and he asked, "How long have you lived here?"

"Six years," I answered.

Shoo! Good. A simple answer that didn't make me sound like an idiot. Thank God.

"What do you do?" he went on.

"I work at Pierson's," I told him.

His neck twisted and his eyes came back to me. "Pierson's Mattress and Bed?"

I nodded. "Yeah."

He looked back at the faucet. "What do you do there? An accountant or something?"

I shook my head even though he wasn't looking at me. "No, I'm a salesperson."

His neck twisted, faster this time, and his eyes locked on mine. "You're a salesperson," he repeated.

"Yeah," I replied.

"At Pierson's Mattress and Bed," he stated.

"Um... yeah," I answered.

He stared at me and I grew confused. I didn't tell him I was a pole dancer. I also didn't tell him I spent my days in my den of evil masterminding a plot to take over the free world. He appeared slightly surprised. I was a salesperson. This wasn't a surprising job. This was a boring job. Then again I was a boring person. He was a police detective. I knew this because I'd seen his badge on his belt on numerous occasions. I also knew this because LaTanya told me. I reckoned, considering his profession, he'd long since figured out I was a boring person. In my mind police detectives could figure anyone out with a glance.

"You good at it?" he asked.

"Um..." I answered because I didn't want to brag.

I *was* good at it. I'd been top salesperson month after month for the last four years after Barney Ruffalo quit (or resigned voluntarily rather than face the sexual harassment charges that Roberta lodged against him). Barney had been my nemesis mainly because he was a dick and always came onto me, along with every woman that worked there or walked through the door, and because he stole my customers.

Mitch looked back at my tap, muttering, "You're good at it."

"Pretty good," I allowed.

"Yeah," he said to the faucet and continued, "put money down that ninety percent of the men who walk in that place go direct to you *and* make a purchase."

This was a weird thing to say. It was true. Most of my customers were men. Men needed mattresses and beds just like any other human being. When they came to Pierson's, since we had excellent quality, value and choice, they'd not want to go anywhere else.

"Why do you say ninety percent?" I asked Mitch.

"'Cause the other ten percent of the male population is gay," he answered the faucet. I blinked at his head in confusion at his words. He straightened, putting the wrench down and lifting his other hand. Between an attractive index finger and thumb was a small, round, black plastic doohickey with a hole in the middle that had some shredding at the edges. "You need a new washer," he informed me.

I looked from the doohickey to him. "I don't have one of those."

He grinned straight out, and my breath got caught in my throat. "No, don't reckon you do," he told me. "Gotta go to the hardware store." Then he flicked the doohickey in my bathroom trash bin and started to exit the room.

I stared at his well-formed back, but my body jolted and I hurried after him.

"No," I called. "You don't have to do that. The water is off now and I have another bathroom." He kept walking and I kept following him and talking. "I'll pop by the management office tomorrow and let them know what's up so they can come fix it."

He had my door open. He stopped in it and turned back to me, so I stopped too.

"No, *I'll* go by the management office tomorrow and tell them how I feel about them lettin' a single woman who pays for their service and has lived in their complex for six years go without a callback when she needs somethin' important done. And tonight, I'll go to the hardware store, get a washer, come back and fix your faucet."

"You don't have to do that," I assured him courteously.

"You're right, but I'm doin' it," he told me firmly.

Okay then. Seeing as his firm was very firm, I decided to let that go.

"Let me get you some money." I looked around trying to remember where I put my purse. "You shouldn't be out money on this."

"Mara, you can buy about a hundred washers for four dollars."

My head turned to him. I stared at him then asked, "Really?"

He grinned at me again, my breath caught in my throat again and he answered, "Yeah, really. I think I got it covered."

"Um...thanks," I replied without anything else to say.

He tipped his chin and said, "I'll be back."

Then I was staring at my closed door.

I did this blankly for a while, wishing I'd shared with *someone* that I was in love with my Ten Point Five neighbor so I could call them or race across the breezeway and ask them what I should do now.

It took a while but I decided to act naturally. So *Mitch* had been in my house. He'd grinned at me. I'd discovered he had beautiful hands and beautiful eyelashes to match all the other beautiful things about him. He actually was a nice guy in a way that went beyond his warm smile, what with turning off my water, going to get his tools, finding my shredded doohickey, planning to have a word at the office on my behalf and then heading out to the hardware store to buy me another doohickey. So what? After he fixed my faucet, he'd be back in his apartment and I'd be alone in mine. Maybe I might say something more than "morning" to him in the mornings. And maybe he'd say my name again sometime in the future. But that would be it.

So I did what I normally did. I changed my clothes, taking off my skirt, blouse, and heels and putting on a pair of jeans and a Chicago Cubs T-shirt. I pulled the pins out of my chignon, sifted my fingers through my hair and pulled it back in a ponytail with a red ponytail holder to go with the red accents in my Cubs tee. Out of habit, I lit the scented candles in my living room and turned on music, going with my "Chill Out at Home Part Trois" playlist, which included some really good tunes. After that I started to make dinner.

I was cutting up veggies for stir-fry when there was a knock on the door and my head came up. I spied the candles, heard the Allman Brothers singing "Midnight

Rider" and immediately panicked. I burned candles and listened to music all the time. I was a sensory person and I liked the sounds and smells. But now I wondered if he'd think he'd walked into a Two Point Five setting the mood for an illegal maneuver on a Ten Point Five.

Crap!

No time to do anything about it now. The scent of the candles would linger even if I blew them out, and he had to hear the music through the door.

I rushed to the door, did the peephole thing and opened it, coming to stand at its edge.

"Hey," I greeted, trying to sound cool. "You're back."

His eyes dropped to my chest and I lost all semblance of cool. There wasn't much to lose but what little existed was quickly history.

Then his eyes came back to mine. "You're a Cubs fan?" he asked.

"Yes," I answered then declared, "They're the best team in the history of baseball."

He walked in and I closed the door. Through this neither of us lost eye contact. This was because he was smiling at me like I was unbelievably amusing and this was because I was staring at him because he was smiling at me like I was unbelievably amusing.

He came to a halt two feet in, and I turned from the closed door, which meant I was about a foot away from him.

"They haven't won a pennant since 1908," he informed me.

"So?" I asked.

"That fact in and of itself means they aren't the best team in the history of baseball."

This was true. It was also false.

"Okay, I amend my statement. They're the coolest, most interesting team in the history of baseball. They have the best fans because their fans don't care if they win or lose. We're die-hard and always will be."

His eyes warmed like they always did before he'd smile at me, and I felt my knees wobble.

"Can't argue with that," he muttered.

I pressed my lips together and hoped I didn't get lightheaded.

"Colorado bleeds black and purple in spring and summer, though, Mara. Careful where you wear that tee," he warned.

"I like the Rockies too," I replied.

He shook his head, turning toward my hall.

"Can't swing both ways," he said as he moved into the hall.

I watched him move. I liked watching him move. I liked it more as I watched him move down my hallway toward my bedroom. I knew I liked it so much I would fantasize the impossible fantasy that such a vision would happen so often it would become commonplace.

I wondered if I could call out to him that I really needed to run an errand. Like say, take care of an old relative who needed me to get her out of her wheelchair and into her bed. Then read her a bedtime story because she was blind. Something I couldn't get out of that would make me seem kind and loving but would really be an excuse to escape him.

Then I realized that would be rude and I followed him.

When I hit the bathroom, he said, "This shouldn't take long and you can get back to making dinner."

Oh boy.

Should I ask him to stay for dinner? I had plenty. He was a big guy, but I still had enough. I just had to cut up another chicken breast or two. Add a few more veggies.

Could I survive a dinner with him? Would he think candles, music and dinner was a play he had to somehow extricate himself out of without seeming like a dick? Or would he know it was just my way of saying thanks?

Crap!

I listened as "Midnight Rider" became America's "Ventura Highway," and I did what I had to do.

"Would you like to stay for dinner as an, um…thank-you for helping out?" I asked. "I'm making stir-fry," I went on.

"Rain check," he told the faucet, not even looking at me, and I was immensely disappointed. So much so I felt it crushing my chest at the same time I was relieved, because his answer meant all was right in Mara World.

Then he continued talking, making Mara World rock on its foundations.

"Knock on my door when you're makin' your barbeque chicken pizza."

I blinked.

Then I breathed, "What?"

"Derek tells me it's the shit."

I blinked again.

They talked about me?

Why would they do that?

Derek was definitely a firm Nine. LaTanya was too. Nines could be friends with Two Point Fives, but male Nines didn't talk to each other about Two Point Fives. They talked about other Sevens to Tens. If they were younger or were jerks, they made fun of Ones to Threes.

But they never talked about Two Point Fives and the really great pizza Two Point Fives could make. *Ever.*

His head tipped back and his eyes hit mine. "Derek tells me your barbeque chicken pizza is the shit," he repeated and explained, "as in, really fuckin' good."

Derek was right. It was really good. I made my own pizza dough and marinated the chicken in barbeque sauce all day and everything. It was awesome.

Seeing as I was unable to respond, I didn't. Mitch looked back at the faucet and carried on rocking my world.

"Or when you're makin' your baked beans. Derek says those are even better. But tonight, I gotta take a rain check because I gotta get back to work."

They talked about my baked beans too? This meant they talked more than a little about me. This was more than a passing comment, "Oh you gotta try Mara's barbeque chicken pizza. It's the shit," or something like that. This meant more than a few sentences. My baked beans were so good they *had* to be a whole other topic.

Ohmigod!

I remained silent and tried to level my breathing. Mitch kept working. Then he kept talking to the tap.

"You got great taste in music, Mara."

Oh God. I liked my music. I liked it a lot. I played it a lot and sometimes I played it loud. Damn.

"I'm sorry, do I play it too loudly that it bothers you?" I asked. His neck twisted to the side but his head was still bent so his eyes were on me but he wasn't exactly facing me, yet he was.

"No, at least not so it's annoying. I can hear it now 'cause I'm in your house. The Allman Brothers' "Midnight Rider," America's 'Ventura Highway,' great taste."

God, of course. I was an idiot.

"Right," I whispered, "of course."

Something happened to his eyes. Something I didn't get but something that made a whoosh sweep through my belly all the same. It was stronger than normal and it felt a whole lot nicer.

"Better than your taste in baseball teams," he stated, and it hit me that he was teasing me.

Holy crap! Detective Mitch Lawson was in my bathroom teasing me!

"Um…" I mumbled then bit my bottom lip and checked the impulse to flee the room.

"Relax, Mara," he said softly, his eyes going super warm. "I don't bite."

I wished he did. I really, really did. Just like I wished I was at least a Nine. He'd never settle for anything lower than a Nine because he didn't have to. As a Nine, I might get the chance to find out if I could *make* him bite me and I'd get the chance to bite *him*.

"Okay," I whispered.

"But I am serious," he went on, his eyes holding mine captive in a way I didn't get but I still couldn't look away no matter how much I wanted to.

"About what?" I was losing track of the conversation.

"I expect a knock on my door, you're makin' pizza or your beans."

"Um…okay," I lied. There was no way I was knocking on his door when I made my pizza or beans. No way in hell. In fact, I was moving the first chance I could get.

"Or just anytime you feel like company," he kept going, and I felt the room teeter.

What did he mean by that?

"Um . . . I'm kinda a loner," I lied again and he grinned.

"Yeah, I noticed that. Your imaginary friend who was over watchin' TV last night sounded a lot like LaTanya though. Now *she* sings loud and it skates the edge of annoying. Luckily it's more funny than annoying and it only lasts an hour."

Oh damn. He'd called me out on a lie. And double damn because I also sang with the kids on *Glee*. Hopefully he couldn't hear me but he wasn't wrong. LaTanya thought she was Patti LaBelle's more talented sister. She diva'ed her way through every episode of *Glee* that we'd watched together. And we'd watched every episode of *Glee* together.

"Um . . ." I repeated, my eyes sliding to the mirror, but I wish they hadn't because I could see his broad shoulders and muscled back leading to his slim hips. I could also see him straightening, which meant I had his full attention. Not that I didn't have it before, just that now I *really* had it.

"Mara," I watched him call, my eyes at the mirror and they slid back to his then he kept talking. "What I'm sayin' is, I get it that you're shy . . ."

Oh God. Totally a police detective. He had me figured out.

He moved his body closer and kept speaking. I held my breath as he held my gaze. "But what I want you to know is that I'd like you to come over, but because you're shy, you gotta walk that breezeway, sweetheart. I'm tellin' you you're welcome, but I made the first move, you need to make the next one. You with me here?"

No. No, I wasn't with him. He'd made the first move? What move?

And he'd called me sweetheart, which made the belly whoosh move through me like a tidal wave.

I was pretty certain I was going to die right there, totally swept away.

Then it it hit me as I stared into his beautiful eyes. They were so dark brown they seemed fathomless, and if I wasn't careful, I would drown in them. But I was careful and I knew who I was and what zone I lived in. So when it hit me, I understood.

Derek and LaTanya were both Nines. Brent and Bradon were firm at Eight Point Fives in the gay world, the straight world or an alien world (both Brent and Bradon were gorgeous, very cool and very, very nice). But they all liked me. We were not only neighbors, we were good friends. And Mitch had been living across the way from me for four years. He was a good guy. He fixed faucets. He smiled warmly.

Therefore, he was trying to be a good neighbor and maybe even a friend.

"I'm with you," I whispered.

He came closer and when he spoke his voice dipped lower. "That mean you're gonna knock on the door tellin' me you're makin' pizza sometime soon?"

"My barbeque chicken pizza takes planning and preparation," I explained. His eyes flashed and I finished, "It'd have to be this Saturday, when I have a day off."

He got even closer. I pulled in a breath because he was now *really* close. His head had to tip down *really* far, and if I moved up on my toes, just a tiny bit, I could actually touch my lips to his.

I felt another belly whoosh.

"Works for me," he murmured.

Oh. Wow.

"'Kay," I breathed.

He stood where he was. I stood and started drowning in his eyes. He didn't move. I didn't either. I felt my body lean toward his a centimeter, such was his hot-guy magnetic pull, at the same time I licked my lip. His eyes dropped to my mouth but not before I saw them get even darker and more fathomless. My heart started to beat in my throat. His cell rang.

Then his eyes closed and the spell was broken as he moved a bit away growling, "Fuck."

He pulled his cell out of his back jeans pocket, hit a button and put it to his ear as his gaze came back to mine.

"Lawson," he said into his phone, and I moved farther away, thinking distance was a good thing. He was a good neighbor. He didn't need to be being neighborly and have the person he was being neighborly toward throw herself at him. That would be wrong. "Yeah, right," he continued. "I said I'll be there, I'll be there. I got somethin' I gotta do. When I'm done I'm on my way. Yeah?" He paused and kept hold of my gaze. "Right. Later."

He shut down his cell and shoved it back in his pocket.

"Work?" I asked.

"Love it most the time, hate it right about now," he answered.

"Uh-huh," I mumbled like I understood what he meant when I didn't. Changing a doohickey wasn't the height of entertainment that you didn't want to be torn away from to do work you loved.

"Gotta get this done, Mara," he told me.

"Okay," I replied.

He stared at me and didn't move. I did the same.

His grin came back and he repeated, "Gotta get this done."

"I know," I said. "You have to get to work."

"Yeah and I gotta get this done."

I blinked then said, "So, um...can I help?"

"You can help by lettin' me get this done."

What did he mean? I wasn't stopping him.

"Please," I motioned to the sink, "carry on."

His grin became a smile. "Sweetheart, what I'm sayin' is," he leaned in, "you're a distraction."

I was?

Oh God! He was saying he didn't need me hanging around chatting with him.

I was such a dork!

"I'll, uh...go make dinner."

"Good idea."

I nodded. "And thanks, um...for, you know," I motioned to the sink again, "helping out, especially when you're so busy."

"Any time."

"Well, I hope it doesn't happen again," I pointed out the obvious. "But thanks anyway."

A sound came from deep in his chest. I realized it was an immensely attractive chuckle, and he said, his voice deep and vibrating with his chuckle, "Mara."

There were many things I wished in my life. Many. Too many to count.

But the top one at that moment in time, scratched at the top of that list in a way I knew it would stay there a good long while, was that I wished with everything that was me that my life would lead me to a new life. One where I would hear Detective Mitch Lawson say my name in his deep voice that vibrated with his laughter time and time and time again.

"I'll just go," I whispered and turned to leave.

"I'll show you the valve to turn off the water another time," he offered to my back.

"Thanks," I said to my bedroom.

Then I was out the door.

Detective Mitch Lawson left not ten minutes later. He was carrying his toolbox. He lifted a hand in a wave as he walked through my living-room-slash-dining-room space. But he stopped at the door, his eyes leveled on mine and he said two words.

"Saturday. Pizza."

Then all I saw was my closed door.

THE DISH

Where Authors Give You the Inside Scoop

From the desk of Roxanne St. Claire

Dear Reader,

Years ago, I picked up a romance novel about a contemporary "marriage of convenience" and I recall being quite skeptical that the idea could work in anything but a historical novel. How wrong I was! I not only enjoyed the book, but *Separate Beds* by LaVyrle Spencer became one of my top ten favorite books of all time. (Do yourself a favor and dig up this classic if you haven't read it!) Since then, I've always wanted to put my own spin on a story about two people who are in a situation where they need to marry for reasons other than love, knowing that their faux marriage is doomed.

I finally found the perfect characters and setup for a marriage of convenience story when I returned to Barefoot Bay to write BAREFOOT BY THE SEA, my most recent release in the series set on an idyllic Gulf Coast island in Florida. I knew that sparks would fly and tears might flow when I paired Tessa Galloway, earth mother longing for a baby, with Ian Browning, a grieving widower in the witness protection program. I suspected that it would be a terrific conflict to give the woman who despises secrets a man who has to keep one in order to stay alive, with the added complication of a situation that can only be resolved with a fake, arranged marriage. However, I never dreamed just how much I would love writing that marriage of convenience! I should have known, since I adored the first one I'd ever read.

Throughout most of BAREFOOT BY THE SEA, hero Ian is forced to hide who he really is and why he's in Barefoot Bay. And that gave me another story twist I love to explore: the build-up to the inevitable revelation of a character's true identity and just how devastating that is for everyone (including the reader!). I had a blast being in Ian's head when he fought off his demons and past to fall hard into Tessa's arms and life. And I ached and grew with Tessa as the truth became crystal clear and shattered her fragile heart.

The best part, for me, was folding that marriage of convenience into a story about a woman who wants a child of her own but has to give up that hope to help, and ultimately lose, a man who needs her in order to be reunited with his own children. If she marries him, he gets what he needs...but he can't give her the one thing she wants most. Will Tessa surrender her lifelong dream to help a man who lost his? She can if she loves him enough, right? Maybe.

Ironically, when the actual marriage of convenience finally took place on the page, that ceremony felt more real than any of the many weddings I've ever written. I hope readers agree. And speaking of weddings, stay tuned for more of them in Barefoot Bay when the Barefoot Brides trilogy launches next year! Nothing like an opportunity to kick off your shoes and fall in love, which is never convenient but always fun!

Happy reading!

Roxanne St. Claire

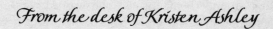

From the desk of Kristen Ashley

Dear Reader,

As it happens when I start a book and the action plays out in my head, characters pop up out of nowhere.

See, I don't plot, or outline. An idea will come to me and *Wham!* My brain just flows with it. Or a character will come to me and all the pieces of his or her puzzle start tumbling quickly into place and the story moves from there. Either way, this all plays in my mind's eye like a movie and I sit at my keyboard doing my darnedest to get it all down as it goes along.

In my Dream Man series, I started it with *Mystery Man* because Hawk and Gwen came to me and I was desperate to get their story out. I'm not even sure that I expected it to be a series. I just *needed* to tell their story.

Very quickly I was introduced to Kane "Tack" Allen and Detective Mitch Lawson. When I met them through Gwen, I knew instantly—with all the hotness that was them—that they both needed their own book. So this one idea I had of Hawk and Gwen finding their happily ever after became a series.

Brock "Slim" Lucas showed up later in *Mystery Man* but when he did, he certainly intrigued me. Most specifically the lengths he'd go to do his job. I wondered why that fire was in his belly. And suddenly I couldn't wait to find out.

In the meantime, my aunt Barb, who reads every one of my books when they come out, mentioned in passing she'd like to see one of my couples *not* struggle before they capitulated to the attraction and emotion swirling around them. Instead, she wanted to see the relationship build and grow, not the hero and heroine fighting it.

This intrigued me, too, especially when it came to Brock, who had seen a lot and done a lot in his mission as a DEA agent. I didn't want him to have another fight on his hands, not like that. But also, I'd never done this, not in all the books I'd written.

I'm a girl who likes a challenge.

But could I weave a tale that was about a man and a woman in love, recognizing and embracing that love relatively early in the story, and then focus the story on how they learn to live with each other, deal with each other's histories, family, and all that life throws at them on a normal basis? Would this even be interesting?

Luckily, life *is* interesting, sometimes in good ways, sometimes not-so-good.

Throwing Elvira and Martha into the mix, along with Tess's hideous ex-husband and Brock's odious ex-wife, and adding children and family, life for Brock and Tess, as well as their story, was indeed interesting (and fun) to write—when I didn't want to wring Olivia's neck, that is.

And I found there's great beauty in telling a tale that isn't about fighting attraction because of past issues or history (or the like) and besting that to find love; instead delving into what makes a man and a woman, and allowing them to let their loved one get close, at the same time learning how to depend on each other to make it through.

I should thank my aunt Barb. Because she had a great idea that led to a beautiful love story.

Kristen Ashley

♥ ♥ ♥ ♥ ♥ ♥ ♥ ♥ ♥ ♥ ♥ ♥ ♥ ♥ ♥ ♥

From the desk of Eileen Dreyer

Dear Reader,

The last thing I ever thought I would do was write a series. I thought I was brave putting together a trilogy. Well, as usual, my characters outsmarted me, and I now find myself in the middle of a nine-story series about Drake's Rakes, my handsome gentleman spies. But I don't wait well as a reader myself. How do I ask my own readers to wait nine books for any resolution?

I just couldn't do it. So I've divided up the Rakes into three trilogies based on the heroines. The first was The Three Graces. This one I'm calling Last Chance Academy, where the heroines went to school. I introduced them all in my short e-novel *It Begins With A Kiss*, and continue in ONCE A RAKE with Sarah Clarke, who has to save Scotsman Colonel Ian Ferguson from gunshot, assassin, and the charges of treason.

I love Sarah. A woman with an unfortunate beginning, she is just trying to save the only home she's ever really had from penury, an estate so small and isolated that her best friend is a six-hundred-pound pig. Enter Ian. Suddenly she's facing off with smugglers, spies, assassins, and possible eviction. I call my Drake's Rakes series Romantic Historical Adventure, and I think there is plenty of each in ONCE A RAKE. Let me know at www .eileendreyer.com, my Facebook page (Eileen Dreyer), or on Twitter @EileenDreyer. Now I need to get back. I have five more Rakes to threaten.

Eileen Dreyer

♥ ♥ ♥ ♥ ♥ ♥ ♥ ♥ ♥ ♥ ♥ ♥ ♥

From the desk of Anne Barton

Dear Reader,

Regrets. We all have them. Incidents from our distant (or not-so-distant) pasts that we'd like to forget. Photos we'd like to burn, boyfriends we never should have dated, a night or two of partying that got slightly out of control. Ahem.

In short, there are some stories we'd rather our siblings didn't tell in front of Grandma at Thanksgiving dinner.

Luckily for me, I grew up in the pre-Internet era. Back then, a faux pas wasn't instantly posted or tweeted for the world to see. Instead, it was recounted in a note that was ruthlessly passed through a network of tables in the cafeteria—a highly effective means of humiliation, but not nearly as permanent as the digital equivalent, thank goodness.

Even so, I distinctly remember the sinking feeling, the dread of knowing that my deep dark secret could be exposed at any moment. If you've ever had a little indiscretion that you just can't seem to outrun (and who hasn't?), you know how it weighs on you. It can be almost paralyzing.

In ONCE SHE WAS TEMPTED, Miss Daphne Honeycote has such a secret. Actually, she has two of them—a pair of scandalous portraits. She posed for them when she was poor and in dire need of money for her sick mother. But after her mother recovers and Daphne's circumstances improve considerably, the shocking portraits come back to haunt her, threatening to ruin her reputation, her friendships, and her family's good name.

Much to Daphne's horror, Benjamin Elliott, the Earl of Foxburn, possesses one of the paintings—and therefore, the power to destroy her. But he also has the means to help her discover the whereabouts of the second portrait before its unscrupulous owner can make it public. Daphne must decide whether to trust the brooding earl. But even if she does, he can't fully protect her—it's ultimately up to Daphne to come to terms with her scandalous past. Just as we all eventually must.

In the meantime, I suggest seating your siblings on the opposite end of the Thanksgiving table from Grandma.

Happy reading,

Anne Barton

♥ ♥ ♥ ♥ ♥ ♥ ♥ ♥ ♥ ♥ ♥ ♥ ♥ ♥ ♥

From the desk of Mimi Jean Pamfiloff

Dear Reader,

After living a life filled with nothing but bizarre, Emma Keane just wants normal. Husband, picket fence, vegetable garden, and a voice-free head. Normal. And Mr. Voice happens to agree. He'd like nothing more than to be free from the stubborn, spiteful, spoiled girl he's spent the last twenty-two years listening to day and night. Unfortunately for him, however, escaping his only companion in the universe won't be so easy. You see, there's a damned good reason Emma is the only one who can hear him—though he's not spilling the beans just yet—and there's a damned bad reason he can't leave Emma: He's imprisoned. And to be set free, Mr. Voice is going to have to convince Emma to travel from New York City to the darkest corner of Mexico's most dangerous jungle.

But not only will the perilous journey help Emma become the brave woman she's destined to be, it will also be the single most trying challenge Mr. Voice has ever had to face. In his seventy thousand years, he's never met a mortal he can't live without. Until now. Too bad she's going to die helping him. What's an ancient god to do?

Mimi

10/23